IN THE WAKE
OF THE
EMPRESS OF
CHINA

IN THE WAKE OF THE EMPRESS OF CHINA

ROBERT LIVINGSTON

IN THE WAKE OF THE EMPRESS OF CHINA

iUniverse books may be ordered through booksellers or by contacting:

iUniverse
1663 Liberty Drive
Bloomington, IN 47403
www.iuniverse.com
844-349-9409

ISBN: 978-1-6632-1635-9 (sc)
ISBN: 978-1-6632-1636-6 (e)

Print information available on the last page.

iUniverse rev. date: 01/12/2021

CONTENTS

DEDICATION

To Those in Our Family Who Answered the Call

INTRODUCTION

1941 – the world is at war. Nazi Germany controls Europe and has invaded the Soviet Union. Fascist Italy is trying to recreate a Roman Empire in North Africa and throughout the Mediterranean. In the Far East Imperial Japan controls Korea, Manchuria and has been at war in China since 1937. Only the United States basks in the last twilight hours of relative peace.

1941 – three people are quietly involved in a conspiracy to keep America out of a war in the Pacific with Japan. If unable to do so, they want to understand why war was seemingly inevitable. And lastly, they struggle to create an intellectual life raft for the post-war survivors to avoid still another future war, one that potentially would endanger Western Civilization. They refer to this life raft as the ARK.

1941 – who are these conspirators? Estelle Stead is the leader. Her father was W.T. Stead, the famous London investigative reporter, who led the first effort in 1910 to avoid a European War. John Marshall Harlan II is also standing on the shoulders of an earlier conspirator, his grandfather, Judge John Marshall Harlan I. The last person is Alfreda Wells. Her mother was Ida B. Wells, the civil rights activist, who also conspired in 1910 to avoid the tragedy now known as World War I.

1941 – the three conspirators, who refer to themselves as "pirates," are plagued by one intractable question: is war inevitable in the Pacific? If yes, there is no hope to avoid a conflict. If no, those who control the reins of government still have an opportunity to pull back from the abyss. Blending "it is what it is" realism with sharp-edged idealism, the new conspirators are determined to reset the human compass in order to save humanity from a final catastrophe.

1941 – to understand the present, the past must be understood by the conspirators. They know this and embark on this task to fathom a century of Japanese-American relations. What they learn explains the current tensions in the Far East, but leaves one question unexplained: how could the historical narrative have been altered? If not possible, a new ARK is doomed to failure, as was the first. If possible, there is hope and it is this tangent of human affairs that the conspirators grasp.

1941 – in the end this is the story of three extraordinary people attempting to put into practice an admonition of President Abraham Lincoln given in the last desperate moments before civil conflict:

The dogmas of the quiet past are inadequate to the stormy present. The occasion is piled high with difficulty, and we must rise with the occasion. As our case is new, so we must think anew and act anew.

PROLOGUE

<u>December 1, 1972 – New York City</u>

They are all gone now. Finally...

First, my personal doctor and private nurse, so predictably somber and apologetic as they departed, their medical arts betrayed by the malevolent spinal cancer eating away at me. So too was my immediate family, having left earlier, all weary of the prolonged struggle, yet emotionally unwilling to accept the inevitable. The lawyers and judges, old colleagues and close friends, have also quietly retreated into the night, fully cognizant of the verdict of time and fate, which had gone against me. A final case to review and no appeal possible... Judgment confirmed. Last to leave was my cherished servant of many years, old and spent himself, a living reminder of quieter days and a more orderly world we both applauded and cherished. A nod and a tear and he was gone, the door to my private study finally closed.

I was, as I must be, as all of us must be when death approaches, alone with my thoughts, undeceived by false hopes, finally accepting an abbreviated future. My destiny proclaimed earlier by the men in starched whites at Walter Reed Hospital. Three weeks, possibly, five at the most. Certainly over by Christmas, little doubt about that. No exchange of presents this year. No Yule time toasts to health and happiness, and the hope of "peace on earth and good will to all." And later, no swaying to the nostalgic lyrics of *Auld Lang Sign*, as balloons were released and noisemakers welcomed the New Year.

All disappearing into the past...

Yet strangely, as others thought they saw me, I accepted my fate with little protest, and apparently with few, if any, regrets. In that, of course, they were terribly wrong, though one could hardly blame them. Years on the judicial bench had cultivated a stoic persona, devoid of clues as to how I might decide a case. No hints, no indication, obliqueness to the extreme before plaintiffs and defendants alike, and all those who represented them before the bench.

But protesting I was, but not against death. That which is inevitable makes a mockery of "screaming into the night." What I rebelled against was the still "unfinished business that was contemptuous of my situation, always reminding me of my mortality, and great failure. Lurking behind my seemingly placid face was one last self-incrimination, shrouding what was left of me in unsatisfied anger and hopeless remorse.

I had failed, as had the others, utterly and completely, in our self-appointed task set so many years ago, first in 1910, later in 1941, to "save the world," from still another global war, a pestilence again bringing death and destruction.

Three times at bats to use a baseball metaphor, and three strikeouts, the game over, another loss racked up. First batter, my grandfather, my namesake, John Marshall Harlan, who served on the Supreme Court from 1877 to 1911, and who was intimate with the "Conspiracy of 1910" to avoid a general war in Europe. Then my own abortive swings to forestall a second European conflict in 1939, and finally, my subsequent ineffectual effort to avoid war with Japan in 1941.

"To save the world," our exalted goal, our high-minded objective, our sublime quest, that's how others portrayed us in '39, and others before us in 1910. Decent people many said retrospectively with an unrealistic, naive view of the world. Decent people unable, nay unwilling to accept the world the way it was, given the ingrained selfishness of individuals and nations, all at home in a Darwinian world of constant struggle and brutal survival. That's what people clamored, reminding us that war and killing came naturally to God's creation, the evicted, forlorn children of Eden. A little cynicism would do us good, many argued. Stop battling the "windmills" of Don Quixote's world. Cervantes was dead, de la Mancha in ruins. Let the poet, they preached, rest in peace.

But, of course, we couldn't do that. Not in 1910, nor in 1939, and then in 1941. Why, some asked? Our answer, always so unsatisfying, won few adherents: "to extol humanity, to be civilized, to stop the killing and drive back the barbarians of our nature."

Still condemnation assaulted us much to our consternation. "Foolish utopians," we were labeled, noble in thought, misguided in practice, and destined to be disappointed. Mankind, it was contended, was still a creature of the jungle, a blood-thirsty savage, which no amount of material abundance, or strictures of law could completely disguise. The species extolled killing.

Of course, we understood that, but what was comprehended we steadfastly refused to fully accept. Always, we sought to ascend, to rise above the blood and gore of history's pages, seeking in some indeterminate future a new chapter in human affairs. In late 1939 the latest dreadful news from Europe rebuked all our hopes, flaunting our dreams. Poland invaded. Poland smashed. And later...Nazi armored tanks and millions of troops invading the Soviet Union, initially crushing the ill-prepared Russian defenders. It was mechanized warfare, "blitzkrieg," the German name for "lightning war," which had only been recently coined. In Asia the world was aflame as Japan consolidated her position as a military power in Korea and Manchuria, while invading China and coveting, if not already threatening, oil rich colonial possessions in Southeast Asia.

Perhaps the challenge was simply too great, or we hadn't sufficiently learned the lessons of the first aborted attempt in 1910, an acknowledgement, I could in good conscience no longer deny. Twenty-five years ago, August 1, 1914 the Kaiser's troops invaded France. And then August 1939 the swastika overwhelmed Warsaw. Two world wars, a quarter of a century between them... Or was it actually one conflict, a thirty-year war, with a temporary respite?

Certainly, there had been enough time to still the insanity of another general war. Yet, we had again failed, our hopes dashed by the vengeful, unrelenting forces of history, too great, it appeared, for mortals to fully appreciate and finally to successfully resist.

I was oppressed by these thoughts. Worse than the cancer they stalked my mind, unrelenting in their prosecutorial charge. The evidence lay barren, as did the indictment. "Justice John Marshall Harlan II, you failed, as did the others in avoiding a second world war. Acquittal denied."

And then the faces... I saw them again, those other conspirators of 1941 In my mind I reached out to them through the fading pages of time and lapsed into a dreamy half-sleep as I recalled how the second conspiracy began.

CHAPTER 1

SEA CLIFF

<u>January 1941 – San Francisco</u>

The large, obviously expensive home at 47 Scenic Way was situated in the northwest section of San Francisco in an affluent area called Sea Cliff, a descriptive term that more than accounted for its location and wealthy residents. The view from the home was magnificent. To the west the vastness of the Pacific stretched past Hawaii and the Philippines to the very shores of Japan already at war with China since 1931. To the north, the engineering marvel of its day, the glorious Golden Gate Bridge, newly completed, spanned the straits of the same name. The glistening towers and cables connected "Bagdad by the Bay" with Marin County, and what was generously called Northern California, a land of vast forests of ponderosas and redwoods, and innumerable rivers, beneficiaries of the Sierra Nevada's yearly snowpack. To the east were the skyscrapers of the city housing the financial "hub" of the West, home to the great banks, all intimate with California's history: Bank of America, Wells Fargo, and Crocker. The same view encompassed the iconic Ferry Building with its great clock at the head of Market Street, and adjacent to the string of piers berthing the cargo and cruise ships, and, if one looked closely, the grey metal of warships refitting for potential combat in a looming Pacific war not yet declared.

Sea Cliff… Little did I know the vital role this residence would play in my life in the last year of peace before the Far East exploded. I suppose my grandfather, the first John Marshall Harlan, felt the same way about the sprawling residence in Chicago, Jane Addams' Hull House, some 25-years earlier when he first spied it. Was this history repeating itself? First one Harlan conscripted into the enterprise to avoid a "general European war in 1910." Then another Harlan, once more enticed into an unappetizing enterprise to head off conflict with Tokyo in 1941. Perhaps, or was this the same moment in history, just the other side of the coin? An intriguing, but unanswerable question…

Conveniently, the owner of a sprawling six-bedroom house, Mr. Sean Murphy, an elderly, widowed man who was well connected in the local liquor and wine business, was taking his annual fall trip to the "Old Country, which in his case meant Christmas in a small fishing village on the east coast, just north of Boston. He would have preferred Ireland, but the war and lurking German submarines around the British Isles made that impossible. As she had tried in 1914, once more Berlin was seeking to starve Britain into submission, and once more the issue was in doubt.

Most fortunately, Mr. Murray's Sea Cliff home would, therefore, be vacant during December. A necessity for what three conspirators had in mind as war raised its ugly head in the Pacific.

Very few knew that the owner had lost two youthful brothers on the Western Front in 1918, and ironically in the numbing last months of the war. One was cut down while fighting for the British in the Argonne Forest. The other lost his life at the Marne. Eventually, a saddened Sean Murray moved to the United States for business purposes and, as some speculated, to simply take his broken heart across the Atlantic. The weight of the twin loss convinced him to adopt pacifism as his guiding light and to support like-minded individuals and groups to avoid future conflicts.

That said, it was my chore to contact Mr. Murray to see if our conspirators could use his home. After a lengthy chat with Mr. Murray over a few stout Irish beers, I confessed the nature of our little conspiracy. He quickly made his home available in December, no strings attached. No charge was required, a sort of real estate pro bono in reverse. He did so with a passion and conviction perhaps only known to those who have lost loved ones in the insanity of wars. Moreover, once he was fully advised of the daunting challenge facing those who would reside in his home, he willingly and without any qualms supported our little conspiracy, providing needed funds for the enterprise, and trusted servants for our stay. He did, however, have one question that, of course, led to more.

"Mr. Harlan, there are many fine homes in Sea Cliff. All might have met your needs. Why did you choose my residence?"

"I didn't, at least not directly."

"I remain baffled."

"Your name was provided by another."

"Who, if I may ask?"

"The daughter of a man you spent less than five minutes with before boarding the *Titanic* in 1912."

To say that Sean Murphy was taken aback by this declaration was all too obvious. For a moment the man seemed unable to speak, which for an Irishman with the "gift of gab" was indeed something. Time and memories contrived, however, to finally loosen his tongue.

"The Southampton pier... Yes, I remember. He was there, gazing at the ship, a bemused look on his face. Stead... W.T. Stead, the London reporter, who enjoyed celebrity status in the world of journalism. We were both looking at the steel-plated side of the unsinkable ship and her four huge funnels that were her trademark."

"That's what I was told."

"By whom, if I may ask?"

"By his daughter, Estelle."

"I remain puzzled."

"Before the *Titanic* collided with the iceberg, Stead wired his family about a memorable moment with, as he said, 'a most enjoyable Irish chap named Sean Murphy.'"

"Blessed are the angels. I do remember. Curiously, we talked about his premonitions concerning the great ship. He had written, I recall, about ship disasters at sea, especially where too few lifeboats were available, or ice warnings were ignored."

"About the *Titanic*?"

"Nothing, really. Only that our fate, such as it might be, would sort itself out."

"He provided exposition as to what this meant?"

"None whatsoever."

"You saw him again aboard the ship, Mr. Murphy?"

"At times chatting with the wealthy, holding them spellbound with his many stories of which he had an endless supply. And, of course, and then only briefly that terrible night."

"Was Stead, as has been said, calming people, trying to organize an orderly movement to the lifeboats?"

"It seems so."

"He gave away his lifejacket?"

"If so, I didn't see that, but I wouldn't doubt such a story."

"You survived."

"Frozen to the bone and barely alive... Pulled out of the sea by miraculous hands at the last possible second. The Saints be praised. Sadly, not Stead's fate."

"As Stead once remarked to his daughter, one cannot elude his destiny, which brings us to our meetings... To why your home has been chosen, Sir."

"Yes."

"You, Sir, cannot evade your destiny."

"Do explain."

"Estelle Stead has carried on her father's work for many years, seeking to reduce the dangers of another general war. In doing so she came across your name and efforts in a similar vein. She also learned about your two sons for whom she shed many tears."

"Both rest now beneath the poppies."

"Further research on her part revealed your successful business enterprises in the beverage industry and why you became an expatriate in America."

"To put some distance between myself and the British Crown is the kindest way I can say it."

"Estelle determined where you lived after much research."

"My sanctuary."

"And that your residence, Sean, might be a refuge for our work. a latter day Hull House for plotting a second conspiracy, if I may be so bold. She truly believed you would understand."

"Completely, but with one other question."

"Which is?"

"What you seek, is it possible?"

"A betting man would argue against the enterprise."

"But?"

"I… We must wager there is always a chance."

"With Il Duce, Mr. Harlan, running wild in the Mediterranean proclaiming it *Mare Nostrum*, 'Our Lake?' With his designs on Africa, especially Ethiopia, to crown his fascist empire?"

"We cannot flag, Mr. Murray."

"With the little mustached one in Berlin envisioning a Reich encompassing the entire European continent and more? With Nazi hoards on the move, strutting through Austria, the Sudetenland, Poland, parading in Paris, and now overrunning Russia, seeking to turn the entire continent into one gigantic concentration camp? In the Far East with the military in control of the Japanese civilian government, and with a million fighting men in China, and everywhere pursuing an aggressive foreign policy, how can that be possible? The Japanese march, proclaiming a new day for Asians at the point of a bayonet. How might this river of aggression be stemmed, this chant for war?"

"The opportunity, I'm afraid, has come and gone. The gods of war are in the ascendancy. They will not be denied. Poland is already history. France is occupied. The Russians are attacked. Europe has already entered a new Dark Age."

"Then what, Mr. Harlan?"

"America is not yet at war. True, we are preparing for a conflict, but for the moment diplomacy carries the day, especially with Japan. What we and the world could not stop in 1939, we hope to avoid in 1941, at least in the Pacific with Japan."

"And if you fail?"

"We will at least leave for the world, as was done before, an Ark with a new vision for the post-war survivors."

"I don't understand."

"Then permit me to explain."

I provided an explanation. Not all that had taken place in 1910, but enough to quench immediate curiosity. And what might still be done in 1941, but again not all that had led to this moment.

"Unable to stop the general war on the European plain, the first conspirators resolved to provide the world with a blueprint of lasting peace. Their *"Seven Points,"* one of which was an international organization to keep the peace, what has become the League of Nations. To a degree, it is thought, the earlier conspirators influenced President Woodrow Wilson in his articulation of the Fourteen Points in 1918, chief of which was his desire for an international body to head off another bloodletting."

"The earlier conspirators, they reached the Oval Office?"

"Indirectly, Mr. Murray. They published their *Seven Points*, their 'Ark,' if you will, and acquainted it with member of Congress, the press, America's religious leaders, and the general public. In retrospect, we also believe that Colonel Edward House, Wilson's personal envoy, visited Hull House on at least three occasions to discuss the 'Ark' with Jane Addams after Stead's death."

"But the Treaty of Versailles failed to keep the peace, Mr. Harlan?"

"That treaty, and most historians agree on this point, was an abomination, too punitive, too harsh, too unrealistic. No question about that. It all but guaranteed another war."

"And the League of Nations, Sir? Has it not failed?"

"Not the concept. Only the nations in it, and those who watch from afar, most notably, the United States."

"You seek to resurrect it, Mr. Harlan a new League? Is that what you're saying? Trying once more to accomplish what your grandfather and the others couldn't?"

"Perhaps the first effort continuing."

"Three of the original conspirators are deceased?"

"Unfortunately, yes Mr. Murphy. My grandfather, the first John Marshall Harlan died in 1911. Of course, W.T. Stead drowned as the *Titanic* plunged to the bottom in 1912. As to Ida B. Wells, she passed in 1931.

"Were there not others?"

"Two others, yes. The quiet grace of Jane Addams: she is gone, lost to the ages in 1935. A benevolent deity will take her, I trust, under his compassionate wings. She deserves no less."

"And Marcus Garvey?"

"In London, June 1940; he died during the blitz."

"To use an American baseball analogy, Mr. Harlan, players on the bench must come forward, replacing those who have passed."

"Fortunately, two daughters will suffice for our purpose."

"And the two women you mentioned earlier, Mr. Harlan. They are also committed?"

"Let me put it this way. The fury of daughters seeking absolution for their parents will not be denied."

"For the London journalist whom I spend a scant few minutes before boarding the *Titanic*?"

"Stead's daughter, Estelle Stead, will have her day."

"And for the other daughter?"

"Alreda Wells, also a civil rights activist, seeks the same goals as her astute and passionate mother, Ida B. Wells."

Sean Murphy considered all that had been said before responding with a slight hiss to his tone.

"That Democrat in the White House, what about him? Can you work with that Hyde Park patrician?"

"I'm a good Republican. Voted against Roosevelt in '32 and '36. But I voted for him in '40, even as he broke with the three term tradition."

"You have your differences with Franklin Delano Roosevelt?"

"Many."

"But?"

"He's a known commodity, Sean. He's astute. He's experienced. He is anti-fascist to the core. He realizes the danger posed by Hitler and Mussolini, and the Japanese expansive goals in the Pacific. He is already attempting to rearm America. He reinstituted the draft. He understands Britain's plight. We will work with him as we did with President Woodrow Wilson. Let's not forget FDR was there in 1919 as Wilson's Secretary of the Navy. He saw first hand Wilson's failure to get the Treaty of Versailles through the U.S. Senate. He saw first hand our failure to join the League of Nations. Hopefully, if a new treaty comes out of another conflict, it will have a better outcome with a new international body. Roosevelt, I hope, will avoid Wilson's mistakes. He also understands that war today far outstrips its benefits. That is a polite way of saying war jeopardizes our Western Civilization, and all too soon the very existence of our species."

"You can't be serious, Mr. Harlan?"

"On my soul, Mr. Murray, I wish I wasn't. The physicists, I am told, both in Germany and the United States, are new envisioning new worlds by splitting atomic matter, which could lead to weapons fraught with unprecedented dangers."

"I don't ..."

"Destructive bombs unparalleled in human history. Bombs that destroy entire cities, while contaminating the land, water, air with something called radiation."

Sean Murphy could only chew on what he had heard. Thoughts that one might find in comic books and science fiction, or even *Buck Rogers* movies. Still, his visitor seemed completely sane, a man not given to irrationality. "Unprecedented dangers..." "Frightful weapons" Dreadful thoughts to consider...

"Such weapons exist?"

"On the drawing boards."

"Difficult to imagine."

"What is theoretical today is possible tomorrow. This only adds to the imperative to launch another peace effort."

"The need for my house again I understand. The unusual connection I have with W.T. Stead I appreciate. What I lack is an understanding as to how this latest conspiracy originated."

"The post office was, I'm afraid, partially responsible. A letter, Sir; l received a hand written note by US Mail requiring a signature. I complied, *John Marshall Harlan II* to distinguish me from my illustrious grandfather, and former Associate Justice of the same name, *John Marshall Harlan I.* The return address, which at first I didn't connect with anything, was Oxford, England, a hamlet approximately 30-kilometers north of London. The note was received at my private residence in Maryland, just an hour's drive from the marble columns where I occasionally slaved on behalf of my clients and our mutual tyrant, the United States Constitution. Again, while the sender's first name was affixed, it broached no recognition on my part. But not the surname; Stead was a household fixture in our family given his role in the failed 1910 effort.

"And the letter?"

"In a moment. Patience please. . Along with others, my grandfather had toiled to head off the Great War, what people now are starting to call World War I since the Germans invaded Poland. He and his cohorts wanted to provide a philosophical framework of positive ideas to ensure no future conflict. This is what Stead and his "gang of pirates" referred to as the "Ark." A repository for truth much like the Jewish Torah, parchment or sheepskin with the architectural plans for a better, more secure world. In avoiding the conflict, they failed. In providing an intellectual basis to maintain the peace, they were only partially successful in the form of the League of Nations and its tenuous grip on international sanity."

"This I grasp. But the letter?"

At that moment I retrieved the letter from my inside jacket pocket. I carefully unfolded it and read:

January 1941
Oxford, England

My dear, Judge Harlan,

Our previous efforts have failed to keep the peace. Europe is at war. What is left for us is an effort to avoid a conflict with the Empire of Japan. I see little hope in this, but we, as always, must try. Regardless of what happens, a second Ark, will be needed. Of course, we must learn from the past in doing so. What has taken place in Europe is fairly understood. Europe Is again at war. Japan tortures China and threatens Dutch and British interests in Southeast East Asia. But America is not yet involved. She still clings to isolationism. We hope to stave off a conflict between these Pacific powers. To that end we need to more fully understand the conditions and motivations, which have led us to the brink of war with Tokyo.

In a few days you will receive from me primary historical materials related to Japan and the present grave situation .For the most part the materials were provided by academics at Stanford University, the University of California, and the University of Hawaii. Scholarly materials were also provided by the

Japanese Center for Cultural Studies in San Francisco. They cover an expanse of almost a century. You will find them most useful since our ignorance of Asia is a detriment to our efforts to create a second Ark.

I have also been in contact with numerous professors well versed in Japanese history, as well as American diplomacy. Beginning this month we will impose upon ourselves a series of lectures as the attached reading and meeting schedule indicates. Certainly, by September or October at the latest we will be well versed in recent Japanese-American history. By December we should meet in San Francisco to complete our "New Ark." By then the situation in Russia will be clarified, and hopefully, the Pacific will not boil over before then. In any event, this is our plan.

I will check in at the Mark Hopkins Hotel on January 22nd and I invite you to join me that evening for a private dinner at 6:00 p.m. One other will also join us, Ida Wells' daughter, Alfreda. This request in made on behalf of my father, W.T. Stead and the others who first conspired to construct an Ark long ago. The sole purpose of this meeting, I remind you, is to eventually resurrect and update the Ark of 1910 in light of the present tense international scene.

Sincerely,
Estelle W. Stead

———————

"You derived what from reading the note, Sir?"

"Sean, I, of course, mulled over the letter, but not for long. My interest was peaked. Stead's daughter was reaching out to me. I responded immediately. 'Yes, I would meet.' I quickly cleared my calendar, citing health issues, which was not a complete fabrication. Plane tickets were booked and hotel accommodations made. My legal clerks were assigned to upcoming cases. Naturally, in doing all this I wondered about an earlier John Marshall Harlan who went through the same charade years ago. Sometime later I boarded a TWA non-stop to San Francisco cognizant of the fact that, as W.T. Stead said, 'destiny rules all.'"

"The meeting was illuminating?"

"More than I could imagine."

"And Mr. Harlan, the outcome."

"That I meet with you."

Sean Murray paced for a few moments, seemingly considering all that had been said before saying, "The Saints be praised. As I said earlier, the residence is yours. Make of it what you will and may the luck of the Irish be with you."

———————

I knew then I was walking where my grandfather had tread years ago. I could only imagine what he would have thought.

CHAPTER 2

TOP OF THE MARK

January 1941 – San Francisco

The fog had swept in late yesterday, quietly laying claim to coastal San Francisco as it moved relentlessly across the Sunset, Richmond, and Sea Cliff districts of the city. What it did yesterday, it would do again today, only to repeat the process tomorrow. One could almost set his watch by this daily atmospheric ritual in the city of St. Francis. The clockwork appearance of the wispy, feather-like strands of fog, really a thick cloud of tiny water droplets, was a continuing inducement to wear warm sweaters and woolen jackets, and, as was to be expected, to hear the mournful wail of the foghorns beseeching those at sea to keep a sharp eye.

Most natives of the city were aware of the fog's hypnotic grip on poets. And, of course, Carl Sandburg had willed it so when he wrote:

The fog comes
on little cat feet.
It sits looking
over harbor and city
on silent haunches
and then moves on.

But another poet might challenge this whimsical portrait, declaring as Walterrean Salley did, that there is a serious side to these "cat feet," which is most appropriate for the story at hand.

> *The fog is an illusion...*
> *A master of disguise,*
> *Which hides the tangible*
> *Before our very eyes...*
>
> *Or late at night,*
> *The fog descends*
> *Upon various sites...*
> *It gives an air of mystery*
> *That has long prevailed,*
> *Dangerously intriguing*
> *Is the fog's foggy veil...*

The Meeting

The Mark Hopkins Hotel is located at the top of Nob Hill in San Francisco. It is the very epitome of luxury comfort and dining. Constructed on the site of a mansion originally built by Mark Hopkins for his wife, Mary in 1878, the hotel is a iconic fixture in San Francisco. As one of the founders of the Central Pacific Railroad, Hopkins had the financial clout to build the mansion for his sweetheart. Chartered by Congress in 1862, the Central Pacific laid track from Sacramento, California to Promontory Point in Utah, thereby completing the country's transcontinental railroad.

The mansion did survive the 1906 earthquake, but the not the great fire that followed. George D. Smith, a mining engineer and investor, purchased the mansion site and constructed the Mark Hopkins, a nineteenth story hotel designed as a French chateau. In 1939 the penthouse suite on the top floor was converted into a restaurant and cocktail lounge, and was aptly called the "The Top of the Mark." As fate would have it, the lounge became a favorite spot for romantic interludes, and a delightful place for servicemen and their female companions in what appeared to be the last days of peace.

It was here that three people met to share Napa Valley white wine, a Caesar salad, warmed sourdough bread, and to talk quietly of a conspiracy to avoid war in the Pacific. They did so in a subdued corner of the room where the sun's light found little purchase and shadows lingered.

"Well, Miss Stead, we're here, as you requested, landlocked under this foggy wet blanket that should put the local chamber of commerce to shame."

"My dear, Mr. Harlan, please call me Estelle. No need for the old Victorian formality and so less easier to say, don't you think?"

"I will comply. After all, you are the daughter of W.T. Stead of whom my grandfather often spoke."

"Favorably, I trust?"

"A man for all seasons, I believe, was his exact expression of devotion and admiration for your father."

"Judge John Marshall Harlan, your grandfather was favored with similar accolades by my father. There was great respect between the two men."

"They did work well together, an Associate Judge on the U.S. Supreme Court contributing to landmark constitutional decisions, and a muckraking, tabloid reporter practicing robust journalism. That said, how should I address you?"

"Harlan will do."

"Not yet a 'Judge?'"

"In my blood, I think. Perhaps in time, Estelle."

"And you, Mrs. Wells. How should we address you?"

"Freda, Harlan. Short for my full name, which is Alfreda M. Bennett Duster, certainly a mouthful."

"Of course. Now that we are on a first name basis, its time to get down to business, isn't it?"

"All too true, Freda. And, yes, it's time to get on with it, but before we do, a moment of tribute to the past, to those who came before us. Sadly, no one is left from the 1910 conspiracy with the passing of Marcus Garvey in London last year. He had hoped, as you all know, to have another bite of the apple. Always so impatient, he wanted to fling himself once more into the maelstrom with hopefully a different outcome. That unfortunately was not to be. Two major strokes left him paralyzed before conveying him into the next world.'

"He's interred, is he not in London, Estelle?"

"Indeed. In a vault in the catacombs of St. Mary's Roman Catholic Church, but with instructions to remove his remains to Kingston, Jamaica when the war is over."

"Given his efforts to treat black Jamaicans as first class citizens of the British Empire, that would appear most appropriate."

"Estelle, always to the salient point. Yes, most appropriate."

The three raised their glasses, clicked, and sipped. Those watching could only speculate as to their toast.

"Harlan, your grandfather, Judge Harlan worked with Marcus, and, Freda, your mother, Ida B. Wells, was also part of that first conspiracy. As for me, I was the daughter of the irritable, irascible rogue who initiated this whole business almost three decades ago, my beloved father, W. T. Stead."

"My memories of your father are quite clear, Estelle. Family lore passed on from my grandfather supports your caricature. You father was so intimidating. He walked with a swagger and flourished with a temper, somewhat mollified by a keen sense of humor as he considered the antics of the human race. And what a teacher… He taught my learned grandfather, it appears, so much about investigative journalism and his belief in the use of the written word to counter the evils of the world. True, he was daunting in the way he prodded all of them, always pushing, shoving, pounding away as he reminded all of the goal to construct an Ark."

"Estelle, you will push as he did?"

"Not as he did, Harlan, only as I can."

"My mother often spoke of your father with undiluted respect. Here, as he told me, was a man of action who challenged the controversies of his day, including childhood prostitution, the jailing of women thought to have a venereal disease, and corruption in government. His God was truth and the newspaper his sacred scripture. A true unredeemed 'Muckraker.' I regret he died before his time."

"My appreciation, Freda, for your thoughts."

"Your father certainly influenced my mother. Perhaps it was their common interest in civil rights issues, the dreaded place of lynching in American society, or the near hopeless state of the underclass in the London's darker regions. In your father's public denunciation of civic action to redress these social problems, both in the 'old world' and in

Chicago, they were kin. And, I think they perceived the looming general European war as a lynching of civilization on a scale almost beyond human comprehension. In sum, my mother, though she clashed at times with your father, cared deeply for him."

"I am grateful for your comments, Freda. We would be remiss if we didn't recall one other, who cannot be here, dear Jane Addams."

"The mistress of Hull House, Estelle?"

"Yes, Harlan. She passed away in 1935, but not before receiving the Nobel Prize for Peace in 1931 for her contribution to the new discipline of Sociology, as well as her charitable work. She was indeed a formidable lady wrapped up in a diminutive package. Always, she provided stability, I believe; she had a most calming influence on Mr. Stead when he tore into a tirade. And the meals her staff prepared, an unforgettable aspect of their little conspiracy."

"My mother always thought there was something more, Estelle, between your father and Jane, an affection that transcended mere friendship and common social propriety. She did stumble upon them once, late in the evening. They were enjoying a late night cup of hot chocolate and a smattering of leftover lemon cookies as they spoke in hushed terms, presumably about the day's events. They did so with an intimacy that was the very soul of innocence, and yes, so charming. But perhaps I read too much into what my mother shared."

"Freda, my father's behavior does not annoy or surprise me. He enjoyed being with women, and, for their part, they adored his company. My father had an immense ego, often stroked by the ladies in his life. He lived, I think, a vicarious life. Obedient to his marriage vows, yet a romantic at heart whose thoughts roamed other realms. Most probably his relationship with Jane bordered, but did not exceed the social proprieties of his day. Still, one can wonder..."

Memories raised and considered... Memories now stored in the human warehouse of the past. It was time, as the group knew, to move on. Estelle Stead understood this.

———————

Automatic Handwriting

"To begin, my dear friends, what do you know about automatic handwriting?"

"Strange question, Estelle, but such handwriting, does it not have to do with producing written words without consciously writing them?"

"Very good, Harlan. The theory is that the words come from the unconscious or from spiritual or supernatural sources."

"Something similar to dreams, where life's challenges of emotions and desires seek an outlet by symbolically percolating to the surface with a resolution of some sort?"

"A fit comparison, Freda."

"What Freud called the 'royal road to the unconscious.'"

"A Jewish psychiatrist of some renown."

"The unconscious, I can handle, but not the rest, Estelle. Automatic handwriting… It disturbs my sense of intellectual inquiry. I accept what I can observe. Facts, derived as such, are the building blocks of my understanding."

"Harlan, many people take your position. They challenge claimed psychic ability."

"Withholding judgment, how does it work?"

"Very simply, Freda, an individual loosely holds a pen against a blank sheet of paper. According to some, a spirit from the other side is invoked to write message."

"That's what clairvoyants claim."

"Yes."

"As do charlatans, Estelle."

"True, Harlan. And, as to the messages… They usually have a moral or ethical aspect to them."

"Not too different from telepathy, Estelle?"

"Yes, if you mean communicating from a distance from a deceased person, Freda."

"Where is all this headed, Estelle?"

"My father, W.T. Stead believed in spiritualism, which was not uncommon at the turn of the century. A such he investigated automatic handwriting in particular, at times attempting it himself."

"What are you getting at?"

"Just this, Marcus. My father has been communicating with me. That among other things is why we're here."

Estelle's remark did not go unheard or unnoticed. Whatever the others felt about spiritualism and the supernatural, they kept to themselves. Decorum dictated such. Curiosity, as might be expected, felt no such compunction. . Inquisitive people, responding to an unusual pronouncement, had a strong desire to comprehend what appeared to be the inexplicable. Harlan, always the most impatient one when facts were needed, was first off the starter's mark.

"You summoned us here because your father communicated across the void?"

"Well, yes."

"And that is why we are meeting at the Mark Hopkins?"

"I do not deny that, Harlan."

"What, if I may ask, is the nature of this communication, Estelle?

"Warnings."

"You understand how strange all this sounds to us?"

"Even more to me, if you can believe that?"

"Perhaps you can share with us exactly what you experienced?"

"I mean to, Sir."

"Sometime in July last year my thoughts turned to my father in a way that seemed most intense. But not in the usual surface banter, to be sure. What he would have thought about this or that, such as my new very fashionable hat, for example, or the car breaking down again? No, none of that. All topics so common and so uninteresting in light of other things."

"After some sleepless nights and the realization that I was deeply depressed by Nazi-dominated Europe, I decided speak to my father somewhat indirectly. That is, I would sit in the parlor holding a photo of him, gazing for a few hours at a time at a face, so young and seeming full of possibilities. One night I placed his photo on a chair, symbolizing his presence in my mind."

"You conversed?"

"I did, Freda, very personally things at first. How much I missed him. How much I needed his guidance. How quiet the house seemed without his incessant strutting and clamorous denunciations of the world's ills, of which I also shared."

"He answered?"

"Nary a word. Silent as the night, his photo stared back at me."

What, then?"

Eventually, Harlan, I decided to pen a note to W.T., as I enjoyed calling him. You know, a short note, acting as if he would read it."

"Go on, Estelle. Pen in hand..."

"I never wrote anything, Harlan, at least of my own volition. My ink pen hovered above the linen paper, my hand steady but unmoving. I found myself merely staring into space, my mind seemingly clear of the mundane, certainly of the bourgeois thoughts of my station."

"And?"

"Harlan, I am unsure. It was like I was in a trance. My hand did move and the ink flowed, but not in the concise, journalistic language, which explained and educated, the twin characteristics marking my father's newspaper writing and my desire to emulate. Rather, only two words appeared:"

Accept It

"Accept what?"

"My first question, Freda."

"Which was answered, how?"

"Well, not by believing I had invoked the spirit of my father in a supernatural sense, or that I had received a message from the other side. That I can state unequivocally. Such thoughts I rejected out of hand."

"Leading to what conclusion, Estelle?"

"In the absence of a better explanation, the reincarnation of my father's dreams and hopes, which had found residence in my mind with a force and passion I could not deny, Harlan."

"Exactly, what are you saying? What is the 'it' you are expected to accept."

"Creating a second Ark even in the face of Hitler's triumphs. That is what I must accept."

For a long moment little was said, though much was thought. Again, respect for W.T. Stead's daughter held more animated expressions of disbelief in check, as did a calming respect for rational argument and considered words. Still…

"Estelle, very pointedly, what is the connection between your own views and your father's admonition?"

"Certainly, the father-daughter relationship. That cannot be denied. But, I openingly confess, a common adherence for the present world situation; that is also a reality."

"But the connection? How was it done?"

"In a word, Freda, mysticism. I had entered a world where the intellect alone cannot access knowledge, but where contemplation and self-surrender may attain understanding. But, as you see, pointedly the original Ark, a copy of which you all possess was at the center of my experiences."

"Something bordering on the supernatural?"

"Harlan, an experience beyond the accepted subject-object rationality of observable facts, for the lack of a better term."

"This has happened more than once, Estelle?"

"At the risk of appearing self-delusional, yes. The pen in hand, the sheet of white paper present, a kind of dreamy moment, and then my hand moves, as if it was detached from my body, acting again independently of my conscious mind as if directed by another hand."

"Difficult to accept, Estelle."

"Again, as for me, Freda."

"You've received other messages?"

"I have, Harlan. Two weeks ago:"

Idealism, not Cynicism

"Which meant what to you?"

"That the dark forces leading us again to the abyss must be challenged. We must never accept them as the 'new normal.' That we should not permit cynicism to erode our hopes for a better world, Harlan."

"Utopia?"

"I don't think so. W.T. was a realist. While he challenged the realities of his day, he never sought perfection in its own right. Rather, he sought a sort of social balance where society redressed its imperfections by wit of the democratic process. He was in that sense, I believe, an idealist, but never yoked to the ideal. I trust, Freda, this clears thinks up?"

"To some degree, yes. But going on. Have there been other manifestations, Estelle?"

"One other and most recent:

Resurrection

"Our Christian belief that the dead will rise at the Last Judgment?"

"In concept, yes, Harlan. In application, I think something far different."

"You will explain."

"No dead will rise. A second calamity will shake ... More to the point, is stalking humanity. And, if no new Ark exists, surely a third even more deadly conflict will occur, much as night follows day. As to the Last Judgment so often tied to resurrection that is a realm I cannot speculate upon except to say this. We the living, those of us here at this table, must make our own judgments in the here and now. And what would that mean, you might ask? Succinctly, the world must choose, war and oblivion, or peace and a future. This is not about the Almighty. God is off the hook."

"As to us?"

"Freda, we can only create a new Ark to enable the survivors to finally still the guns."

"A moral understanding, devoid of the Deity?"

"Our work. Freda."

Again, much like Sandburg's 'little cat feet', quiet crept into the room on 'silent haunches' and then departed, taking with it all illusions. Europe was at war. In the Pacific war was on the horizon. Death by the millions was again prancing before them, a social disease, a pandemic once more assaulting civilized societies. The specter was almost too much for those cloistered in the Mark Hopkins.

"Your desire to, if I may be so bold, to resurrect your father's work cannot be denied, nor the value of his efforts, all of which withstands challenge. That is on one side of the ledger. And then there is the process you have articulated, automatic handwriting. Delving into the mystical. Here a trained therapist might challenge the relationship between truth and fact."

"I do not reject that possibility, Freda."

"But still you wish us to act?"

"I ask you to separate the message from the process. Whether self-induced, as some might conclude, or truly beyond the pale, the process is of little concern, is it not? The message, however, is of concern regardless of its origin."

"What you ask requires faith."

"A leap of faith in ourselves, Freda."

"And in the Ark, does it not?"

"As always, on point, Harlan, as was the poet:"

The fog is an illusion...
A master of disguise,
Which hides the tangible
Before our very eyes...

CHAPTER 3

THE LETTER

<u>1941 – San Francisco - A Moment Later</u>

"Estelle, I feel there something more you wish to share?"

"You are incisive in your perception, Harlan."

"It is a useful skill when dealing with clients, some of whom are not always fully responsive to their legal representative."

"You prod?"

"Indeed, Estelle. To defend one must have clarity."

"What is called truth?"

"Or some acceptable version of it."

"Then you wish to know more. That is what you're saying?"

"If so, yes, especially if it bears upon our conspiracy."

"Does it, Estelle?"

"Without question, Freda."

"Then we are here to listen."

"My father's legacy, as you might expect, is never far from my heart. Since his passing, I have researched his life, written about his journalistic

23

career, and fought off those who would disparage his reputation. This last effort was not always easy since he aroused emotional responses with his devilish ink pen and sensationalized headlines. Some were just disagreements; others wanted his head on a plank. All that he didn't mind as he fought for women's suffrage, the limitation of arms sales, and a more active Parliament to reduce abject poverty among other things. He, of course, was never without a cause.

"In his advocacy of world peace, he was ahead of his time. Thus in his latter years it became the issue that most motivated him. Some thought he was too extreme in his desire to ward off war, even describing him as 'hysterical' in foreseeing the imminent collapse of Western civilization. His vision of the future, I'm afraid, inhibited him from being overly optimistic."

"But he did join many peace groups, isn't that so, Estelle?"

"Correct, Harlan, and with one particular group."

"The Carnegie Endowment for International Peace."

"You never fail to amaze me, Sir."

"Endowed by the industrialist, Andrew Carnegie."

"You know of this, Harlan?"

"A few general facts. Carnegie provided a gift of $10 million dollars in the form of first mortgage bonds, which paid a 5% rate of interest, sufficient to fund the peace foundation. This was in 1910."

"My father always believed he had something to do with Carnegie's generous gift."

"They did meet on numerous occasions, so perhaps he did."

"And the purpose of the endowment?"

"Freda, as Carnegie hoped, ' to hasten the abolition of international war, the foulest blot upon our civilization.'"

"An internationalist, Estelle?"

"Influence by many views, and, I believe, by my father's editorials and investigative reporting into arms sales. They were kin in their desire to hold off the gods of war."

"Through international cooperation."

"Peace conferences, Harlan."

"And unfortunately his last task and perhaps his lasting legacy."

"You speak of the peace conference in Washington D.C. in 1912?"

"None other."

"Though he had little faith in any real progress, still your father was willing to attend."

"He purchased a first class ticket on the *Titanic*, Harlan. To be on the maiden voyage of the great ship fascinated him as a reporter and, of course, provided --- hopefully --- the source of many possible stories."

The conspirators, perhaps numbed by their last exchange, retreated into a cocoon of silence, there to contemplate the vicissitudes of life, if not the ironies of unanticipated circumstances. The *Titanic*... Always the ship held sway. William Thomas Steed, the driving force behind the first Ark, would forever be tied to the ship, and a chunk of ice for whom human hubris amounted to nothing. *Unsinkable*... The word still stabbed at Estelle and the others, as did its warning never to tempt the gods.

"Estelle, you muse."

"I do, Freda."

"The ship again?"

"Not entirely."

"Then?"

"I'm afraid have not been completely candid with you, my dear colleagues. Before our Mark Hopkins gathering, and certainly before our new arrangements for the Sea Cliff residence, I received another message from my father."

"Mystical handwriting again?"

"Yes, if you wish to portray it that way, Freda?"

"Another word?"

Persist

"At what?"

"That I could not determined. Only retrospectively do I have an explanation"

"Which is?"

"An unopened letter, Harlan, I recently discovered lodged between two books in my personal library dated 1912. Apparently, it arrived just after the *Titanic* sank. In my grief I somehow misplaced it. Those first days of the disaster left me in a daze, and what some might call clinical depression. In any event it was forgotten."

"How did you find it?"

"Freda, it unnerves me to say. A strange feeling came over me one evening to read a certain book, a child's book that my father often read to me. The urge to find it became quite overpowering. I stayed up half the night searching. Eventually, I found the book, thin in width, only ten pages in length. Sandwiched between other books, it was all but invisible. In removing it from the shelf, the letter appeared, almost as if by magic."

"Your father communicating to you?"

"On some level, yes, Harlan."

"You opened it?"

"I did."

"And?"

"The letter was written to me before his ill-fated voyage."

"The contents of which you desire to share?"

"Which I must share, Harlan."

———————

1912
London

Dearest Estelle,

I embark soon on a journey to the New World in an effort to save the old one. I do so with forbearance since I feel little will be accomplished at the peace conference, though all who attend are good people of high purpose. The problem seems to be three-fold. First, the leaders of great European empires have not and will not accept our conclusions and recommendations to keep the peace. Second, we have no mechanism by which to enforce our views on sovereign governments, whether democratic or authoritarian. Third, the general public, ignorant of the coming war, does not appreciate the calamity before them. In this they cannot be fully blamed. People are still thinking in terms of the relative short Franco-Prussian War of 1870. That is the mold that constricts their understanding. The magnitude of the looming tragedy will be far different in its consequences. Still, I do what I can.

My dear daughter, do not be put off about what I am about to say. I am at the moment feverish and famished. I have not slept for days. And I fear I am experiencing a nervous breakdown. That is, your father's sanity is eroding. What has caused this? A vision... A prelude of what is coming... Not the general European war of which I have warned. Not that. Rather, a sequel, far more destructive and a final threat to civilized men. The vision came to me periodically during the past few months. It is if the future is communicating with me on a psychic level. It is if the future has already occurred and I remain the only witness to it.

I am frightened by all this and loath to share the vision with others. I fear many would consider me unbalanced. But I must speak. I must share. I do so now, fearful that our little Conspiracy of 1910, of which you are now fully aware, will fail. Keep in mind I am not crazy, though what I predict and describe is communal insanity.

Estelle, the coming conflict will occur. Consider it past tense. A peace treaty will be signed. It will have in it the seeds of another unavoidable war within two decades. One war will give birth to another. The vision has made this abundantly clear to me.

The physicists tell us that for every action there is a reaction. This is also true of history. A peace treaty will be enforced on the defeated by the victors. It will be stringent. Unduly harsh... Colonies will be taken from the vanquished, as will land-portions of the defeated in Europe. Impossible reparations will be made on the losing side. They will be imposed harshly. Again, in my vision what will happen has already occurred. Call it, if you will, a form of historical telepathy.

———————

"Estelle, you accept all of this?"

"Harlan, do I really have a choice? My father was given to hyperbole, not ranting in the night."

"But telepathy."

"Perhaps just the convoluted workings of his agile mind, or maybe an astral presence existing in two different realities, yet able to converse. I have no clear answer."

"Still, you ask us to act on the basis of this letter?"

"I do Harlan, but not entirely. Leave aside its origin; deal only with its content. Either it has persuasive value, or it doesn't. You must decide."

"There is more?"

"Yes, Freda, and most alarming..."

———————

Estelle, for a time there will be an enforced European peace after the former empires of the continent are dismembered into ethnic states. But all this will be an illusion. Beneath the surface, the disgruntled, those who see themselves as victims, will attract each other, much as a magnet attracts metal filings. They will meet, coalesce around sinister ideas of revenge and seek to gain political and police power. From this mindless morass of human frustration and craven anger will emerge a leader before whom the world will tremble in fear. All this cannot be stopped. In one sense, as I have already said, it has already happened.

"Are you saying, Estelle, that your father predicted the rise of Adolf Hitler and the Nazi regime?"

"No, Freda. Something deeper. He saw the rise of a demonic leader willing to turn the world into a vast wasteland of unredeemed suffering."

"How can that be?"

"The vision he had… It wasn't about what was coming. It was about what already existed."

"Hard to accept."

"What choice do we have, Harlan. Hitler exists. Belgium and Holland are gone. France is prostrate. An independent Poland is no more. The rumors of death camps exist. Does it really matter how my father came to know this? We have in writing his statement of fact, understood as a vision, prepared before his death in 1912. We can dismiss him as deranged or, as I hope, honor his legacy and act."

"That being the case, Estelle, what should we do?"

"His very last words, Freda."

"Given all this, Estelle, what should we do? Tragically, I am now convinced nothing can avoid the coming war in Europe, what's immediately up ahead and its aftermath. And with the greatest misgivings, I foresee little hope in our Ark at the current time to forestall the post-war problems I've alluded to. An an even greater war will follow that which looms before us. A new Ark will be needed twenty or thirty years from now. If our little 'Conspiracy of 1910' fails, another will be needed, and given my age and others in the gang, this

responsibility will fall to you and perhaps, Marcus, and if they are willing, the children of Ida B. Wells and Judge Harlan. This weight I bequeath to you and them with the greatest sadness. I know what I am asking; I have nowhere else to turn. But be aware that my vision foresees still another conflict, distant and barely discernable, but so terrible in its possibility as to threaten the human specie. These terrible conflicts, as if they were railroad cars, line up, one after the other, each a further insanity, the final folly of the human race. I do not think I can ward off this aberration that so haunts my soul and disturbs my mind.

Your loving father, W.T. Stead

––––––––––

"What are we going to do?"

"Precisely, Harlan. Or better said, what should we do? For Europe it is too late. If possible, we must try to keep the peace in the Pacific to avoid a conflict between the United States and Japan."

"Dear lady, will not America, as once before, be drawn into the European conflict regardless of what happens in the Pacific?

"Perhaps. But what choice do we have? Where peace is still possible, we must act."

"And if we fail?"

"Then, Harlan, we will still resurrect a new Ark, bequeathing it the survivors. In that we must persist. Marcus Garvey and the others would want us to do this.

CHAPTER 4

THE EMPRESS OF CHINA

<u>February 1941 – Seattle</u>

The conspirators were enjoying their lunch at Ben Paris' Restaurant located at 1609 Westlake. Thanks to Estelle, who always seemed to be on top of things, much like her father, they had reservations on the tenth anniversary of the well-known eatery. Not only that, they were enjoying prices that were in effect in 1931 when the place opened. Of course, the restaurant was full, locals and visitors to town enjoying good food and an outrageously low tab. What could be better?

"How's your lunch, Harlan?"

"At $.60, what can I say? The roast leg of pork cooked with a homemade dressing is just fine, along with the warm rolls and tangy butter. Good choice, Estelle."

"And, Freda, your meal?"

"Veal fricassee and vegetables at an embarrassing $.40 per plate... I think I'll make do. And your food, Estelle, your cream chicken a la king on a biscuit?"

"Delightful."

Traveling by rail and bus at Estelle's urging, Freda and Harlan found themselves in Seattle with a typical Stead command still ringing in their ears.

"That's right, every so often we'll meet in a different city to review and discuss what we've digested. That way, there's less of a chance anyone will catch on to our little conspiracy of incognito 'pirates,' as my father often referred to his gang. And before I hear objections, recall that travel is good for the soul. It will also give us an opportunity to see the country we're trying to keep at peace even at this late date."

"Time for dessert. Harlan?"

"Apple pie a la mode."

"Freda?"

"Chocolate pudding."

"And I'll have a baked apple. Then, I think, it's time for us to discuss the materials you received earlier in the month."

Three packages, each wrapped in heavy brown paper, arrived on a Wednesday as expected by the sender, Kenneth Tanaka, a Stanford University Professor of Japanese Studies. In no particular order, the lawyer Harlan received his package in New York City where he resided pleasantly with his family and an enjoyable legal practice. Another package traveled to Chicago, where the activist-Freda quickly put aside her latest editorial on race relations in the Windy City. Almost as quickly, she found a pair of sharp scissors to cut the twine holding the contents securely in their wrapping. The last package found its way to San Francisco, only a few miles north of Palo Alto, home to Leland Stanford's legacy to the "gold rush of 1849," and the transcontinental railroad he helped to build that provided the cash for an institution bearing his name. The instigator-Estelle, of course, knew in general what was in the bundle, since she had first proposed the idea to the university academic.

Once unwrapped each conspirator found seventy or more pages, along with a few charts and maps. Of course, what got their immediate attention was the envelope addressed to them, containing for each the same message.

To those involved,

I have provided you with materials concerning America's initial involvement in Asia as requested by Estelle Stead to assist you in your efforts to create an Ark, about which she conveyed little clarity. Indeed, she was quite mysterious about this. As a historian I was, of course, quite curious given her request for information about the Empress of China. As you will soon learn this has little to do with any Chinese personage, but a great deal to do with a ship and America's first attempt in the 1870's to trade with China, as were the English, the Dutch, and the Portuguese. Retrospectively, the implication of this first voyage was more than obvious in time. One of the newest nations in the world was commencing relations with one of the oldest civilization known. But it would also mean that America would slowly become inextricably entangled in the Far East and, as subsequent events would show, with the Imperial Japan.

Before proceeding further, a word about myself. My grandfather migrated from Japan in the 1880's to work on the railroads. In time he sent for my mother, a "picture bride." My father and his family started a nursery in the Central Valley of California, near Madera. They specialized in camellias, an Asian shrub similar to the tea plant. It is known for its snowy white flowers and shiny leaves. The business flourished, the Great Depression notwithstanding, as did the size of their family. As the youngest of five I was the first to attend college. Attracted to history I pursued a doctorate at Stanford in Japanese-American relations. This is where I now teach as the Chair of Japanese Studies. My own family lives in Redwood City not far from the campus.

Given the present tense situation with the Empire of Japan, I trust what follows will be useful to you. As you read recall that all events have a past that influences the present, and is sometimes a sign of what is to come.

Professor Kenneth Tanaka
February 1941

The Story of the Empress of China

February 22, 1874 marked the fifty-second anniversary of George Washington's birthday. It also marked the day a 360-ton wooden, squared rigged ship maneuvered out of New York harbor to begin an 18,000-mile trip to Canton, China and back. It would be at sea for fourteen months and twenty-four days before it again birthed in New York Harbor. The *Empress of China*, originally constructed as a privateer during the American Revolution, had been refitted into a commercial cargo ship after the Treaty of Paris (1783) ended the conflict with Great Britain.

The ship reached Canton on August 28, 1784, and America's history would forever be altered by this voyage.

The 43-man crew was led by Captain John Green, a seaman with considerable command experience, both in peacetime and war. Fortunately, the good captain maintained a diary throughout the voyage. Entries will be included from time to time. They lend local color to life at sea.

The *Empress of China* carried 30 tons of cargo worth $120,000. The voyage was financed by many of America's richest men, including Robert Morris of Philadelphia, the banker who help fund the American Revolution. He had a half-interest in the venture.

The cargo included:

- Barrels of pepper   ... Furs
- 600 beaver skins   ... Chest of Spanish silver
- 242 casks of ginseng ... Raw cotton

The cargo would be exchanged for China's valuable exports, which were most sought after:

- Black tea – 2,460 loads (800 chests)
- Green tea – 562 loads
- Silk – 490 rolls
- Porcelain – 962 loads (64 tons)

The eventual profit from this transaction was $30,727, a 24% return on the investment. The items brought back were a sensation, as people purchased them and wanted more. Traders quickly understood there was a market for Chinese goods and fortunes to be made. This was particularly true of porcelain for which there was an almost insatiable demand. On the other side of the world, Chinese factories were constructed to just deal with the American demand.

Between 1784 and 1790 some 28 American ships sailed to China. By 1790 Chinese imports accounted for 1/7th of all imports and nine Yankee companies were registered and operating in Canton. The first crop of American millionaires, many contend, were those involved in the China trade.

A word, if you will, about the valuable ginseng plant. The Chinese have always valued this plant for medical reasons because of its healing powers. The *Shen-Nng Pharmacopoeia* was written in China in 196 A.D. Ginseng was characterized as a medicinal herb. Li Shizhen described the plant as a "superior tonic" for patients with chronic illnesses in 1596 (*Compendium of Materia Medica*). Technically it is a root plant in the genus Panax, which means "all-healing." That being the case, many Chinese men concerned about their virility were not unopposed to purchasing the plant. A last point: this plant root has a forked shape, which resembles the legs of a person, but not the gender.

The voyage was by no means easy. Once leaving New York, the *Empress of China* went to Cape Verde off the west coast of Africa. This was followed by extended sailing down the coast of Africa and around the Cape of Good Hope. Then there was the expanse of the Indian Ocean to be navigated before reaching the Sumatra Straits, the watery corridor between Java and Sumatra, two colonial outposts of the Dutch between Australia and China. Once through the "straits," the next stop was the Portugal's trading center in Macao, and then to the Pearl River in China, which led the *Empress of China* to Canton, also known by its Chinese name, Whampoa.

LEAVING NEW YORK HARBOR

Sunday, February 1784 – This morning commenced with pleasant weather. The winds at WNW... At daylight, hove the ship from the wharf into the stream. Got all hands on board. At passing the Grand Battery, a great number of inhabitants saluted us by giving three cheers, which we returned. We also saluted the Fort with 13 guns, which they returned with 12.

A host of questions remained unanswered when the *Empress of China* sailed for China. First and foremost, would the profits of such a venture be worth the risk? Would commerce between the two countries be mutually advantageous? As already noted the first question was answered in the affirmative. There was money to be made in the China trade.

Would the commercial conditions and practices in Canton be conducive to trade? Again, the question proved academic. The Chinese were skilled traders with an entrepreneurial spirit that would do justice to any New England merchant. Chinese merchants were "enthused" by the prospect of trade with America after seeing the size of he country on a map. For their part, the perennial hope of U.S. merchants to capture the presumably rich China market seemed to be realized. In short, future trade and profits were possible, especially with spices, such as:

- Cloves
- Cinnamon
- Nutmeg

How would the Chinese receive a ship flying the American flag? Would there be a clash of cultures? In general there was no problem as long as the *Empress of China* adhered to Chinese regulations. Indeed, those in Canton wanted to know about America. The Chinese were receptive of the officers and crew and desirous of acquiring information about these foreigners. Where was America? Why do you speak the same language as the British? What products do you produce?

WILDLIFE AT SEA

Sunday, June 20, 1784 – Wind blowing fresh all this 24 hours from ESE. Mostly the reefed topsails set, close handed by the wind. Saw numbers of fowls like gannets as to their plumage but fly like seagulls or a bird called boobies. Numbers of flying fish in sight as well as the tropicbirds. At noon, saw a plank, which had been in the water for some time by its appearance.

HARSH WEATHER

Wednesday, July 7, 1784 – Dark, cloudy, squally weather… No such thing as trusting much sail set, the weather looks so bad. At 6 P.M., reefed the three topsails. Handed the mainsail. Set the forestay sail, main and mizzen-staysails with the foresail and topsails. At 8, sounded. No ground 120 fathom. The hardest rain I ever saw. We catched in our water sail near 600 gallons of excellent water. The latter part, calm. All hands drying their clothes. Out of reefs to dry. Mending the main and mizzen-topsails, which were blown from the foot-rope.

The voyage of the *Empress of China* brought America to the shores of China and soon after to Japan. There would be no turning back. America now had Asiatic interests as prophesied by Senator William H. Seward two decades earlier:

> *Who does not see, then, that…the Pacific Ocean, Its shores, its islands, and the vast regions beyond, will become the chief theatre of events in the world's great hereafter? (1852)*

The "great hereafter" came sooner than Seward might have expected in the form of America's Open Door Policy, a topic we will next take up with implications for our present foreign policy toward Japan.

REACHING CANTON

Tuesday, August 24, 1784 – At 4 A.M., several of the greatest quantities s of Chinese boats I ever beheld were out fishing. At 5, a Chinese boat came on board, took down the ship's name, master's name, quantity of men and guns on board, where from, and what nation; then left us. Soon after came several boats with eggs, sugar, breadfruit, and shoes with sundry other articles for sale. A Canton pilot was sent for taking us to Whampoa.

The journey of *Empress of China* was now history. What the future would bring was beyond the scope of those who sailed into Asiatic waters, but in time their story would be told. But here one must be careful. As Napoleon Bonaparte said, "History is the version of past events that people have decided to agree upon."

To commemorate the voyage, the American poet, Phillip Franeau, penned a poem extoling the enterprise, representing as it did, a newly independent country finally freed of the British trade yoke and free to do business in the Far East.

> With clearance from Bellon won
> She spreads her wings to meet the Sun,
> Those golden regions to explore
> To countries placed in burning climes
> And islands of remotest times
> She now her eager course explores
> And soon shall greet Chinesian shores.
> From thence their fragrant teas to bring
> Without the leave of Britain's king;
> And Porcelain ware, enchased in gold,
> The product of that finer mould.

CHAPTER 5

THE OPEN DOOR
POLICY

———————◦∿◦———————

February 1941 – Seattle

The conspirators needed a few days to digest what they had read
and to converse with each other before moving on to Professor Tanaka's
next topic, the Open Door Policy of President William McKinley. The
Empress of China still sailed gallantly, however, in their minds, the wind
at her stern pushing her forward, even as the bow cut through the waves,
spraying those on deck with a fine mist. They could see the men in
their daily routines: The Captain plotting his course; the steady hand of
helmsman keeping China always on the horizon; the deckhands high in
the clouds clearing sail; the gunner testing his armaments; the barrel maker
rechecking the provisions below deck.

Of course, the conspirators wondered if the men knew they were making
history? Did they comprehend the invisible line that curved across great
oceans to Canton and past that moment to the present day? Most probably
no; they lived in their day, as the conspirators must in their own time.

Once again, they turned to a preamble written by their mentor,
Professor Tanaka.

Americans are prone to risk-taking. The American Revolution itself was a roll of the dice. Imagine, taking on the British Empire. Heading westward into hostile lands was a decision not easily made by those stranded along the eastern seaboard. "Wagons West" was the cry no matter the dangers. Later choosing sides, free state, slave state and a civil war, placing the entire American experiment in democratic government at risk. Laying rail across a continent, or digging a ditch across the Isthmus of Panama to connect two great bodies of water, two unprecedented challenges and each successfully met no matter the odds. Yes, America is a land of risk-takers, including, as in this case, a quiet unassuming statesman who bluffed the world in 1895, pulling off the diplomatic stunt of his day, and in doing so guaranteed America's involvement in Asian affairs, then and now.

Or at least that's what some say.

John Hays' Problem

As Secretary of State under Presidents William McKinley and later Theodore Roosevelt, John Hay faced many diplomatic challenges, none more serious than the question of how to maintain free trade in China for American business interests, while dealing with the emergence of a powerful Japanese military in the Far East? That was the question and the Secretary's problem.

To some extent, at least for the United States, it all began in Shimonoseki, Japan on April 17, 1895. In that city the Treaty of Shimonoseki was signed between the Empire of Japan and the Qing Dynasty of China, thereby ending the Sino-Japanese War of 1894-95. Driven by Japan's overwhelming victory, the terms of the treaty were exceedingly harsh:

- China would recognize the complete independence of Korea (and indirectly Japan's nominal control of the peninsula, one cause of the war).
- China would cede to Japan the Pescadores, Formosa, and eastern portions of the Bay of Liaodong Peninsula.
- All fortifications, arsenals, and public properties in these areas would fall under Japanese control.

- China would pay an indemnity to Japan of 16,534,599 pounds of silver.
- China would also grant to Japan a "most favored nation status" in the area of foreign trade on the mainland equal to any trade relationship already enjoyed by the British, French, Germans, the Dutch, and the Americans. Additionally, Japan could use any Chinese port and navigate any river without question.

The Japanese military victory humiliated China. Chinese possessions were ripped away. More than that, it emphasized Japan's emergence as an Asian power and the weakness of the Chinese government, sealing the country's reputation as the "sick man of Asia." European powers were now in a position to carve up the "living carcass" of China into strong "spheres of influence" under the guise of "long-term lease holdings." Within each sphere, the imperialistic power had political and economic control, providing its nationals with preferential treatment over other foreign nationals. This could amount to control of port fees, railroad costs, and tariffs, all of which had a direct influence on trade. It also meant that revenues to the Chinese government might be reduced, even eliminated, leaving the nation starved for cash.

As Secretary of State, John Hay realized that something had to be done to protect America's commercial ties to China caused by the imperialistic frenzy by Europeans and Japan to create further areas of foreign control. Those economic ties were significant. Since the 1980's, China had evolved into a major trading partner for the United States, so much so that approximately one-third of the China trade was carried in American ships. Hay concluded that Russia, Germany, and France were attempting to exclude both Britain and America from the China trade. Something had to be done about this.

Hay outlined a number of basic principles that should underpin America's foreign policy in order to keep the "door" open to Chinese trade. They included:

1. The United States was opposed to colonial acquisitions in China by any nations.

2. Equality of trade opportunities for all nations was paramount.
3. The United States desired free and equal access to the Chinese market, which amounted to 2% of the nation's foreign trade in 1884, but was growing.
4. Chinese territorial sovereignty should be maintained in order to keep a balance of power in Asia (Japan vs. China). The partitioning of China should end.

Hay concluded that a statement of the U.S. position on freedom of trade in China would "appease American businessmen and possibly earn some goodwill among the Chinese that might benefit the United States commercially. It would convince "expansionists" at home that the United States was prepared to live up to its responsibility as an Asian power."

Straightforward, could Hay craft a workable trade policy, which the European powers and Japan would accede to that included the Secretary's principles? Without the power of law or any enforcement provision, how could this be done? And why would Berlin, St. Petersburg, London, and Paris consider such principles from an upstart nation late on the imperialistic scene? And, of course, there was Japan. Would she abide by an American sponsored Open Door Policy? Given this, Hay decided to play poker. He would, if possible, gain international support by a diplomatic bluff.

On September 6, 1899 he sent a note to the capitals alluded to, which became known as the Open Door Policy. The note sought unanimous approval regarding the following points:

1. Within any "sphere of influence," no power would interfere with foreign nationals and their use of any treaty port.
2. The Chinese tariff treaty would be applicable within all "spheres of interest."
3. Chinese authorities would collect all tariffs.
4. No power would discriminate in favor of its own nationals within its area of control.

Essentially, Secretary Hay was seeking the fairest and most equable system of trade opportunities, which would protect America's commercial interests. He was not ending areas of foreign control, nor was he advocating for the extensions or enlargement of such areas. As Hay stated:

41

> *The United States earnestly desirous to remove any cause of irritation and to insure at the same time to the commerce of all nations in China the undoubted benefits which should accrue from a formal recognition by the various powers claiming "spheres of interest" that they shall enjoy perfect equality of treatment for their commerce and navigation within n such "spheres," the Government of the United States would be pleased to see His German Majesty's Government give formal assurances, and lend its cooperation in securing like assurances from the other interested powers, that each, within its respective sphere of whatever influence.*

Having sent out his "Note," he awaited responses.

Almost all nations responded affirmatively, but each with a major qualification and less than subtle caveats. Full acceptance was contingent upon the "unqualified approval" of other nations. Russia hinted at rejection, which would have released any nation from the agreement. To avoid this and a host of changes Hays sent out a second statement indicating that all countries had assented, and that the policy was now "final." This, of course, was his great gamble. Would he be able to bluff the other parties to the agreement, most importantly, Britain.

In the end he was able to do so. Why was this possible? The direct answer was this: the great powers did not trust each other or their ambitions in China. Suspicion reigned. Conflict was in the air. Some resolution was necessary to mediate the situation. Hay's policy depended on this. His declaration provided a face-saving way out for all nations. The Open Door Policy allayed fears by providing a sense of equal treatment that nations gave tacit agreement to, even as they exploited China.

Historians later asked hard questions of the Open Door policy. Did Hays actually pull off the bluff, or did others simply go along with it? Acquiesce was better than conflict. Did the policy actually provide equal opportunity in every "sphere of interest?" Not necessarily. Nationals were still generally treated preferentially compared to foreigners. Did the policy insist on Chinese territorial integrity? Again, not really; the foreign enclaves continued to extract mining and railroad concessions from the Chinese government. Did the Open Door Policy pry open a door for increased American trade? Generally, yes.

The China Policy of the United States was now to:

> *... promote permanent safety and peace to China, preserve Chinese territorial and administrative entity... and safeguard for the world the principle of equal and impartial trade with all parts of the Chinese empire.*

The implications of Hay's policy were easily perceived, not only in hindsight, but also at the time by keen observers. America was now entangled in China's affairs and opposed to any effort that threatened the sovereignty of the country, and/or its trade with the West. That threat, as then understood at the turn of the century, would come over time from an expansive Tokyo marching to the drumbeat of Japanese imperialistic designs in China. If so, what would be America's response?

Professor Tanaka added a postscript:

> *On point; the current crisis in Asia reflects this continuing concerns. The American administration under President Franklin D. Roosevelt opposes the Japanese recent takeover of Manchuria and the more recent invasion of China, which began in 1931. Japan's aggressive foreign policy threatens the territorial sovereignty of China and adherence to the Open Door Policy. The Japanese, however, take a different view. Japan, lacking in major resources such as coal, oil, and iron ore, needs to expand beyond her borders, not only in Korea, Manchuria, and China, but also in Southeast Asia. Japan contends she needs additional resources and new markets, even at the point of a bayonet, to support her notion of "manifest destiny" in the Far East. Unless these contrasting views could be reconciled, the danger of a Pacific War exists.*

What began with the voyage of *Empress of China* now sailed into the high seas of American foreign policy. If you look closely enough you can still eye her just over the horizon.

> *A gray day, and the gulls are gone.*
> *Visor of mist o'er the sun is drawn.*
> *The cordage creaks and sails all strain,*
> *The deck is drenched with the rushing rain,*
> *The saves leap strong at the struggling keels,*
> *And the ship rides madly with plunge and reel.*
> *But the sailors shout as they haul away,*
> *And merrily sing, for it's naught care they*
> *For the wind that screams on the lee,*
> *Or a gray day out at sea…*

And again, if your eyes are keen enough you'll see other ships plying the Pacific, stretching out from San Francisco to the shores of Nippon.

CHAPTER 6

OPENING UP JAPAN

March 1941 – Seattle

As was his way, Professor Tanaka prefaced each topic in a manner to engage the reader; that is, the conspirators. That was appreciated by all since history can be deadly if carried to the lowest common dominator: names, facts, and dates floating in a universe of time, but signifying what?

Friends… By now I think of you as such. Now that we've pried open an American market in China, it's time to turn our attention to Japan, which for over two-hundred-years had resisted European efforts to open up the country to foreigners. All good things, at least from one point of view, must come to an end; the end for Japan's resistance to foreign trade began quietly on November 24, 1852 in the naval harbor of Norfolk, Virginia. Aboard the steam-powered flagship USS Mississippi Commodore Matthew Perry cast anchor and, along with other ships of the East India Squadron, fired up all boilers for an arduous cruise to Japan. Prodded by his boss, President Franklin Pierce, Perry's mission was to succeed where others had failed; that is, to establish diplomatic ties with Edo (modern day Tokyo) and to further America's economic interests in the Far East. Ostensibly this task would be accomplished diplomatically. If not possible, however, "gunboat diplomacy" would be utilized. Perry's considerable number of naval guns would threatened to fire away until the diplomats reconciled the situation in an agreement satisfactory to all.

As always, you should be asking yourself important questions. What had motivated President Pierce to force open the Japanese door, so to speak? If successful, what were the implications for both countries? In answering these questions, a number of other topics will be discussed beyond Perry's mission itself. These topics include the Convention of Kanagawa, the Harris Treaty, the Meiji Restoration, and the Sino-Japanese War of 1894-95. Again, you might ask, why these topics? The succinct answer is this: the present tensions with Japan in 1941 stem from what happened almost 90-years ago on the day Perry sailed into Tokyo Harbor.

All of this, of course, will be taken in small bites. History is better digested in this manner.

Perry's Mission

A number of factors motivated President Millard Pierce to send Perry to the ends of the earth, including:

1. Concluding a commercial treaty to provide for trade between the two countries.
2. Protection of shipwrecked American sailors, especially whalers operating near Japan, and their safe return to the United States.
3. Establishing a coaling station for America's new steam-powered ships.
4. Executing an agreement with Japan before the Europeans did so, as they had done in China, and doing so through negotiations, not at the point of a cannon.
5. A sense of "manifest destiny" to spread America's civilization, not only throughout a vast North American continent, but also to the Far East.

Perry was the right man for the job. He was a commodore in the navy. He had fought bravely in the War of 1812 and the Mexican War of 1846-48. He also took part in the Barbary War off North Africa and the efforts in the West Indies to end the slave trade.

He had helped to establish the curriculum for the new United States Naval Academy. He was also a leading advocate to switch from sails to a steam-powered navy, so much so that he is considered the "father of the steam navy." Beyond that, he came from a family of sailors, one of who was the hero of Lake Erie in the War of 1812 against Great Britain, Oliver Hazard Perry known for his iconic cry, " I have not yet begun to fight."

Though not a professional diplomat, Perry had the instincts, constraint, and keenness of focus, all necessary qualities for his mission to open up Japan. Pierce had picked the right man for the job.

On July 8, 1853 Perry's fleet of four black-hulled ships, sprouting 61-guns and a crew of nearly 1,000 men reached the entrance to Edo Bay. He ordered his ships to steam past Japanese troops to the capital. The Japanese had never seen steamships belching black smoke moving up stream against a heavy wind, apparently without a problem. This was surprising to them, as they were when Perry trained his guns on local towns, indicating he would fire if there were a lack of cooperation. It was difficult for the Japanese not to panic as the "burning ships" took up position. This was something of a ploy, since Perry was really under orders to avoid using force except in self-defense.

He was told to dock at Nagasaki, the only port open to the Dutch, who had a limited trade relationship with Edo. Perry refused. Straightforward, he told the Japanese he had a letter for the Shogun, the hereditary leader in feudal Japan, even more so than the weak Mikado or emperor. His fleet then fired blank shots from all guns to intimidate the Japanese. Following this, he ordered his ships to survey the coastline and surrounding waters against Japanese resistance.

Forewarned by the Dutch of the American fleet, the Japanese government was still "paralyzed," as to how to deal with the Americans. The reigning Shogun Tokugawa was ill. There was indecision by his advisors as to what actions should be taken. Eventually, Pierce's letter was accepted by delegates of the Shogun, and Perry was allowed to make landfall on July 14,1853. Soon after he departed for Hong Kong, the first part of his mission accomplished. He promised to return the following year to negotiate a treaty. The beginnings of a diplomatic relationship were in place.

It is prudent to ask, what was in the Pierce's letter to the Japanese Emperor upon which so much depended?

Assurances:

I have *directed Commodore Perry to assure your imperial majesty that I entertain the strongest feelings toward your majesty's person and government, and that I have no other object in sending him to Japan but to propose to your imperial majesty that the United States and Japan should live in friendship and have commercial intercourse with each other.*

Proximity:

The United States of America reach from ocean to ocean and our Territory of Oregon and California lie directly opposite to the dominions of your imperial majesty. A steamship can go from California to Japan in eighteen days.

Trade:

The ancient laws of your imperial majesty's government do not all of free trade, except with the Chinese and the Dutch, but as the state of the world shows new governments are formed; it seems to be wise, from time to time, to review old laws. There was a time when the ancient laws of your imperial majesty's government were first made. If your government were to change the ancient laws as to allow a free trade between the two countries, it would be extremely vital to both.

It was clear that Japan's selective isolation was over. The United States was going to pry open trade, one way or another. Japan got the message, no matter how nuanced.

The Convention of Kanagawa

Six months later Perry returned, this time with ten ships and over 1600 men. The size of his force was intentional. He was determined to pressure the Japanese government by an implied threat of naval guns blasting away. He landed at Yokohama. The date was March 8, 1851.

Perry now sought to impress the Japanese with the "power and greatness of the United States." Abroad his ships were large quantities of champagne and vintage Kentucky bourbon, which he shared with his unwilling hosts to their delight. He also showed off a pair of Sam Colt's six-shooters, making the point that America had thousands more plus other armaments. Technology was also on display, as when Perry produced a scale model train for their hosts, who were again delighted in watching the locomotive work. Progress was being made if the use of Kentucky bourbon imbued can be considered a yardstick.

Intense negotiations were carried on for a month and under the threat of military conflict, and because the Japanese were unsure what policy to pursue. Always the Chinese situation was in the background, and only recently, the aggressiveness of Russian warships plying in Japanese waters. In the end national survival won out; the Americans had knocked on the door, the Japanese would open it. Better to deal with the Yankees than the British or others. Better to make limited concessions than to have exploitative agreements forced upon them

Ultimately, after considerable negotiations, the first treaty between the two countries was arrived at, the Treaty of Peace and Amity (1856). It included the following provisions:

1. Mutual peace between Japan and the United States.
2. Two ports would be opened for trade.
3. Shipwrecked American sailors would be assisted and safe.
4. There would be freedom of movement by temporary foreign residents in treaty ports.
5. Trade transactions would be permitted.
6. Currencies could be exchanged.
7. The provisioning of American ships would be a government monopoly.
8. Japan would give the United States any favorable advantage, which might be negotiated by Japan with any other foreign government in the future.

Point 7 was of great importance to the United States: Japan would become a coaling station for American ships as requested in Pierce's letter:

> *We wish that our steamships be allowed to stop in Japan and supply themselves with coal and other provisions,*

On February 21,1855, the Treaty of Pace and Amity was ratified by both countries In doing so, over 200-years of Japan's self-imposed isolation ended. No longer would the Dutch and Chinese have exclusive trade privileges with Japan through the port of Nagasaki. A new day in the history of Japan and the United States was at hand. Japan was opening up to the world and America had her foot in the Far East door.

Professor Tanaka added an important note here:

> *Once more, beyond the looming big guns of Perry's ships, why did the Japanese capitulate? Why did they give the Americans all that they requested? From the perspective of the Japanese they feared that trade and a desire to spread Christianity would provide the imperialists powers with a pretext to carve up Japan, as had been the case in China. A militarily weak Japan was in no position for a military confrontation. She had to be pragmatic. She had to buy time.*

Townsend Harris

Soon after President Pierce appointed Townsend Harris the first Consul General to the Tokugawa government in 1856. Harris was an exceedingly good choice. He was a successful New York City merchant and importer. He was an avid reader who taught himself French, Italian, and Spanish. He also founded the Free Academy of the City of New York, which is today known as the City College of New York. He did so to provide educational opportunities for the city's working people. He was also acquainted with Asian customs and societies having been to Thailand, and the Dutch and British East Indies.

Harris summarized his conception of his role and mission as Counsel General, stating, as he had earlier about Thailand:

> *The United States does not hold any possessions in the East, nor does it desire any. The form of government forbids the holding of colonies. The United States therefore cannot be an object of jealousy to any Eastern Power. Peaceful commercial relations, which give as well as receive benefits, is what the*

> *President wishes to establish, and such is the object of my mission.*

Harris opened the first US consulate in Japan with little fanfare. Life was not easy for him. He was housed in a run-down temple with, as he recalled, "rats, bats, and enormous spiders" in a small and rather isolated village of Shimoda. For months he heard nothing from Washington, referring to himself as the "most isolated American official in the world."

It was obvious that though the door was open, the Japanese were not going to indulge the interloper. However, Harris was a patient man, who came to appreciate the Japanese culture. He had to wait eighteen months before being permitted to have a personal audience with the Shogun in the royal palace. He then presented a letter from the President to the Shogun. Four months later he concluded the Harris Treaty of 1858, which amplified the earlier treaty provisions concluded by Perry. For example, improved trade rights were gained and foreign concessions were established. Five new ports were opened to trade. Though reluctant, the Japanese accepted the principle of extra-territoriality. American nationals would be under American law in their own enclaves, not Japanese law.

What had finally turned the tide? Harris contended persuasively that Japan would be better off yielding to America voluntarily than forced concessions the European imperialists would force on the country by Again, the Japanese were quick to grasp his meaning.

Now a bit of trivia that cemented the treaty... The Harris Treaty made provisions for a Japanese mission to travel to America and exchange treaty ratifications. A party of over seventy persons, envoys and their retinue, were transported on an American warship in 1860. Congress appropriated $50,000 for their entertainment of what was described as wide-eyed visitors. They toured America for seven months before returning home, fascinated by what they had seen. They would eventually be the kernels of change in Japan.

As to Harris... He held a favorable view of the Japanese. He said of them:

The people all appeared clean and well fed, well clad, and happy looking. It is more like the golden age of simplicity and honesty than I have ever seen in other counties.

When Harris returned to the United States in 1861, a Japanese diplomat described him this way: "You have been more than a friend. You have been our benefactor and teacher. Your spirit and memory will live forever in the history of Japan."

Professor Tanaka summarized the implications of Perry's venture, stating:

Japan was not opened to the world and the country was at a crossroads. The Japanese, though jealous of their traditional customs and certainly their history, were being brought unceremoniously into new circumstances. As a nation what would happen to the Japanese people? On the one hand, there was the example of China, where imperialistic carving knives were sharp and out. But what was in the other hand? Was it possible for Japan and adopt Western ways and adapt quickly enough to avoid China's fate? And, if possible, how would the West respond, especially the United States in the long run?

Bayard Taylor, a journalist, was aboard one of Perry's ships. He reported this first most favorable view of Japan's coastline near the port of Naha:

The shores of the island were green and beautiful from the water, diversified with groves and fields of freshest verdure. The rain had brightened the colors of the landscape, which recalled to my mind the richest English scenery. The swelling hills, which rose immediately from the water's edge, increased in height toward the center of the island, and were picturesquely broken by abrupt rocks and crags, which, rising here and there, gave evidence of volcanic action. Woods, apparently of cedar or pine, ran long the crests of the hills, while their slopes were covered with gardens and fields of grain. To the northward, the hills were higher and the coast

jutted out in two projecting headlands, showing that there
were deep bays or indentations between.

President William McKinley hoped that the future of Japanese-American relations would be as bright as Taylor's imagery.

Let us ever remember that our interest is in concord, not in conflict, and
that our real eminence rets in the victories of peace, not those of war.

A loosely translated Japanese poem suggested a more complicated future:

The steam-powered ships
Break the halcyon slumber
of the Pacific;
a mere four boats are enough
to make us lose sleep at night.

CHAPTER 7

THE MEIJI RESTORATION

<u>March 1941 – Los Angeles</u>

At the direction of Estelle, the conspirators were now meeting in the "City of Angels" and enjoying the restaurant fare of the city. As always, Estelle insisted on dining where the food was scrumptious, the service excellent, and the prices something less than a "stagecoach holdup." That being the case, they were at the House of Murphy in Beverly Hills, an affluent enclave in the heart of Los Angeles. Estelle, it appears, had a strong need for affirmation, at least when it came to gastronomic issues.

"Well, Harlan, from the way you attacked your dinner, I assume you enjoyed your meal?"

"The corned beef and cabbage would bring tears of joy to any Irishman worth his salt."

"Freda, care to comment?"

"Chicken curry roasted to perfection. I may never leave the table. The world will have to save itself."

"And your choice, Estelle?"

"Broiled pork chops and mashed potatoes, each done to perfection."

Though not immune to the crisis in the Far East and the blood shedding in Europe, the conspirators understood, as Napoleon had once pointed out, "an army travels on its stomach." With Estelle's prompting they had taken this nostrum to heart.

As dessert was served, apple pie for all, the conversation turned naturally to their task at hand.

"You have to admire the Japanese. Perry knocks on the door and in an unbelievably short time the Japanese turn a feudal society upside as they converted to Western ways."

"Certainly, an industrious people, Harlan, to accomplish so much. Still, here we are, two younger nations, contending for influence in the Far East and close to a shooting match over China"

"It seems incomprehensible, doesn't it?

"Perhaps Professor Tanaka's scribbling will lay bare what happened."

"A good idea, Harlan."

By now you've had an opportunity to mull over America's role in ending Japan's isolation, as well as John Hay' Open Door Policy in China. Most probably, you have noted our Asian foreign policy was becoming entangled in the destinies of both countries. We now turn to Japan's response to her experience with Commodore Matthew Perry and Council General, Townsend Harris.

As a working definition, the term restoration as I now use it in reference to Japan can refer to "the time of Honorable Restoration," the Meiji Renovation, or the Meiji Reform. Regardless, it refers to a period in Japanese history when the power of imperial rule was restored under the Emperor about 1868. To do so, the feudal power of the Shoguns was broken and a modern central government established. As to the term Meiji, it means "enlightened rule," the goal of the new Japanese government to convert a feudal society into a modern nation-state, modernized, industrialized, and militarized. In short, Japan decided to emulate the Western Powers.

The Meiji Restoration

Almost immediately, Japan recognized her situation in the Far East following Perry's second visit. As one diplomat put it, "if we take the initiative, we can dominate; if we do not, we will be dominated." That said, the imperial role had to be restored to strengthen Japan as a bulwark against the colonial powers. A new system of government had to evolve, more democratic, more Western, yet still one that honored past traditions and a rich culture. Isolation, therefore, had to end; Japan had to open her arms to Western technology, meaning she had to rapidly industrialize, an enormous change for an agricultural nation. For this to happen, Japanese nationals had to leave the country to learn the ways of the West. The mantra driving this change was straightforward: knowledge must be "sought all over the world and thereby the foundation of imperial rule shall be strengthened."

The Emperor Meiji ascended to the throne on February 3, 1867 after the death of his father. A year later he announced "to all the sovereigns of the world of all foreign countries and to their subjects that:"

> *Permission has been granted to the Shogun Tokugawa Yoshinbu to return the governing power in accordance with his own request. We shall henceforward exercise supreme authority in all the internal and external affairs of the country.*

What did that mean? Succinctly, the feudal lords were giving up their power, even if reluctantly, to centralize political authority in the Emperor. In doing this, the Meiji leaders were creating a "civic ideology" centered on the emperor who was viewed as a symbol of Japanese culture and "historical continuity." He was also the head of the Shinto religion, since he descended from the sun goddess and was, therefore, semi-divine. The Japanese people were taught to honor the emperor and the unity of the Japanese people, which he represented.

The Charter Oath

The key to the whole business was the Charter Oath, or the Imperial Oath; this document spelled out a number of articles, as articulated by the government in 1868 by Emperor Meiji to bring Japan into the modern world. The articles or principles stated:

Article 1 – A deliberative assemble shall be established and all government matters shall be determined by public discussion.

Article 2 – All classes, high or low, shall carry out vigorously the plan of government.

Article 3 – All classes shall be permitted to fulfill their just aspirations.

Article 4 – Evil customs of the past shall be discontinued. New customs shall be based on just laws of the nation.

Article 5 – Knowledge shall be sought throughout the world to promote the welfare of the people.

In addition to the government's Charter Oath, other actions were taken, including:

- Switching from a feudal economic system to a market-driven economy. The abolition of feudalism made possible tremendous social and political changes. Millions of people were now free to choose their occupation and move about without restrictions.

- Implementing a standard language to replace regional dialects, while providing a national system of free public education with a focus on reading, mathematics and science. "Moral training" was emphasized. It focused on the importance of duty to the emperor, the nation, and to the family.

- The military was reorganized along Western lines. This began with a nationwide conscription law instituted in 1873. It required all men to serve four-years in the armed forces after they turned 21. Once trained, they were obligated to three more years in the reserve.

An important lesson had been learned by Japan. Only a strong military and a modernized government would stave off the colonial powers. Stated another way, if Japan couldn't beat the Western powers, she would join them.

To become an industrial nation Japan had to improve its infrastructure, which initially meant creating an improved road system and constructing a national railroad entity, as well as an up-to-date communication system. Shipyards had to be built. Iron smelters had to be constructed. Spinning mills were necessary. The government led the way in this effort, especially in industries making sugar, glass, textiles, cement, and chemicals. Beginning 1880 private investors were encouraged to participate in remaking the economy.

Without question, the Japanese were quick learners, as indicated by the following statistics:

Annual Raw Silk Production and Exports
(in tons)

Years	Production	Exports
1868-1872	1026	646
1883	1682	1347
1889-1893	4098	2444
1899-1903	7103	4098
1909-1914	12460	9462

Size of the Japanese Merchant Fleet

Years	Number of Steamships
1873	26
1894	169
1904	797
1913	1514

Length of Japanese Train Track

Years	Miles
1872	18
1883	240
1887	640
1894	2100
1904	4700
1914	7100

The rapid industrialization of Japan was hastened by three factors: first, a centralized industrial policy was implemented; second, Japanese citizens went abroad to learn the skills of the West; third, European nations invested in Japan's economy. In time, however, a problem emerged with far-reaching implications. Due to a relative lack of resources, coal and later oil, there were limits to Japan's economic growth. In addition, her increasingly large population was outstripping domestic agricultural production. To be an industrial power, Japan would need raw materials sources and foodstuffs beyond her own borders. Also, Japan needed new markets for her products. How would these be obtained was the question facing the country? The world did not have long before the question was answered.

Mr. Darwin

The Meiji Restoration occurred within the context of Charles Darwin's *Origin of Species* in which he theorized that plant and animal life had evolved through the ages on the basis of raw, aggressive competition.

That being the case, only the "fittest survived." Others fell by the biological wayside. In time these ideas coalesced under the guise of Social Darwinism and were applied to the struggle of nations to survive, and as a justification for the pursuit of power and wealth, and the world's resources. Thus imperialism was accepted as a biological norm in human enterprises. Opportunities for success had to be grasped in a world of nations, each seeking to further its vital interests. Social Darwinism was not lost on the Japanese. They understood its implications and acted accordingly.

The world recognized the considerable achievement of the Meiji Restoration. Japan had successfully reorganized itself as an industrial, capitalist state on Western models. The rub concerned her foreign policy, which mimicked Western imperialism through her later designs on Korea, Manchuria, and China. Overtime European colonial powers viewed Japan as an "upstart," a nonwhite nation joining the race for natural resources and markets, and, of course, not accepted as an "equal." In short, Japan sensed a double standard; European imperialism was acceptable, rising Japanese colonialism was not. This situation continues today.

Perhaps the Emperor Meiji put this moment into perspective when he said:

I dreamed of a unified Japan. Of a country strong and independent and modern... Now we have railroads and cannon, Western clothing, but we cannot forget who we are or where we come from.

A footnote, if you will before we move on. In order to modernize their navy, the military encouraged students to attend the American service academies. The first Japanese cadet to do so was Junjo Matsamura, who completed his course of study in 1868. Curiously, the United States was to play an instrumental hand in the training of the Japanese navy, the same force that challenge us today in the Far Pacific. Such are the whims of history.

CHAPTER 8

CRISIS IN THE FAR EAST

<u>March 1941 – Los Angeles</u>

Old friends… By now we certainly must be this. A new day and a new topic, not unrelated to our past efforts to understand America's relationship with Japan. We will begin with a question to whet your appetite for further peeling back of the Pacific onion. What made Kittery, Maine, a small town near the city of Portsmouth, the center of the diplomatic world in 1905? A small hint: the Portsmouth Navy Yard was located there, as was one of the shipyard's buildings, the General Stores Building, once known as Building 86. If you took a wild guess and said President John Adams established the naval shipyard on June 12, 1800, making the facility the oldest continuously operating "yard," you would be quite right. However, that is not the answer we're looking for. Perhaps another hint would be useful: in August 1905 it was not uncommon for two delegations of diplomats to spend considerable time negotiating an agreement behind closed doors, spurred on by a "Roughrider" in the White House, President Theodore Roosevelt. Any suggestions as to what was transpiring? Perhaps a last hint will suffice: Mukden, and Tsushima. Still no thoughts; don't be disheartened. Most people would be equally perplexed. Besides that, I was just having a little academic frivolity with the past. But now it is time to be serious.

61

Hard Negotiations

The Treaty of Portsmouth ended the Russo-Japanese War of 1904-1905. It was signed on September 5, 1905 by negotiators from Tokyo and St. Petersburg. The White House occupant who pushed and prodded both sides to the peace table was Theodore Roosevelt (TR to his supporters). That's right, the onetime dashing "Roughrider" who charged up San Juan Hill in Cuba and loved the drama of battle, evolved into a peacemaker, claiming:

> *We have become a great nation and we must behave as beseems a people with such responsibilities. The United States has a moral duty to preserve the peace.*

Unlike some presidents, TR loved to be at the center of the action, whether it was his unwillingness to flinch before Spanish guns, or enjoying shoving dirt in Panama to construct the canal. Intervention in the Russo-Japanese conflict gave him a stage big enough for his flowering ego to deal with the diplomatic intractability that continued a useless war. He was now a warrior for peace and loved every moment of it. Though TR never participated directly in the negotiations, his "behind the scenes efforts" would win him the Nobel Prize for peace. That in a nutshell is why Portsmouth was for one month the center of the diplomatic world.

Naturally, the question arises as to why the belligerent nations were at the peace table? In summary because:

1. The war fought in Manchuria was increasing unpopular in both Russia and Japan.
2. The casualty and death numbers were beyond all calculations of each country due to the advent of the machine gun.
3. The cost of the war was driving both nations into a debt crisis causing great harm to both economies.
4. The war aims of each country had not been realized.
5. A long-term conflict was no longer in the interest of either nation.
6. Each side was looking for a mediator to broker peace negotiations. They found one in President Roosevelt.

Of course, the next question must be, why did the Russian Empire go to war with the Emperor of Japan? Why did Japan, a newly industrialized country, go to war with the Russian army, the largest military force in the world? The basic answer was this: an aggressive foreign policy by Russia was moving her sense of "manifest destiny" eastward through Siberia to Manchuria, and, if possible, into Korea. At the same time, an equally aggressive Japan was moving northward into the same areas. A collision of ambitions was inevitable.

Besides the general imperialistic impulse for raw materials, food stuffs, and new markets, the Czarist government sought a warm-water port on the Pacific for its navy and maritime commerce. The only port under Russian control facing the Pacific was Vladivostok, which was only operational during the summer. There was, however, another possibility; Port Arthur was a naval base in Liaodong Province in China, which the Russians had leased from the Chinese. It was an open-water port year round. Russian ambitions were perceived by the Japanese as leading to "spheres of influence" in both Korea and Manchuria, which was also their goal. Of course, neither country considered the right of the Korean people to be free of foreign control, nor the Manchurians. The Japanese in particular considered the Korean people to be "backward," since they had not modernized, and deserved to be conquered. In harsh terms, a superior society was ordained by history to take over an "inferior people." To a large extent, the Japanese people supported this position, partially because they were indoctrinated and imbued with the spirit of Bushido (spirit of the warrior) and the code of the Samurai.

When the war began between the two countries, it was the considered opinion of military analysts that Russia would win easily. That said, when Japan prevailed in a series land and sea battles, the world was astonished. How could an Asian nation, newly industrialized, defeat a powerful European nation? To some extent, the answer rested in the changing nature of war itself.

The Battle of Mukden, March 10, 1905

Mukden is not a locale generally known by Americans. It was located in Manchuria, north of Korea. Mukden is today called Shenyang and is the capital of Liaoning province in China. The battle fought there was the largest land battle prior to World War I. It was also the final and most decisive battle of the Russo-Japanese War, which was fought between February 20ᵗʰ and March 10ᵗʰ 1905. The result was Japan's victory over Russia, and the occupation of Mukden. Nothing like this war had ever been seen before, a reality caused by the use of machine guns, more accurate rifles, and improved artillery by vast armies.

The Russians had an army of 340,000 men; the Japanese 270,000. The Czar's troops had 1,386 field guns and 56 machine guns. The Emperor's troops had 1,062 field guns and 200 machine guns. Together, over 600,000 soldiers were involved in the battle with over 164,000 combatant casualties. Over 25,000 were killed. The amount of ordinance used was unprecedented. The Japanese, by way of example, fired over 20,000,000 rifle and machine gun rounds, plus 279,394 artillery shells in a little over ten days of fighting. The Russians expended even more ordinance. For each side, this was more than both sides in the Franco-Prussian War of 1870 that lasted 191 days. The final result of this carnage was the defeat of the Russian Manchurian army in Mukden, which meant the loss of Southern Manchuria. The Japanese, however, had a pyrrhic victory. Exhausted and with extended supply lines, they could not pursue and destroy a retreating Russian army. Enduring terrible casualties and bitter cold weather, neither side was in shape for another immediate bloodletting.

The Naval Battle of Tsushima

This was the major naval battle of the Russo-Japanese War, fought May 27-28, 1905. It was the first decisive sea battle fought by modern battleships constructed of steel. It was also the first naval battle in which wireless telegraphy or radio played an important role.

Once war was decided upon, the Czar sent his Baltic Fleet to the Sea of Japan, an 18,000 nautical miles journey. To do so was a logistical nightmare. Over 500,000 tons of coal was needed. Since recoiling could not be done in neutral ports, a fleet of colliers had to accompany the fleet. Once in Asia the Russian fleet headed for Vladivostok. The route taken passed through the Tsushima Straits between Korea and Japan, a most dangerous passage. In the ensuing battle, 28 Russian capital ships were sunk. Over 126,792 tons were lost. The Japanese lost three torpedo boats or 450 tons. Over 4,300 Russian sailors died compared to 117 Japanese. By any account, the Japanese victory was total.

Historians generally agree that the destruction of the Russian navy induced the Czar to enter into peace negotiations. And in the Far East, Russia's defeat altered the balance of power in the region. The Japanese were now the major power in Asia. The first defeat of a European power increased nationalistic aspirations in colonial possessions. The notion of white supremacy was called into question. And finally, and most dangerously, the overwhelming Japanese naval victory emboldened Japan's military to consider more aggressive ambitions in the future. In that Japan had perhaps misread her victory. Great as the victory was, it was over a weak opponent. Though victorious, Japan's navy was not invincible.

The Negotiating Table

Czar Nicholas II's instructions to the Russia delegation to Portsmouth indicated that, despite the severe military setbacks, he was not amendable to negotiated compromise. The Czar demanded:

1. No territorial concessions.
2. No reparations.
3. No limitations on the deployment of Russian forces in the Far East.
4. Recognition of their interests in Korea and Manchuria.

For their part, the Japanese, some thought, were both stubborn and delusionary in their demands. They wanted:

1. Total recognition of their interests in Korea and Manchuria.
2. Removal of Russian forces from Manchuria.
3. Control of Sakhalin Island.
4. Substantial reparations to pay for the cost of the war.

As in any negotiations compromise were necessary. The final Agreement included:

1. An immediate ceasefire.
2. Recognition of Japan's claims to Korea.
3. Evacuation of Russian forces from Manchuria.
4. Russia must relinquish her leases in southern Manchuria (Port Arthur) to China.
5. Russia was required to turn over to Japan the South Manchurian Railway and her mining concessions.
6. Russia was allowed to retain the Chinese Eastern Railroad in Northern Manchuria.
7. No reparations.
8. Russia would keep half of Sakhalin Island.

Effects of the Treaty

The agreement settled the immediate difficulties between the two countries and provided a degree of peace for three decades. The conflict confirmed Japan's emergence as the preeminent power in Asia. The Russians were forced to forgo their expansionist policies in Asia, mainly Manchuria and Korea.

The agreement was not received well in Russia. The Czar's army and navy had been humiliated. The cost of the war had placed the country's economy at risk. The pressure to effect change in Russia's government, either by democratic means or revolution was increasing.

The Japanese too were unsettled by the agreement. After all, they had won the major battles, beaten a European power, but were not awarded reparations, or additional land acquisitions, mainly all of Sakhalin Island. There was unhappiness with President Roosevelt who appeared to be favoring Russia by pressuring the Japanese to forgo reparations, which were needed to pay for the war and to assist families who lost someone in battle. Japanese citizens were also displeased that --- in the absence of needed reparations --- taxes would be increased. Riots in the streets punctuated the Japanese frustration with the outcome of the war as reflected in the terms of the treaty.

As a matter of record, two years later Japan annexed Korea with little protest from the West. In time Japan would use Korea as a steppingstone toward control of Manchuria and China. But all that was still in the future. TR took some criticism for what was later considered the loss of Korea and direct commercial ties with the country, thereby casting the Open Door Policy into the North China Sea. All dealings would now be with Japan. Roosevelt, always the realist, protested, saying:

> *Many people are still angry because we did not keep Japan from taking Korea. There as nothing we could do except fight Japan. Congress wouldn't have declared war and the people have turned out the Congress if they had. All we might have done was to make threats, which we could not carry out.*

Worst Fears

Though not as obvious as it is today, an unanticipated consequence of the war concerned alliances. Russia, as always, feared being isolated in any European conflict where Germany would attack. That being the case, she looked to France as a natural ally, placing Berlin in a two-front war. On the other hand, the Japanese feared a two-front conflict with Russia and possibly Great Britain, or even the United States given their sympathy for the Chinese in any war. Already in 1904 the geometry of future alliances and possible conflicts were influencing foreign policies. As one historian said:

> *The Japanese wee undeniably the victors, although they might not have been without Roosevelt's vigorous mediation. Not only had they established themselves the dominant power in the Far East, but they had emerged with considerable territorial gains.*

Japanese later expansionism into Korea, Manchuria, and China had many causes. It is wise to summarize then at this point before moving on:

1. The determination to transform Japan into a Western-style power.

2. The desire for equality among Western powers.
3. Japan's belief in its destiny as the leader of Asia's millions.
4. The need to obtain raw materials and to secure markets.
5. The need for a strategy to promote Japan's security.
6. Growing popular In Japan support for Tokyo's decisions to eventually invade Korea, Manchuria, and China with the goal of creating a Far Eastern Empire. .

Retrospectively, three nations by 1900 were engaged in empire-building: Moscow had extended eastward from European Russia into Siberia and southward toward Mongolia and Manchuria. The United States had expanded westward to the Pacific, and in time to the Philippines. Tokyo moved northward into Korea and beyond. At sometime in the indeterminate future a collision of interests was inevitable. What would happen then?

Residual Challenge – Exclusionary Policies

Negative Japanese feelings toward the United States increased the next year (1905) due to a "diplomatic slight" from an unlikely source, the grand state of California. So what happened? In two words, a "tidal wave" of Japanese citizens migrating to the West Coast, upwards to 1,000 people per month. Driven by a desire to escape the rice paddies of Japan, young men in particular sought the land of "milk and honey." No crime in that, but the influx was too great. It reminded Californians of their previous experience with the Chinese two decades earlier when white laborers felt the competition of Asians in the workplace. These anxieties were inflamed by "yellow journalism," which distorted the problem and heightened anti-Asian feelings.

For native-Americans it seemed like Washington wasn't listening to their concerns. That being the case the San Francisco School Board took matters into it own hand in October 1906. The Board ordered all "Oriental" students to be in segregated classes. At the time there were only 95-students in the school district. They were not, as the Board argued, causing schools to be overcrowded. Essentially, this was a roundabout way to get the TR's attention. Always sensitive to accusations of inferiority, the

Japanese press, driven by its own "jingoistic press," slashed back at the perceived slight:

> *Stand up, Japanese nation! Our countrymen have been HUMILIATED on the other side of the Pacific. Our poor boys and girls have been expelled from the public schools. Why do we not insist sending warships?*

Try as he might, President Roosevelt found it difficult explaining the concept of federalism to the Japanese. Though he was personally opposed to the School Board's policy, describing it as a "wicked absurdity," public education was a state affair. The President confessed he was "horribly bothered about the Japanese business," referring to the School Board as "infernal fools in California." Clearly, he was opposed to their "reckless policy," which could get the nation into war. To alleviate emotions on both sides of the Pacific, the President put consider pressure on the Board to rescind its policies by promising do something about the immigration problem. Conferring with Japanese officials who also wanted to dampen the rhetoric, a Gentlemen's Agreement was worked out n 1907 by an executive arrangement. The provisions were:

1. Tokyo voluntarily agreed to issue no more passports to coolies.
2. Coolies, however, could go to Hawaii.
3. Coolies could not migrate from Hawaii to the mainland.
4. Passports could be issued to Japanese women, the "picture brides," who were married in absentia to men already residing in the United States.

The agreement worked. Immigration declined to a trickle. Both sides had worked to smooth over the alleged slight to the satisfaction of each. Sensitivities were temporarily appeased.

Residual Challenge – Pacific Diplomacy

Reinforcing efforts to reduce tensions, the Root-Takahira Agreement was hammered out in 1908. The provisions included:

1. The status quo in the Pacific would be maintained.
2. The territorial possessions (or influence) of each country would be respected.
3. For Japan that meant Korea, Manchuria, and Formosa.
4. For the United States that meant Hawaii, Guam, and the Philippines.
5. Each side would uphold the Open Door Policy in China.
6. Each side would support by pacific means the independence and integrity of China.

The implications of the agreement were profound. First, both nations were no longer insular, tied to some form of isolationism. They were world powers in the Pacific with vital interests, which were not always in concert.

The Open Door Policy was a potential "firecracker" when applied not only to China, but to the possessions already noted. If supported by each, the Far East was stabilized. If not...

One question lingered. Japan had gone to war in 1894 against China, and in 1901 with Russia. Was she prepared to do so again? As to the Open Door Policy, it was not law, only voluntary acceptance. If pledges of support ended by Japan, what would happen? Finally, the territorial integrity of China swayed in the air. If Japan plucked Manchuria and advanced toward China, what would the American response be? But for a moment, the Agreements provided for the status quo. The lingering question, of course, was how long would they last?

Roosevelt and the American people were delighted with this unprecedented achievement, and the nation's newly gained prestige in the world. The American navy gained considerable experience in fleet operations, including:

- Formation steaming and the need for auxiliary ships for resupply.
- Coal economy and the need for coaling stations.
- Gunnery exercises, and the need for greater fleet accuracy.
- Maintaining fleet morale.

That said, the President had made his point, perhaps only too strongly. The country was strong and prepared. Without question, however, the fleet's voyage encouraged naval construction in Japan, the United States, and elsewhere. A naval race was on to build dreadnaughts, and in more recent times, the aircraft carrier. This was a consequence that was unintended.

Residual Challenge – Admiral Mahan's Little Book

Alfred Thayer Mahan was called the must important "naval strategist" of the 19th-century. Two books sealed his reputation: *The Influence of Sea Power Upon History* (1890) and *The Influence of Sea Power Upon the French Revolution and Empire* (1892). All seafaring nations read the books, no more so than Japan's military.

Mahan became the President of the American Naval War College in 1886 after a long career aboard naval ships. Importantly, he became a close friend and advisor of TR, who was most interested in naval power. His basic concepts can be summarized as follows:

1. Control of the seas was the key to protecting any nation.
2. Control meant commercial advantages in peacetime and an equal military advantage in wartime.
3. Choke points should be noted, such as canals, coaling stations, and naval bases –Gibraltar for the British and Pearl Harbor in the Pacific.
4. The primary mission of the navy was to secure control of the sea by destroying or neutralizing the enemy. To do so meant concentrating your forces in a decisive battle. In short the best defense was an offense.

As Pacific powers with widely scattered possessions, both American and Japanese war planners took notice of Mahan's contentions. Was the vastness of the Pacific both a temporary impediment to war, or merely a conduit for modern navies in a future conflict?

There you have it, the ascension of Japan and the rise of America on the international scene. China, as always, was a wild card in the Far East. Ultimately, what were Japan's interests in Manchuria and China, and the wider Pacific region? What was the future of the Open Door Policy? And what would America's foreign policy be in a potential clash with the Empire of Japan, the "Big Stick," or the "Olive Branch?" The answer to that question rested partially in the depths of Havana Harbor.

CHAPTER 9

SAVING FACE

<u>March 1941 – Los Angeles</u>

A short introduction to three crises swirling around and influencing Japanese-American relations in the first decades of the new century is in order: the San Francisco School Board incident; the Immigration Act of 1924; and the Racial Equality Amendment of 1919. What do these crises have in common? First, they validated a major theme of physics, for every action there is a reaction. Historians know this to be only too true. Second, nations have long memories, particularly where they experience humiliation requiring some form of redress. Third, historical events can be simultaneously both linear and circular. That is, events may occur in the present, only to quickly be drawn into the past, while in the same moment offering a glimpse of the future. At the same time, events may also orbit each other, contemporary companions in any given moment, unfettered by dates and the winding second hand of time.

No nation enjoys being disrespected, embarrassed in public, or forced to "lose face" before its peers. Such an experience is disgraceful, a humiliation calling into question a nation's self-respect, honor, and perceived reputation. In the Japanese culture there is no greater dishonor.

When a nation is insulted, however that experience is defined, there are always ramifications in its foreign policy. Grudges? Anger? Forces unleashed? All that and more...

Immigration Act of 1924

As an issue, immigration refused, however, to go away. In 1924 it was again front and center. The Japanese envoy in Washington D.C. was Masanao Hanihara. Instructed by Tokyo, he wrote a note to Charles Evans Hughes, the American Secretary of State, stating:

The object is single out Japanese as a nation, stigmatizing them as unworthy and undesirable in the eyes of the American people.

What was the envoy getting at? What would stigmatize the Japanese people, causing them to be seen as unworthy?

The Emergency Quota Act of 1921 was expiring. A large segment of the population wanted severe limitations on immigration, particularly from Eastern Europe and especially Jews. Justification for this centered on a desire to maintain America as a distinct identity and to provide for ethnic homogeneity; that is, Western European and Christian so that the county's "stock would be up to the highest level, or standard." Other arguments included keeping out the ill, the starving, and those who couldn't contribute to the culture, since they refused to assimilate. Though directed at Europe, the Japanese took notice and were appalled. Jingoistic newspapers, such as the McClatchy Company and the Heart papers, did not nuance the issue:

They come here (the Japanese) specifically and professedly for the purpose of colonizing and establishing here permanently the proud Yamato race.

The details of the Immigration Bill of 1924 erected stringent bars against Eastern Europeans and Asians. Specifically, foreign nations could only send on a yearly basis a maximum of 2 percent of the "number of nationals residing in the United States in 1890. Using that formula, no more than 250 people would be allowed from Japan each year. Drastic reductions also hit Eastern Europe and Russia. Overall, the total immigration quota was only 165,000 from outside of the Western Hemisphere. This was an 80% reduction from the pre-war years.

The legislation also made "aliens ineligible for citizenship." The term "aliens" referred to all Orientals, but was really aimed at Japanese citizens, and Japan knew it. Hanihara alluded to this, saying:

I realize, as I believe you do, the grave consequences, which the enactment of the measure retaining that particular provision would inevitably bring upon the otherwise happy and mutually advantageous relations between our two countries.

The anti-Japanese crowd responded to what many considered a "veiled threat of war." The *Seattle Times* called his comments "the most insolent message this Government has ever received." In Japan there were anti-American demonstrations, even a National Humiliation Day when the legislation became law by President Calvin Coolidge, May 24, 1924.

Tokyo readily admitted that the United States had the legal right to adopt any type of immigration act it chose. That point was not in doubt. The Japanese objected to what amounted to an "exclusion clause" within the 1924 legislation directed against them. Once more tensions between the two countries were in play. Congress, as some historians claim, forgot that "purely domestic laws can often produce the most serious foreign complications" Continuing *The goal of Japanese exclusion could have been achieved, and the good will of a powerful nation could have been retained, by more diplomatic methods. Congress paid much too high a price in hate for the spiteful satisfaction of excluding about 200 Japanese immigrants a year."*

Racial Equality Amendment of 1919

Following the Armistice ending World War I on November 11, 1918, the world prepared to meet in Paris to conclude a treaty. Each nation attending Versailles had an agenda, goals, and aims, which it considered important. That was, of course, true of the Japanese delegation, which wanted:

1. Japan should be recognized for her contribution to winning the war given her support of the Triple Entente (Britain, France, and Russia).
2. Japan should receive and control German-held island in the Central Pacific.

3. Japan should keep the German concessions in Shandong, China, which had been seized during the war.
4. Settle outstanding immigration problems.
5. Reaffirm Japan's place as a great power.

A sixth aim came in the form of a proposed amendment to the actual final treaty. The proposal was entitled the Racial Equality Amendment (REA). Initially, the proposal was not intended to be a universal statement that all people should be treated equally, and were equal regardless of their racial, religious, or ethnic background. The original intent was more qualified; nations within the proposed League of Nations would be equal before each other. As stated:

> *The equality of nations being a basic principle of he League of Nations, the High Contracting Parties agree to accord as soon as possible to all alien nations of states, members of the League, equal and just treatment in every respect taking no distinction either in law or in fact on account of their race or nationality.*

Written in the spirit of President Woodrow Wilson's Fourteen Points, the proposal enjoyed initial wide support, yet almost immediately became enmeshed in controversy leading to its final rejection. For the Japanese, this was a bitter defeat leading to heightened nationalism and an increased focus on militarism, which still stirs the waters of today's crisis in the Pacific.

Why was the proposal rejected?

The British government, as did the French, perceived a threat in the Japanese proposal to their continued colonial power in Africa, Southeast Asia, India, and the Middle East. How, for example, would control over natives be justified if all people were equal and, therefore, entitled to certain legal rights, including President Wilson's notion of self-determination? And, if this was the case, what did it mean for immigration? Would this proposal limit a sovereign nation's right to control immigration? What would it mean for Australia and her "white only" immigration policy? By implication, what would this mean for the United States with respect to Cuba, Guam, Puerto Rico, and the Philippines?

President Wilson found himself in an impossible situation. He needed the support of Japan to establish the League of Nations. He desired Tokyo's assistance in maintaining the Open Door Policy in China. He wanted Japan to remove more than 70,00 soldiers from Siberia, there to keep Russia in the war. He also wanted to mitigate Japan's expansionist policy in the Pacific, especially with Korea, Manchuria, and China. In short, an amiable relationship with Japan was in America's best interest.

At home Wilson faced difficulties. America was not ready for a "racial equality " proposal. This was especially true in the South where Jim Crow laws held sway, and discrimination and segregation were a way of life for the majority white population. As noted earlier, it was more than evident in California where anti-Asian sentiment ran high. As a country, which was white. Christian, and European in background, attitudes ran counter to equality of races.

And then there was the math… Wilson would need 2/3rds of the Senate to eventually support the Treaty of Versailles and America's entry into the new League of Nations. Supporting the Japanese proposal would put the Senate vote in jeopardy. Wilson was reaching the limits of his idealistic Fourteen Points. He would be forced to reject the proposal if the Japanese demanded a vote. To that end, he urged the Japanese to withdraw their amendment. He said:

It was a mistake to make too much fuss abut racial prejudice. That would only stir up flames that would eventually hurt the League. Everyone in the room knew that the League was based on the equality of nations. There was no need to say anything more.

The Japanese insisted on a vote. A majority voted for the amendment. Wilson then claimed there was wide and strong objections to the amendment and it would not carry. The Japanese chose not to challenge Wilson's ruling and the racial equality clause did not become part of the Covenant of the League of Nations. As expected, the Japanese press was bitterly critical of the "so-called civilized" nations of the world. The Japanese were, as they saw it, still being treated an "inferiors." For some historians, this was a turning point:

> *The failure to get the racial equality clause was an important factor in the interwar years in turning Japan away from cooperation with the West and toward more aggressively nationalistic policies.*

Root-Takahira Agreement

The equality issue boiled in Paris, but had simmered earlier regardless of earnest efforts to lower the diplomatic heat. By way of example, Elihu Root and Takahira Kogoro, each representing a Pacific power, signed an accord on November 30, 1908 to avert the drift toward war. Root, the American Secretary of State, followed President Theodore Roosevelt's foreign wishes to maintain, if possible, the preservation of good relations with Japan. Takahira, representing the Emperor, sought the same outcome. After negotiating for almost a year, the two men hammered out an agreement, which essentially maintained the status quo in the Far East. The specific provisions were as follows:

1. The territorial possessions (or areas of influence) of each country would be respected. For Japan that meant her interests in Korea, Manchuria, and Formosa would not be challenged. Equally so, American interests in the Philippines, Guam, and Hawaii were acknowledged and accepted.
2. Both Japan and the United States would honor and uphold the "Open Door Policy" in China.
3. Each side would support efforts to maintain the independence and integrity of China.

The accord, of necessity, was purposely vague with respect to more concrete enforcement. Certainly, it was binding on a voluntary basis as long as it was in their interests to maintain it. The accord did recognize that both countries were no longer insular, tied to some form of isolationism. They were world powers in the Pacific with vital interests, which were not always in concert. Hay's trade policy in China was always a potential "firecracker." The question of China's integrity loomed dangerously in the future if Japan's aggressiveness continued northward from Manchuria.

TR considered the accord acceptable given the situation in the Pacific stating:

> *The recognition of Japan's dominance in the Far East was realistic. He implied that his decisions of 1908 had been part of a wise and well-planned policy. His long-rang policy had been to respect Japanese sensitivity regarding Manchuria and not to interfere there.*

Roosevelt was a realist who "sought to extort concessions in exchange for accepting what he did not have the military strength to prevent." Japan sway in Korea and Manchuria was the price the "Roughrider" paid. America's preeminence in the Philippines and Guam was the price Tokyo paid. Unstated, but obviously present, was the price both countries were willing to pay concerning the integrity of China.

America's role in the world had changed. TR understood that:

> *Much has been given us, and much will rightfully be expected from us. We have duties to others and duties to ourselves, and we can shirk neither. We have become a great nation, forced by the fact of its greatness into relations with the other nations of the earth, and we must behave and be seen as a people with such responsibilities.*

CHAPTER 10

THE GREAT
WHITE FLEET

<u>April 1941 – San Diego</u>

"Freda, why are you laughing?"

"Estelle, your choice of lunch, grilled swordfish."

"So?"

"Well, Harlan's choice, grilled barracuda, for one thing. Almost sounds like a prize fight, swordfish vs. barracuda, know what I mean?"

"And your choice, Freda?"

"I'm the referee. I ordered grilled halibut steak."

The conspirators were now in San Diego at the Red Sails Inn located at the foot of G Street on Fisherman's Wharf. Again, at Estelle's urging and planning they were enjoying an excellent meal in a restaurant festooned with nautical items provided by local fisherman, who also brought in their fresh catches each day.

"Estelle, like your father, you know how to treat a 'gang of pirates.' My hat is off to you."

"Harlan, I've never seen you with a hat."

"Someday when I'm on the Supreme Court, you will. Stick around, dear woman."

"Well, until then, what do you think of the music?"

"Familiar and certainly cute?"

"Cute, Harlan?"

"Something to do with our topic for today?"

"Indeed."

> *All the dames of France are fond and free*
> *And Flemish lips are really willing*
> *Very soft the maids of Italy*
> *And Spanish eyes are so thrilling.*
>
> *Still, although I bask beneath their smile,*
> *Their charms will fail to bind me*
> *And my heart falls back to Erin's isle*
> *To the girl I left behind me.*

———————

Professor Tanaka was holding forth, at least on paper.

By now you are beginning to see a somewhat schizophrenic relationship between Japan and the United States in respect to their foreign policies in the Far East. Each country, as already noted, had vital interests in the area, Tokyo by proximity, Washington by extending her reach cross the Pacific. Without question both countries wanted to protect those interest, but at what cost? Neither nation wanted a war regardless of the inflammatory headlines spit out by their "yellow journalistic presses." Diplomat, as was their penchant, sought to calm the waters through the "give and take" of protracted negotiations leading to acceptable agreements, which to be effective needed to be honored. Always in the background was, of course, the existence of the two largest navies in the Pacific. On occasion they were put on display in what were called "Navy Days." The ships would be reviewed in public as they steamed past dignities and supportive citizens. The review reminded all of the military potential of each country. These peacetime naval ceremonies were predictable and enjoyable. However. That predictability was about to end in a most unusable way.

———————

The presidential yacht, *Mayflower*, was anchored in the quiet waters off Hampton Roads, Virginia. The date was December 16, 1907. Standing on the weathered deck that warmish, cloudy morning was President Theodore Roosevelt flashing his "famous broad, toothy smile" as he gazed at the mighty armada passing in review before him. On the nearby shore, hundreds of people gathered to see the spectacle and to join the TR in expressing their "pride and exhilaration" as 16 battleships of the Atlantic Fleet passed before them. The ships were all painted in a brilliant white; they glistened in the morning sun as they steamed in a long "majestic column" out of Hampton Roads to the open sea. As they did, the familiar sounds of a popular song floated in the air, *The Girl I left Behind Me.*

The first ship in the column, the *USS Connecticut (BB-18)*, steamed ahead to start what would be an improbable cruise around the world. She was followed by newly commissioned ships, including the *USS Kearsarge (BB-5)*, the *USS Kentucky (BB-6)*, the *USS Illinois (BB-7)*, the *USS Alabama (BB-8)*, the *USS Maine (BB-10)*, the *USS Missouri (BB-17)*, the *USS Ohio (BB-12)*, the *USS Virginia (BB-13)*, the *USS Georgia (BB-15)*, the *USS New Jersey (BB-16)*, and other battleships, all named after states as was the custom of the United States Navy. All the ships passed before the President at 400-yard intervals with their crews on deck and "smartly" fitted for the occasion.

The battleships put to sea flanked by their auxiliary ships, some of which carried coal for the fleet. All the ships were cloistered in four squadrons and "dubbed by the local press as the Great White Fleet." The 14,000 sailors and marines aboard were under the command of Rear Admiral Robley Evans, affectionately known as "Fighting Bob" Evans." The fleet was embarking on a 43,000 mile, 14-mnth circumnavigation of the world with 20 port calls scheduled on six continents. The ships would cross the equator five times and consume 435,000 tons of coal at a cost of $ 1,967,553. The total cost was $20,000,000 to showcase America's naval prowess. The ships wouldn't return to Hampton Roads until February 22, 1909. This would be the first such cruise by fleet of steam-powered steel battleships. Nothing like this had ever been done before in naval history.

The schedule was audacious as shown below:

LEG	DESTINATIONS	NAUTICAL MILES
1st	Hampton Roads to San Francisco	14,556
2nd	San Francisco to Puget Sound RT	347
3rd	San Francisco to Manila	16,336
4th	Manila to Hampton Roads	12,455

Some of the nations visited included:

DATE	COUNTRY
May 6, 1908	San Francisco, California
July 16, 1908	Honolulu, Hawaii
August 29, 1908	Melbourne, Victoria, Australia
October 2,1908	Manila, Philippine Islands
October 18, 1908	Yokohama, Japan
October 29, 1908	Amoy, China
January 3,1909	Suez, Egypt
January 31, 1909	Gibraltar
February 22, 1909	Hampton Roads, Virginia

The famous US Navy ad, "Join the Navy and see the World" was certainly true of the Great White Fleet.

Of course, the obvious question arises: why was the fleet circumnavigating the world's oceans" The answer is both simple and complex.

President Roosevelt wanted to impress the Japanese with the naval strength of the United States. That was his major motivation for the unprecedented effort. Show the flag of the world's second largest navy behind the British Japan was 5th and closing the gap. Remind the Japanese that America was prepared for any emergency, regardless of where the fleet might be deployed, but especially in the newly acquired Philippines. That message was not lost on the Japanese.

Of course, the cruise would have other benefits. Naval recruitment might increase. Congressional appropriations would be more generous, it was assumed if the voyage was successful. Hopefully, wherever the fleet traveled and docked, it would engender good will. And that is exactly what happened. Everywhere the fleet birthed, crowds came out to see the ships. The officers and crew were, as they say, "wined and dined."

Only one question remained: what would happen when the fleet arrived in Japan? Would the ships, as some speculated, be victim of a sneak attack by the Japanese? Would the arrival of the warships be seen as a provocation? Would the Japanese public be openly hostile to the crews?

The answer to these questions was heartening. On October 24, 1908, some ten months after the ships embarked, the *Japan Daily Mail* carried the following statement:

> *The Fleet of East and West --- of the two greatest naval Powers on the Pacific --- met yesterday in peace and amity. The delay of a day in the arrival of the White Sixteen, as the visiting Fleet may not inaptly be termed, served only to whet the popular appetite and add to the enthusiasm of the greeting, which rich and poor, young and old, are voicing to the no halting tones.*

Behind the scenes the Japanese government had prepared for the visit beginning with a proclamation in Yokohama for appropriate public behavior, including the following behaviors:

1. Courtesy and cordiality shall be observed in the treatment of foreigners.
2. No comments or ridicule and mean words shall be given in regard to the dress, bearing, and words of foreigners.
3. Seats shall be given to foreigners in streetcars and trains.
4. People shall not gather around foreigners in crowds.
5. The age of foreigners shall not be asked unless some special necessity demands it.

In addition, other somewhat amusing requirements were posted such as:

6. Staring shall not be made at foreigners except when necessary.

7. It shall be borne in mind that foreigners are disgusted with the habit of spitting anywhere and of scattering about the skin of fruits.
8. Handkerchiefs shall be used in the clearing of nostrils.

For their part the Navy responded in kind. When ship's crews were invited to the first garden party, by way of example, the following order was sent to each ship:

> *You will therefore detail one hundred and fifty first-class men for this party. Select first-class men whose records show no evidence of previous indulgence in intoxicating liquor. The men will be made to clearly understand that this, though an entertainment, is a matter of military duty.*

Both sides wanted to avoid an "incident." Was the Japanese reception to the Great White Fleet heartfelt and legitimate and beyond question? Yes, it appeared, as far the people went. They were delighted to see Americans. As to the government, that was another question. Yes, in a diplomatic sense. Maintaining the peace in the Far East, which was being forged by he Root-Takahira Agreements, was important to both countries. Recall, the accord called for respecting each other's territorial possessions. While this protected the American in the Philippines, it also gave Japan carte blanche in Manchuria and her increasingly paramount interests in China. Both sides wanted to maintain this applecart full of status quo fruit.

Of course, behind the scenes, the Roosevelt Administration had many concerns. Japan had gone to war in 1894 against China. She had gone to war against Russia in 1901. Was she prepared to do so again? As to the Open Door Policy, it was not law, only the beneficiary of voluntary acceptance. Finally, the territorial integrity of China hung precariously in the air. If Japan plucked Manchuria and aggressively advanced toward China, what would be Washington's response? The question now turned on itself. Was America willing to support China to the point of war? For the moment, however, diplomacy prevailed but for how long?

Roosevelt and the American people were delighted with the unprecedented achievement when the fleet safely returned Hampton

Roads. Following on the successful Spanish-American War in 1898, the nation had gained prestige in the world. America was now a power to be reckoned with in the Pacific. That, however, was also true of Japan.

Planning

Though they publically proclaimed their desire for peace, behind the scene military planners in both Japan and the US were hard at work in anticipation of a Pacific conflict. Their strategies were based on the work of Alfred Thayer Mahan and his two influential books: *The Influence of Sea Power Upon History* (1890) and *The Influence of Sea Power Upon the French Revolution and Empire* (1892), Mahan was the President of the American Naval War College and a close friend and advisor of TR, who was always interested in naval power. Mahan's basic concepts can be summarized again as follows:

1. Control of the seas was the key to protecting any nation.
2. Control meant commercial advantages in peacetime and an equal military advantage in wartime.
3. Choke points should be noted, such as canals, coaling stations, and naval bases such as Gibraltar and Pearl Harbor.
4. The primary mission of the navy was to secure control of the sea by destroying or neutralizing the enemy. To do so meant concentrating your forces in a decisive battle. In short, the best defense was an effective offense.

On the basis of Mahan's strategies, the United States developed a war plan code named Plan Orange. The plan was adopted in 1924 and assumed that the United States would fight Japan alone. The plan stated:

1. The Japanese navy would blockade the Philippine Islands.
2. American land forces would be expected to hold out.
3. The Pacific Fleet would be marshaled at bases in California and Pearl Harbor.
4. The Panama Canal would be protected.

5. The mobilized fleet would sail westward to relieve American forces in the Philippines and Guam.
6. The fleet would then sail northward for a decisive battle against the Imperial Japanese Navy.
7. The Japanese home islands would be blockaded.

The Japanese counter-plan included:

1. Permitting the American fleet to sail across the Pacific.
2. Submarines and aircraft carriers would be used to weaken the American fleet as it crossed the Pacific.
3. A decisive battle would be fought by surface ships, as battles had been fought for 300 years, near Japan.

The planners in both countries initially underestimated the future role of naval aviation and the roles and effectiveness of aircraft carriers and submarines. In the crucible of war both countries would learn this lesson. Until then, both countries were in the process of answering a difficult question. Was the vastness of the Pacific both a temporary impediment to war, or merely a conduit for modern navies in a future conflict?

————————

There you have it, the ascension of Japan and the rise of America on the international scene. China, as always, was a wild card in the Far East. Ultimately, what were Japan's interests in Manchuria and China, and the wider Pacific region? What was the future of the Open Door Policy? And what would America's foreign policy be in a potential clash with the Empire of Japan, the "Olive Branch," or the "Big Stick?" The answer to that question rested partially in the depths. of Havana Harbor.

CHAPTER 11

HAVANA HARBOR

———— ∞ ————

<u>April 1941 – San Diego</u>

Here we are again, plowing through history, trying to make sense out of the past. As you've learned by now, this is no simple task peeling back the onion layers of past events, all open to various interpretations, each the result of a multitude of influences and motivations, leading to consequences no one would have predicted in advance. Such is our challenge today as we seek to understand what happened on the evening of February 15, 1898 in the quiet harbor of Havana, Cuba, and how one incident would forever shape America's future in the Far East.

<u>Good Will Mission</u>

She was commissioned in 1895, a modern armored cruiser for her day named after the state of Maine. Initially, she represented the most advanced American warship design. Unfortunately, due to a nine-year construction period, she was obsolete the day her boilers were finally lit, a victim of more advanced ships nearing completion or already in service. The calendar explained all:

August 3, 1886	Construction Ordered
October 17, 1888	Keel Laid
November 18, 1889	Launched
September 17, 1895	Commissioned

Even at a cost of $4,677,788 dollars, there was nothing to really distinguish the ship from others in the American fleet. Unfortunately, her lasting fame would come from her infamous ending. It all began in Key West, Florida where orders were issued to send the ship to Havana Harbor to protect US citizens and interests during the latest Cuban War of Independence. The country was in near anarchy with rioting in the streets and pitched fighting between the insurgents and Spanish troops. So to speak, Americans and other foreigners were caught in the middle. The presence of the *USS Maine* would hopefully defuse the situation, at least temporarily, protecting American lives and interests.

On February 15, 1898, the ship lay at bay in the beautiful harbor. Just before 10:00 PM, the ship was at ease. In the forward area of the ship sailors were resting, some playing cards, others reading, some writing letters. In the aft area the officers, having gone over plans for the next day, were also resting. At exactly 9:40 a terrible explosion ripped the ship in half. The forward area was obliterated, killing most of the sailors aboard. The Captain and his officers were spared for the most part. Overall, 266 men died. The ship settled to the shallow bottom of Havana Harbor, an inglorious fate.

Immediate inquiries into what caused the explosion led to controversial findings.

The Spanish Inquiry

Spanish naval officers examined the remains of the *USS Maine*. They concluded a spontaneous combustion of the coal bunker, which was located adjacent to the munitions stored on the ship, as the most likely cause of the explosion. Further, their report indicated:

1. A column of water would have been seen if a mine had been the cause of the explosion.

2. No dead fish were found in the harbor; dead fish would have been expected if a mine had been used.
3. When sunk by a mine, munitions stored do not usually explode.
4. Calm harbor waters that night would have made it difficult to detonate a mine by contact; only by using electricity could this have been done.
5. No electric cables were found in the harbor.

This investigation concluded an explosion of the forward magazines caused the destruction of the ship. This view strongly suggested that the ship's magazines were ignited by a spontaneous fire in a coal bunker. The coal in question was bituminous, which was known for releasing fire-dam, a mixture of gases composed primarily of flammable methane that is prone to spontaneous explosions. The inflamed American press did not report this conclusion at the time.

The American Inquiry

This investigation considered a hypothetical situation of a "coal bunker fire igniting the reserve six-inch ammunition, with a resulting explosion sinking the ship." The inquiry concluded hat the *Maine* "had been blown up by a mine, which, in turn, caused the explosion of her forward magazines." They reached this conclusion based on the fact that the majority of witnesses stated that they had heard two explosions and that part of the keel was bent inwards."

In the opinion of the court, the Maine was destroyed by the explosion of a submarine mine, which caused the partial explosion of two of her forward magazines.

This information was quickly reported to the American press, even though exhaustive research years later concluded the "catastrophe almost certainly resulted from an internal explosion."

The Cofferdam Investigation

In December 1910, a cofferdam was built around the wreck. This was a watertight enclosure from which water was pumped "to expose the bed of a body of water," and the *USS Maine*. The cofferdam was made by driving sheet pilings into the bed to form a watertight fence. The vertical piles are held in place by horizontal framing that are constructed of heavy timber, or steel. The pumping created a dry working area so that an investigation could be carried out safely. Between November 20, 1911 and December 2, 1911, a court of inquiry inspected the wreck. The conclusion was that "an external explosion had triggered the explosion of the magazines."

As a footnote: the newly located dead were later buried in Arlington National Cemetery. The hollow, intact portion of the *USS Maine's* hull was refloated and unceremoniously scuttled at sea on March 16, 1912.

Yellow Journalism

Newspaper coverage, as one might expect, captured the headlines and in the process ignited an outraged American public.

THE U.S. MAINE SUNK IN HAVANA HARBOR

SPAIN AT FAULT

AMERICA SHOULD GO TO WAR

Two newspapers in particular contributed to a frenzy of war talk, the *New York World* run by Joseph Pulitzer, and the *New York Journal* published by William R. Hearst. The two papers were in head-to-head competition in New York for readership. In their mutual drive for circulation, they sensationalized the news with less than well-researched articles, even as they exaggerated the news in a tabloid fashion. It was what was called "yellow journalism," based on bold headlines, large and flashy illustrations, unnamed sources, faked interviews, and misleading information, including in the case of the *USS Maine*, a drumbeat for war. As Hearst declared:

THE WARSHIP MAINE WAS SPLIT IN TWO BY AN
ENEMY'S SECRET INFERNAL MACHINE

THE WHOLE COUNTRY THRILLS WITH WAR FEVER

THE MAINE WAS DESTROYED BY TREACHERY

Of course, such headlines never asked some difficult questions before condemning Spain for the atrocity. For example:

1. Why would Spain destroy the ship knowing full well such an action might lead to war?
2. Would the insurgents fighting Spain do so knowing it might bring the US into the war?
3. Would certain American commercial interests want a war with Spain at any costs?

Regardless, public restraint was lost and with it a fair judgment of the situation; Spain was guilty of treachery. The country was ready for, as TR would later say, "a splendid little war."

> *Remember the Maine!*
> *To hell with Spain!*

The Insurgency

That the country was prepped for war was more than obvious. But the sinking of the *USS Maine* alone was not the cause of war hysteria. That prize went to the furious and deadly struggle of the Cubans to be free of Spain colonial rule. The latest incarnation of Cuban restlessness began in 1895 with a "scorched earth policy." The rebels would devastate the island so drastically and mercilessly that Spain would consider just leaving. The former would happen, but not the latter. Valerian Weyler, a Spanish general was sent to Cuba with orders to:

1. Pacify the Cuban rebellion.
2. End the insurgency.

3. Restore political order.
4. Return sugar productivity to profitable levels.

Weyler was instructed to use whatever methods were necessary to accomplish these goals. He recognized immediately the nature of the struggle. The Cubans were engaging in guerrilla warfare; they used hit and run tactics rather than being drawn into a pitched battle. They lived off the land. And finally, they blended into the general population making it difficult to find them. To counter the rebel strategy, Weyler tried to separate them from the general population by confining people in towns or nearby forts where the Spanish army offered protection. Over 300,000 people were forced into "relocation camps." In addition, crops were burned and replanting was prevented. Livestock was driven away from rural areas. The entire countryside was being made inhospitable to the guerrillas.

The result of Spain's policy was a disaster for the Cuban people and a gift of the gods to "yellow journalists." At least 150,000 people died from disease and famine in the relocation camps where adequate housing in a tropical climate was unavailable. Weyler was characterized as "Butcher Weyler," and "Wolf Weyler." He was called a "mad dog," a "hyena." It was claimed that Spanish solders massacred prisoners, even throwing them to the sharks, or dragging them from their beds to shoot them, and then feed them to their dogs. A sympathetic America found itself in concert with blazing editorials driven by Pulitzer and Hearst.

> *It is not only Weyler the soldier... but Weyler the brute, the devastator of haciendas, the destroyer of families, and the outrager of women... Pitiless, cold, an exterminator men ... There is nothing to prevent his carnal, animal brain from running riot with itself in inventing tortures and infamies of bloody debauchery.*
> *New York Journal*

As for the Hearst's *New York World*:

> *Blood on the roadsides, blood in the fields, blood on the doorsteps, blood, blood, blood. The old, the young, the weak,*

> *the crippled --- all are butchered without mercy... Is there*
> *no nation wise enough, brave enough, and strong enough o*
> *restore peace in this blood smitten land"*

Naturally, Hearst and Pulitzer had the same question. With circulations above 800,000 each, their readers wanted to know what would President William McKinley do? Though an expansionist at heart, he was a cautious man and reluctant to go to war. Shrewdly he let Congress initiative, demanding and then declaring the nation at war with Spain. This, by the way, was the first and only time in American history that this has occurred. McKinley finally gave into the public's passion and Congress' pressure, asking for a declaration of war on April 25, 1898. Congress enthusiastically obliged. A joint resolution passed with the following provisions:

1. The United States declared Cuba free of Spain's control.
2. Spain was required to withdraw from the island.
3. The President was directed by Congress to use the armed forces to accomplish the above.
4. The United States declined any intention to annex Cuba.

A bit of trivia invades our thinking now. Even as the United States was caught up in the Cuban revolution against Spain and the impending war with Madrid, a letter dropped out of the heavens much to the delight of the "yellow press" and those promoting war. On February 9, 1898 the *New* York *Journal*, a Hearst paper as you will recall, published what came to be called the De Lome letter. What's the story behind this story?

The Spanish Ambassador to the United States, Senor Don Enrique Dupuy de Lome, wrote a note to Don Jose Canalejas, the Foreign Minister of Spain. Happens everyday, one might think and one would be right. Cuban revolutionaries intercepted the note. Once they were aware of its contents, they forwarded it to the Hearst papers. The note revealed de Lome's opinion about Spain's involvement in Cuba, and his undiplomatic statements about President McKinley. The *Journal* immediately called for de Lome's resignation, which soon happened, even as the paper "stoked the flames" for war.

What had de Lome said about the insurrection?

I am entirely of your opinion, without a military end of the matter nothing will be accomplished in Cuba, and without a military and political settlement there will always be the danger of encouragement being given to the insurgents by a part of the public opinion (in America) if not by the government.

A rather realistic assessment of the situation, don't you think? The press, however, focused more on the next comment"

McKinley is weak and a bidder for the admiration of the crowd besides being a would-be politician who tries to leave a door open behind himself while **keeping** *on good terms with the jingoes of his party.*

Creative sloganeering and ingenious political caricatures are as American as "apple pie." McKinley had been derided much worse by his political foes, and even somewhat comically by his Secretary of the Navy, who said in 1897, "He has no more backbone than a chocolate éclair." It was, however, one thing for a fellow American to criticize and quite another for a foreigner to do so.

America was going to war with Spain, but what did that mean in terms of the nation's future relationship with Japan in the Far East, then and now? What invisible line connected the *USS Maine* with Japan's aspirations in Korea, Manchuria, and China? The answer rested with the diplomats who met in Paris in 1899 to end the Spanish-American War, thereby crowning a defining America victory over Spain, as significant as Japan's defeat of Russia in the same decade.

CHAPTER 12

TREATY OF PARIS

———⌢———

<u>April 1941 – San Diego</u>

So there you have it. President McKinley, heeding the voice of America's destiny, declared war on Spain to free the Cuban people of Madrid's colonial yoke. The war would last from April 25, 1898 to August 12, 1898. The final treaty to conclude all issues would be signed on December 10, 1898. With victories on land and at sea, the war was "splendid," as TR described it later. Americans, once divided by the Civil War and its aftermath, enjoyed a special unity that a satisfying war makes possible. Whether it was Commodore George Dewey's modern ten ship fleet that smashed the outdated Spanish navy in the Philippines, or TR scampering up San Juan Hill, a generally good time was held by all, regardless of those who died from bullets or disease in Cuba.

Of course, as in all wars, when young men are through doing battle, the old men scratch out a treaty to have a "cessation of hostilities." How diplomats do love that term.

Even before our diplomatic delegation arrived in France, a preface to the conflict and the later treaty was working its way through Congress, what America's post-war relationship would be with Cuba? The proposal was referred to as the Platt Amendment. It would have implications, not only in the Caribbean, but also in the Far Pacific.

The Teller Amendment

Senator Henry M. Teller, Republicans from Colorado, was worried. President McKinley's speech of April 11, 1898 suggested a long term involvement in Cuba's affairs once the war was over.

To ensure in the island the establishment of a stable government, capable of maintaining order and observing its international obligations, ensuring peace and tranquility and the security of its citizens as well as our own, and to use the military and naval forces of the United States as may be necessary for these purposes.

Teller was fearful the United States would annex Cuba. Considerable commercial pressures were being exerted on the President to do just that. Teller wanted assurance that Cuba, once freed of the Spanish, would be an independent country. To that point, he proposed the following words:

The United States hereby disclaims any disposition of intention to exercise sovereignty, jurisdiction, or control over said island except for pacification there of, and asserts its determination, when that is accomplished, to leave the government and control of the island to its people.

In short he was saying, the war has been won, now it's time for the Cubans to rule. Stated in another manner, he was placing conditions on America's continued presence on the island. Inherent in his amendment were three choices: (1) annex Cuba; (2) control the island in some quasi-colonial fashion; or (3) leave Cuba to the Cubans.

The Senate passed the Teller Amendment 42 to 35. In the House it passed 311 to 6. America would not engage in imperialism. Point one was out; point three was aspirational. Point two was the transition and ultimately the American policy. Where idealism, realism, and cynicism clashed, this was about the best that could be hoped for. It was, you see, what it was.

Hawaii

Even before the diplomats converged on Paris, another topic of interest was percolating to the surface. President McKinley was determined to annex the sun-drenched islands in the face of anti-imperialistic opposition. Already at the turn of the century, Japan was a perceived threat in the

Pacific and naval war planners were considering the acquisition of scattered bases, including the Hawaiian Islands. Not surprisingly, Japan was opposed to such planning.

McKinley submitted to Congress a resolution for annexation, arguing that:

1. Hawaii had undaunted strategic importance in the Pacific.
2. German and Japanese expansion in the Pacific reinforced this point.
3. If in the looming war with Spain, the US acquired the Philippines, Hawaii would play a significant role in supplying American troops in the far Pacific.

Summarizing, McKinley declared Hawaii a "naval and military necessity" and the "key to the Pacific." His resolution passed by wide majorities in the Congress. Tokyo was not pleased.

As the Spanish-American war progressed, other territorial acquisitions came to the forefront, including the Philippines, Guam, the Wake Island atoll, and Puerto Rico, a potential "Malta of the Caribbean" because it could protect both the Pacific Coast and any proposed canal through Central America. With Guam and Wake Island, the United States would have steppingstones across the Pacific. The Navy quickly seized both areas in 1899, once more cheered on by "expansionists," but derided by the Japanese.

The Treaty of Paris

The outcome of the treaty negotiations was, as one might expect, heavily in favor of the United States. The provisions of the treaty were as follows:

1. Spain gave up all claims to Cuba.
2. Three Spanish colonial possessions would be transferred to the United States: Guam, Puerto, Rico, and the Philippine Islands.
3. Spain would receive $20,000,000 in compensation.

The Treaty of Paris marked the end of the Spanish empire. It also marked the beginning of an America as a world power. The New World had replaced the Old World.

Both parties generally supported the Treaty of Paris. Needing a two-thirds vote, the treaty eventually passed the Senate 57 to 27. One significant question, however, still claimed attention. What would be done about post-war Cuba? What should be done about the Philippines?

Did the United States want to control a subject race in the Pacific? The anti-expansionists thought such control would violate the Constitution. Did the United States have the right to pass laws that governed colonial people who were not represented by lawmakers? Anti-imperialists said, "No."

Expansionists argue the country must honor the Treaty and the President. Rejection would mark the nation as less than a major power unwilling to take on global responsibilities. America, as the argument went, did not come as a despot, but rather to spread her Christian civilization. Finally, the Constitution did not apply to non-Americans, only to US citizens.

The expansionists won the day. Still, what would be done about the Philippines? Most Americans, if asked, didn't even know where the archipelago was on a map. President McKinley confessed as much after Dewey's resounding naval victory in the Pacific:

When we received the cable from Admiral Dewey telling of the taking of the Philippines I looked up their location on the globe. I could not have told where those darned islands were within 200 miles.

Be that as it may, the Philippines were now tied to America's destiny in the Pacific. Three courses of action were open to McKinley. First, grant the Filipino people their independence and say "adios." Second, treat them as a colonial possession within the new American empire. Third, find a position somewhat between; occupation now, independence later. To a degree, the options were analogous to Japan's situation in Korea and Manchuria, the demands of empire pitted against the nationalistic impulses of an occupied people. Back to the Philippines in a moment; the Cuban situation still needed to be settled.

The Platt Amendment

March 2, 1901... Supported by Senator Orville Platt of Wisconsin, an amendment bearing his name was passed by the Senate. It stipulated various conditions for the withdrawal of the remaining American troops in Cuba. The conditions, when implemented, would turn Cuba into a quasi-protectorate of the United States until full independence was granted at some future time. The main provisions were:

Treaty Power - Cuba could not make any treaty with a foreign power, which would endanger her independence.

Indebtedness - Cuba could not incur foreign debts beyond her means to payback in order to avoid foreign intervention.

Intervention - The United States could intervene in Cuba's domestic affairs to maintain order and Cuban independence.

Public Health - Cuba would agree to an American sanitation system to eradicate yellow fever.

Coaling Sites – Cuba would lease or sell to the United States sites for coaling stations and/or a naval base such as Guantanamo Bay.

The Platt Amendment passed the Senate by a vote of 43 to 20. Though initially rejected by the Cuban assembly, the amendment was finally approved by a vote of 16 to 11 and integrated into the 1901 Cuban Constitution.

Cuba, as determined by the Platt Amendment, wasn't a territory or a colony, certainly not a state, but rather some mix of all under American control for better or worse. But whatever it was, it wasn't independent.

The Philippines

Cuba was one thing, a relatively small island only 90-miles from Key West, Florida, and certainly within America's "sphere of influence." The Philippines, composed of 7,641 islands, were quite another task, situated some 4353 miles from San Francisco, and only1882 miles from Japan. With 7.5 million people in 1900 she was many times larger than Cuba with 1.5 million people. Distance, population, and proximity, all factors to consider in 1900.

President McKinley was unsure what to do about "the gift from the gods," as he called the islands. His choices, as they seemed to him, were not altogether clear at first:

1. Give the Philippines back to Spain, but that would be, of course, both dishonorable and cowardly.
2. We could turn the Philippines over to the French or Germans, but that would be bad business and discreditable.
3. We could leave the Philippines to themselves, but they were quite unfit for self-government.
4. We could keep the Philippines and educate the Filipinos.

McKinley's decision to keep the Philippines was influenced by business interests who felt they were being shut out of China and Korea and that the Open Door was closing. Manila, the thinking went, could be an American Hong Kong with access to East Asia where half the people in the world lived. An advisor to the President, Mark Hanna, stated the case:

It is commercialism to want the possession of a strategic point giving the American people an opportunity to maintain a foothold in the markets of that great East country (China), for God's sake let us have commercialism.

Humanitarian interests were also influencing the President. A half-naked and half-civilized people needed a mentor to prepare them for later independence. Chaos would result without America's presence, which would encourage German and Japanese intervention, possibly dragging the United States into a Pacific War. Having destroyed the Spanish we were, as many contended, the new guardians of the islands.

In the end, three "D's" forced McKinley's hand: "duty, destiny, and Dewey." The Philippines would be absorbed into the American orbit.

February 4, 1898 brought home the realities of annexing the Philippines. On that day, the Filipinos, realizing the United States had replaced the Spanish as overlords of the islands, rose in rebellion against their erstwhile saviors. The cost of empire was about to be learned.

The Filipino Insurrection

That's what we called it, the Filipino Insurrection. Characterizing the clash as such branded the rebels as the enemy of legitimate constitutional authority. Of course, the Filipinos saw it differently; it was a war for independence, much like America in 1776. Emilo Aguinaldo, a nationalist, led the struggle against the United States. The revolt, some contended, against American rule could have been avoided if Congress had stated unequivocally that it would grant full independence to the Filipinos once order was restored. This did not happen. The war lasted two years from February 4, 1899 to July 2, 1902. For Filipino nationalists it was a continuation of their struggle for independence beginning in 1896 against Spain.

By any standard the war was harsh and savage. At least 200,000 civilians were killed, mainly due to famine and disease. Some 5,000 or more Americans were killed and over 2,000 were wounded. From 16,000 to 20,000 Filipino fighters were killed in the war. Atrocities were committed by both sides, including torture, butchering, and the use of the "water cure." Butcher Weyler's strategy was commonplace. In the end the United earned an inglorious victory.

A vocal critic of the war, Mark Twain, summed up the entire situation, arguing the "betrayed the ideals of American democracy by not allowing the Filipino people to choose their own destiny."

I thought we should act as their protector---not to get them under our heel. We were to relieve them from Spanish tyranny to enable them to set up a government of their own, and were to stand by and see that it got a fair trial. It was not to be a government according to our ideas, but a government that represented the feeling of the majority of the Filipinos...That would have been a worthy mission for the United States.

Even as the deadly war was raging, post-war policies were evolving to induce a framework of Filipino governance leading to future independence, the Philippine Organic Act of 1902, the Jones Act of 1916, and the Tydings-McDuffie Act of 1934. Each act of Congress was an incremental, but a necessary step to end the existing colonial relationship.

Philippine Organic Act of 1902

Introduced by Congressman Henry A. Cooper, this legislation became law on July 1, 1902. Specifically, the Act called for a Philippine Assembly, an elected lower house. Three pre-conditions were necessary: (a) there had to be two consecutive years of peace; (c) a census had to be completed and published; (c) US authority had to be recognized. An appointed upper house would complete the bicameral legislature.

The Cooper Act, as it was sometimes called, also guaranteed a Bill of Rights to the Filipino people, including the right to (a) live, (b) acquire property, (c) practice religion, and (d) have freedom of expression. In addition, all citizens would be subject to due process. The Act also called for the appointment of two Filipinos to represent the country in the US Congress.

The Jones Law of 1916

Proposed by Congressman William Jones, this legislation superseded the Philippine Organic Act of 1902. Significantly, both houses of the legislature would be elected by popular vote. This arrangement made the two houses more autonomous of US influence. The Governor-General of the Philippines would be appointed and American.

This Act fulfilled TR's vision, first stated in 1901:

We hope to do for them what has never been done for any people of the tropics---to make them fit for self-government after the fashion of really free nations.

Recognizing the power of Filipino nationalism, TR anticipated the Jones Act in 1907:

We shall have to be prepared for giving the islands independence of a more or less complete type much sooner than I think advisable.

President Woodrow Wilson signed the legislation on August 29, 1916. Significantly, this was the first official declaration of Congress that the United States was committed to independence of the Philippines.

Tydings-McDuffie Act of 1934

This legislation sometimes called the Philippine Independence Act, created the Commonwealth of the Philippines. It sought to increase self-governance in advance of independence, which was scheduled for 1944. It also required the first directly elected President of the Philippines. Beyond this, the Filipino and American armed forces would be combined in the event of an emergency. Given the current situation in the Far East, this provision has proved providential.

The Spanish-American War represented a turning point in the nation's history. As a people, America had slipped the bonds of a continental nation by acquiring foreign territories, most particularly the Philippines. No longer did the Atlantic Shore and the Pacific Coast constrain our influence in the world. Dewey's victory at Manila Bay had seen to that, even as America's intervention in the Great War (1917) had finally and fully ended the traditional policy of "non-entanglements" in Europe's "embroilments." In the shadows of this change was a belief in a "divine will" active in the country's foreign policy of expansionism. Whether it was the acquisition of Texas, the Mexican War, reaching out to Hawaii and Alaska, the Oregon Territory, or the Spanish-American War, the hand of a higher entity was perceived. But then, the victors always claim God's favor.

Manifest Destiny

This belief --- Manifest Destiny --- held currency among many Americans in the 19th-century that its people, prompted by land in the West, was carrying out a divine mission to expand across North America. John O'Sullivan, a newspaper editor, first coined the term in 1845. It was never a precise policy of the national government. Rather, it was a generally held belief, or historical rationalization that Americans were destined to expand across the North American continent. O'Sullivan believed Americans had a "divine destiny" based upon values such as "equality, rights of conscience, and personal enfranchisement to establish on earth the moral dignity and salvation of man." The continent, the argument went, only awaited the advancement of covered wagons and sturdy Americans headed west. On December 27, 1845 he wrote in the *New York Morning News*:

And that claim is by the right of our manifest destiny to overspread and to possess the whole of the continent, which Providence has given us for the development of the great experiment of liberty and federated self-government entrusted to us.

But did the romantic notion of divine intervention apply beyond the nation's coastline? In 1898 President McKinley answered that question in justifying the annexation of Hawaii, stating:

We need Hawaii just as much and a good deal more than we did California. It is manifest destiny.

Three important themes motivated America's view of manifest destiny.

1. The American people had special virtues, especially their adherence to democratic practices and free enterprise.
2. The mission of America was to remake the continent in its own image.
3. It was the essential duty of America to carry out this irresistible destiny.

Whatever the validity of these views, they were, as many believed, a wellspring of national motivation and justification for the nation's expression of expansionism. Of course, no nation had a monopoly on such views. Great Britain held similar views, attested to by her empire. Earlier, Spain's colonial possessions in the New World were supported by divine support for Madrid. And, of course, there was Japan in the Far East, a late player on the stage, proclaiming a new day for Asians under the "Rising Sun?" And looking ahead, what would happen when the two emerging powers, Washington and Tokyo, confronted each other in the Far Pacific?

———————

That's it, a prologue to today's crisis in the Pacific. Hopefully, I have assisted you in your quest, be that still a mystery to me. I leave you, then, to return to my academic pursuits with a perspective for you to consider. While war in the Pacific is not inevitable, the culmination of many factors may sometimes suggest that. At this moment in 1941 we cannot know for sure how history will turn. That is not within our province. But one thing can be said with absolute clarity: the bellowing sails of the Empress of China still accompany us into an uncharted future, reminding us, as did Oliver Wendell Holmes, Sr., that inertia in human events is unknown to the historian:

> *To reach a port we must sail,*
> *sometimes with the wind, and*
> *sometimes against it. But we*
> *must not drift or lie at anchor.*

CHAPTER 13

WILSON'S IDEALISTIC VISION

May 1941 – St. Louis

The White Duck Deli is a local favorite in St. Louis, especially if you were into seafaring lore. A maritime motif gave the place a decidedly nautical feeling. On all walls there were shelves with models of civilian and naval ships, each painstakingly constructed to precise ratios, and painted in exacting colors. There were models of expensive yachts, musty old freighters, cavernous oil transports, and, as one would expect, luxurious cruise liners. Of course, there were the warships, destroyers, cruisers, battleships, aircraft carriers, and submarines. Against two walls were anchors from famous ships, all rust removed and a healthy coat of paint added to keep them ship shape. There were symbols, too, of rank, particularly the stars, shoulder boards, and sleeve stripes of US Navy captains. In short, the deli, which claimed the best clam chowder on the Mississippi or, if you so desired, an excellent variety of fish fare, was the perfect harbor for those who go down to the sea.

Located literally in the "middle of America," St. Louis was a perfect meeting spot for the three conspirators. Estelle Stead flew in from San Francisco on a two-engine TWA, propeller-driven plane. Freda Wells jumped on a Greyhound Bus from Chicago and headed for the "Queen City of the Mississippi River." Disliking air travel, John Marshal Harlan II, decided to cater to his boyhood fantasies and climbed aboard a Central Pacific passenger car. Regardless of their mode of transportation, all arrived unscathed by their journey; they all checked into the Delta House near Grant Park, where the proprietor provided comfortable rooms and accepted meals, if so desired. He also provided his boarders with a degree of anonymity in exchange for a generous bonus.

On this day, their second in St. Louis, the conspirators choose to meet at the White Duck Deli, where they were engaged in serious talk in a shrouded corner of the eatery.

"Estelle, a wise choice, this deli."

"You enjoyed your sliced ham, diced potatoes, and scrambled eggs, Harlan."

"Indeed. And you, Freda?"

"My rye bagel and cream cheese was satisfying, as was the thick coffee."

"Estelle, if I maybe presumptuous, you've hardly touched your food. Are you feeling okay?"

"Harlan, my zest for food is diminished today."

"Because?"

"My father paid me a visit last night."

If words could stop a freight train or move a mountain, Estelle's utterance certainly qualified.

"More automatic handwriting?"

"Yes, Freda."

"And?"

"This."

Estelle produced her diary, turned to the page in question before pointing to some scribbling written in indented dark lines, almost as if the pen had pressed hard against the paper multiple times.

WW/4/1941/RX

"You know what your father was communicating?"

"Only an educated guess, Harlan, after a few sleepless hours tying to decode this cryptic message."

"And you came up with what?"

"Possibilities, Freda, **WW** could stand for World War, or Woodrow Wilson. The number **4** was troublesome. It could refer to Wilson's 4-year term of office, or the Big Four who attended the Paris Peace Conference in 1919. As to **1941** it refers perhaps to apprehension in our own time of another conflict. **RX** might stand for royalty, or possibly a medication. If royalty, this might refer to the Kaiser's abdication and the end of the German monarchy, or the downfall of the Romanov's in Russia. Of course, the end of the Hapsburgs in Austria suggests still another aristocratic line lost to history."

"Your conclusion?"

"My father wants us to focus on Paris in 1919."

"The Treaty of Versailles?"

"That and the Covenant of the League of Nations, Freda."

"Leaving only..."

"Wilson's Fourteen Points, Harlan, which is why you are our expertise today."

"And why all this, Estelle?"

"We, I believe, cannot write a new Ark unless we fully understand where the first effort fell short. It all begins and ends with Paris in 1919."

"Then I shall do my best Estelle. It is true I am knowledgeable in this field, hearing my grandfather talk about it so often, as well as my academic studies at Cornell University, which provided a year-long seminar on the topic. At Estelle's request, I have prepared a "mini-lecture, which will satiate your need for a information, but not for sleep."

Drifting Toward War

At the outset it should be noted that President Wilson was most resistant to entering the European War. He had to be pulled, prodded, and pressured before finally entering the conflict in mid-1917. An affinity for Britain's long history and democratic practices, pulled at him to deny a German victory over Shakespeare's "emerald isle." The German strategy of "unrestricted submarine warfare" that denied "freedom of the seas" to American shipping prodded him toward a belligerent position. American loans to England and France, not to Germany, pressured Wilson to support the Entente Alliance, not the Central Powers (Germany, Austria-Hungary, and the Ottoman Empire).

Before entering the conflict, Wilson wanted a statement of principles for peace, which could be used in peace negotiations to end the war. and to influence the post-war period. He desired a set of moral aims, progressive in nature, to counter the secret political dealings that brought Europe to the abyss. He wanted to end:

1. Nationalistic disputes concerning ethnic groups.
2. Long-standing disputes concerning foreign possessions.
3. Obstacles to freedom of the seas.

He wanted to implement progressive ideas, such as:

1. Free trade and limited tariffs.
2. Self-determination of ethnic and national groups.
3. Democratic governments.
4. Open agreements.
5. Reductions in armaments.
6. Adjustments in colonial claims.

To this end, Wilson convened in September 1917 a group known as *The Inquiry.* This group was charged with the task of researching the past to provide Wilson with the intellectual arguments to support his principles once the war ended. What the first conspirators in 1910 had tried to do, the President would complete in negotiating a peace treaty. Over 150 experts in various fields, including geography, history, and government, were organized to do this, first as researchers, then as advisors to the President. Essentially, *The Inquiry* sought to explain the cause of the war and how to prevent a new one, again as the first conspirators had tried.

Colonel Edward M. House

All presidents have a special advisor, a close friend, sometimes elected, sometimes appointed, but always a trusted individual, often taking on difficult jobs for the White House. Colonel House was Wilson's man. He delighted in this, "to serve wherever and whenever possible" the President. This was the role of Colonel House, who helped Wilson to win in 1912, and then in 1916 as his campaign manager. He was also the President's point man in foreign policy, brokering where possible Wilson's efforts to negotiate a peace through diplomacy. In doing so, House felt that the war was a titanic struggle between democracy and autocracy. Eventually, it was his job to chair *The Inquiry*.

The research was done in New York City. Over 2,000 reports were prepared, along with 1,000 maps. Everything was analyzed --- economic, social, and political factors influencing European nations and various ethnic groups. In time and in a systematic manner, the research was digested and distilled for the President as America's war objectives, and Wilson's vision for a post-war world. On January 8, 1918 the President outlined these "war aims" and "peace terms" before a generally supportive Congress. The aims and terms would be known as the Fourteen Points. Wilson's speech was made without prior consultation and coordination with the British and France, who were not always in agreement with the President. However, at this moment it was Wilson's show.

George Creel

In 1918 George Creel was the director of the American Committee on Public Information. He was in charge of propaganda, not only in America, but throughout Europe and the world. Once enunciated, it was his job to share Wilson's views with the world. To that end, he distributed 60,000,000 copies of the Fourteen Points in pamphlet form. By balloon and plane, the skies over Germany were filled with floating leaflets to undermine the German will to fight, or, if you will, to give people a reason for capitulating on the basis of the Fourteen Points.

"What our legacy of conspirators tried to do in 1910."
"Quite so, Freda."
"Was Creel effective?"

111

"To a degree, yes, Estelle. Germany finally made peace, many argued, on the basis of Wilson's "Points." On November 11, 1918 the war ended."

"I am somewhat familiar with the Fourteen Points, but not the contrasting views, which made them so controversial."

"There I can help."

"And the relationship to Japan and the current crisis so many years later?"

"Again, I will, if possible, part the clouds. But before I do, some sobering statistics, which will cause us to pause as we trace the past:

Country	Combat Deaths	All Deaths (Disease)	Wounded
Britain	950,000	1,118,000	2,100,000
France	1,250,000	1,350,000	2,100,000
Germany	1,800,000	2,000,000	4,200,000
Austria/ Hungary	1,000,000	1,300,000	3,800,000
America	53,000	226,000	200,000

These numbers are approximations, but they do indicate the magnitude of the disaster. They do not include all the other combatants. When factored in:

9,600,000	Military Deaths
12,600,000	Civilian Deaths
2,600,000	Military Illness and Disease
21,200,000	Wounded
7,800,000	POW and MIA

Wilson's Fourteen Points, the eventual Treaty of Versailles, and the Covenant of the League of Nations must be seen though the "historic lens" of the European slaughterhouse of 1918. The blood of "Flanders Field" pervaded all.

<u>Wilson's Vision</u>

Point #1: Open covenants of peace, openly arrived at, after which there shall be no private international understandings of any kind but diplomacy shall proceed always frankly and in the public view.

Did secret treaties, agreements, and understandings contribute to war? Generally, historians believe so. To what extent is difficult to determine. However, the various existence of such diplomacy leads to suspicions with the worst of intentions attributed to the "other country." Of course, in the absence of public debate, even awareness, entire populations are obligated to events beyond their control. In "raw terms" secret treaties are the mother lode of "power politics" on an international scale. As an example, the British French, and Germans made promises to the Arab world to gain their oil resources and support during a conflict. Additional promises were made to Jews concerning a "homeland in Palestine" in the absence of Arab consultation and agreement. Duplicity is the end result of secret treaties.

Realistically, most governments, weather democratic or authoritarian, prefer secrecy to public scrutiny. Here Wilson was pushing against a large boulder. Paradoxically, he would engage in this business in securing a treaty to end the conflict.

Wilson violated his own principles?"

"He did but not willingly, Estelle."

"I don't understand."

"Every nation attending Versailles, including representatives including representatives of various ethnic groups, had their own post-war aims, which they were often at odds with each other. Through protracted negotiations and less than satisfying compromises, decisions were made but not always in a public forum. In an imperfect world, deals were cut, map were altered, and ethnic, nationalistic aspirations were churned through the treaty making process."

"Wilson went along with this, Harlan?"

"He had to, Freda, as did Clemenceau of France, David Lloyd George of Britain, and Orlando of Italy --- the so-called "Big Four." The final treaty was a composite of conflicting national goals, domestic political considerations, and compromise, all necessary for passage of any sort of treaty."

"Then what was the war all about?"

"That is the question, isn't it, Estelle?"

Point #2: Absolute freedom of navigation upon the seas, outside territorial waters, alike in peace and in war, except as the seas may be closed in whole or part by international action for the enforcement of international covenants.

"Harlan, how can freedom of the seas lead to war? Shouldn't ships be able to navigate free of restrictions?"

"Yes, certainly in peacetime, Freda. But in wartime, does the same theme apply? That's when the question becomes sticky. Perhaps President Thomas Jefferson might best answer that question. During the Napoleonic Wars, French ships sank American vessels headed toward England. British warships captured American ships headed to France, and "impressed" seaman into English warships. Though he demanded "freedom of the seas," it was all the Virginian could do to keep the new nation out of the European conflict."

"A problem we observed again in the last war."

"Correct, Freda."

"In more recent times the German policy of "unrestricted submarine warfare" led to the sinking of a British passenger liner *Lusitania* on May 7, 1915 with the loss of 1198 dead, including 128 Americans. Wilson demanded that Germany respect neutral rights and avoid sinking merchant and passenger ships. Berlin chose not to do so and Wilson was eventually pushed into war."

"Wilson's idealism crashing on the jagged rocks of power-politics."

"Well put, Estelle. Realistically, great naval powers such as the United States, Britain, and Japan supported (and would have demanded) absolute freedom navigation, only to curtail it when it was in their interests. In no way would they permit any limitations on their naval forces at Versailles. While freedom of the seas provision made its way into the treaty, it did so without any enforcement mechanism. Great naval powers still ruled the waves."

"That left, Harlan, two great naval forces in the Pacific, did it not, Japan and the United States?"

"And on a collision course."

"We need to talk more on this."

"After lunch, Estelle."

CHAPTER 14

IDEALISM CHALLENGED

An Hour Later

"The chicken salad wasn't bad, Estelle."

Since peer pressure overwhelmed us, and we all ordered the same, I must agree with you, Harlan. What say, Freda?"

It's hard to go wrong with chicken salad."

The early lunch was over. It was time for Harlan to get back in the saddle. After last sip of his Napa "something," he did so, saying, "Back to the Fourteen Points."

Point #3 – The removable, so far as possible, of all economic barriers and the establishment of equality of trade conditions among all the nations consenting to the peace and associating themselves for its maintenance.

"It was desirous from Wilson's perspective to ensure the economic development of newly created nations, as well as to assist the near bankrupted of the war. Self-interest also played a role here. America's surplus production needed a strong European market, particularly with the end of wartime contracts. Reduction in economic barriers was good for business. That's the plus side of he equation.

"What we're really talking about here is an effort to avoid protective tariffs that insulate one country's businesses or economy against another. Obviously, this is difficult to do when nations must import as well as export. Economic barriers inhibit both transactions. Nations such as Japan are particularly sensitive to foreign markets for both raw materials and markets for their goods. Tariffs, if used unwisely, may be perceived as a weapon to influence another nation's foreign policies. This is a claim the Japanese are making about America's recent boycott of scrap iron and refined oil. Of course, there are dangers lurking in boycotts. What will the affected nation do in response? That is our situation in 1941."

FDR is aware of this situation, Harlan?"

"Yes. His administration is playing a high-risk game, Freda. To entice Japan to remove troops from China, and to ward off a threat to Southeast Asia, President Roosevelt has instigated a severe boycott, really a blockade in all but name."

"Prohibiting the export of scrap iron to Japan?"

"Again, yes, and also crude oil."

"Is this economic gunboat diplomacy?"

"Of course, Estelle. That's the way the Japanese sees it, a quasi-military act."

"And if Japan doesn't accede to FDR's demands?"

"War is a definite possibility."

"Wilson's idealism gone astray."

"That's one way of looking at it, Freda. Remember, Japan has 1.000,000 men in China, others in Manchuria and Korea. At great cost in coin and flesh she has pursued an aggressive foreign policy. It's difficult to envision Japan backing down to economic threats."

"Roosevelt's advisers know this, Harlan."

"Certainly."

"What can be done at this late hour?"

"That, as always, is the question, Freda. What can be done?"

Point #4 – Adequate guarantees given and taken that national armaments will be reduced to the lowest point consistent with domestic safety.

"Few would dispute the need for disarmament and/or that arms contribute to international tensions. But what to do about has always been the question. What does "consistent with domestic safety" really mean? How are "adequate guarantees" enforced? If a nation is at war, as his Japan in China at the present moment, to what extent can armaments be reduced? Does the notion of "national sovereignty" and "independence of action" hinder arms reduction? Is parity the goal where every nation has equality of weaponry, but not more or less?" By way of example, should the American navy and Japan's sea force have equivalency though Tokyo needs only a one-ocean fleet and America requires a two-ocean armada? And, of course, the weapon's industry everywhere will not look kindly in reductions."

"You have studied the issues, Harlan."

"I have, that I admit, Estelle."

"Concluding?"

"I have more questions than answers."

"Then where are we, Sir?"

"Striving to create a second Ark that takes Wilson's idealism into account yet forges a rationale way to implement his approach to foreign policy."

"But not while Hitler reigns?"

"Only after that psychopath is removed or is dead, and most probably Germany is in ruins., Freda."

"And Japan?"

"Estelle, if war can be avoided, armaments can be reduced regardless of the difficulty."

"The chances?"

"Slim to nothing at this moment."

"There are still more 'Points,' Harlan?"

"Indeed."

Point #5 – *A free, open-minded and absolutely impartial adjustment of all colonial claims based upon a strict observance of the principle that in determining all such questions of sovereignty the interests of the populations concerned must have equal weight with the equitable government whose title is to be determined.*

The diplomats do go on an on. What a mouthful? It seems at first glance such an easy "point" to understand. But is it that? I think not. As an example, if Germany, as she did, capitulates, what happens to her Pacific possessions, her colonial outposts in Africa, and "spheres of interest" in China? Does she maintain control? Are these areas simply released from Berlin's yoke? Are they the "fruits of war" for the victors? And what of the Ottoman Turks and the various nationalistic groups in the Middle East? Naturally, there is the ethnic puzzle of Berlin's ally, the Austro-Hungarian empire. And what does "equal weight" really mean? Who is to determine this? How is this to be determined? How does all this apply to Korea and Manchuria, or for that matter the Philippines? Onion layers of questions for an illusionary simple "Point."

"In short how is the nationalistic, self-determination pie to be sliced and diced, Harlan?"

"You do add to the already complicated situation, Estelle."

"As I am told of W.T. Stead, it is my nature. The questions flow, Harlan, a force of their own."

"We will endure this through all the "Points?""

"Nay, Freda, only one more."

"The others are less important?"

"No, they are merely reflections of each other. For example"

Point #6 -The settlement of all questions affecting Russia.

Point #7 dealt with the restoration of Belgium as a freed nation. Point #8 concerned Alsace-Lorraine. Point #9 tried to resolve the adjusting Italy's borders. Point #10 focused on the autonomous development of the people of Austria and Hungary. Point #11 asked what wound happen to the people of Roman Serbia and Montenegro? Point #12 asked the same question, this time concerning the people of Turkey and the Ottoman Empire? Point #13 emphasized an independent Polish state, erected with free and assured access to the sea?

"You appear fatigued, Harlan."

"No more so than Wilson and others trying mightily to make adjustments of people and territories in Europe and elsewhere. Perhaps it was all beyond anyone's reach, Estelle. Dissolving an empire is not the same thing as liquidating a business. Redrawing the map is not the same thing as satisfying nationalistic and ethnic aspirations. Recreating the world is, in the absence of a deity, perhaps more than mortal hands can accomplish."

"And with our new Ark?"

"Estelle, we can but hope."

"One Pont still to go, Harlan, which you have left for last."

"Only because it is the last of Wilson's hopes, as it was for my grandfather, to maintain the peace in the post-war period."

"The first Harlan conceived of an international assembly of nations to do so, is that not so?"

"That is the case and Wilson brought the concept to Paris."

Point #12 – A general association of nations must be formed under specific covenants for the purpose of affording mutual guarantees of political independence and territorial integrity to great ad small states alike.

"A general association of nations? What was Wilson alluding to? The present League of Nations, of course, was what the President had in mind, an international organization to maintain the peace, to avoid another even worse calamity.

"Once more the question of guarantees haunts us? What is the nature of such guarantees? What happens if they are violated? Mutual guarantees; are these really alliances by another name?

What would the specific covenants say? Would they be made public? Would all nations carry equal weight in the "general association?" As always, too many questions, or perhaps not enough, one might ask? In any event, Wilson's idealism, whether misguided or not, perceived the new entity as the world's last hope to resolve issues related to the war and future challenges still to manifest themselves. It was at the center of all that he believed and the vision that would finally break his heart and cost him his life."

"His life, Harlan?"

"Tragically, yes, Freda."

"The battle for the Versailles Treaty?"

"Again, yes, but that is to get ahead of the story."

"In the interim?"

"A final question."

––––––––––––

What was the impact of the Fourteen Points on America and the belligerent countries? The answer perhaps begins with Wilson and his use of the "bully pulpit." He began the tortuous route from nonintervention to direct participation in the war, first stating the "world must be made safe from the submarine." That evolved into this must be a "war to end war," and finally, a struggle to "make the world safe for democracy." The Fourteen Points encapsulated and articulated these themes, both on a philosophical basis and as a form of propaganda emphasizing, as they did, Wilson's desire for a "just, permanent, and open peace."

"He was ahead of his time, Harlan."

"As some said Stead and his gang were, Estelle."

"As some will speak of us?"

"Most assuredly, dear person."

"But Wilson's views did play well in Germany?"

"Indeed, his views had a pronounced effect on Germany, particularly his argument that the American people had no quarrel with Germans, only with their "military master." In effect, that meant the High Command and the Kaiser. Fatigued by the war, the German people quickly and accurately read Wilson's mind. The Kaiser would have to go if the war was to end without a large-scale invasion of Germany. On November 9, 1918, it was over. The Kaiser was forced to abdicate and to flee to Holland, where he lived for the next twenty-three years. Two days later an armistice was signed. There is no question the Germans threw in the towel, so to speak, on the basis of Wilson's Fourteen Points. They fully expected the final treaty to reflect the idealism and progressivism, if not the leniency of the President's expressions. In the end this proved to be a miscalculation of immense import."

"You're hinting and implying, Harlan."

"True. Freda."

"To what end?"

"Estelle can answer that."

"Tomorrow Harlan gets a well-deserved reprieve. He will rest. Professor Eleanor Longstreet will be with us tomorrow. She's an expert on the Treaty of Versailles. She will help us to understand what happened in Paris in 1919 where, for better or worse, a post-war world was hammered out by the great powers. And this is important for us if we are to construct a new Ark, since the present war in Europe, and the looming crisis in the Pacific is, as some historians claim, an outcome of an overly harsh treaty. As a bridge to our speaker, I leave you with two quotes: the first is from the *New York Nation* in 1919, the second from President Wilson.

> *Six million young men lie in premature graves, and four old men sit in Paris partitioning the earth.*
> *New York Nation*

> *My urgent advice to you would be, not only always to think first of America, but always, also to think first of humanity. You do no love of humanity if you seek to divide humanity into jealous camps. Humanity can be welded together only by love, by sympathy, by justice, not by jealousy and hatred. I am sorry for the man who seeks to make personal capital out of the passions.*
> President Woodrow Wilson

CHAPTER 15

ALL ROADS LEAD
TO VERSAILLES

May 1941 – St. Louis

"And so without any further introduction, we will begin with the aims of the French government, which in this case meant the Prime Minister, George Clemenceau."

"The one called the 'Tiger of France?'"

"That one, Freda, yes. He was an older man, tenacious, unforgiving, and revengeful, and with the power to punish the Hun, once and for all. And this was the time. Seventy delegates representing twenty-seven nations had gathered in Paris at the French Foreign Ministry in Paris to bring a legal end to the Great War."

The conspirators were again meeting at the White Duck Deli and, as before, they huddled in the shadows, having once more finished breakfast, though still savoring their meal. No longer was Harlan holding forth. As promised by Estelle, Professor Eleanor Longstreet was their guest and mentor.

"To understand Clemenceau's anger, one had only to recall the price France paid in the conflict. Over 1,300,000 soldiers buried across the flowery landscape. At least 25% of Frenchmen between the ages of 18-30 dead, never to be husbands and fathers, shopkeepers, and scientists, all gone... The beautiful countryside physically destroyed by the ravages of a war mainly fought in France. The coal and iron ore areas devastated, no longer supportive of industry. Railroads upturned, bridges collapsed in heaps, factories in ruins, and mines flooded. This was victorious France on January 18, 1919, the day peace discussions began."

Professor Longstreet was middle-aged, tall and willowy, with long brown hair cascading to her shoulders. She had a pleasant face and a enticing smile, which gave way to an intensely studious demeanor once she shifted into her topic, which was today, the Treaty of Versailles. Attached to the history department, she taught at the University of St. Louis and was considered an expert on the "Treaty," assuming that three books on the subject qualifies one as an expert. She knew little about the conspirators and their goals. As always, Estelle had revealed little, much as her father had done in gaining access to information. But the professor was not without a sharp eye.

――――――――――

You have an interest in understanding the current tensions with Japan and the strong possibility that war is imminent this year. That you would like to do something about this I get. But, as you appreciate, Japanese-American relations do not function in a vacuum or only in the present. The world is again at war. The Nazis have seen to that, as have Mussolini's hoards. What happens in the Pacific will not have begun in 1941. There is a history here, which includes the Paris Peace Conference and the world it bequeathed to Tokyo and Washington. To learn about one is to comprehend the other.

――――――――――

"I take it you're not related to the Longstreet of Gettysburg fame?"

"Not even a distant relative, Harlan, though I would have enjoyed the connection, having been born not far from the battle. But, as I understand it, your grandfather was of that vintage."

"Indeed. A witness to all."

"And a unique Associate Judge of the Supreme Court, most often it seems, the contrarian."

"And, of course, Freda, the daughter of Ida B. Wells, a special person in my life given my mother's family's abolitionist sentiments and support of the Underground Railroad before the Confederates bolted."

"Any thoughts about W.T. Stead?"

"Estelle, after your entreaties to meet, I did some research. The man does take one's breath away, historically speaking. So daring, so charming… But now we must get to the subject at hand."

French War Aims

Though many nations attended the peace conference, only four had the real power:

> George Clemenceau, Premier of France
> Vittorio Orlando, Italian Prime Minister
> David Lloyd George, Prime Minister of Great Britain
> Woodrow Wilson, President of the United States

Collectively, they were known as the "Big Four." They would meet for 145 closed sessions and make the major decisions about the eventual treaty. Each came with a laundry list of goals. We begin with the French.

First and foremost, France wanted security to avoid another conflict with Germany. She had lost in 1870 in the Franco-Prussian War and had barely survived the Great War. And, of course, in the present moment, Berlin has overrun Paris in a third conflict. But in 1919 Clemenceau expressed the French view to Wilson:

America is far away, protected by the ocean. Not even Napoleon himself could touch England. You are both sheltered; we are not.

Security for France meant Germany would be weakened, economically and militarily. How was this to be done? By making the German military incapable of future aggressive action. That is, end her ability to go on the offensive again.

1. Permit only an army of 100,000 men.
2. Dissolve the German high command.
3. Limit the number of military schools.

4. Limit the number of paramilitary groups.
5. Demilitarize the Rhineland.
6. Destroy all fortifications on the Rhine.
7. Limit the size and power of German weapons.
8. Prohibit the stockpiling of chemical weapons.
9. Reduce the navy to 15,000 men.
10. End any submarine threat in the future.
11. Prohibit Germany from having an air force.
12. Forbid Germany from importing planes for six months.
13. Demilitarize the Rhineland.
14. Permit French occupation of the Rhineland for 15-years.

When eventually presented with these demands and others, the German government balked, but there was little her delegates could do. It was a "take it or leave it" proposition. Accept these terms or be invaded. Massed Allied troops would carry the war all the way to Berlin. The army was disintegrating; soldiers were deserting. Civilian strikes were limiting war production. Sailors of the Imperial German Navy at Kiel mutinied. Food shortages enveloped the country. Resistance was no longer an option.

Woodrow Wilson had his Fourteen Points, as did the French Premier, and each would prevail to some extent. Both leaders were confronted with a simple question: What kind of treaty did they want? There were in Paris at least three possibilities. First, there was a peace of accommodation, which permits the victors to "forgive and to forget" as far as is humanly possible. Such a treaty recognizes that in a new post-war period nations must establish new relationships to ensure a peaceful world. Treating the vanquished in a fair way is the key. President Lincoln attempted to do this, desiring to welcome back the rebellious South once allegiance to the Constitution and the abolition of slavery was accepted, what the President called "mild reconstruction." He was opposed to a military occupation of the former Confederacy if at all possible. Unfortunately, things turned out differently.

The second type is a "victor's peace," harsh, needlessly unfair, and humiliating. Such a treaty makes a future war almost inevitable, since the vanquished, if able, will want to undo it. The Treaty of Guadalupe Hidalgo, signed near Mexico City on February 2, 1848, was a disaster for Mexico. The entire Southwest was lost, over half of Mexico's land possession. While Mexico could dream of a future change of borders, in this case the "Colossus of the North" was too powerful. The "victor's treaty" would stand.

The third type of treaty is something in between, vengeful enough to arouse the vanquished for revenge, but not harsh enough to keep them controlled for more than one generation. To the point: victors can have peace or they may have vengeance, but they can't have both in the same treaty. Of course, the Treaty of Portsmouth is a perfect example. Both the Russians and the Japanese were dissatisfied with President Teddy Roosevelt's sponsored agreement. No final victor; no final foe vanquished. That being the case, each side lived to fight again.

———————

"Wilson, of course, wanted "accommodation, Professor Longstreet?"

"Correct, Freda."

"And Clemenceau desired a "victor's mantle?"

"Estelle, without doubt, yes."

"And in the end, they got neither, right?"

"Unfortunately, Harlan."

"Wilson would have preferred 'Peace without Victory?'"

"As did the British who wanted 'reconciliation with Germany,' if Berlin was to be a future trading partner without a crippled economy. Always the pragmatic, the British government wanted to maintain a 'balance of power' in Europe. A vibrant, post-war Germany could off-set France's determination to be dominant on the continent, while at the same time be a counterbalance against Bolshevik Russia."

"Still, Britain sided with France. A harsh treaty was proclaimed."

"True, Harlan. Two factors forced the issue, the infamous 'Guilt Clause' and the question of 'reparations.' The two issues are so intertwined that it difficult to separate one from the other. Together, however, they were to define the Peace Conference's outcome as a 'victor's treaty.'"

———————

The Guilt Clause

How do wars begin? Such a simple question, is it not? Country A attacks Country B. Of course, that's the "what," not the "why." Is war an outcome of conscious decision-making? Is it caused by a miscalculation? Public misunderstanding? Governments overwhelmed by events, questioning their ability to handle a crisis? Do years of propaganda create a national mindset conducive to accept war as the only acceptable outcome? Does hubris play a role, either individually or collectively? Or is war simply the outcome of some primitive human need for bloodletting? The choices abound and at Versailles they mingled and mixed, emerging as Article 231, the War Guilt Clause.

The Allied and Associated Governments affirm and Germany accepts the responsibility of Germany and her allies for causing all the loss and damage to which the Allied and Associated Governments and their nationals have been subjected as a consequence of the war imposed upon them by the aggression of Germany and her allies.

On an academic basis a number of questions are immediately apparent. The term "accepts." At the point of a bayonet Berlin was "*forced*" to acknowledge Article 231. The words, "*all the loss and damage*" suggests that Berlin alone was responsible for war-related destruction. Was the word "*imposed*" really an explanation of why Britain and France went to war with Germany? Did they have no choice in the matter?

Notice the word "guilt" was not used in Article 231. Still, Germans viewed this clause as a national humiliation. German politicians and historians were defiant in their opposition. Allied justification for the clause accepted the view that the war was "premeditated by the Central Powers," and that such actions made "war unavoidable" despite repeated efforts by the Entente to be "conciliatory."

Of course, there was another way of looking at the clause in question, war reparations. The term "guilt" served as a legal basis to compel German to pay for damages caused by the war, a legal basis to extract compensation from Germany. This was really an assumption of guilt in order for reparations the victors would demand. Without an admission of "guilt," reparations would not be possible. If that was the case, the entire treaty might collapse, since responsibility for the war would be shared. Therefore, there was a legal necessity to unequivocally place responsibility on Berlin. It was not alone a moral issue; it was also a financial one. Ultimately, a Reparation Committee fixed the tab at 50 billon gold marks or $12.5 billion in U.S. dollars. A payment schedule was set up for this purpose. Germany could pay in cash or kind, including coal, timber, chemical dyes, factory machinery, livestock, and pharmaceuticals.

Generally speaking, the British and French populations accepted this outcome with various degrees of glee. Others, perhaps more somber in their analysis, saw this business as vindictive and greedy, if not difficult to enforce, leaving Europe in a constant state of turmoil because the treaty itself was unstable. As for the Germans:"

> *We know the full brunt of hate that confronts us here. You demand from us to confess we were the only guilty part of war; such a confession in my mouth would be a lie. It would be a violation of honor.*

In response Clemenceau bitterly address the vanquished, saying in highly dramatic terms:

> *It is neither the time nor the place for superfluous words... You have before you the accredited plenipotentiaries of all the small and great Powers united to fight together in the war that has been so cruelly imposed upon them. The time has come when we must settle our accounts. You have asked for peace. We are ready to give you peace.*

As to the reparation bill, the famous British economist, John Maynard Keynes, referred to the Treaty of Versailles as a "Carthaginian peace." He considered it a misguided attempt to destroy Germany on behalf of France. For Keynes, it would have been better to implement the fairer principles for a lasting peace "set out in President Wilson's Fourteen Points," which Berlin had accepted as a prerequisite for peace. Keynes stated the proposition as such:

> *I believe that the campaign for securing out of Germany the general costs of the war was one of the most serious acts of political un-wisdom for which our statesmen have ever been responsible.*

"I get it."

"Get what, Estelle?"

"If the Nazis are defeated, any new treaty must avoid the faults of Versailles, professor. If the United States ends up in a Pacific War with Japan, the same theme must apply."

"That is the lesson."

"But is it true that Germany alone was not responsible for the conflict?"

"Harlan, historians has debated that question since Versailles."

"And?"

"They reached various conclusions."

"You have a favorite?"

"I do, Freda. Before divulging, let me share a few facts about the origin of the conflict. Then before I share, you take a position."

---

1. June 28, 1914 — The Archduke of Austria-Hungary and heir to the throne, Franz Ferdinand, is assassinated. A Serbian nationalist is blamed.
2. Austria-Hungary declares war on Serbia after consulting with her major ally, Germany.
3. The Serbians reach out to the "big Slavic brother, " Russia.
4. Russia consults with Paris; Paris consults with London.
5. Germany consults with Vienna; Vienna consults the Ottomans.
6. All countries warn others to avoid mobilization of armed forces.
7. The Central Powers mobilize --- Austria-Hungary, Germany, and the Ottoman Empire.
8. The Triple Entente mobilizes --- France, Russia, and Great Britain.
9. The Japanese watch, unsure where to throw their weight.
10. The United States tries to stay neutral.
11. The alliance system works; previously developed war plans are implemented.
12. Germany attacks France by way of the Low Countries. Belgium's neutrality is violated.
13. Europe is at war.
14. Colonial areas participate; the world is at war.

"There you have it. Within thirty days Europe goes off the cliff into an abyss."

"And most responsible, Professor Longstreet?

"Germany, Estelle. Two reasons: first she gave Vienna the famous "blank check," meaning Austria could make impossible demands on Serbia. Second, always fearful of a two-front war, Germany chose to attack France before the Russians were fully mobilized."

"I pick England."

"Because, Harlan?"

"If London had stayed out it, the French might not have mobilized. British troops and Britain's control of the sea were needed by Paris."

"Your view, Freda?"

"I am a pacifist. Why the death of one man should lead to the deaths of millions I still do not understand. Be that as it may, the two alliances made a choice to go to war. No country pulled back. That being the case, they are all at fault."

"Well stated, Freda. Many historians would agree with you, though some might add, "alliances don't kill; countries in alliances kill."

"That is a lesson for the future?"

"Yes, Harlan, it is. But how to eliminate them is a difficult question.'

"We're done?"

"Almost. We need to look at the question of mandates."

The Mandate System

Two conflicting views emerged after Germany agreed to the Armistice and the victors met at Versailles. First, what should happen to Germany's overseas possessions, and in the same vein, what should happen to those areas controlled by the Ottoman Empire in the Middle East? Cynically, who should get the "spoils of war?" Of course, this view was countered to Wilson's notion of self-determination and respect for indigenous people in colonial possessions. How would the two views be reconciled?

Article 22 of the League of Nations (June 28, 1919) Covenant provided an answer. Territories once controlled by Germany and the Ottomans, but now under League supervision, would be doled out to various countries as mandates with the following provisions:

1. There would be no annexation of any territory.
2. Each territory involved would be a "sacred trust of civilization to develop the area for the benefit of its native people."
3. Native people would be prepared for self-government.
4. The possessions would not be protectorates to be used for the benefit of the trustee nation.
5. Trustees were prohibited from fortifying a possession.
6. Freedom of religion and conscience must be guaranteed.

Two countries in particular received former German and Ottoman possessions, Britain and France as follows:

France	Britain
Lebanon	Palestine
Syria	Transjordan
Iraq	

The two countries were also awarded mandates in Africa, while Japan received former-German possessions in the Pacific with the exception of New Guinea, which went to the Australians, while New Zealand got West Samoa. Africa, always an area of colonial rivalry, continued that way with London and Paris inheriting former-German areas in Togoland. While the mandate system wasn't perfect, it did recognize Wilson's concern for self-determination and self-rule. Overall, it mirrored the entire Versailles Treaty in that what was possible found its way to Paris. Wilson's advisor, Colonel House, summed up the situation as such in June 1919:

> *I am leaving Paris, after eight fateful months, with conflicting emotions. Looking at the conference in retrospect, there is much to approve and yet much to regret. It is easy to say what should have been done, but more difficult to have found a way of doing it. To those who are saying that the treaty is bad and should never have been made and that it will involve Europe in infinite difficulties its enforcement, I feel like admitting it. But I would also say in reply that empires cannot be shattered, and new states raised upon their ruins*

without disturbance. To create new boundaries is to create new troubles the one follows the other. While I should have preferred a different peace, I doubt very much whether it could have been made, for the ingredients required for such a peace as I would have were lacking at Paris

---

"As always, I ask what lessons can be learned? Harlan?"

"In the courtroom there is the decision you desire for your client, and there is what the jury confirms, a fair comparison for the challenges at Versailles."

"Freda?"

"Lofty goals and the most idealistic vision always confronts what some call the "real world," where negotiations and compromise provide something less than what our heart desires."

"Estelle?"

"We must learn from the past and prepare for a better future, when war rages in Europe and threatens in the Pacific."

"Well, then, if this was your final examination, all have received an A+, assuming, of course, you'll treat for a large size cheese burger. We have been at this all morning and I'm starved."

"And after lunch, Professor Longstreet?"

CHAPTER 16

THE USS GEORGE WASHINGTON

<u>June 1941 – St. Louis</u>

Professor Longstreet was holding forth, even as she resisted the temptation to be pandemic and, fearfully boring. Rather, she sought to engage her new friends with what color she might add to the subject at hand.

"It was built in 1908."

"Of course, but what was it, Professor?"

"Curiously, it was constructed in Germany, Freda?"

"You're sharing a puzzle?"

"To be solved, Harlan. It was launched with great fanfare befitting the third largest steamship in the world, designed to comfortably care for 2,900 passengers. Her original name was the *SS George Washington*.

"It is of some importance?"

"Indeed, Freda, given the fickleness of history."

"Which you will share?"

"Naturally."

"The ship was in an American harbor in 1914 when the European war broke out. Since she was birthed in a neutral harbor, she was soon interred. Upon entering the war in 1917, American authorities seized the cruise ship. The ship was quickly pressed into service and renamed the *USS George Washington*. During the war the ship would ferry over 48,000 troops to Europe. On December 4, 1918, its most famous passenger boarded. Nine days later, on December 13, 1918, the ship reached Breast, France along with a protective convoy of ten battleships and twenty-eight destroyers. I wonder who the passenger was?" Freda? Harlan? Estelle?"

"Much too easy, Professor. It had to be President Wilson."

"As you say, Freda. Now, where was he headed?"

"To Paris, of course, and to Versailles."

"Nailed it, Estelle. And what tradition was he breaking, Harlan?"

"On November 11, 1918 the war ended. One week later Wilson broke tradition with his predecessors in the Oval Office. He decided to attend the Paris Peace Conference in person, thereby becoming the first president to visit Europe. As already noted, he sailed on the *USS George Washington*."

"Well done. Now what was ironic about this, Sir?"

"Wilson was sailing in the face of American history, most specifically President Washington's famous 'Farewell Speech,' which had cautioned the new nation to avoid entanglements in Europe's conflicts. Our first president wanted to follow policy of neutrality and necessary isolationism by avoiding entering into alliances. This was especially true in Washington's mind as France and England were embroiled in the Napoleonic Wars. For Washington, alliances were entanglements, which would drag the young country into trouble. Paradoxically, all this, of course, was what Wilson was about to do. He hoped to entangle the country in a lasting treaty agreement to end the Armistice and to create a League of Nations. In doing so, he would exchange neutrality and non-involvement for engagement and collective security."

"Excellent. Naturally, one question still remains. Want to take a stab at it, Freda? Why had Wilson broken with tradition?"

"Apparently, Professor Longstreet, the president felt his presence was necessary to conclude a 'just treaty,' which would not lead to another conflict. His critics, however, said he suffered from a 'messiah complex,' and that this dictated his decision. Whatever the case, he sailed forth from the 'new world' to save the 'old' one."

"Concisely done. In some respects, it should be noted that Wilson was greeted as a 'savior.' He was the man who had forced an Armistice and envisioned a new millennium of peace. One woman reportedly said:

> *You have saved our fiancés, love blooms again. Wilson,*
> *you have saved our children. Through you evil is punished.*
> *Wilson! Wilson! Wilson! Glory to you, who like Jesus, have*
> *said: Peace on Earth and Good Will to Men!*

"Surely, Wilson went with advisers?"

"Plenty of them, Freda, but with one notable and problematic exception."

"You will explain."

"Wilson formed a Peace Commission with himself, as would be expect, the leader. The others on the Peace Commission included:

Robert Lansing	-	Secretary of State
Colonel Edward House	-	Personal Advisor
General Bliss	-	Military Advisor
Henry White	-	Career Bureaucrat

"House's name is familiar,"

"It should be, Estelle. As noted earlier, House was Wilson's closest advisor. He was also the person who visited Hull House and spoke with Jane Addams about the work of the first conspirators. Presumably, much of their views found their way into Wilson's Fourteen Points."

"The 'exception,' Professor Longstreet?"

"Freda, the US Senate was not consulted, nor were key members of the Republican majority included in the Peace Commission. The Senate was slighted. No other way to describe it. Why was this important? In a nutshell all treaties must be approved by a 2/3rds Senate vote according to the Constitution:

> *He (the President) shall have Power by and with the Advice*
> *and Consent of the Senate, to make Treaties, provided two-*
> *thirds of the Senators present concur...*

"The Republicans held a slim majority, 49 to 47. The Democrats alone, if everyone voted along partisan lines, could not approve a treaty, certainly the complicated and controversial Treaty of Versailles. Unfortunately, Wilson did not appoint a Senator to his Peace Commission, and worst of all, the Chairman of the Senate Foreign Relations Committee was bypassed, Henry Cabot Lodge. The Senate felt ignored. Lodge felt ignored. That meant that no treaty, regardless of its merits, would be approved without Lodge's endorsement and the concurrence of the Senate."

"Professor, a mistake by Wilson? A mishap? Distain?"

"Perhaps all, Freda, but certainly not bipartisanship. To a degree, Wilson had moved in this direction during the 1918 Congressional Elections when he initiated a highly partisan appeal to the public, saying:

> *If you have approved of my leadership and wish me to continue to be your unembarrassed spokesman in affairs at home and abroad, I earnestly beg that you will express yourselves unmistakably… by returning a Democratic majority to both the Senate and the House of Representatives.*

"The public, exhausted by the sacrifices of war, including inflation at home, and having second thoughts about the involvement in the European turmoil, turned away from Wilson. The Congress went Republican."

"A lesson to be learned by FDR?"

"Quite right, Estelle, one of many lessons."

"You're hinting at something."

"I am. Once in Paris, Wilson came face-to-face with European realities. The first was the need for speed in writing and concluding the Treaty of Versailles. Europe was exhausted and hungry. More than Germany, much of France was in ruins. The Kaiser had abdicated; he found a new home in Holland, unloved and unwanted. A new German government, absent of the monarchy, was forming hoping to avoid anarchy. The Russian Revolution was history and the threat of Bolshevism moving westward was real. Ethnic groups were at each other's throats. Everywhere the 'wolf was at door.' By physically attending the Peace Conference, Wilson couldn't help but be caught up in the emotions and pressures of the moment, leading some to think he should have remained in Washington. At home he could have made unhurried decisions. It is important to remember that treaties are made by men, who are susceptible to every human emotions, fear, anger, jealousy, hate, and greed, emotions that can find their way into all things."

"No matter the best of intentions."

"Correct, Harlan, especially when treaty options are available."

"You're driving at what, Professor Longstreet?"

"There are at least three kinds of peace treaties as described earlier. First, there is the **victor's peace,** which makes a future war all but inevitable. Second, there is a **peace of accommodation**, which permits the vanquished to forgive and forget. The provisions here are milder, recognizing that all belligerents had some capability in causing the conflict. Then there is the third option, what happened eventually in Paris, **something in between.** This treaty was vengeful enough to arouse the vanquished people to thirst for revenge, but not harsh enough to keep the defeated people controlled for more than one generation. This was, of course, what would occur at Versailles, only to lead to revulsion by Berlin, and to assist in the rise of Nazi Germany."

A routine had set in. Breakfast followed by a meeting. Lunch followed by a nap, quiet time, and, if necessary, some research. Late afternoon, and another meeting before dinner… Estelle, very much like her father, organized and schooled the daily events, even as she pushed and prodded, driving each "pirate" toward the ultimate goal, a new Ark. On more than one occasion, Harlan remarked, "Estelle is truly a reincarnation of W.T.

Professor Longstreet was, as a mentor, in fine fiddle. Hardly looking at her notes, bounced right into her topic.

"By way of review… The treaty draft arrived at was over 200 ages long. Small print… Put together by legions of dissent men, all experts in their fields, such as history, economics, geography, and political science, the first draft was the result of copious research, facts and details by the thousands, yet in the end the treaty represented the work of the 'Big Four:'

"It might be argued they had stumbled into war. Now it appeared they were stumbling into peace, planting, as they did, the seeds of another European conflict. Collectively, they produced a harsh treaty as perceived by Germany.

1. Guilt Clause   -   Germany was blamed for starting the war.
2. Reparations   -   Germany would pay for war damages.
3. Rhineland   -   France would occupy the area for 15-years.
4. Saar Valley   -   Administered by the League of Nations.
5. Military   -   Severe limitations on Germany.
6. Possessions   -   Became mandates under the League of Nations

"The fault for all this, Professor?"

"Collectively, the victors. Individually, Clemenceau, it can be argued.

He prized security and frowned on Wilson's idealism embedded in the Fourteen Points. Needing to answer to the French voters, he wanted compensation in full for the death and destruction caused by the German invasion. Fear of a future German invasion motivated him for 'guarantees' against another war from Britain and the United States."

"He got them?"

"No, Freda, only vague promises at best and the prospect of the League of Nations to keep the peace."

"Berlin would sign the treaty?"

"At the point of bayonet, yes."

"A treaty harsh, but not harsh enough?"

"Again, yes, Freda."

"A question, Professor Longstreet."

"Harlan?"

"Where was Japan in all this?"

"That is our next chapter in this troublesome story of Versailles. Tomorrow we take it on."

CHAPTER 17

MANDATES

<u>June 1941 - The Next Day – St. Louis</u>

Professor Longstreet had a glint in her eye today, an academic, it might be said who had cast aside the professional decorum of the cloistered classroom for the rough and tough rugby field. Stored up anger and a desire to release it, that's what her voice and body language conveyed. It was obvious that something was up.

"The Japanese government and the Versailles mandate system, that's what we're into today. It is not a charming story. Three challenging problems concerning Germany's colonial possessions faced the peacemakers. First, what should happen to Germany's overseas possessions? In the same vein, what should happen to those areas controlled by the Ottoman Empire? Third, how should the Austria-Hungarian Empire be broken up in Europe? Cynically, who should get the 'spoils of war?' On the other side of the coin was Wilson's idealism and his staunch stand on self-determination and respect for indigenous people. How could these two views be reconciled? And how did Japan, a non-European power, fit into this puzzle? That's what we're into today.

"Wars change things, as did the fields of France where so many died. Empires were lost. Berlin, Vienna, Moscow, and Constantinople would attest to that. Imperialist ambitions were repudiated; colonialism was languishing in the backwaters of history. All true but not without a final farewell, a last attempt to maintain the past, the assumed superiority of Europeans over millions of others deemed less fit to govern themselves, all in the face of Wilson's views.

"Remapping the world was challenging. On the positive side, ethnic and racial distinctions and aspirations for independence would emerge in the aftermath of war. On the negative side, if not handled right, anarchy and chaos might explode across the globe. The Mandate System devised in Paris tried mightily to thread between these possibilities."

"You're referring to Article 22 of the League of Nation Covenant (June 28, 1919)?"

"I am, Harlan. This article provided the legal status for 'certain territories transferred from the control of one country to another.' That is, it was the legal instrument that 'contained the internationally agreed upon terms for administering the territories on behalf of the League.'"

"On what basis, Professor Longstreet?"

"Former colonial possessions and areas of regional ethnic agitation were now under League supervision. That being the case, such entities would be doled out to various victorious countries with the following provisions:

1. There would be no annexation of any territory.
2. Each area involved would be a "sacred trust of civilization to develop the area for the benefit of its native people."
3. Native people would be prepared for self-government.
4. The possessions would not be protectorates to be used for the benefit of the trustee nation.
5. Trustees were prohibited from fortifying a possession.
6. Freedom of religion and conscience must be guaranteed.

"The League could enforce these provisions?"

"Not necessarily, Harlan. Self-policing was the coin of the day based on signatures and pledges. This issue we'll return to in a moment, but first we must deal with the alphabet, in particular the A, B, C Plan forged by the delegates at Versailles."

"You will explain, Professor Longstreet."

"Of course, Freda."

A, B, C Mandates

The proposed mandates were divided into three distinct groups based on their level of development as defined by the League of Nations. This determination would decide the exact degree of control by the 'mandatory power' on an individual area basis. To that end the mandates were divided into three classes:

Class A – territories once controlled by the Ottoman Empire that were deemed to "have reached a stage of development where their existence as independent nations can be provisionally recognized subject to the rendering of administrative advice and assistance by a Mandatory until such time as they are able to go it be alone." Presumably the wishes of these communities would be a principal consideration in the selection of the Mandatory. Eventually, that led to France controlling Lebanon and Syria, while Great Britain administered Iraq, Transjordan, and Palestine. By definition, these areas were closest to becoming independent nation-states and would be dealt with on that basis. But what was that basis? Was a mandate a quasi-form of colonialism, imperialism on a more accepted form for Wilson's sensitivities? Was this a way to control self-determination for the benefit of the Mandatory? Did the question of oil reserves and strategic location play a role? Of course, only the most naïve would reject this view.

Class B – these territories were formerly possessed by Germany in West and Central Africa and were deemed to "require a greater level of control by the mandatory power." In such cases the Mandatory 'must be responsible for the administration of the territory under conditions which will guarantee freedom of conscience and religion. The League also 'forbade the construction of military or naval bases within the mandates. By design or necessity, Great Britain benefited greatly, gaining province in Tanganyika, East Africa, Togoland, and the Cameroons. As viewed by her critics, the British won the 'Oklahoma Land Rush.'"

Class C – these territories included South West Africa and certain South Pacific Islands, which were considered to be "best administered under the laws of the Mandatory as an integral portion of its territories." Australia, by way of example, would receive New Guinea as a mandate. New Zealand would supervise a portion of Samoa. The real rub was what would happen to Germany's possessions in the Central Pacific?"

"Japan again?"

"Freda, on point. Recall the question of fortifications and the absence of any viable enforcement policy beyond trusting the Mandatories adhering to the spirit of the Covenant of the League of Nations. Given this, what would happen if Japan received, as she did, four island chains in the Central Pacific once controlled by Berlin: the Marshall Island, the Marianas, the Carolinas, and the Pelew Group, and did fortify the islands? Who could stop them short of war? The League of Nations, you suggest? Without its own independent military force probably not. Feeling endangered, another Pacific power, such as the US? A possibility, but only if attacked, one would think."

"In other words, Japan could, if she decided, fortify her mandates."

"Yes, Estelle."

"But why would they?"

"Freda, recall Plan Orange of the United States. To attack Japan directly, American forces would have to cross the Pacific. Island fortresses, really unthinkable aircraft carriers, would play havoc with American ships and landing forces steaming eastward."

"These island chains were that important to Japan's defense of her home islands?"

"Exceedingly, Harlan. The islands were scattered over a vast stretch of ocean between the equator and 20 degrees north latitude, and between the meridians 130 degrees and 170 degrees east longitude. They contain only 2,149 square kilometers, and the total population in no more than 60,000 of whom 5,500 are Japanese."

"But their importance?"

"This is not to be measured by their small size and population, but by their location in relation to America's possessions in the Pacific, particularly Guam and the Philippines. Closer to Japan than the United States and in the midst of Japanese mandates, these US possessions were obvious military targets in case of war, including Guam, Wake, and Howland Island. On the other side of the ledger, a ring of Japanese islands awaited any intruder challenging Japan --- Tarawa, and Makin in the Gilberts, Kwajalein Atoll in the Marshall Islands, Saipan in the Mariana Islands, and Truk in the Caroline Islands."

"Professor, you're getting at something."

"I am, Estelle. Japan has fortified these mandates."

"Against the express will of the League?"

"A murky situation, at least at first. Some economic improvements may also have military value, such as expanding port facilities, or the roads, even the water system, and, of course, airfields. Since 1921 the Japanese military began making survey and plans for the 'rapid deployment' of men into the mandates in the event of hostilities. The militarization of the mandates increased after Japan left the League in 1933 due to her takeover of Manchuria. She made it clear she had no intention of giving up her Pacific mandates."

"The League couldn't stop her?"

"Couldn't or wouldn't, Freda, it didn't. Anyway, there was a flip side to all this. The United States commenced fortifying Guam and the Philippines, also Wake Island, and an insignificant atoll called Midway. The Pacific, unless something were to change, was preparing for war."

"That is what is upsetting you, Professor Longstreet?"

"Something more. War looms with Japan. These mandates will in time be bloodstained."

"That is what we're trying to stop/"

"True enough, Harlan. But you, I'm afraid, are late. Events have overtaken us. If we are not at war with Japan by the end of the year, I would be most surprised."

"That soon?"

"Japan's war in China staggers the Japanese economy. Scrap iron by the ton is needed, as well as crude oil by the tanker to support Tokyo's aggression in China. She has, according to some experts, no more than a six-month supply of crude, possibly 18-months if used conservatively. Either she gets it from the United States, or Japan will have to invade the oil-rich Dutch East Indies. FDR's sanctions on the sale of oil will, I think, force the issue. Japan will not, as desired by the President, retreat from China under any circumstance. War, I'm afraid, is a forgone conclusion. The only question is when?"

"And our little conspiracy?"

"To provide, as always, something for the survivors to grasp, your Ark, to avoid still another conflict."

"Then the Versailles Treaty failed? The League failed. The first Ark failed!"

"Perspective is needed, Estelle, and more information about the League of Nations. That is our next topic. For now, I'll defer to President Wilson's challenge in Paris:

> *The man who is swimming against the (rapid) stream knows the strength of it.*

CHAPTER 18

THE COVENANT

Professor Longstreet was lecturing, sharing a Greek tragedy with the conspirators. A great sadness enveloped her, which not even two cups of strong, black coffee and a massive bear claw would dispel.

"All wars, it has been said, begin with a gunshot, an artillery blast, or a torpedo leaving in its wake a sunken ship. And, of course, all wars must come to an end, sometimes with the belligerents exhausted to the point of death, sometimes with the victors marching triumphantly through the streets of the vanquished. But always in the end distinguished men sign a document, a treaty of some sort attesting to who won or lost. As you know, that's happened in 1919 in Versailles, thereby ending the Armistice and bringing a legal end to the insanity of "Flanders Field."

"Sometimes those who affix their signatures, having learned harsh lessons, see beyond the moment with a vision encompassing a better world to avoid another tragedy. That occurred, at least to some degree, on June 28, 1919 when the Covenant of the League of Nations was signed as Part I of the Treaty of Versailles. It became effective, along with the rest of the Treaty on January 10, 1920, over two decades ago."

"The high water mark of Wilson's hopes?"

"Yes, Estelle, the victors had acted. Birth pangs aside, the League was now a reality."

"Now came the hard part, would the League be effective."

"Consider the Covenant a preface to desired world peace, or, if you will, an agreement to abide in a civilized manner when disputes occurred among nations. It was, it could be said, the blue print for the League, the architectural design for the international organization to maintain the peace. Certainly, the Covenant was for President Wilson the key to his Fourteen Points and to all the difficult compromises he made in Paris. As he said:

> *The League would grow and change over the years. In time,*
> *it would embrace the enemy nations and help them to stay on*
> *the paths of peace and democracy. Where the peace settlement*
> *needed fixing, one by one the mistakes can be brought to the*
> *League for readjustment.*

"The Covenant attempted to deal with each of the main proposals, that emerged in Paris: collective security, arbitration and judicial settlement of disputes. It did not satisfy extreme pacifists, who rejected any use of force, even to resist aggression. Nor were the extreme internationalists happy, since they wanted the League to have its own military forces and to "impose all of its decisions, if necessary, by force. Wilson and others sought a middle road.

"Wilson rightly understood, as did others who were realistic, that the Versailles Treaty was an imperfect document, but the best that compromises and the emotions of the moment permitted among sovereign states. Could it have been better? Of course; it also could have been worse. So much depended on the League of Nations to sort things out, and on nations willing to make that happen. What was concluded in Paris ended one chapter, no matter how incompletely. In envisioning a League of Nations, however, regardless of doubts about its future effectiveness, another chapter opened in human progress."

Harlan and his co-conspirators were listening intently, reluctantly understanding in advance what was about to be shared over the remains of breakfast. They would have preferred it to be otherwise.

146

"Today the Covenant of the League, and the institution itself, is in disarray, for many a shopworn idea, which couldn't live up to its promise to maintain the peace. Look all around and you will see the ruins of a noble idea smashed by Fascist Italy in Ethiopia, the Nazi Regime triumphant throughout conquered Europe, and the Japanese invasion of China. Everywhere war or the threat of war is in the air. Everywhere diplomacy is distained by aggressive military action. The gods of war are on the ascendency. In the words of the poet, the League split asunder."

The dream lost ... Oh, what might have been.

"Only to be replaced by the present nightmare, concentration camps in Europe, atrocities in China, and, as always, the multitude displaced civilians caught in the middle. My god, we're doing it all over again."

"Freda, a legacy we would prefer to disown. World events had proven Wilson wrong. He had hoped that Article X of the Covenant would prove a refuge for mankind:

> *... and that no matter what their differences arise amongst them they will never resort to war without first having done one or other of two things --- either submitted the matter of controversy to arbitration ... or submitt6ed it to the consideration of the council of the League of Nations.*

"At the Peace Conference in Paris in 1919, a commission was appointed at Wilson's urging to agree on covenant for the League of Nations, diplomatic architects at work, if you will. The members met ten times to hammer out differences. It wasn't easy.

"France, always fearful of Germany, wanted the League to form an international army to enforce its decisions. The British, fearful the French would dominate the military force, opposed the plan. Wilson was caught in the middle, since only the American Congress could declare war. If necessary how would sanctions be enforced? For this there was no good answer. Then there was the question of resources. How would the League be funded? Voluntary contributions provided the only answer with the richest nations paying the most. Who would be in charge of the League? A permanent Secretariat was the answer, voted upon the League members. What venue would be provided the smaller nations of the world? All member states would be in a General Assembly. A select group, note that as the powerful nations, would be in an Executive Council. Initially, this included France, Italy, the United Kingdom, and Japan. Why not the United States? That is a sad story still to be told."

"Wilson's greatest failure, Professor Longstreet?"

"Or the failure of his vision to fully influence the Senate, Harlan."

"A difficult judgment."

"Be that as it may, member states were 'expected to oppose external aggression.' The territorial integrity of members was paramount. But what happens if a member state violated this pledge? What then? All members were required to "submit complaints for arbitration or judicial inquiry before going to war. A Permanent Court of International Justice was created to hear such cases. Again, the tough question: what if a member didn't accept the Court's decision?

"Unanimity was required for decisions of both the Assembly and the Executive Council except in matter of procedure and the admission of new members. The League sought to lead by consent, not by dictation. The League counted on the 'good will' of its members. With 44-natons initially, that was a lot to ask. A veto was a constant shadow."

"Without it there would be no League, Harlan. The great powers jealously guarded their right to act independently of the League in pursuit of their vital interests."

"The great paradox. How do you maintain a system of world order, while at the same time being unable to stop nations from calling into question the preservation of peace?"

"That is the crux of the problem, is it not? What Wilson was trying to establish was collective security. By 1935 this was impossible. Events had overtaken the League. The US never joined the League of Nations. The Soviet Union did and was expelled after invading Finland (1939). Germany withdrew (1933), as did Japan, Spain, and Italy (1937), all aggressor nations. The League had no answer for this. It could not stop aggression. It could not end war."

"A challenge the next Ark must address?'

"Freda, the key challenge and with some small print. It is important to recall the world's desire for not only world peace, but a guarantee of such a state, and how Wilson responded to this desire of millions:

… You will say, "Is the League an absolute guarantee against war? No, I do not know any absolute guaranty against the errors of human judgment or the violence of human passions.

"One word of caution, however, before moving on from this unhappy verdict of history. The League was really a large committee. When its members worked in unison, it was effective. When members accepted judicial renderings, it was useful. To be successful, the League needed members who wanted it to work. Many didn't, and today we have the consequence of such shortsightedness, war in Europe and conflict in the Pacific."

"Professor Longstreet, you provide a painful perspective."

"Estelle, it is the lot of the historian to denote the *what* of our times, and to share the *why* of history among, as it always seems to be the case, the multitude of possibilities, and then to make sense of the whole business. It is not his job, however, to sugarcoat the past or to chisel and sculpture an acceptable version to placate contemporary needs, or even his own prejudices."

"You're setting us for something, aren't you?"

"Indeed, Freda."

"Dare I ask?"

"We have before us difficult questions, all of which bear on your enterprise."

"The Ark?"

"What else, Freda? As did others in 1910, you're preparing for the post-war period, hopeful to avoid still another conflict."

"And Japan?"

"At this late hour, little hope, I'm afraid. War looms, as does the need for your new Ark, Estelle. That is why we turn away from Paris, retreating to our own shores to take up the Senate battle over Versailles, and the tragedy of a failed vision. There is much to understand and lessons to be learned if your next Ark is to be more successful."

"The Covenant to the League of Nations was, as said earlier, that which would nourish peace. In the dreamy world of the idealist, Wilson stated his case:

"We are all citizens of the world. The tragedy of our times is that we do not know this."

And:

> *"War isn't declared in the name of God; it is a human affair entirely".*

Finally, in speaking to those who would listen:

> *"You are here in order to enable the world to live more amply, with greater vision, with a finer sprit of hope and achievement. You are here to enrich the world."*

"That is our hope and pledge, too, Professor Longstreet."

"And a worthy one, Estelle."

"In our new Ark there is hope?"

"Harlan, there is always the possible."

"And the pain of failure?"

"Indeed, Freda, as Wilson found out when he carried the Versailles Treaty home."

"Our next topic, I assume."

"Of necessity, yes, if your hopes are to be realized. But beware. There are almost immutable challenges to be met:

> *We would not have our country's vigor exhausted or her moral force abated, by everlasting meddling and muddling in every quarrel, great and small, which afflicts the world.*

Senator Henry Cabot Lodge

CHAPTER 19

THE GREAT CRUSADE

———————◆◆◆———————

<u>June 1941 – A Few Days Later – St. Louis</u>

The conspirators took two day off. Professor Longstreet needed to do some personal research at St. Louis University. Harlan had some legal business to do. Estelle was talking to a Hollywood-type who was considering a film about her father. As for Freda, she had been asked to speak at an NACCP meeting. In short, people had things to do. The truth, however, was that they needed time out from "saving the world." So to speak, they needed to come up for air. The history of the League's origins and present plight, the escalating tensions in the Far East, plus the continuous rain of bad news from Europe was more than they wished to handle. This being the case, tailor-made excuses were fortuitously present for all. The respite could last and it didn't. Two days later…

"Okay, Professor Longstreet, the podium is yours again, though we are seated at a round table in Mexican Joe's Restaurant."

"And on an extremely muggy day, high temperatures and humidity, and not even a slight stirring of the air off the Mississippi, Estelle."

"Makes one want to take a siesta."

"Harlan, I will endeavor to keep your attention, as well as Freda's gaze."

151

"Do so, please, my lunch of delightful refried beans, a large chicken burrito, and more freshly baked chips that I wish to count have filled my stomach and fatigued my eyes. Sleep is calling to me."

"I'll see if I can compete with your nocturnal demands, Harlan.

"We travel to the White House?"

"We do, Freda."

"President Wilson returned from furious political jousting in Paris to the equally turbulent arena of American politics. He brought with him the Treaty of Versailles including and the Covenant to the League of Nations, which he handed off to the Republican, fully believing they would hitch a ride to the stars and pass the treaty. He was unprepared for the criticism leveled against the treaty and his beloved League."

"The critics were waiting, Professor Longstreet?"

"Yes, with their knives out." Estelle."

"As expected, the German people criticized what they considered a harsh treaty. Since Germany was not invaded and occupied, a delusional myth emerged. Germany had not really been defeated. Jews and Communists had betrayed the country. The Versailles Treaty was 'shameful' and needed to be repudiated."

"Adolf Hitler's later claims, Professor Longstreet?"

"Yes, Estelle. But he was not alone. Also critical but for a different reason were liberals everywhere who were 'shocked and bitter' at Wilson's apparent abandonment of the Fourteen Points. American progressives were disillusioned by the terms of the treaty."

"They didn't have to deal with Clemenceau."

"True enough. And then there were the colonial groups, where the application of Wilson's 'self-determination' concept seemed only tied to Europe. India remained under British rule. Southeast Asia felt the combined yoke of British and French rule. North Africa and the Middle East remained under European control. Oppressed people disillusioned and angry about the hypocrisy of Wilson's idealism marched to an impassioned 'anti-colonial movement.'

"This theme of the future resonated in Asia?"

"Strongly, Harlan. Korea and China were restive under Japanese rule, as the Egyptians under London's seal."

"Wilson was bringing home a tinderbox, Professor."

"One he signed in the ornate Hall of Mirrors of the palace of Versailles on June 28, 1919."

"Why is that date disturbing me?"

"Perhaps, Harlan, because it marked the anniversary of the assassination of the Archduke and his wife in Sarajevo, the event that sparked the damn war."

There it was again, the same lingering, troubling question. How could the death of two people cause a world war and the death of millions? And even more concerning, was there ahead an incident in Asia that would finally cause America to go to war with Japan? Would millions more die because a few, by comparison, did?

"There were also domestic ethnic critics. German-Americans castigated the Wilson's treaty, calling his birth child the 'League of Damnations.' Italian-America also jumped on Wilson for his opposition to Italy's territorial claims. Not unexpectedly the Irish-Americans attacked the President for failing to free Ireland of London's control.

"Criticism was also personal. Henry Cabot Lodge, the Chairperson of the Senate Foreign Relations Committee, and a history professor from Yale University was Wilson's implacable foe. Many historians saw him as 'out to defeat and humiliate his arch enemy,' also a professor of history but from Princeton University. The 'Ivy League' was at war over the League of Nations.

"As stated earlier, there was the slight of the Senate. The President did not take a Republican senator to Paris. As fate would have it, it was also a presidential election year' 1920 beckoned. If there were to be a treaty, it would never be a Wilson agreement alone. The Republicans would have a large say in the final product. The Republicans were very public about this, warning Wilson:

> *Resolve… That it is the sense of the Senate that while it is*
> *their sincere desire that the nations of the world should unite*
> *to promote peace and general disarmament, the constitution*
> *of the League of Nations in the form now proposed to the*
> *peace conference should not be accepted by the United States.*

"What changes did the Republican want?"

"First and foremost, Freda, they wanted changes, which were called reservations, sufficient to design a treaty they could vote for in response to the public sympathy for a League of Nations. All this came out when debate began on March 4, 1919."

"What reservation was most important to them?"

"Article 10 dealing with collective security."

Members of the League of Nations would assure the territorial integrity of other member nations.

"This was a sticking point for Senators, but mainly Republicans. If necessary, did this mean the use of force to protect member nations? If so, that meant war and that was the rub. Article 1, Section 8 of the Constitution granted to the Congress the right to declare war. Republican opponents of the treaty were willing to follow the League's Article 10, but only if Congress declared war. American sovereignty trumped any future international League obligation when it came to war."

"Professor Longstreet, the Senate was of one mind on this?"

"Not entirely, Freda. Within the Republican Party there were three distinct groups:

20 – Strong Reservationists
12 – Mild Reservationists
12 - Irreconcilables

"The Irreconcilables were against any treaty. They would not be budged. They were not open to compromise. Senator Frank Norris of Nebraska summed up their position: they feared the treaty 'would perpetuate the status quo and bind the United States to the reactionary great powers.' Senator Hiram Johnson of California expressed 'horror at the thought of surrendering American freedom of action to a world organization.'

"Strong vs. mild was a matter of degree. How many changes? What changes? Senator Lodge led the strong reservationists. As for the Democrats, they would go along with mild changes if given the green light by the White House. On March 19, 1919 the first of many votes was taken after numerous changes, proposed and supported in various degrees by both sides. The final vote was 49 to 35 for the treaty. Seven more votes were needed to reach a 2/3rd super-majority. It would never happen. The treaty was dead. Unwilling to accept this outcome, Wilson played his last card to pass the treaty.

"Which was?"

"A crusade, Estelle, by train to harness public opinion and to pressure the Senate for an affirmative vote. He would take the debate to the American people.

"He would fight to the end?"

"As you say, Estelle, to the end."

"On September 3, 1919, Wilson's embarked on an 8,000-mile railroad trip in 22 days to promote the passage of the Versailles Treaty and membership in the League of Nations. He would take his case to the American people, barnstorming across the nation, making multiple speeches each day to generally supportive crowds. The trip, arduous for a younger man, all but killed him. He was 63-years old. He suffered constant headaches during the 'tour,' as some called it. He had difficulty sleeping. He grew weaker by the day. His hands trembled. He was physically played out.

"Advised by his personal physician, Rear Admiral Cary Grayson, that he should consider his health given the schedule ahead, Wilson's answer still brings tears to me today.

I do not want to do anything foolhardy, but the League of Nations is now in its crisis, and if it fails, I hate to think what will happen to the world... I cannot put my personal safety, my health, in the balance against my duty.... I must go.

"On September 25, 1919, Wilson's train reached Pueblo, Colorado. There he was to give a speech in the new City Auditorium. When introduced, the audience applauded him enthusiastically for ten minutes. With tears in his eyes, he began to speak. After a few minutes, his hands shook. He began to perspire. A few minutes later he collapsed. He was suffering acute heart problems. He was immediately taken back to Washington. On October 2, he suffered a massive stroke, which left him partially paralyzed on the left side, as well as blind in the left eye. He was bedridden and unable to meet with his cabinet during a seven month period."

"Who was in charge, Professor Longstreet?"

"Some say his wife, Edith. She cared for him during the last 17-months of his administration. Except for trusted advisers, no one knew the full extent of the president's health. Not the press... Not the opposition... Not the public, while he was convalescing."

"Another victim of the war."

"A touching sentiment, Freda. It is, I must tell you, instructive to know what Wilson was going to say in Pueblo. A few excerpts provide a light into is thoughts.

At the front of this great treaty is the Covenant of the League of Nations. Unless you get the united, concerted purpose and power of the great Governments of the world behind this settlement, it will fall down like a house of cards. There is only one power to put behind the liberation of mankind and that is the power of mankind. It is the power of the united moral forces of the world and in the Covenant of the League of Nations the moral forces of the world are mobilized.

And what do they unite for? They enter into a solemn promise to one another that they will never use their power against one another for aggression.

"Nobel words."

"Perhaps too noble for our times."

"Professor?"

"Wilson's dream destroyed by Nazi armies in Poland. Wrecked by Fascist armies in Africa. Called into question by Japan's planes bombing Nanking. No willingness to submit grievances to arbitration. No desire to permit the League to reconcile problems. Only the use of force is the clarion call of these rouge nations, which threaten a second global conflict."

"Why didn't the League act?"

"The basic reason, Estelle, is that the aggressors were willing to use force. They were willing to go to war. They were prepared mentally to risk war. Britain and France, even Russia were not so inclined to use force."

"And today?"

"At this hour, Estelle, only force will stop Berlin and Rome. That is the great contradiction."

"And in the Pacific?"

"Only the threat of force."

"We cannot stop these wars?"

"Harlan, provide for the next generation. There your Ark may find a home."

"Had he lived my father would have been horrified, Professor."

"Estelle, not to discount your father's feelings, he would have also applauded Wilson's crusade, for that's what it was. A noble effort to undo the past... A noble effort to build a constructive future... And with some pride, I think, he would note that the work of the conspirators in 1910 influenced President Wilson's views. In that, the first Ark, there was some success and reason for hope.

"Perhaps you are right. But..."

"Go ahead, Estelle."

"Wilson wanted to end war, yet with the American Expeditionary Force, the military was used. For my father, and I think for Wilson, there were no heroic sacrifices, no martyrs for a cause, only the gruesome deaths by the millions. Had it been possible, both would have pointed to the Battle of Verdun. Ten months of slaughter and 800,000 casualties. The Battle of the Somme... Over 57,000 British casualties on the first day... So many young men... So many dead... Europe awash in blood."

"That was for Wilson, and perhaps for us, the lesson. Countries must be willing to use force to stop conflicts."

"What are we left with, Dr. Longstreet?"

"Estelle, your hopes for a new Ark, and Wilson's own words, bequeath to us:

> *There is one thing that the American people always rise to*
> *and extend their hand to, and that is the truth of justice and*
> *of liberty and peace. We have accepted the truth and we are*
> *going o be led by it, and it is going to lead us, and through us*
> *e world, out into pastures of quietness and peace such as the*
> *world has never dreamed of before.*

"That, I think, should serve as the preamble to our new Ark. What say you Harlan and Freda?"

CHAPTER 20

SHANDONG AND YAK

———————————————

<u>July 1941 – Atlanta</u>

Three weeks later the conspirators, having said goodbye to Professor Longstreet, met at the Golden Buddha Restaurant in Atlanta for lunch and tea. Owned by a Korean-American family, the restaurant was known for its authentic Asian dishes, especially scrumptious sweet and sour chicken or pork, along with fried rice, and egg drop soup. Their former mentor suggested that they meet there, hinting that there was more than good food on the menu. It turned out she was right.

In her last remarks, Professor Longstreet said, "I've taken you as far as I can. Today I hand the baton to Professor Hamilton Loo. He is an expert on Chinese-Japanese relations in the post-World War I period, the 20's and 30's. Of course, as a Korean, he has a perspective unique to his heritage and the history you wish to understand. You should also know his family owns the Golden Buddha so be attentive, as I know you will be, to his thoughtful remarks, and the delectable green-tea ice cream that will be on the house."

True to her word the green tea ice cream was on the house, delicate and sweet tasting, a fitting way to end a delightful meal. Professor Loo then introduced himself for the first time.

"Thank you and welcome to my family's humble establishment. Before getting into today's topics, I must say how delighted I am to meet all of you. Conspirators all, I am told, to avoid war with Japan even at this late hour. Your self-imposed task is of consequence, but I'm afraid, beyond all of us. I fear war is coming with Japan, but, as you have gathered, I'm sure, the conflict will be the result of a long relationship disturbed by challenging events and contesting foreign policies, some of which will get to soon. But first, however, a word about my family background, if I may.

"My father took a circuitous route getting the United States. He was born in Korea in 1888 near Seoul, the capital. By 1915 he was barely making a living as a day laborer, having only a rudimentary education. But at the age of 26 events conspired to change his life. It seemed that the British and the French were hiring workers to dig ditches in France, or what came to be known as trenches. Somehow, along with thousands of others, mainly Chinese coolies, he traveled by steamship to France at Allied expense. There the 'Asian imports' relieved troops of the "digging" task, at least to a point. Somehow my father survived the war, skinny as a beanpole, but unscathed by the German machine guns. He always claimed that working in the trenches and caked with mud made it hard for the Germans to see him. The war ended and somehow he connected with the Americans and came to New York with the "doughboys." We were never quite clear how he managed that. A few theories circulated in the family. Was he a stowaway? Had he bribed a Colonel? Had some compassionate Yankee aided him? We'll never know for sure.

"Once in the states he headed south to Georgia where he heard agricultural workers were needed. Three things happened there. First, he got involved in agriculture. Hard working and friendly, he made a name for himself as a useful worker. Second, he met my future mother. She was Japanese and it took a while to pry her away from her family. Fortunately for me he was successful. Third, he self-taught himself English and determined to be a good citizen in his adopted country. In time they opened a restaurant. The present Golden Buddha is the third incarnation of that effort.

"After I came along, he used all his Buddhist tricks to push me for a college education, which I did at Georgia State, historically not a school for Negroes. For whatever reason I was accepted. I desegregated the school in a reverse sort of way. There I majored in history. In time I specialized in Asian Studies, and eventually made a small name for myself in the field after receiving my doctorate at Georgia Tech. *'Go rumbling wrecks.'* Truth be told, I think I was the token Korean on campus.

As fate would have it, I was doing research in St. Louis when Professor Longstreet called me. Naturally, I jumped at the opportunity to speak to you. Not many people, of course, want to know about Japan and the Versailles Treaty. And, as I understand it, not many people out of government are trying with your dedication to head off a tragedy in the Far East, or to build an Ark for those who will survive still another war. Of this Professor Longstreet has advised me. Please include me on your team."

"With joy, was Professor Loo, consider yourself a paid up member of our little conspiracy."

"Please call me Brandon; no title is necessary. I've been told to refer to you as Harlan, Estelle, and Freda. Before I start, however, a confession. As a Korean, I am not totally against the brewing Asian war. It is possible that, through a war, and assuming the United States wins, that my country might be unshackled from the Japanese Empire. This is not easy for me to admit, but there is precedent. The new Poland… The new Czechoslovakia… The new Yugoslavia… All came into existence with the fall of Vienna. My father's adopted country arose out of the ashes of a revolution against England. China will not gain her freedom until the Japanese are vanquished. So you see I am of two minds. Certainly, I wish to head off a war in the Pacific, but the same violence might free Korea. It is a conflict I have not fully resolved."

"We take your confession under compassionate advisement, Sir."

"Thank you, Harlan. That said we should get started?

Today we will cover the Shandong Problem (1919-1920), the outrageous 21 Demands forced on China by Japan (1915), the unknown Yap Crisis (1920), and the Washington Naval Conference (1920's). You're wondering, of course, what these topics have in common? That is, how are they related? Imagine, if you will, three countries, China, Japan, and the United States, as if they were celestial spheres revolving around each other, all hovering above the vast Pacific, each seeking to avoid an orbital collision. That's what we're dealing with. As for my former country, also imagine Korea also orbiting, unable to break from their gravity. That's Korea's situation.

The Shandong Problem

"Perhaps it all began in 1897 in the Shandong Province. Two German missionaries were killed in a local disturbance. Kaiser Wilhelm II, pushed by expansionists in Berlin, recognized a splendid opportunity to gain a German foothold in China, as had the British, the French, and the Dutch among others.

Politely, they were called spheres of influence, rather than areas of foreign military occupation in disregard of China's territorial integrity. If a treaty legalized the situation, it was called a concession. In any event, the Kaiser sent a naval squadron to Kiachow to take over the port, and to exercise a belated imperialistic land grab. The Chinese protested but to no avail. With a divided, splintered government, a questionable military force, and faced with a powerful European nation, the Chinese gave way.

"In 1898, under protest, an agreement was signed with Germany, providing for a 99-year lease for 100 square miles of land around Kiachow Harbor. Berlin also received the right to build railroads, open mines, modernize the harbor, construct a sewage water system, build schools, and garrison German troops to protect the interests of its nationals. Thirty million Chinese citizens were now under German influence, both as cheap labor and as a market for German goods. To a great extent, this is what happened in Korea once the Chinese invaded and occupied the country regardless of Korean sentiment."

"This advantageous situation for Germany in China was upset by Great War?"

"To the point, yes, Harlan. Japan joined Britain and France as an ally, and quickly attacked the Germany enclave. Shandong was overrun, but not returned to China. The Japanese wanted to retain control. China felt otherwise. That question was put off until after the war."

"Until Versailles, Hamilton?"

"Until 1919-1920. Before that, however the 21 Demands situation occurred throwing the whole dispute into the air, and putting the United States right square in the middle."

"Of which you will speak?"

"Yes. On January 8, 1915, Japan secretly made 21 demands of the Chinese government, which if accepted, would mean that China was clearly a protectorate of Tokyo. Once the demands were leaked to the public, the United States unequivocally opposed them. Three points motivated the US response. First, the demands would have ended the Open Door Policy, still important to Washington. Second, the territory integrity of China was at risk. Third, Japan's aggressive foreign policy had to be challenged."

"America was supporting China/"

"Strongly and openly, Estelle, regardless of Japanese sensitivities."

"Was this a Rubicon of some sort, Hamilton?"

"One of many leading to the present crisis in the Far East, Freda."

"What were the demands?"

"The most aggressive demands, really an ultimatum backed by what Japan called dire consequences, if not accepted, included:

1. A 99-year lease extending Japanese control of the South Manchuria Railway Zone, Manchuria generally, and eastern Inner Mongolia.
2. Extraterritoriality would be extended in these areas.
3. Appointment of Japanese financial and administrative officers to the Chinese government.
4. Priority to Japanese investments in those areas.
5. Access to Inner Mongolia's raw materials.
6. The use of Mongolia as a strategic buffer against Russian encroachment in Korea.
7. China would hire Japanese advisors to take effective control of the country's fiancé and police.
8. China would confirm Japan's recent seizure of Shandong Province from the Germans.

"Japan was really exercising her expansive muscles."

"Indeed, Estelle."

"America's immediate response?"

"The Secretary of State under President Woodrow Wilson, William Jennings Bryan, issued the Bryan Note on March 13, 1915, stating:

While the United States affirms Japan's special interests in Manchuria, Mongolia and Shandong, the government has expressed concern over further encroachments to Chinese sovereignty.

"The Japanese could read between the lines, Hamilton?"

"Of course, Harlan. As expected, Tokyo pushed its position, arguing that their 'special interests' represented a sort of 'Asian Monroe Doctrine' modeled after American policy in the Western Hemisphere."

Just as the United States for its own security treated Latin America as its backyard. So Japan has to worry about China and neighbors such as Korea and Mongolia.

"The situation was complicated. The Wilson administration acknowledged Japan's special interest in China, since most of the 'white world' was closed off to Tokyo. Wilson's advisor, Colonel House stated the case.

We cannot meet Japan in her desires as to land immigration, and unless we make some concessions in regard to her sphere of influence in the East, trouble is sure, soon or later to come.

"House sought a compromise to keep the Open Door Policy, while rehabilitating China, and also satisfying Japan. But, of course, that was asking a great deal."

"Was it possible, Hamilton?"

"The current situation, Estelle, suggests no, then and now. That being the case, some felt that opposition to Japan's policies in Korea and Manchuria would lead to a armed conflict within one generation. That position was underpinned with the view the United States would not accept any agreement that undercut America's trade (commerce rights) in China."

"Wilson seemed trapped."

"Freda, the President Wilson had the oldest of conflicts. On the one hand, he could be pragmatic and find a way to cooperate with Japan. On the other hand, he could remain loyal to China, maintaining an idealistic sentiment based on his Fourteen Points. That quandary led to two questions: first, could China even be saved from a combination of Western and Asian imperialism? Second, was opposition to Japan worth the risk of war?"

"What did the Chinese have to say in the matter?"

"Good question, Harlan. First and foremost, China disavowed any and all treaties signed under duress with Japan. The United States supported this view. China was grateful that Japan had driven the Germans out of the Shandong Province. However, she didn't want to exchange German control for Japanese occupation. Again, Washington supported China. As a military consideration, under Japanese control, Shandong was a dagger pointed at the heart of China."

"President Wilson appealed to the Japanese to give way, to put the Versailles Treaty and the League of Nations ahead of purely national interests. In the end that was not to be; Japanese public opinion was for keeping the Shandong concession even if that put the peace treaty in jeopardy. Was the Japanese government bluffing? Wilson couldn't take that chance. Italy had already left Paris over a territorial dispute. If Japan walked out... Plus there was an awkward question of fairness. Wilson understood that:

> *Japan had already lost in the racial equality clause; it would*
> *be very serious if it were to lose over Shandong.*

"The Japanese would continue to control Shandong. China had a persuasive moral position but Japan had the largest navy in the Asia. The Versailles Treaty and the League of Nations came before the notion of self-determination. The best Wilson could get from the Japanese delegation was a verbal assurance that Tokyo would 'eventually give back sovereignty in Shandong to China.' The suggest date was 1922. This statement, however, would not be put in writing. The government believed 'any appearance of giving way would inflame public opinion at home.' In a statement to the press Wilson described the settlement as 'satisfactory as could be got out of the tangle of treaties in which China herself was involved.' In response to this, the Japanese left Paris 'convinced that the United States was out to stop them in China.'"

"Compromises, always compromises."

"The way of the world, Estelle, if you want to get something done."

"He went against his own view of self-determination, Hamilton."

"Not completed, Freda."

"I don't understand."

"The term self-determination had never really been defined with any clarity. As one historian said:

In its practical application in regions of mixed nationalities and ethnic groups the concept proved nightmarish.

"Wilson admitted that 'he had no idea what demons the concept would unleash.' Retrospectively, definitions not withstanding, the demons were loose. A sort of organized international anarchy existed as Wilson and others sought to adjust the claims of nationalistic groups. It wasn't a perfect situation. Shandong was an example of that."

"Where do we go from here, Hamilton?"

"To a tiny spot in the vast Pacific.

Mysterious Island

"What do you call an island 4319 miles from Pearl Harbor, Hawaii?" No response. Okay, I make it easier for you. What coral reef located in the Caroline group in the Central Pacific is 1804 miles from Tokyo? Still no takers, I see. Try this, then. What 39 square miles of real estate, four islands clustered closely together, is about 917 miles from the Philippines with a high elevation of only 584 feet? Still silence prevails. That being the case, let's switch from geography to international knockdown politics in 1919. Why would a flyspeck in the middle of the Pacific almost cause a war between the United States and Japan?"

It was obvious Professor Hamilton Loo was enjoying himself asking questions about a tiny, almost microscopic piece of land no one in the group knew anything about with the possible exception of his colleague, Professor Longstreet. Harlan, always one for details, was at a loss. Estelle, who usually did her homework, was quiet. Freda, a reporter at heart, had nothing to report. Perhaps because of all this, Professor Loo took mercy on his captive audience in a round about way.

"A last hint and a big one, a popular little something called *Yap for the Yappers.*

Give us Yap! Give us Yap!
The Yanks have put it,
The Yanks have put it,
The Yanks have put it,
On the Map!

"Yap, I should have known."

"Harlan, you have something to add?"

"It was the key cable connection, was it not, between the United States and the Philippines, Guam, and Shanghai."

"So far so good, Sir."

"It was awarded to Japan as a mandate?"

"Correct."

"More to the point, Japanese troops, as allies of France and Britain, ripped it away from the Germans in 1914."

"And?"

"President Wilson wanted to internationalize Yap because of its cable importance. The Japanese were opposed to this. Tensions rose in the US and Tokyo."

"Harlan, you know your Yap history."

"But not how the tension was reduced."

"Succinctly, a special US-Japanese Treaty went into effect as of February 11, 1922 providing guarantees that communication would not be hindered. The 'Yellow Press' on both sides of the Pacific was disappointed, but not without a lasting consequence. The papers in Seattle and Hiroshima had it right.

*American public opinion generally settled on Japan as the rival to watch ---
and the Japanese knew it. War talk seethed in the Pacific. In Japan, student
mass meetings were arguing methods of fighting the United States; in America,
the 'inevitable' war in the Pacific was bing widely discussed.*

"Inevitable, Hamilton?"

"Estelle, more than speculation, and already in the planning for a Pacific war."

*Yap suggested to a number of Americans in the Navy and State Department
that war with Japan must entail a bloody island hopping campaign across the
Pacific.*

"Yap was symbolic what American military planners most feared. Though the mandates were forbidden to establish fortification, to establish military bases, it was near impossible to stop the practice. The League of Nations had no enforcement provision. Obscure mandated islands were marked for future battles if war came to the Pacific, Tarawa, Tinian, and Saipan."

"You read tomorrow as if it is already yesterday, Hamilton."

"We have gone from hours to minutes, and now, I'm afraid, we're in the last seconds, Freda."

"But we must try."

"As others did in Washington, London, and Geneva in the 1920's in a failed attempt to stem the buildup of naval forces and fortified possessions. What started out with the highest intensions left a legacy of suspicion and increased tensions in the Far East. That will be our next topic, disarmament, a forlorn hope of President Wilson.

CHAPTER 21

PARITY IN THE PACIFIC

July 1941 – Atlanta

"A question for you, my devoted students. Is a battleship the cause of war, or merely a symptom of war?"

"Professor Loo, are you asking if naval ships and military armaments are generally a cause war?:

"Hamilton, please, and yes, Freda, I am."

"Well, if you took away all weapons, it would be difficult to wage war, would it not?"

"Indeed."

"But, as I think about it, I've never heard of a battleship or a big tank declaring war on someone. Yet, people with lots of big tanks might Isn't that so, Hamilton?"

"That seems to be the way things are."

"You referred to symptoms to begin this conversation. Are you really referring to causes of war?"

"Factors, Estelle, other than weapons, yes."

Professor Loo was in his element, proffering a question, responding, and then parrying with an oblique answer leading to another question, and so it went. He did enjoy the exercise.

"There are many causes of war, Hamilton."

"Quite so. Care to suggest the unfortunate title holder, the king of all causes, Harlan?"

"At the risk of sounding like a "shrink," a need for security drives war; all other possibilities fall under that heading."

"And weapons?"

"The outward steel to maintain security in a world of competing nations."

"That said, Harlan, what would be the challenge to any seeking disarmament?"

"Maintaining security while reducing, not eliminating, weapons. There would need to be, I believe, a precarious balance between the two possibilities."

"Let's check out your proposition, Sir. Not long ago it was put to the test."

Scuttling the Fleet

"As Secretary of State, Charles Evans Hughes was meticulous in his work, a detail man not given to off-the-cuff remarks, or anything which had not been judiciously thought through. But that was, according to some, until November 12, 1921 at the beautiful Memorial Continental Hall in Washington D.C. That's when Hughes, hosting the great naval powers of the world, suggested an unheard of proposal. A British reporter captured the immediate and astonished response of those present, especially admirals in the tome-like silence of the room:

> *They (the British and the Japanese) should scrap 19 and 17 capital ships respectively. The United States and other would also do this. In less than fifteen minutes, he (Hughes) destroyed 66 ships (of all types) with a total tonnage of 1,878,043, more than all the admirals of the world have sunk in a cycle of centuries.*

"And, of course, Hughes had done it without firing one cannon, but only with a broadside of carefully chosen words, which we'll shortly get to."

"You will provide some background, Hamilton?"

"Certainly, Estelle. Perhaps we should start with Senator William E. Borah of Idaho, a state not known for its nautical heritage beyond white water rapids, and mirror-flat, pristine lakes. The good Senator, weary of war and the great expenditures in flesh and wealth, wanted to try something new to end the cycle of peace, tensions, war, again and again. He introduced a mild resolution designed to bring about a disarmament conference by putting pressure on President Warren Harding. That was in December 1920."

"He seemed well meaning?"

"Quite so, Estelle. Surprisingly, the public got behind him in a big way. Petitions were filed. The chambers of commerce across America voiced their support. A tidal wave of sentiment inundated Washington. Somehow Borah had tapped into a national desire to push back against armaments. In mid 1921 hIS proposal passed the Senate unanimously and with only four dissenting votes did the same in the House."

"The Secretary of State was forced to act?"

"Freda, that was the case. He invited many nations to Washington, though four countries were his chief concern: Britain, Italy, Japan, and France. For a variety of reasons, they all accepted his overture."

"I sense an irony here, Hamilton."

"Which is, Harlan?"

"Though not in the League, the United States was entering into international agreements."

"The goals of Washington paralleled those of the League. Where, at least to this point, the League had failed to advance disarmament, Hughes was going to give it a try through a series of treaties."

The Five-Power Treaty

"Almost immediately, problems arose which hindered discussions. For example, assuming naval reductions were possible, but not the total elimination of combat ships, what formula would be used to determine final numbers for each country? If, by way of example, Britain wanted ten battleships, does the United States get the same number or more? What about Japan? If old ships are scrapped, does each country have to sink the same number? And, of course, what ships are we talking about? The queen of the navy, the battleship, certainly... But what about cruisers and destroyers" Though in its infancy, would aircraft carriers be included in the final treaty? Of course, just lurking beneath the surface was the issue of submarines. What should be done about them?"

"Hamilton, you offer such easily solved issues."

"Then Estelle let me add this. How do you measure ships, by tonnage or by the actual number of ships? More to the point, is the size of your navy, by way of example, based on a "proportional formula;" that is, the number of warships necessary to protect your interests. Or, again, if proportional, is the size of your navy related to the size of other navies? And naturally, do the two questions overlap?"

"Do they?"

"They do, Freda. Britain and America argued, for example, since they have global interests, they require a two-ocean navy. From their perch the Japanese, needed fewer ships, since Tokyo was overwhelmingly a one ocean, Pacific power. Italy and France were concerned mainly with the Atlantic and the Mediterranean, and needed the fewest ships."

"Professor Loo, how would all of this finally be settled?"

"Hughes suggested first the most obvious principle: to disarm you first have to disarm." Therefore, scrap old, unnecessary ships. Then limit the number of new ships under construction. Align your foreign policy to reduce dependence on capital ships. Somewhat brazenly, he made this argument. A mathematical system would be needed to do all these things, a ratio formula would be factored into the final agreement,."

"He had a formula in mind?"

"Hughes had thought it through. He introduced the controversial, if not simplified 5-5-3-1.5-1.5 formula. What did this mean? On a practical basis, this meant the US and the British would have 500,000 tonnage pounds, while Japan had 300,000, and Italy and France had approximately 175,000. America, he pointed out, would immediately sink 30 ships with an aggregated tonnage of an astounding 845,740 tons under this formula. What the Germans couldn't do in the recent war, he would do with the stroke of a pen. His declaration captured the imagination of the world. He became a hero to all of Europe's rank and file. Nothing like this had ever been done before."

"What about the Japanese? Weren't they being asked to take third place, or second depending on how you calculated things?"

"Quite right, Harlan. As would be expected, Tokyo wanted a different ratio among the three major powers: 10-10-7. That ratio gave Britain and the United States more ships, but Japan considered that acceptable in terms of her security needs. On the emotional side, she wanted to be treated, as always, with respect as a great power, but in the end she went along. Why? Historians are in general agreement that:

> *Tokyo consented to the Hughes ratio on December 15, 1921. The alternative to concession was a ruinous naval race. But Japan insisted upon important safeguards. America agreed not to fortify further her Pacific Islands (except for Hawaii), particularly the Philippines, Goam, Wake, and the Aleutians. Without adequate bases on these outposts, the United States, even with a 5-3 ration, could not expect to attack Japan successfully in her home waters.*

"Though an agreement was signed, one thorn remained, the British-Japanese Treaty of 1902, which obligated each side to support the other if either was attacked. In theory, if a war broke out in the Pacific, the US would have to face both London and Tokyo. But to abrogate the treaty meant Japan might conceivably face Washington and London. How to resolve this situation was the focus of the Four Power Treaty. An agreement was reached on December 3, 1921. What were the provisions?

1. The 1902 British-Japanese Treaty ended.
2. All signatories, including France, agreed to respect one another's rights in the Pacific.
3. Future disputes would be referred to a joint conference.

"Was there an enforcement provision, Hamilton?"

"As with all the treaties signed in Washington, Estelle, none beyond the hope all countries would act honorably in their own self-interest."

"More than a 'mere scrap of paper?'"

"A workable enforcement policy is elusive."

"Even in the United States?"

"Especially in the Senate, Freda. Always cautious about its war-making power, the Senate tacked on a reservation on the Washington treaties declaring that 'there is no commitment to armed force, no alliance, no obligation to join in any defense.' This, of course, was the old problem with the League of Nations. When it came to sending soldiers off to battle, the Senate would call the shots."

"And where was China in all this?"

"Good question, Harlan. The 'Sick Man of the Far East,' as many characterized the country, was dealt with in a third treaty, the Nine Power Pact signed on February 6, 1922 in Washington. Nine countries bound themselves to respect the 'sovereignty, the independence, and the territorial integrity of China.' Additionally, they pledged themselves to uphold the 'principles of the Open Door and to assist China in forming a stable government.'"

"Other provisions?"

1. The 'internationalization of the Open Door Policy; it was no longer an American policy per se.
2. Recognition of Japan's dominance in Manchuria and Korea; Japan's proximity to the area, and her large navy was the reality check.
3. All nations could do business in Manchuria without discrimination; Japanese businesses would not be favored (or at least not too much).
4. Shantung, by a separate agreement, would be returned to Chinese control, along with the railroads in the provenance. Japan, however, would still be influential in the area.
5. Equal access of all countries to Yap Island for cable and radio facilities.

"And the enforcement provisions?"

"Estelle, it was common knowledge that the Nine Powers Treaty was toothless. That was on purpose in order to get an agreement. Basically, countries gave a self-denying pledge. Those who signed on were not bound to defend the Open Door Policy by force. Everything was a matter of good faith."

"Your views as to the value of these agreements, Hamilton?

"The agreement recognized existing realities in Asia. An effort was made to freeze into play the status quo in the Far East. As with any compromise, no nation was completely satisfied with the final treaty draft. On the positive side:

> *It was the first general agreement for naval limitations. It did*
> *bring about a temporary halt to frantic naval construction.*
> *It did, to a degree, reduce tensions in the Pacific.*

"Permit me to add this. The Nine Power Treaty established what has come to be known as the **Washington System** and it successfully maintained the peace in the Pacific. We should not underestimate its contribution to the world of diplomacy.:

"Hamilton, it worked because its members wanted it to?"

"Yes, Harlan."

"Then what happened?"

"The short answer is this. Japan felt constricted by the Nine Power Agreements, especially when it came to Manchuria and China. From her perspective, the only way to pursue her foreign policy goals was to unshackle herself from the Washington System."

"How would she do that?"

"Freda, by constructing a new system for the Far East with Japan as the dominant power at the expense of the Western Powers."

"A clash of systems?"

"Aptly put."

"Japan was taking on the entire world?"

"On a regional basis, yes."

"This has already occurred?"

"With Japan's take over of Manchuria in 1931, yes, and in 1937 with her invasion of China. In the first case, she left the League of Nations. In the second case, she jettisoned the Washington system."

"Hamilton, was Tokyo justified?"

"As with most things, a matter of perspective. Three things do stand out, however. First, in all these agreement Japan felt the sting of Western disrespect; that is, a sense she was never fully being treated or taken as an equal. Second, continuing an aggressive foreign policy in Manchuria and China would eventually lead to a clash with the West. Third, naval parity on paper was one thing. Naval superiority, however, was what really mattered and toward that view Japan would eventually turn."

"Where do we go from here?"

"If you're thinking about the Far East, the prospects are dim, Estelle. We want Japan out of China. Japan refutes that view. War in the Pacific, I'm afraid, is stalking us."

"And our potential Ark, does it still have value?"

"Only if the survivors take it to heart. Except for infrequent periods of peace, war has been, I regret to say, a continuing human folly. Still, you must try and you have my support."

"You're leaving us?"

"Yes, I'm off to do some research. Professor Longstreet will be back to captivate you again with a challenging look at the League of Nations in the 1930's. Before going, however, I would like to leave you with a Chinese proverb. Possibly it will help you through the coming storm:

> *If there is light in the soul,*
> *There will be beauty in the person.*
> *If there is beauty in the person,*
> *There will be harmony in the house.*
> *If there is harmony in the house,*
> *There will be order in the nation.*
> *If there is order in the nation,*
> *There will be peace in the world.*

CHAPTER 22

THE LEAGUE CHALLENGED

<u>July 1941 – The Next Day - Atlanta</u>

The "pirates," mindful of their age and various physical ailments, had enjoyed a few extra hours of blissful sleep. At some point they collectively roused themselves to review notes or reconsider their research to date. Outside a typical St. Louis day welcomed them, hot, humid, and nary a stirring of a breeze. Fluttering above all this, a canopy of birds drifted in the wind currents as they went about their business apparently oblivious to the human dramas played out below. In short, they were decidedly uninterested in the Ark or the desire of a few buccaneers to "save the world."

Eventually, a light brunch was served at the hotel that imprisoned them and then it was back to work. Always the whip hand, Estelle emulated her father, and corralled her cronies.

"Before Professor Longstreet tackles her topic today, a few questions for Harlan."

"Yes, dear woman."

"What was it your grandfather most wanted the Ark to include in 1910?"

"Without doubt, some sort of international association of countries to maintain the peace through arbitration and negotiations. Through diplomacy… He placed a great deal of hope on this concept."

"And, as a follow up, what was the mechanism by which this dream would be realized?"

"The notion of collective security by which nations pledge to stop aggression."

"And the goal of all this?"

"Very simply to prevent war and the renewal of suffering and destruction."

"Lastly, what unstated principal was he up against?"

"Unfortunately, there is no natural law or, if you will, some supreme law that makes war a crime, or an entity that stops conflict before it starts."

"A difficult situation, Harlan.

"One he challenged with all his heart."

Estelle paused with her inquires before saying, "Your grandfather was ahead of his time, as were the others in 1910."

"Indeed, they all were, Estelle,"

"Keeping that in mind, permit me to welcome back Professor Longstreet.

Without any preamble, the erstwhile mentor of the "pirates" launched herself into her presentation with pent up energy.

"The goals of the League of Nations were self-evident, as pointed out by Harlan. I will focus on the weaknesses of the League, which you must understand if you include such a body in your new Ark. We will begin with membership, or the lack of it. Between 1919 and 1939, six nations, all very powerful and each with different agendas never entered, or, if they did, left in a huff. The rogues gallery reads as follows:

Germany – 1920… initially excluded as a member because she was blamed for starting the war. Enters the League in 1926. The Nazis exited the League seven years later in 1933.

Russia – 1919 - initially excluded because of the Russian Revolution and the Russian Civil War, Communists vs. Royalists, Reds vs. Whites. Moscow entered the League in the 1930's and stuck around.

Japan – 1919 – an original member. Exited the League in 1933 after being condemned for her invasion of Manchuria and aggressiveness toward China

Italy – 1919 – withdraws from the League in 1937 after being condemned for her invasion of Ethiopia. How dare the League criticize her thrashing of a backward African people?

Spain – 1919 – exits the League in 1938 after General Franco wins the Spanish Civil War.

America – 1919 – Never joined the League due to the Senate's rejection of the Versailles Treaty. The US was Incognito…

"What do we have here? Italy, Japan, and German went AWOL for purely selfish reasons, to either make war or to prepare to make war. There really was no middle ground, and the League of Nations lacked the institutional fortitude to halt this parade of troublemakers. At least three reasons can initially explain this unholy situation:

<u>Veto power</u> *– unanimous votes were necessary; therefore one veto could stymie efforts to impose sanctions, to enforce rules of law, or to raise an armed force. The veto was demanded by the great power, since no nation wanted its fate in the hands of other nations.*

<u>Revenue</u> *– the League was dependent on contributions from its members. It had no other revenue-producing mechanism.*

<u>Armed Forces</u> *– the League did not have an independent armed force at its disposal. It was totally dependent on member nations contributing forces.*

"These weaknesses made it difficult, even impossible, for the League to conduct its affair. National sovereignty trumped international action?"

"But what about collective security? Surely, the League's members saw the wisdom in maintaining such a security system?"

"They did and they didn't, Harlan."

"That makes no sense."

"Depends on your perspective and understanding some relevant contradictions.

1. The League supported disarmament. It also supported armed intervention. Question: can you have both at once?
2. Most countries were unprepared to go to war. Only the aggressor country was prepared for war. Such countries had built up their military. The unprepared had not; they felt vulnerable. Appeasement on some basis was preferable to conflict.
3. Selfish national economic interests collided with collective security needs. Members often sought short-term profits rather than support boycotts and embargos established by the League.
4. Pacifism in many countries competed with militarism. High public morality vs. autocratic, dictatorial henchmen in political power, an unfair match.

"When you challenge the contradictions, what emerges? First and foremost, armed intervention by the League required the willingness of nations to (1) arm themselves and (2) be willing to use force in order to keep the peace. Stated this way, disarmament acted as an incentive to aggressive nations to militarize their foreign policy. Pacifism was not a disincentive to nations bent upon aggression. The unfortunate lesson was that only force can inhibit force.

"Professor, you paint an unusually dark picture."

"Do I, Freda? Did the 'rule of law' keep Hitler from invading Poland? Did it keep Japan from invading Korea and Manchuria?" Did it stop Mussolini from marching into Africa? Did the very existence of the League of Nations constrain Franco in Spain?"

"But Article 8 of the League Covenant stated that armaments should be reduced to "the lowest point consistent with national security."

"Indeed, it does, Harlan, but how is that to be done? By mathematical strictures of the League, determined by bureaucrats in Geneva? And what is the 'lowest point?' Is it the same for all nations? Probably not... And how do you enforce any agreement? How do you stop cheating, for example?"

"But what about alliances? Wouldn't that help? Countries pledged to assist each other?"

"In theory perhaps, Harlan. But wasn't the alliance system one cause of the war, along with the secret treaties which produced them?"

"Such a thicket."

"Estelle, you are so right, as our the questions that still haunt your hopes for a determinant Ark:

1. Was the League of Nations too American for a Europe unfamiliar with our notions of democracy?
2. Did the victors, France and Britain in particular, enter the League reluctantly given Wilson's popularity and influence in Paris?
3. Was it wise to tie the Covenant of the League to the final Versailles treaty?
4. Was too much asked of the League to actually stop war?
5. Could a League, inclusive of many authoritarian states, actually keep the world safe for democratic countries?
6. Did the notion of self-determination unleash more problems than the League could handle?
7. Must nations maintain a robust military in order to ward off aggressive nations?
8. Is peace better maintained if an aggressor state actually believes force will be used against it?

"Professor, perhaps you brought a large dose of scholarly aspirin to douse the headaches caused by these questions?"

"Freda, the questions noted I share easily, but not answers to them sufficient to satisfy you. But answer you must, if your new Ark is to prevail in the aftermath. However, I don't want to leave you completely in a lurch. Historians have suggested two lessons to be considered:

#1 - Undoubtedly much of the troubles with the League was that it was formed after and not during the first World War when Allied Nations no

longer had to find answers to the thousand and one reasons why men do not want to cooperate.

*#2 — Today those powers which did not feel the League useful to safeguard their own security, have to recognize that international order through collective security has become essential for the survival of strong states as well as the preservation of weaker ones. Unfortunately, today an aggressor left alone in his preparations for war can get a **death jump** on a strong state as well as a weak one.*

"Death jump, an unhappy turn of words, Professor."

"Isn't it, Estelle?"

"Nazi Germany, you're suggesting has already jumped?"

"With Rome, yes."

"Leaving Japan about to do so?"

"Can you reach any other conclusion, Freda?"

"About which we can do what?"

"We must learn from what's taken place."

"We will be forced to jump?"

The Mukden Incident

Professor Longstreet let the question remain unanswered. She went on to her joyless lecture.

It is sometimes referred to as the 'Manchurian Incident.' What it really was, according to a consensus of historians, was naked Japanese aggression in Manchuria brought about by troops in the Kwantung Army under the order of Japanese army officers. On September 18, 1931 a small explosion took place along the South Manchurian Railroad line. Some two to three feet of rails were only slightly damaged. Apparently, the Japanese lit the fuse, so to speak, in order to blame the Chinese as a pretext for war. The officer in charge telegraphed his superiors that:

> *... the time was ripe for the Kwantung Army to act boldly and assume responsibility for law and order throughout Manchuria.*

Within a short period both Mukden and Changchun (the northern terminus of the South Manchuria Railway) were seized by Japanese troops in an orchestrated move. Soon all of Manchuria was occupied and renamed Manchukuo under a 'puppet leader' subservient to Tokyo. That was on March 9, 1932."

"What did the League do?"

"In consideration to China's view that she had been attacked, observers, Harlan, were sent to the area to determine what occurred. The commission spent six weeks in the area on a fact-finding mission. The Lytton Report (October 1932) declared Japan an aggressor and demanded that Manchuria be returned to China. The report, authored by Victor-Bulwer-Lytton of Great Britain urged that Manchukuo should not be recognized, and recommended Manchurian autonomy under Chinese sovereignty. The League Assembly accepted the report by a vote 42 to 1. Importantly, two conclusions were reached that led to far-reaching consequences: first, the actions of the Imperial Japanese Government could not be 'regarded as legitimate self-defense." And secondly:

> *The new state (Manchukuo) could not have been formed without the presence of Japanese troops; that it had no general Chinese support; and that it was not part of a genuine and spontaneous independent movement.*

"The report also proposed that China and Japan should be given three months in which to accept or reject the provided recommendations. It was hoped that the parties would agree to direct negotiations. That didn't happen. In September 1932, even before the Lytton Report was made public on October 2,1932, the Japanese government formally recognized Manchukuo. After discussion, the General Assembly of the League considered a resolution to condemn Japan as an aggressor in February 1933. The Japanese delegation walked out before this could happen. Added to this, three countries immediately recognized Manchukuo and applauded Japan's stance."

"Let me guess, Fascist Italy, Nazi Germany and autocratic Spain?"

"Bingo, Harlan.

"Japan remained in control?"

"Yes, Freda. The League didn't have the power to enforce its decisions. That weakness of the League was present for all to see. In Tokyo, Berlin, and Rome it did not go unnoticed."

"What was the position of the United States?"

"Henry Stimson, the Secretary of State under President Herbert Hoover, issued a lengthy statement, which I now share with you in detail:

> *The American Government deems it to be its duty to notify both the Imperial Japanese Government and the Government of the Chinese Republic that it cannot admit the legality of any situation de facto nor does it intend to recognize any treaty or agreement entered into between those Governments, or agents thereof, which may impair the treaty rights of the United States, or its citizens in China, including those that relate to the sovereignty, the independence, or the territorial and administrative integrity of the Republic of China, or to the internal policy relative to China, commonly known as the open door policy.*

"Beyond the diplomatic jargon, what was Stimson saying? At least the following:

1. The United States was supporting China in this clash.
2. Manchukuo would not be recognized by the United States.
3. Japan was guilty of aggression.
4. The Open Door Policy was vital to the United States.

"Stimson's note became known as the Stimson Doctrine of Non-Recognition. Historians stated the doctrine as such:

> *Thus Washington, while avoiding economic sanctions or other strong-armed measures, established a moral sanction against aggression. The diplomacy of condemnation was a cheap and conscience-satisfying substitute for armed intervention.*

"Just words, Professor Longstreet."

"Stimson would agree with you, Freda. America was not prepared to go to war. As might be expected, most people in America perceived no vital interests in Manchuria. Though they sympathized with China, any support was always just short of showdown with Japan according to the polling of that day. Stimson knew he was armed with little more than 'spears of straw and swords of ice.' His doctrine did nothing to stop the Japanese in Manchuria. The simple fact was this; in 1931 the Western powers 'lacked both the will and the means to hinder Japanese conquests.'"

"And, as a consequence of all this?"

"Harlan, I'll answer your question with one; just how far was the United States willing to go to avoid war, then or now?"

"Your view?"

"The clock is ticking. Negotiations and compromises have come to an end in the Pacific. Where a few years ago America was unwilling to stop Japan in Korea or Manchuria, today we are prepared, it seems, to do so in China. Some invisible line has been crossed. All that is needed is an incident to break the back of peace."

"Something in Europe?"

"Old news, Estelle, but with a lesson, at least indirectly for the world if the League were to survive."

"You're getting at what, professor?"

"Africa."

Ethiopia

"In October 1935 some four years after the Manchuria crisis, Benito Mussolini, the Fascist leader of Italy, unleashed war on a small African country. Over 400,000 troops invaded Ethiopia. It was an unfair fight from the beginning. Italy had modern airplanes and crack troops. The Italians had mustard gas, which they used on innocent villagers when they weren't bombing them. They poisoned wells, depriving people of water supplies. Still, the outmanned Ethiopians fought. It wasn't until May 1936 that the Italians captured Addis Ababa, the capital. Emperor Haile Selassie was forced to flee the country."

"The League's response, Professor Longstreet?"

"What we've come to expect, Freda. Italian aggression was condemned, again with words. Economic sanctions were placed on Italy with little follow through, and almost no enforcement. That was pretty much it. What wasn't done was, however, of interest."

"Which was?"

"Oil sales were continued. Modern armies run on the 'black stuff.' An oil embargo would, if successful, put a crimp in Mussolini's military. Unfortunately, the United States continued to export large quantities of crude to Italy in opposition to the League's policy. The Suez Canal, under British control, remained open to Italian shipping, including naval vessels and troop ships heading for Ethiopia. Profits again ruled the day in some capitals."

"Sanctions without muscle?"

"Britain didn't want to antagonize Rome. Two reasons, really. First, she shied away from direct military confrontation in the Mediterranean, while also dealing with an aggressive Japan in the Far East. Second, she didn't want to drive Italy into an alliance with Nazi Germany."

"Which in the end happened anyway?"

"Quite right. By July 1936 it was all over. Ethiopia fell. Mussolini's dream of a new Roman Empire under his sway was a reality. King Victor Emmanuel of Italy received a new title, Emperor of Ethiopia."

"Didn't Haile Selassie appear before the League of Nations, seeking assistance?"

"Yes, Estelle, in June of 1936. In an unprecedented action, he became the first head of state to appear before the League. There he spoke eloquently on behalf of his country with words, which ultimately went unheeded:

> *There is no precedent for a people being victim of such*
> *injustice and being at present threatened by abandonment to*
> *its aggressor. Also, there never before been an example of any*
> *Government proceeding to the systematic extermination of a*
> *nation by barbarous means, in violation of the most solemn*
> *promises made by the nations of the earth that there should*
> *not be used against innocent human beings the terrible poison*
> *of harmful gases. It is to defend a people struggling for its*
> *age-old independence that the head of the Ethiopian Empire*

has come to Geneva to fulfill this supreme duty, after having himself fought at the head of his armies.

"A powerful indictment."

"Words that also included a warning to the League, Harlan."

Throughout history, it has been the inaction of those who could have acted; the indifference of those who should have known better; the silence of the voice of justice when it mattered most; that has made it possible for evil to triumph.

"But to no avail, Harlan."

"Haile Selassie's final words captured the pathos of the time:

I ask the fifty-two nations, who have given the Ethiopian people a promise to help them in their resistance to the aggressor, what are they willing to do for Ethiopia? And the great Powers who have promised the guarantee of collective security to small States on whom weighs the threat that they may one day suffer the fate of Ethiopia. I ask what measures do you intend to take?

"He predicted what has come to pass, Freda."

"What the Czechs learned…"

"What the Poles recently experienced.?"

"What China was going through, professor?"

"There was, it seemed no collective security, only a nasty word, which was finding its way into the headlines, *appeasement*. Estelle tells me that is your next topic. A working definition might prove useful. It is, I believe, an action to avoid war by giving into the taunts and demands of a bully on the international scene."

"A Hitler?"

"Or a Mussolini, Freda."

"But bullies with big sticks!"

"That is generally the case, but giving into one only encourages more demands."

"Like blackmail?"

"As you say, Estelle."

"But if you stand up to the bully?"

"You better make sure you have a stick, too, Harlan."

"Perhaps we should move on, Professor Longstreet?"

"Good. Before I take my leave of you and this sad League business, a bit of history generally unknown to Americans."

"Do explain."

"Among Negroes in America, Freda, there was an especially strong response to Italy's invasion of Ethiopia. The African country was symbolically very important to Negroes because it was one of the few places in Africa not colonized by white Europeans. Negroes protested Italian aggression and demanded embargoes on trade with Italy. They also boycotted Italian-American businesses. They raised funds for Ethiopia, while some Negroes actually volunteered to fight in the war. They also petitioned the Pope to restrain Mussolini. Their opposition to Italy was balanced, as one would expect, by Italian-Americans who generally supported Mussolini. As always, hyphenated Americans were brought into conflicts, even those a continent away."

"Professor Longstreet, you have been an excellent mentor."

"Then I leave you with this. Your new Ark must take into account the failures of the League of Nations. In the aftermath of what is ahead, a new international body will be needed to prevent, if possible, a third such conflagration. Your job... Your self-imposed obligation is to design an Ark, which takes that into consideration. That must be your guiding light for all the children yet unborn as noted by one poet.

> *Listen, children:*
> *Your father is dead.*
> *From his old coats*
> *I'll make you little jackets;*
> *I'll make you little trousers*
> *From old pants...*
>
> *There will be in his pockets,*
> *Things he used to put there.*
> *Keys and pennies*

Covered with tobacco;
Dan shall have the pennies
To save in his bank;
Anne shall have the keys
To make a pretty Rose with…

Life must go on,
And the dead be forgotten;
Life must go on,
Though good men die;
Anne, eat your breakfast;
Dan, take your medicine;
Life must go on;
I forget just why.

Lament by Edna St. Vincent Millay

CHAPTER 23

TROUBLE ON
THE YANGTZE

August 1941 – At Home

The conspirators were home. Atlanta was yesterday. Now it was time to catch up on their personal lives, at least for a few days, and to digest all they had learned. Harlan and Freda knew instinctively their hiatus would be short run given Estelle's penchant for pushing forward. This, of course, proved to be the case. Five days passed and then a ubiquitous, brown-wrapped package arrived, once more via the United States Postal Service, Ben Franklin's greatest contribution beyond the stove named in his honor. Estelle had forwarded research materials for their consideration. As always, there was an accompanying note:

The sands of time are drifting away. Enough of the R and R. It's time to advance our quest for a new Ark, don't you think? So up and at them with your foot to the pedal and full steam ahead. There's no time to dilly, dally. Oh, how I detest clichés.

Enclosed are materials for your perusal from my good friend, Henry Lee. You'll recall that when we last met a warning was ringing in our ears. What was it Professor Longstreet had said? The tension in the Far East was explosive; all that was needed was an incident to set the Pacific on fire. Well, that's what we're into now, an "incident" with a curious, unexpected outcome; the spears were shelved as the world backed away from war at the last moment. Hopefully, these few words have whetted your quizzical appetite for more details. After looking at Henry's materials (yes, we're on a first name basis), we'll be in touch.

One last thing; I heard from my father again, just too uncomfortable words:

TOO LATE

Obviously, the first question that came to mind was, "too late for what?" Naturally, many interpretations are possible. For now, all that is on the back burner. I just don't know what to make of it. For a man who wrote voluminously, his cryptic comments are most frustrating. At the moment you need to take a cruise up the Yangtze and Henry is our tour director.

Dear Friends,

Estelle, somewhat obliquely, has told me of your Ark, and what you hope to achieve. In that vein I hope to assist you.

A word about myself: I shelter at the University of Oregon where I'm in the history department specializing in Asian History. How I got to Eugene is a long story. Leave it at this; in 1937 my father, though seriously wounded, survived a Japanese attack on an American gunboat on the Yangtze River. Though not in the US Navy, he worked in the engine room, where he had an aptitude for motors and grease. After short stay in a Chinese hospital, he was brought to Hawaii. There he met my mother before migrating to Portland, Oregon when I was born. Not too exciting a story with, however, one exception. The ship attacked by the Japanese was the USS Panay.

In 1937 the Imperial Japanese Army attacked the capital of China, Nanking (now known as Nanjing), about 150-miles west of Shanghai on the Yangtze River. In what the world would describe as the "Rape of Nanking," the city was bombed from the air while shelled by ground forces. It was the blitz before the term was coined, the indiscriminate destruction of a city's population. Over 300,000 civilians and prisoners of war died in the attack and occupation. Though it's hard to believe, that wasn't the worst of it. An undisciplined Japanese military committed unspeakable atrocities including rape and the brutal killing of women in the most obscene manner. As an eyewitness to what happened, the Reverend James M. McCallum, wrote in his diary:

> *Never I have heard or read such brutality. Rape! Rap! Rape!*
> *We estimate at least 1,000 cases a night and many by day.*
> *In case of resistance or anything that seems like disapproval,*
> *there is a bayonet stab or a bullet… People are hysterical…*
> *Women are being carried off every morning, afternoon, and*
> *evening. The whole Japanese army seems to be free to go and*
> *come as it pleases, and to do whatever pleases.*

Given this situation, both the British and American consulates attempted to evacuate their nationals from the holocaust. In addition, two British ships, the *HMS Cricket* and the *HMS Scarab*, the *USS Panay* were ordered to pick up those fleeing from the Japanese. The ships accomplished their mission and headed up the Yangtze River, steaming about 27- miles above Nanking where they anchored. Three Standard Oil tankers, also with company families and employees, joined the little flotilla. The Captain of the *Panay*, Joseph Hughes noted the date: December 11, 1937.

A word about the *Panay;* she was a river gunboat built for the American Asiatic Fleet on the Yangtze River. Her primary mission was the protection of American lives and property. What made the *Panay* special was her draft, 5-feet, 3-inches, which was excellent for the, at times, shallow, meandering river. In addition to her 59 officers and crew, she was armed with 2 3"/50 caliber guns and a number of machine guns. With all boilers lit and her two towering smoke stacks belching a dark cloud, she could travel at 15 knots (17 mph).

December 12, 1937 – Sunday, 11:00 A.M.

The US Consulate in Shanghai was informed of the *Panay's* disposition and exact location. The Consulate in turn sent word to Japanese authorities hoping to avoid an attack by mistake. Also, to ward off any misunderstandings, two huge American flags, 18 X 14, were painted on the ship's awnings that covered the upper deck. An enormous ensign was also flown from the mizzenmast. The precautions should have been sufficient even in the confusion of war.

1:35 P.M.

Visibility clear… Lookouts on the *Panay* reported strange aircrafts coming toward the ship from the SW. The aircrafts, as it later turned out, were from the Imperial Navy's 13th naval air group. The planes were strung out in a long line. Suddenly, three planes rolled over and went into a dive, the prelude to a bombing run and attacked the *Panay*. Direct hits… The *Panay* was immediately disabled; the ship's engines were knocked out and the rudder was damaged. The Captain, severely wounded by the attack, grounded the ship before giving the order to abandon the vessel. The survivors in the two wooden lifeboats were continuously strafed as they made for shore. This was also true of those swimming. The Japanese planes bore in and fired again and again. Before it was over with, two sailors were killed and 30 people were wounded.

A cameraman from the National Newsreel Service, Norman William Alley was on the *Panay* and, believe it or not, filmed the attack. What he filmed documented the Japanese planes at low altitude as they made their bombing runs. The film evidence was conclusive. The planes could not have missed the American flags. The *Panay* was too plainly marked. It had been a deliberate attack. In time Alley's footage was shown in movie houses across America and Japan, leading to widely different perspectives.

Why had the Japanese attacked? The initial Tokyo explanation was that rogue pilots saw numerous small boats situated around the *Panay*. The pilots thought these boats were bringing Chinese military officers and weapons to the ship. In attacking the pilots didn't first check with their headquarters. Was it a mistake? No, the Japanese said. Was it a provocation? Again, no... Did the Japanese believe the *Panay* was assisting the Chinese government? Yes!

On both sides of the Pacific newspapers defended or attacked this explanation. Again, as expected, the press made of the "incident" what it wanted, sensationalizing every aspect of the "incident, and demanding retribution. What really mattered, of course, was the response of Washington and Tokyo.

Negotiations and Settlement

The United States demanded an apology. That was given almost immediately by Japan and by thousands of Japanese citizens who sent notes of regret. The United States wanted an indemnity payment for the victim of the attack. This was also done to the tune of $2,214,000.36 after serious negotiations. The United States wanted Japanese assurances to avoid another "incident." They were quickly forthcoming. The entire process took only two weeks, something of a record for diplomats. Why did the Japanese settle so quickly? The answer seems to be this: caught up in a bloody war in China, Tokyo wanted to maintain, if possible, cordial relationships with the United States. If war was to break out in the Far East, it was not yet the appropriate moment from Tokyo's perspective.

The public response in the United States was quite different than when the *USS Maine* exploded in Havana Harbor before the turn of the century. Then the country wanted to go to war against Spain, no questions asked. Though angry and belligerent, most Americans did want to get into a shooting war with Japan. She was far stronger than Madrid. Also, the country was still in a depression and the European situation was just beginning to slide out of control. Militarily, the country was not prepared for a protracted conflict. According to the pollsters, though sympathetic toward the Chinese, most Americans wanted to limit their support to anything short of bullets flying. Going to war over the *Panay* was not in the cards.

President Franklin D. Roosevelt understood the isolationist sentiment in the United States and acted in concert with public opinion. He did not want the sinking of the *Panay* to be a catalyst for "the severance of diplomatic ties" and war with Japan.

The cry for peace was a bellow for neutrality and pacifism bordering on a policy of isolationism. To make that point, Congressman Louis Ludlow from Indiana introduced a controversial amendment in the House of Representative. Essentially, his amendment would do the following: in order for the government to go to war, a nationwide referendum was required unless the country was actually attacked. It was a sort of legislative insurance package to restrain the government's war powers. Some 73% of the public supported Ludlow. After overriding the Democratic leadership in the House and the opposition of FDR, the whole business came up for a vote. That was on January 10, 1938. Ludlow's amendment was defeated in a surprising narrow win, 209 to 138.

Final Perspective

Navy cryptographers decrypted radio traffic related to the attacking planes, which "clearly indicated that they were under orders" during the attack, and that it had not been a mistake of any kind, suggesting that:

> *The chaos in Nanking created an opportunity for renegade factions within the Japanese army who wanted to force the US into an active conflict so that the Japanese could once and for all drive the US out of China.*

With that in mind, Secretary of State Cordell Hall put the "incident" into perspective, stating:

> *On this side our people generally took the incident calmly. There were a few demands that the Fleet should be sent at once to the Orient. There were many more demands that we should withdraw completely from China. It was a serious incident but, unless we could have proven the complicity of the Japanese Government itself, it was not an occasion for war.*

Admiral Yamamoto concurred, pointing out that:

> *The Imperial Japanese Navy, which bore responsibility for this incident, takes this opportunity to express its gratification at the fairness and perspicacity shown, despite a barrage of misunderstanding propaganda, by the American public in appreciating the true facts of the incident and Japan's good faith in dealing with it.*

The potential for an "incident" in the Pacific still rang true. The *Panay* attack brought the Far East to the brink, but not over the edge. Both nations were now warned. Another incident, should it occur, might strain relations beyond repair leading to an armed clash ... On December 12, 1941, only a few months from now, and almost four years since the *Panay* was sunk, the country will recall what happened on the Yangtze River. Hopefully, we can get to that day without a further "incident" in the Pacific.

———

Professor Lee left a final note for the conspirators, reminding them that their next topic awaited, the "neutrality craze of the 1930's. They needed to get on with their reading. They would, of course, and with a sense of desperation. Time was running out in the Pacific. They felt it in their bones.

CHAPTER 24

THE NEUTRALITY FRENZY

<u>August 1941 – At Home</u>

"You know his name. You've seen his picture in the newspapers, *Life* and *Time* magazines, and in the movie newsreels. You know, that non-descript fellow from North Dakota, the Republican with the childish bowl haircut and an unsophisticated way about him, Gerald P. Nye. That's right, the outspoken middle-America isolationist so popular with the non-interventionists and the pacifists, who are trying desperately to keep us out of war. You're remembering now; that's good. You can see him in the Senate, arms waving, eyes blazing, thundering his clarion call to restrain, if not eliminate, the "merchants of death," those industries guilty of war profiteering, and having undo influence on the Wilson Administration, sufficient to get America into an unnecessary war."

In their different locations the three conspirators were reading William Lee's materials on the frenzy of neutrality legislation passed in the 1930's in face of White House opposition in the form of President Roosevelt. And, yes, they did recognize Nye's name and the multitude of committee hearings he chaired to get at two questions:

What role did the financial and banking industry have in influencing American foreign policy, 1914 – 1918? Was it true the industry loaned $27,000,000 to Germany, but over $ 2.3 billion to France and Great Britain? Conclusion: yes, there was influence. Implication: it's hard to collect from a loser.

What role did the armament's industry play in getting America into the European war? Was it true there was price-fixing and profiteering, and other scandals related to government military contracts? Conclusion: yes, there were scandals. Implication: these industries needed to be hemmed in and staunchly watched, or they could get us into another war.

Did these industries influence American public opinion through the use of propaganda? To a degree, yes… Was it true the public was suckered into a war to save profits rather than democracy? Conclusion, yes, propaganda played a role in forging attitudes and actions. Implication: Make sure there is greater public involvement in influencing America's foreign policy.

Was it difficult to determine was the extent to which these industries actually influenced Wilson's foreign policy? Try as it might, the Nye Committee chaired provided no satisfactory answer though the investigation was extensive. There was plenty of circumstantial evidence, but after that things got muddy.

By 1935 a majority of Americans, including our conspirators, shared some of the following sentiments: the political bickering at Versailles, and the endless compromises devalued Wilson's Fourteen Points, leaving many Americans disillusioned with the whole matter. Others were merely cynical about the colonial powers still grasping their foreign possessions in opposition to Wilson's emphasis on self-determination. The huge reparations bill fostered on Germany had its critics of what came to be known as the debt problem. The "guilt-clause" of the Versailles Treaty had also turned heads, especially among German-Americans.

All of this led to a reaction to war, creating an impulse for:

1. Isolationism – America, protected by two oceans, should remain aloof from Europe's conflicts.

2. Non-interventions – regardless of the sympathies for victimized countries by naked aggression, America should not intervene. Victims and aggressors should be treated equally as belligerents.
3. Pacifism – Wars were folly. Unless attacked, America should avoid measures leading to war.
4. Military preparedness – the country should remain prepared for war to defend her interests.

Senator Nye captured the nation's feeling, stating:

> *Getting into this war is not inevitable for America. It is fair to say that our staying out of war is inevitable… Getting into this return engagement of war to Europe is only as inevitable as we, the people of America will permit it to be.*

There is no question that the Nye Committee influenced the Congress' desire to rein in the "road to war" through a series of "neutrality acts." As to whether this was ultimately a good foreign policy in 1930's, that was another question to be researched. What is known is this: most Americans were hesitant to get into another European squabble. To that end, they bought into the a period of "neutrality frenzy."

> *The popular mood was anti-banker, anti-munitions manufacturer, and anti-war; and by stressing the scandalous the Nye investigators succeeded in stirring up a maximum of publicity with a modicum of new facts. The public became aroused over the wrong things, and this state of mind contributed powerfully to the passage of the head-in-the-sands neutrality legislation of the 1930's*

The Neutrality Act of 1935

Passed by the Congress on August 31, 1935 during the invasion of Ethiopia by Italy the legislation had the following provisions:

1. A general embargo on arms and war materials to all parties in a war.

2. American citizens traveling on belligerent ships did so at their own risk.

3. No distinction was drawn between the aggressor and the victim.

The problem, of course, was to get private companies and sovereign nations to avoid trading in arms with countries at war. Without doubt, war is a dastardly business, but there are profits to be made. As to traveling, unless required by law and enforced, Americans were free to travel on belligerent sHips. In treating belligerents the same, no distinction was drawn between the aggressor and the victim. As such, neutrality had its limits.

Neutrality Act of 1936

1. Renewed provisions of the 1935 legislation for 14-months.
2. Forbade all loans or credit to all belligerent countries.
3. Weakness: the legislation didn't account for civil war.
4. Problem: what was war material? Oil sold by Standard Oil or Texaco, for example, could be used for civilian purposes or to power an airplane. Trucks sold by Ford and General Motors had duel purposes.

Again, problems emerged. Tightening credit demanded compliance, always a difficult thing when profits are on the line. As to a civil war, such as was seen in Spain, just who is the belligerent? General Franco and his political supporters, or the elected government and its defenders? As to oil and machinery, any definitive policy was elusive.

Neutrality Act of 1937

1. The earlier provisions were kept.
2. No expiration date.
3. No sales to either side in a civil war as in Spain.
4. US ships were forbidden from transporting passengers and war materials to belligerents.

5. US citizens were forbidden to travel on belligerent ships of any nation.

This legislation attempted to tie down the loose ends. As would be expected, various industries wanted exemptions to the neutrality acts, or a provision by which the law could be legally circumvented. Congress accommodated both the President (to a degree) and industry (to a degree).

Profit-conscious America, though wedded to neutrality was unwilling to deny herself all such trade. As a compromise, the law provided that the President could list certain commodities, and these would have to be paid for upon delivery and taken away in the ships of the buyer.

Cash and Carry Provision

1. President could permit the sale of war materials to belligerents.
2. The buyer had to make arrangements for the transport of such materials.
3. The buyer had to pay immediately in cash for the materials.
4. Loans were prohibited.
5. Cash and carry provisions favored big navy nations, such as Britain. Their ships could reach the United States.

The elephant in the room was, as always, Japan. How would America respond if Japan was involved in a war? How would the neutrality acts be applied? Washington didn't have long to wait.

Sino-Japanese War

Japan attacked China, July 7, 1937. Fighting broke out at the Marco Polo Bridge between Chinese and Japanese soldiers near Peiping. Japanese reinforcements poured into North China; there was no formal declaration of war on Tokyo's part. The incident evolved into the "China Incident" or the "China Affair." Either way, it led to a full-scale invasion of the country by Tokyo.

The US government supported China and public opinion generally supported Washington policies, short of war. Making use of a technicality, FDR didn't invoke the neutrality acts since the parties had not declared war. Application of the law would have hurt China more than Japan because of the so-called equal treatment of all belligerent parties. Not unnoticed by Tokyo, the President imposed a "moral embargo" on American exporters of aircraft to Japan.

Quarantine Speech, October 5, 1937

Beyond the neutrality acts, FDR had to respond to Japan's invasion of China. On October 5, 1937 he did so in Chicago where he came to dedicate the Outer Drive Bridge built by the PWA. That was the excuse provided reporters. In truth he had come to the center of the isolationist movement and sentiment to make his case for military preparedness. He focused on "international lawlessness," stating the country couldn't remain immune to what was happening in China and Europe. He pointed out that aggressor nations were stirring up "international anarchy" and they should be quarantined. That was the key action and the theme of the speech: dangerous nations needed to be quarantined.

The peace, the freedom, and the security of 90 percent of the population of the world is being jeopardized by the remaining 10 percent, who are threatening a breakdown of all international order and law.

There was no doubt what countries were in Roosevelt's 10 percent category, Italy, Japan, and Germany. So to speak, the die was cast. Since Rome, Tokyo, and Berlin would not change their aggressive policies, war was all but assured at some point. FDR put that point across next.

Surely the 90 percent who want to live in peace under law and in accordance with moral standards that have received almost universal acceptance through the centuries, can and must find some way to make their will prevail... There must be positive endeavors to preserve peace.

To better explain his views, the President suggested a medical analogy:

When an epidemic of physical disease starts to spread, the community approves and joins in quarantine of the patients in order to protect the health of the community against the spread of the disease. War is a contagion, whether it be declared or undeclared. There is no escape through mere isolation or neutrality.

What did the President mean by "positive endeavors?" Was he prepared to place extreme economic sanctions on Japan to alter her behavior? Was he willing to risk war by starting down this road? If so, would the isolationists rise up against his policies? Of course, the answers were yes, yes, and yes. The President had to back off. The country was still captive to noninterventionism.

The President ended his speech with a warning:

Without a declaration of war and without warning or justification of any kind, civilians, including vast numbers of women and children, are being ruthlessly murdered (by Japan) with bombs from the air. In times of so-called peace, ships are being attacked and sunk by submarines without cause or notice (Nazi Germany). Nations are fomenting and taking sides in civil warfare in nations that have never done them any harm (Italy in Spain).

Neutrality Act of 1939

1. Cash and Carry provision lapsed. It was renewed.
2. Mandatory arms embargo remained in place.
3. Germany attacked Poland; Britain and France declared war on Nazi Germany. FDR invoked the neutrality acts, thereby giving passive aid to Germany.

There were weaknesses in the 1939 act. Armaments could be sold to neutral countries and then resold to belligerents. As an example, Rome could buy armament from Washington, only then to sell later to Berlin. Also, companies would relocate in Canada in order to bypass American laws.

Lend-Lease

FDR needed a way out of the entanglement of the Neutrality Acts. Great Britain was hanging on by a thread once Germany defeated France. The "Battle of Britain" was taking a toll; daily bombings were leveling British cities. The U-boats encircling the island were cutting off oil and food shipments. Britain's survival was in doubt.

In 1941 the President received a jolting letter from Winston Churchill. The Prime Minister wrote:

> *The moment approaches when we shall no longer be able to pay cash for shipping and other supplies.*

Already sympathetic to Britain's plight, the President had stated earlier in the year:

> *In the present world situation of course there is absolutely no doubt in the mind of a very overwhelming number of Americans that the best immediate defense of the United States is the success of Great Britain in defending itself.*

The President's problem boiled down to this. He needed a method by which to aid Britain while not running afoul of the neutrality acts. He also needed to explain this to the American people in a way they could best understand the situation. To do so he used the analogy of helping a neighbor whose house was on fire:

> *Suppose my neighbor's home catches fire, and I have a length of garden hose... If he can take my garden hose and connect it up with his hydrant, I may help him to put out his fire.*

The President then asked the salient question: do I charge my neighbor for use of my garden hose? Of course not; if the fire is put out, my home is spared. If the hose is returned damaged, so what? My house still stands untouched by the fire. In other words:

> *If you lend certain munitions and get the munitions back at the end of the war, if they are intact haven't been hurt---you are all right; if thy have been damaged or have deteriorated or have been lost completely, it seems t ome you come out pretty well if you have them replaced by the fellow to whom you have lent them.*

What the President needed was a garden hose. On March 11, 1941 he got one. The Congress passed the Lend-Lease Act to assist specifically three countries, Britain, the Free French, and China. Stated in another manner, the United States was now prepared to actively support nations fighting Nazi Germany and Imperial Japan. The new policy effectively ended any pretense of neutrality. It was a final decisive step away from non-intervention. It had been a difficult fight in Congress. On February 9, 1941, the House the final vote was 317 to 71, mainly along party lines. The same was true in the Senate where 50 Democrats, joined by 10 Republicans, turned the tide. Public opinion generally supported the policy:

> 54% favored giving aid to England.
> 15% favored aid with qualifications.
> 22% were unequivocally against any aid.
> 69% of Democrats favored aid, only 38% of Republicans.

What did the Lend-Lease legislation provide?

It permitted the President to "sell, transfer title to, exchange, lease, lend, or otherwise dispose of, to any such government whose defense the President deems vital to the defense of the United States any defense article

The legislation was not without staunch critics who saw it as a "blank-check bill" and coined a frightening rebuttal:

Kill Bill 1776
Not our Boys

The opposition did have one exceedingly powerful argument, actually a prediction. Extensive aid to Britain would require convoys through submarine infested waters of the North Atlantic. American vessels would be needed for this duty. Inevitably, US warships would be sunk, which must lead to war. As such, the United States was becoming a de facto ally in the war against Germany, and the US Navy would be at war in advance of any declaration of war. Unfortunately, this prophecy proved true, as we will see later.

As was his way, Churchill weighed in, mobilizing the English language in support of the Lend-Lease legislation. He delivered the following note, written out in longhand, and quoted from an American poet, Henry D. Longfellow:

> *Sail On, O Ship of State!*
> *Sail on, O Union, strong and great!*
> *Humanity with all its fears,*
> *With all the hopes of future years,*
> *Is hanging breathless on they fate!*

After passage of the legislation, Churchill told the House of Commons that Lend-Lease was "the most unsordid act in the history of any nation." He telegraphed President Roosevelt, saying: "Our blessing from the whole of the British Empire go out to you and the American nation for this very present help in time of trouble." At the conclusion of a radio broadcast on April 27, 1941, he again thanked the American people in the most eloquent terms:

> *In front the sun climbs slow, how slowly,*
> *But westward, look, the land is bright.*

In response to the Lend-Lease legislation, Japan accelerated a similar program, but in reverse. Determining that she would be cut off from oil and scrap iron from the West, Japan sought another avenue of self-sufficiency; that is, she would invade and occupy Asian areas rich in the sinews of war. The policy name for this was the **Great East-Asia Co-Prosperity Sphere**. The purpose, beyond self-sufficiency, was to drive the imperialistic countries out of Asia. This, as seen by Tokyo, would end Japan's dependency on the West. This policy targeted Southeast Asia and meant war with the ABCD countries, Australia, Britain, China, and the Dutch, all supported by the United States. What began at the Marco Polo Bridge was now turning into a global conflict unless cooler heads prevailed.

President Roosevelt saw no practical alternative to assisting China and Britain. They were "carrying the battle for all civilization," and led by an overwhelming majority of Americans prudent assistance would be provided by the Roosevelt Administration. As the President said:

There can be no reasoning with incendiary bombs.

CHAPTER 25

DESTROYERS AND DRAFTEES

August 941 – At Home

In May 1940 President Roosevelt received an urgent message from Winston Churchill describing the dire situation England found herself in as Nazi Germany prepared to invade the island, an event unknown since Napoleon or William the Conqueror. Church wrote:

> As you are no doubt aware, the scene has darkened swiftly.
> We expect to be attacked here ourselves, both from the air and
> by parachute and air borne troops in the near future.

Going on, the Prime Minister than shared a warning:

> The voice and force of the United States may count for nothing
> if they are withheld too long. You may have a completely
> subjugated Nazified Europe established with astonishing
> swiftness, and the weight may be more than we can bear.

Then Churchill got to the heart of the matter:

Immediate needs are first of all, the loan of forty or fifty of your older destroyers. Secondly, we want several hundred of the latest type of aircraft. Thirdly, anti-aircraft equipment and ammunition... Fourthly, we need to purchase steel in the United States.

The conspirators were reading Professor Lee's research materials about the famous or infamous destroyer deal with Britain, depending on your point of view. For the interventionist, the right decision by the White House. For the isolationist, still another step toward pushing America into the war. For the uninitiated, of course, one or two questions: first of all, what is a destroyer, and next, why did Churchill so badly want them?

By definition, a destroyer is a very fast, highly maneuverable warship intended to escort larger ships, such as troop ships, battleships, and aircraft carriers. It also provides a protective ring around convoys in submarine infested waters. Carrying 5-inch guns and a load of torpedoes and depth charges, destroyers are a killing machine, the archenemy of undersea craft.

An unstated task of a destroyer is to, if necessary, take a torpedo hit rather than permitting it to hit a larger ship, especially one carrying troops. In that sense they were expendable.

In response to Churchill's plea for assistance, the United States on September 2, 1940 transferred 50 old US Navy destroyers to the Royal Navy in exchange for land rights in British possessions in the Western Hemisphere. The ships went by unique names, flush-decks, or four pipers (for their four funnels). All were surplus of the First World War. Once transferred, each ship was renamed for a town with a common name in both countries. After refitted, the ships were used to ward off a Nazi invasion across the English Channel, to escort convoys ferreting supplies from the US, and to keep the lifelines open through the Mediterranean to Egypt.

To pull off this hat trick; that is, to circumvent the neutrality laws, President Roosevelt acted on the basis of an executive agreement rather than seeking Congressional approval. There would be no protracted debate in the Senate. There would be no "advise and consent." For some, the

President's actions were illegal, for others expedient and necessary. All agreed, the President had blurred the line between legal and illegal. How had this master politician done it?

First, he got his surrogates to espouse the idea of an exchange, apparently independently of the White House, a sort of heavy handed trial balloon. As the idea caught on, the military declared the ships obsolete and of little use to the United States. In addition, if an exchange took place, the British promised to never surrender their navy to Germany. In other words, the destroyers wouldn't come back to haunt the United States. In addition, the British promised to lease for 99-years various possessions deemed important to American security, including areas of the Bahamas, Trinidad, and Jamaica, British Guiana, and Antigua. All these new bases would protect the east coast of the United States, the Gulf of Mexico, and the Panama Canal. Finally, the Roosevelt's Attorney General concluded and supported the contentious notion that foreign policy was the purview of the president, and, therefore, the executive agreement was legal.

President Roosevelt also caught a break from an unusual source, the political opposition. Wendell Willkie, the Republican presidential challenger in the upcoming 1940 election, pledged not to make the destroyer deal a "big deal." That is, at least initially, Willkie, an internationalist and supportive of the President's foreign policy, did not take advantage of the situation. His partisanship ended at the water's edge. He also recognized that popular opinion was turning in the Roosevelt's direction. As the polls indicated:

> *Many voters believed that Roosevelt's experience was needed in the crisis, that he would prove more effective than Willkie in achieving preparedness; that one should not "swap horses in mid stream;" and that Roosevelt would be a more inspiring war leader should the United States be sucked into the abyss.*

The meaning of the destroyer deal was not lost on the Japanese. The United States was stepping less than gingerly into the European War, and, by extension, opposing Japanese aggressiveness in the Far East. Their foreign policies would take all this into consideration.

Peacetime Draft

They could have called it the Conscription Act of 1940, pure and simple, or even more to the point, The Draft Act. One word might have sufficed: Conscription. Everyone would have known what you were talking about. But not Congress, something more ornate or illusive was needed like the title *The Selective Training and Service Act of 1940* (STSA). Thinking about it, perhaps the name put politicians off, leading to a close vote in the House of Representatives, 203 to 202. That's right; one vote gave America its first peacetime draft in its history, August 12, 1941. Much easier in the Senate; perhaps the Senators liked the name better. Who knows?

With the backing of President Roosevelt, the legislation was introduced in a bipartisan manner by Edward R. Burke, D-NE and James W. Wadsworth, Jr., R-NY. As you would expect, the proposal was controversial in the extreme. The anti-internationalists asked if the legislation was even necessary given "Admiral Atlantic," which separated the US from Europe's war? They answered their own question, asking if this was just another effort by the White House to sally up to Britain? And what, they argued, would Japan think of such a conscription law? They would see it for what it was, a step to bolster America's defense of its Pacific possessions, mainly the Philippines.

A majority of the public was taking a different tack. Public opinion was evolving from strict isolationism to defensive precautions to intervention just shy of war. Polling in 1940 indicated that 67% of the respondents now believed a German/Italian victory in Europe would endanger the United States. Over 71% supported immediate adoption of a compulsory military training program as a necessary insurance policy. Pushing aside the notion of "cannon fodder," 69% of high school seniors agreed. When the legislation passed, President Roosevelt said what he had repeated many time during the debate:

> *America stands at the crossroads of i s destiny. Time and distance have been shortened. A few weeks have seen great nations fall. We cannot remain indifferent to the philosophy of force now rampant in the world. We must and will marshal our great potential strength to fend off war from our shores.*

How would draftees be chosen? A lottery would be used to determine who would serve an initial 12-month period and remain in the reserve for another 10-years. The lottery would be administered by 6,443 local draft boards, which would register young men between the ages of 21 to 30. Once registered, they could not leave the country, and once the conscription began in October 1940 no more than 900,000 could be in the service at any given time. The goal was to train 9,000,000 men by 1943. In an emergency, the required age could be reduced to 18 and the months of service could be extended. In an protracted emergency the length of service would be for the duration of the crisis.

Once registered local draft boards had to determine the fitness of an individual for the military. Three categories were established:

I – physically and emotionally fit for military duty.

II – exempted by reason of having an occupation deemed critical to the war effort.

III – deferred status because of family dependents.

IV – rejected for being physically and emotionally unfit for military duty.

There was, of course, an additional category. As in the 1918 war, what should be done with "conscientious objectors?" The answer was:

> *The act protected conscientious objectors. Nothing contained in the act shall be constructed to require any person to be subject to combatant training and service in the land and naval forces of the United States who, by reason of religious training and belief, is conscientiously opposed to participation in war in any form.*

Naturally, the question emerged, under the law, what work could they could be assigned? The answer, almost anything as determined by officials:

> *... noncombatant service as defined by the president, or shall if he is found to be conscientiously opposed to participation in such noncombatant service, in lieu of such induction,*

be assigned to work of national importance under civilian direction.

All those found fit for service were given the Army General Classification Test composed of 150 questions to take in 40-minutes to determine aptitude traits. An example question… Don't be too hasty in your answer.

Mike had 12 cigars. He bought 3 more and then smoked 6. How many did he have left?

As it turned out, a disproportionate number of low scorers ended up in the infantry. At the same time, the higher scorers ended up in the air corps. Somewhere in the middle were recruits for the navy.

Camp life was for many a rude awakening to military life. A typical day included:

6:05 A.M. – reveille.
8:00 – to 5:30 P.M. – cleaned barracks, trained and took evening mess.
7:00 P.M. – back in barracks.
9:45 P.M. – "lights out."

Eventually, there were over 242 hastily built training camps, most of which wer constructed in the South. Each camp had to meet certain necessary requirements, such as:

- 40,000 acres of varied terrain for weapons practice and maneuvers.
- a reliable water source good weather.
- adequate roads.
- access to rail transport.
- proximity to an urban center for recreation

One unanticipated consequence of the draft was the health of youthful recruits. The military improved the standard of living of a generation of Americans who had barely survived the depression. For the first time in their lives many were receiving 4,300 calories per day. The ubiquitous

C-ration and K-ration meals provided 3,400 calories if you ate everything, in addition to chewing on your four sticks of gum, and smoking an allotment of four cigarettes.

The draft was necessary in a world at war with itself. For the draftee, the change from civilian pursuits to military life was dramatic, for many life changing. One recruit, however, tried to put the whole business in perspective, suggesting that the first time a man goes into battle is:

> *... strangely like the first time a man makes love to a woman. The anticipation is overpowering, the ignorance is obstructive, the fear of disgrace is consuming, and survival is triumphant.*

Apparently, there is more than one way to prepare for a war.

The Speech

The British got their destroyers and America threw its neutrality stance into the Atlantic. At home the draft boards went to work removing any last doubts that the country would stay out of the European war. All that was needed now was a rallying cry to stir the country. On December 29, 1940 President Roosevelt provided the unforgettable words. Speaking on radio for 36-minues, at 9:30 P.M. EST, he pledged the nation to provide all out support to Britain and those fighting Nazi Germany. His theme was a sobering one, the mobilization of the country for war. A restive nation listened intently, when he stated America would be the "great arsenal of democracy."

The President provided a dose of realism to support his policy, pointing out:

> *If Great Britain goes down, the Axis powers will control the continents of Europe, Asia, Africa, Ausralasia, and the high seas --- and they will be in a position to ring enormous military and naval resources against this hemisphere.*

213

He went on to describe the situation in Europe and what it portended for America, stating:

> *The fate of these (occupied) nations tells us what it means to live at the point of a Nazi gun.*

He didn't mention Imperial Japan occupation of Korea, Manchuria, and China, but the message was clear; there was a global threat. Though he wanted to keep America out of a shooting war, the last hope for doing this now was to help Britain and China to save Americans from having to fight. He didn't explicitly pledge to keep the country out of war, only to try to remain out of one. The country understood the nuances of his words.

The President then justified his policies, pointing out that:

> *Europe does not ask us to do their fighting. They ask us for the implements of war, the planes, the tanks, the guns, the freighters, which will enable them to fight for their liberty and for our security. Emphatically, we must get these weapons to them, get them to them in sufficient volume and quickly enough, so that we and our children will be saved the agony and suffering of war which others have had to endure.*

Discerning listeners and certainly the isolationists comprehended the implications of the president's words. The only way to secure the shipment of military equipment to Britain in particular was by a convoy, which, because of the German submarine menace, would have to be escorted by destroyers. That meant, and there was no doubt about this, American naval ships would have to assist the British. America would be in the war even if it was undeclared. On the other side of the world it was all but the same with aid going to China.

The President reminded industry and labor of its obligations, really sacred responsibilities from his perspective, to maintain the splendid cooperation between the Government and industry and labor, and warned against disputes, saying:

> *The nation expects our defense industries to continue operation without interruption by strikes, or lockouts. It expects and*

insists that management and workers will reconcile their differences by voluntary or legal means.

Unsaid was an implied threat; the White House would settle disputes if labor and management failed to do so. Profits and wages were important, but so was getting the job done. And what was that job? As already noted, America had to be the "arsenal of democracy." He sounded the clarion call, explaining:

For this is an emergency as serious as war itself. We must apply ourselves to our task with the same resolution, the same sense of urgency, the same sprit of patriotism and sacrifice as we would show were we at war.

The speech ended. America was at war.

CHAPTER 26

THE LONELY SHIPS

September 1941 – At Home

The words still resonate with us...

It follows then as certain as that night succeeds the day, that without a decisive naval force we can do nothing definitive, and with it, everything honorable and glorious.

It was November 15, 1781 and President George Washington was writing to the Marquis de Lafayette about the importance of the navy to the young nation. The words still hold true.

—————

Alone they stay guard... Gracefully they patrol the seas, guarding convoys and their crews. Always, they understand, if necessary, they will place themselves between a torpedo and a troopship or a larger warship. They are always on duty, these destroyers, these lonely ships.

—————

The South Atlantic

The old steamship navigated ahead in the relatively calm waters of the South Atlantic, her crew going about their duties and the few passengers reading or dozing in the quiet sunlight on deck. Only the two lookouts, one at the bow, the other at the stern, were alert to the drama about to fall on the *SS Robin Moor*. It was May 21, 1941.

She had sailed under the American flag since she was built in 1919 at Hog Island, just outside of Philadelphia by the American International Shipbuilding Corporation. For that reason she was called a "Hog Islander," a name given to ugly but sturdy merchant vessels built for wartime duty.

There were 9 officers and 29 crewmen aboard the ship, plus 8 passengers, all headed from New York to Mozambique via South Africa, just another cargo ship with a full hull: 450 automobiles and trucks, steel rails, assorted tools, agricultural chemicals, 48,0000 US gallons of lubricants in drums, and a few cases of shotgun shells. A typical haul for a tramp steamer, aging nicely, one routine trip after another.

The forward lookout saw the submarine first, the U-69 as it surfaced, water flowing off its menacing hull. Signals were sent; the *Robin Moor* should heave to and stop. She did so in the tropical Atlantic, some 750 miles west of British-controlled Freeport, Sierra Leone and far from her original destination.

The ship's crew and passengers were forced to board the *Robin Moor's* four lifeboats. The *U-69* then fired one torpedo at the ship's rudder before using her deck gun to sink the steamer. This occurred even though the *Robin Moor* was flying the flag of a neutral country, the United States. The explanation for the incident, as stated by the U-69's captain was that the ship was carrying supplies to Germany's enemies. This view, however, was contradicted by the official naval policy of Admiral Erich Raeder that. "… in the next weeks all attacks on naval vessels in the closed area should cease." Apparently, this was an effort to avoid provoking the United States. Hitler didn't want the US in the war along side Britain.

Captain, Metzler, the master of the *U-69*, refused to let the *Robin Moor's* wireless operator radio her position. No "mayday" warning was permitted. The four boats were cast adrift with two tins of butter and four tins of pressed black bread, which proved to be too tough to chew.

It would be 18 days before a Brazilian merchant ship, the *Osorio*, rescued the crew and passengers.

Reaction in the United States was mixed. At first, our old friend, Senator Gerald Nye, blamed the British for sinking the *Robin Moor*, believing Germany had no reason to provoke the US. In time he changed his view to, "the evidence is confusing, unclear, and contradictory. Finally, he altered his view once again, arguing the "evidence that the *Robin Moor* was sunk by a German submarine is too complete." Senator Theodore F. Green (D-RI) stated, "I don't think the sinking will have any more effect than the sinking of the *Panay* by Japan. Representative Andrew J. Maas (R-MN) compared the two incidents, pointing out that Japan "not only failed to rescue the *Panay's* survivors but machine-gunned them afterward and we didn't go to war." Others supported this neo-pacifist attitude. Representative John William McCormack said it was "unfortunate but there is no reason now to get unnecessarily excited over this incident." Representative Andrew J. May, who was chairman of the House Military Affairs Committee, took a different, more aggressive stance: "We ought to convoy with battleships and let the shooting start and see who shoots first and who can outshoot.

Speaking on behalf of the American First Committee, Senator Burton K. Wheeler said, "70% of the *Robin Moor's* cargo constituted contraband, providing Germany with a justification for sinking the ship. He characterized the President Roosevelt's policies as "wanting to get the United States into the war in Europe." He also opposed arming American merchants ships.

On June 20, 1941, Roosevelt answered his critics with a message to the Congress. He made these points:

1. The *Robin Moor*, a neutral vessel, was sunk within 30-minutes after being stopped on the high seas
2. The ship was clearly marked as a neutral.
3. The *U-69* did not display a flag.
4. The *U-69* did not provide provisions for the safety of the crew and passengers.

The President then defended America's right to freedom of the seas, stating:

> *In brief, we must take the sinking of the Robin Moor as a warning to the United States not to resist the Nazi movement of world conquest. It is a warning that the United States may use the high seas of the world only with Nazi consent. Were we to yield this we would inevitably submit to world domination at the hands o the present leaders of the German Reich. We are not yielding and we do not propose to yield.*

The President made his case, arguing:

> *The sinking of this American ship by a German submarine flagrantly violated the right of the United States vessels freely to navigate the seas subject only to a belligerent right accepted under international law.*

The President then sent a less than subtle message to Berlin, Rome, and Tokyo:

> *The present leaders of the German Reich have not hesitated to engage in acts of cruelty and many other forms of terror against the innocent and the helpless in other countries, apparently in the belief that methods of terrorism will lead to a state of affairs permitting the German Reich to exact acquiescence from the Nations victimized.*

Beyond the *Robin Moor Incident* was an equally important issue; the right of the United States to escort a convoy of cargo ships across the North Atlantic to Britain, or across the Central Pacific to China. Conservatives had argued forcibly that "escort protection" would eventually lead to clashes with Germany and Japan. In that, their prophecy proved true.

The *USS Niblack (DD-424)*

On April 10, 1941, while bringing occupational troops to Iceland, the destroyer *Niblack* picked up three boatloads of survivors from a torpedoed merchant ship. Not long after, a submarine was detected and a depth charge attack was ordered, which drove off the *U-52*. This "bloodless battle" stands as the first action between American and German forces to that moment. Because of this incident and later ones, President Roosevelt went before the American people on September 11, 1941. In his broadcast he declared:

> *Henceforth the United States, not content with merely repelling attacks, would defend freedom of the seas by firing first at all Axis raiders operating within the American defensive areas.*

Essentially, the President was calling for "shoot-on-sight." The isolationists howled, protesting that the White House was "usurping the ear-declaring powers of Congress." Be that it may, American merchant ships were now armed and naval units were preparing to shoot and ask questions later. Another fateful step has been taken.

The USS Greer (DD-145)

The official written report by Admiral Harold R. Stark, Chief of Naval Operations, stated:

September 4, 1941

0840 - The destroyer *USS Greer* was carrying mail and passengers to Iceland. A British plane informed the *Greer* "of the presence of a submerged U-boat about 10 miles directly ahead. The *Greer* proceeded to search for the submarine.

0920 - The *Greer* located the submarine directly ahead of her by use of her underwater sound equipment. The *Greer* trailed the submarine and broadcasted the submarine's position.   These actions were in accordance with her orders to give out information but not to attack.

1032 - The British airplane left the area but not before dropping four depth charges in the vicinity of the submarine.

1240 – The submarine changed course and closed on the *Greer*.

1245 - An impulse bubble was detected. The submarine had fired a torpedo at the *Greer*.

1249 - A torpedo track was sighted crossing the wake of the ship from starboard to port, about 100 yards astern.

1250 – The *Greer* lost contact with the submarine.

1300 – The *Greer* again started to search for the submarine.

1512 – The *Greer* made underwater contact with a submarine. The *Greer* attacked immediately with depth charges.

The report indicated that the result of the encounter was undetermined. It was assumed the *U-652* survived. It had. Germany claimed:

> … that "the attack had not been initiated by the German
> submarine; n the contrary, the submarine had been attacked
> with depth bombs, pursued continuously in the German
> blockade Zone, and assailed by depth bombs until midnight.

Germany accused President Roosevelt of: "endeavoring will the means at his disposal to provoke incidents for the purpose of baiting the American people into the war."

President Roosevelt responded as follows:

> I tell you the blunt fact that the German submarine fired first
> upon this American destroyer without warning and with the
> deliberate design to sink her.

He declared Germany guilty of "an act of piracy" and officially announced his "shoot-on-sight" order. He claimed that Nazi submarines "present in any waters which America deems vital to its defense constitutes an attack." Continuing, he said:

In the waters we deem necessary for American defense, they (U-boats) do so at their own peril... The sole responsibility rests upon Germany

President Roosevelt's message was quite clear; war was coming with Germany and her allies, one of which was Japan.

The USS Kearny (DD-432)

October 17, 1941... Most people might not remember where they were that day, but the crew of one American destroyer would never forget. Earlier in the week the *Kearny* was docked at Reykjavik, Iceland, along with other American warships. Word reached the ship that a "wolf pack" had attacked a nearby British convoy. Her Canadian escorts were overwhelmed by the U-boats. The *Kearny* and three other destroyers were dispatched to assist. It was a rescue party by any other name. The ships reached the convoy and threw themselves into the fray, dropping depth charges to drive the submarines away.

The Germans, of course, fought back. A set of three torpedoes was fired by the *U-568*. One of them struck the Kearny on the starboard side. A huge hole was blown open in the middle of the ship. Smoke and fire immediately filled the air. Somehow the crew confined the flooding to the forward fire room. This enabled the ship to get out of the danger zone with power from the aft engine. Fortunately, she also regained power in the forward engine room and was able to steam (or limp) to Iceland at 10 knots, not her usual 30 plus speed.

As always, there were mixed responses from the United States. The isolationists insisted on avoiding war, and, of course, blaming President Roosevelt for putting American lives in harm's way. Interventionists saw it differently, and the White House steered a middle road, muting a push for war, while reminding Nazi Germany there were limits to the present neutrality policies. As the President said:

> *America has been attacked. The USS Kearny is not just a Navy ship. She belongs to every man, woman, and child in this nation... The purpose of Hitler's attack was to frighten the American people off the High seas --- to force us to make a trembling retreat. This is not the first time that he has misjudged the American spirit. That spirit in now aroused...*

The USS Reuben James (DD-245)

It was only a matter of time before it would happen. And then it did... On October 31, 1941 the destroyer, *Reuben James*, was torpedoed by a German U-boat and sunk some 600-miles west of Iceland. With four other destroyers, she had sailed from Newfoundland, escorting Convoy HX-156. At daybreak the *Reuben James* found a position between an ammunition ship and potential U-boats. As part of a "wolf pack," the *U-552* fired a torpedo at the merchant ship. The torpedo missed and hit the forward magazine of the *Reuben James* blowing the entire bow off the ship. The bow sank immediately. The aft section five minutes later. All seven officers were killed; 100 enlisted men died. Only 44 shipmates survived. Even as the ship sank the depth charges exploded, adding to the carnage.

A naval artist in the convoy described what he saw.

With a terrific roar a column of orange flame towers high into the nigh as her magazines go up.

Others saw the instantaneous damage: "The whole front of the ship lifted up and it was gone. Gone in an instant."

Response to the news differed widely. The *New York Times* editorialized: "The sinking brushes away the last possible doubt that the United States and Germany are now at open war in the Atlantic."

Senator Alben Barkley of Kentucky accused the Germans of trying "to drive Americans off the seas." He added, "I don't believe the American people are ready to be driven off." Taking a different stance, Senator George Aiken of Vermont said that Roosevelt was "personally responsible for whatever lives may have been lost because he had ordered convoy duty." Senator Gerald Nye added his two-cents, saying: "You can't expect to walk into barroom brawl and hope to stay out of a fight."

Not unexpectedly, Winston Churchill cabled President Roosevelt that he "grieved at the loss of life you have suffered with *Reuben James*. The *London Daily Mail* predicted on its editorial page that the United States was "marching down the last mile to a declaration of war." Japanese officials were strangely silent.

President Roosevelt was in a tangle. On the one hand, he wanted to smack back at Berlin. Or the other hand, the American military was not ready for war, especially with Germany's recent agreement with Japan, pledging each to help the other in case of war. Unlike President McKinley who only had to take on Spain after the *USS Maine* exploded, FDR was facing a potentially global conflict. Though Americans were upset, there was no general outcry for war. They too understood the gravity of the moment. The *New York Times* reported that: "The people, their Representatives in Congress and even many high officials of the government are deeply divided on the subject."

At least for the time being, officially America would remain neutral, but with periscopes peeking above the waves, and depth charges clanging into the sea, an uneasy peace couldn't last. In the meantime, the country would make do with a ballad by Woody Guthrie:

The Sinking of the Reuben James

> *Have you heard of a ship called the good Reuben James*
> *Manned by hard fighting men both of honor and fame?*
> *She flew the Stars and Stripes of the land of the free*
> *But tonight she's in her grave on the bottom of the sea.*

> *Tell me what were their names, tell me what were their names*
> *Did you have a friend on the good Reuben James?*
> *What were their names, tell me, what were their names?*
> *Did you have a friend on the good Reuben James.*

Well, a hundred men went down in that dark watery grave
When the good ship went down only forty-four were saved
That was the last day of October we saved the forty-four
From the cold ocean waters and cold icy shore.

Tell me what were their names, tell me what were their names
Do you have a friend on the Good Reuben James?
What...

CHAPTER 27

EINSTEIN'S LETTER

<u>October 1941 – New Orleans</u>

"If I appear somewhat irritable, Estelle, it's because of my hurried three train ride changes to New Orleans. That and the fact I left a guilty client in the hands of a young, inexperienced trial lawyer."

"Harlan, your grievance is noted."

"I trust my all day, all night bus ride from Chicago deserves some sympathy."

"Of course, Freda."

"I was right in the middle of a pitched fight with the police department. Two young men in the ghetto had been handled roughly, to say the least. On going story..."

"Still, you came. That's what counts."

"You said it was an emergency, Estelle, one we couldn't discuss on the phone, not even in writing. All very dramatic..."

"I too have been disjointed. My past two weeks at Berkeley interviewing brainy types at the University of California Department of Physics have left me both fearful and exhausted. I do wish, however, I had the luxury of chastising myself as you have."

"Okay, sensitivities aside, what's up, Estelle?"

"A new world that threatens all we hope to accomplish, Freda. A new world of molecular particles, which could blow up in humanity's face."

The conspirators, as noted, were meeting in New Orleans at the urgent request of their unofficial leader. They gathered at Horn's Restaurant, a neighborhood spot on Dauphine Street known for its appetizing fare, always modestly priced and generously served. Breakfast was over, which led to the spontaneous mini-rebellion by Harlan and Freda, and now to a degree of astonishment and incredulity.

"That remark, Estelle, requires exposition."

"Of course. But before we charge into the night, a little light. How was your breakfast?"

"Estelle, my Creole Slammer was delightful. A pile of golden hash browns topped with two eggs and crawfish thrown in; it was a wise choice."

"Harlan, your critique?"

"Something from the local synagogue, I think. Two potato latkes, plus two eggs, fresh grilled spinach topped with crawfish. Not bad for an unredeemed Christian with a Unitarian persuasion. And your choice, Estelle?"

"Cornbread waffle topped with two scrambled eggs."

"Estelle, as always, you picked wisely. Another good eatery... Now as to our meeting?"

"Harlan, I heard from my father again."

"Another cryptic message?"

"One word:

MAUD

"From which you divined what?"

"At first, nothing. Then a second communication a few days later, one I did recognize, which didn't mean I understood it.

CYCLOTRON

"Again, the same problem. What was my father getting at? A little research garnered little beyond this. A cyclotron is some sort of elaborate apparatus in which charged atomic and subatomic particles are accelerated. I had a working definition and no idea what it really meant. That's when I took a bus ride across the San Francisco Bay Bridge to Berkeley to look up an old friend who played with sophisticated mathematical equations beyond my struggles with algebra. After listening to my definitional woes, he smiled and sent me off the Physics Department for an impromptu education that led us to this meeting. What I learned on the QT startled me, as it will you. What I share does not go past this room."

"It influences our Ark?"

"As one might juggle TNT, yes."

The conspirators shared knowing looks with each other, checking as they did those around them for ears too attentive. Assured of their privacy, Freda beckoned to Estelle, saying, "Share."

"MAUD, as I learned in hushed voices was not an acronym; it was, however, a codename for a British committee to study the feasibility of producing a radically new weapon, what my source referred to as an atomic bomb."

"A what?"

"A weapon so powerful it could destroy a city, Freda."

"That weapon exists?"

"It's on the drawing board. The MAUD Committee determined that a 'sufficiently purified critical mass of uranium-235 could lead to fission. That said, the MAUD report estimated that a critical mass of ten kilograms would be 'large enough to produce an enormous explosion.' A bomb of this size could be loaded on an existing aircraft and be ready in approximately two years.' In other words a bomb could be produced in time to affect the outcome of the European war."

"The scientific jargon aside, such a bomb is possible?"

"Probable, Harlan. There is evidence that something called fission was discovered by the Germans almost three years ago and that since the spring of 1940 a large part of the Kaiser Wilhelm Institute in Berlin had been set aside for uranium research.' As to what fission is I cannot say anything beyond this. It is a necessary factor in the bomb making process. Apparently, the Nazis are hard at work to create such a weapon.

If what I was told is accurate, Berlin has at least a two year head start in manufacturing this unholy weapon."

"This is difficult to comprehend."

"And somehow my father, Harlan, divined this."

"And this cyclotron gadget?"

"The instrument by which the physicists unravel the secrets of the atom."

"The Germans are really in this monstrous race?"

"Indeed. A message intercepted by a British operative in Berlin noted that a German physicist wrote to Hitler's War Office, pointing out:

> *We take the liberty of calling your attention to the newest development in nuclear physics, which in our opinion will probably make it possible to produce an explosive many orders of magnitude more powerful than conventional ones. The country which first makes use of it has an unsurpassable advantage over the others.*

"Hitler is building a bomb?"

"Freda, it appears so."

"Such a weapon in the hands of that sociopath is too much to contemplate. Is our government is attempting to do this?"

"Freda, spurred by MAUD report, our country is in a deadly race with Berlin, our expatriated European physicists vs. those under Hitler's control."

"You're hinting at something, Estelle."

As was her father's attraction to the dramatic moment, Estelle found herself unwilling to immediately speak. She permitted curiosity and impatience to brew intolerably slowly before answering. She had been trained well by W.T.

"Some names... Leo Szilard... Emilio Segre... Enrico Fermi... Albert Einstein... J. Robert Oppenheimer... Edward Teller...Notice anything?"

"They sound European, German and Italian, I think."

"Right. Anything else, Freda?"

"Well, for whatever reason, they migrated to the United States."

"And why might they do that?"

"A wild guess. They were Jewish?"

"Yes. File this date away, April 7, 1933, Germany. The Nazi regime forced all non-Aryan civil servants to retire. Hundreds of university professors lost their jobs, including one-fourth of all German physicists, many of whom would later receive a Nobel Prize in Physics. In Italy, Mussolini employed the same racist policies, stating 'Jews do not belong to the Italian race.' The upshot of all this was a migration of scientists to England and the United States, providing the future allies with a 'priceless intellectual endowment' in the race to build an atomic bomb.'"

"Anti-Jew policies, though repugnant, actually had a positive consequence."

"No question about it, Freda. For example:

Leo Szilard – Hungarian Jew who first determined the possibility of a controlled chain reaction while at the University of Berlin. He realized he 'could make an explosion.' Forced out of Germany, he went to London, then to America. In some respects he's the Paul Revere of the Nazi threat."

Enrico Fermi – An Italian physicist who heard he had received the Noble Prize for Physics on November 10, 1938. That same day he also heard about the horrors of Kristallnacht when the insanity of anti-Semitism spread like a wild fire throughout Germany. Broken glass… Broken bodies… Broken dreams… Realizing his precarious position in Italy, he used his Nobel "winning'" to leave for the United States.

Albert Einstein – seeing the writing early on after Hitler came to power, he departed Germany for the Institute of Advanced Study at Princeton University in New Jersey where he could continue his theoretical studies without the Gestapo lurking in the shadows.

Edward Teller – A Hungarian physicist and Jew who also migrated beyond the reach of the Nazi grasp.

J. Robert Oppenheimer – A second generation German Jew and a top physicist at the University of California, Berkley, he was part of the intellectual drain on Berlin, at least indirectly.

"It's hard to believe but 30 top scientists and scholars, almost all Jewish, left Europe in 1933, and 32 the next year before the Nazi door closed, slamming shut escape from Germany."

"Those physicists who stayed in Germany, certainly they must have been concerned about this exodus, Estelle?"

"Of course. Chief among them was Werner Heisenberg who had questions not only about the loss of talent, but also whether or not the bomb should be built.

The psychological situation of American physicists, and particularly of those who have emigrated from Germany and who have been received so hospitably, is completely different from ours. They must all be firmly convinced that they are fighting or a just cause. But iN the case of an atom bomb by which hundreds of thousands of civilians will be killed instantly, warrantable even in defense of a just cause? Can we really apply the old maxim that the ends sanctify the means?

Heisenberg was asking uncomfortable questions. His rhetorical answers were less than comforting.

On other words, are we entitled to build atom bomb for a good cause but not for a bad one? And if we take that view... who decides which cause is good and which is bad? All in all, I think we may take it that even American physicists are not too keen on building atom bombs. But they could, of course, be spurred on by the fear that we may be doing so.

"In many ways the race to build a bomb was now between America's German scientists and Berlin's cadre of physicists. Certainly, there would be others from Canada and Britain. Nevertheless, there was an element of 'an in-house squabble' with a lot up for grabs."

The conspirators understood this, all too well.

———————

"Where do we go from here, Estelle?"

"October 11,1939, Harlan."

"Okay, because?"

"On that day Alexander Sachs, a longtime friend and unofficial economic advisor to President Roosevelt, brought a letter (dated August 2, 1939) to the Commander-and-Chief. The letter was from Albert Einstein, the celebrity scientist with the wild hair and shapeless clothing. He had written, along with Enrico Fermi, a message to sound an alarm by informing tRoosevelt that:

> *... recent research on fission chain reactions utilizing uranium made it probable that large amounts of power could*

be produced by a chain reaction and that, by harnessing this power, the construction of "extremely powerful bombs" was conceivable.

This new phenomenon would also lead to the construction of bombs, and it is conceivable --- though much less certain --- that extremely powerful bombs of a new type may thus be constructed. A single bomb of this type, carried by boat and exploded in a port, might very well destroy the whole port together with some the surrounding territory.

"Einstein indicated the 'German government was actively supporting research in this area and urged the United States to do likewise.' The President heard the warning and accepted the challenge. On October 19, 1939, the President sent an acknowledgement letter to Einstein thanking him for his recent correspondence."

I have convened a board consisting of the head of the Bureau of Standards and a chosen representative of the Army and Navy to thoroughly investigate the possibilities of your suggestion regarding the element of uranium.

In doing so, the President also gave credence to a second concern noted by Einstein:

I understand that Germany has actually stopped the sale of uranium from the Czechoslovakian mines, which she has taken over. That she should have taken such early action might perhaps be understood on the ground that the son of the German Under-Secretary of State, von Weizsackere, is attached to the Kaiser-Wilhelm Institute in Berlin, where some of the American work on uranium is now being repeated.

"The old theoretician was pointing out the need to gain control of the world's uranium supply, especially in the Belgium Congo. This warning was also heeded."

"We were certainly fortunate that Roosevelt acted, Estelle."

"True enough, Harlan. He didn't flinch from the challenge and costs, even before we were actively at war. Some credit, however, must be given to Alexander Sachs, who was picked by Einstein to deliver the letter to the White House. He would be the middleman, so to speak. That was indeed a good decision. No one was better equipped to make relevant the scientific material in an intelligible way to the President. No scientist, many have concluded, could have done it."

"Why was that?"

"Freda, in taking on this responsibility, Sachs was adamant that the letter be delivered by him in person, and that he actually read the letter aloud to Roosevelt in order to make the necessary impression and, if necessary, to answer any questions. On October 11, 1939 Sachs got his opportunity to speak to FDR for a long stretch. He put forth his own summary and conclusions. He explained the peaceful prospects of atomic energy and then turned his attention to the bomb, pointing out:

> *Personally I think there is no doubt that sub-atomic energy is available all around us, and that one man will release and control its almost infinite power. We cannot prevent him from doing so and can only hope that he will not use it exclusively in blowing up his next door neighbor.*

In response, the President said, "Alex, what you are after is to see that Nazis don't blow us up." Sachs quickly answered "Precisely."

"One question, Estelle."

"Harlan?"

"Were the Japanese also in the race?"

"Yes. And the Russians…"

"Then we need to build it. Such a weapon in the hands of our potential adversaries would be unthinkable."

"Estelle, you have that look."

"Which one, Harlan?"

"That, 'How do we deal with this look?'"

"I was just thinking… This terrible bomb… If it is built and used in the war my father predicted, the destruction will be unimaginable."

"And this business of radiation… A kind of lingering death even for the survivors."

"Freda, I had forgotten about that, a manmade virus threatening attempts at recovery."

"This is something else we'll need to account for in creating a new Ark. Always before, it was a question of controlling, if possible, what might be called conventional weapons. That was already a difficult proposition. How do we control the proliferation of atomic weapons? More challenging yet, how do we eliminate them? Where is all this headed?"

"If such weapons sprout like destructive weeds in the aftermath of the carnage we see today in Europe, only two possibilities come to mind. Either we will eventually destroy our civilization, or countries will live in mutual terror of each other, thereby providing some semblance of an uneasy peace."

"Harlan, is such a peace viable over the long run?"

"Humanity, it appears, is going to find out, and let's not forget what Einstein said in a moment of introspection: "We cannot solve our problems with the same thinking we used when we created them.""

CHAPTER 28

CONTRADICTIONS

<u>November 29, 1941 – San Francisco</u>

"I welcome you all."

Sean Murray was standing in his living room, a radiant smile on his face, exclaiming, "I finally meet all of you for the first time."

Outside the mid-morning fog was dissipating, leaving the Sea Cliff area of San Francisco sparkling bright as the sun's first rays warmed the affluent residential neighborhood. An uncommon Indian summer day beckoned.

"Tomorrow, as you know, I leave for my yearly excursion to Ireland by visiting a great number of Irish pubs in Boston for a few weeks. The U-boats have made it difficult to visit the old country. Hitler's stranglehold on Britain is so damnned inconvenient. Can't wait for that little man to be kaput. But for one day at least, I will enjoy your company and your intrigue. From what Estelle tells me, you are well traveled, well fed, and more knowledgeable than most about that live grenade called the Far Pacific."

As Sean Murray spoke, a trusted older Filipino man quietly and efficiently gathered the breakfast dishes, leaving only coffee cups to be refilled. It was obvious he was practiced at his arts.

"Javier has been with me for years, a trusted member of my family who will take good care of you in my absence. Maria, his wife, is in the kitchen, a lady who is a wizard with pots and pans, as I assume you noticed at breakfast. In her able hands you will not lack for nutritious meals with a bit of a southwestern flair due to her many years in New Mexico as a fast-order cook along Old Route 66."

If the morning meal was an indicator, Sean Murray was acknowledging what was already understood. Maria's breakfast omelet with bits of bacon, mild peppers, tangy cheese, chopped green onions, and a light touch of salsa made for a fantastic egg dish. The hot, homemade biscuits with a layer of butter only added to the fare. The coffee, a Colombian import from high in the local mountains, was especially flavorful.

"Permit me to introduce Doctor Evelyn Flores, whom you've met earlier at breakfast. At the urging of Estelle, I contacted her. She will be your mentor for the next few weeks. Estelle, perhaps a word before Dr. Flores speaks?"

"Two special words, actually, Sean, 'Thank you' for making your home available for us. As did my father, W.T. Stead and others, all those who came before us in their Hull House hideout twenty-years ago, we appreciate the generous use of your home."

"I also add my gratitude, as does Freda. Your Sea Cliff sanctuary is most appreciated."

"Harlan, the least I could do. That it helps in your work is all that I can ask. With that, let's hear from our speaker."

"It's a pleasure to be with you. Estelle has provided me with a glimpse into your secretive enterprise and, of course, the 1910 origins of the effort. How much I can assist you is a matter of conjecture. At this point war in the Pacific appears to be a foregone conclusion, as will be the need for your Ark in the aftermath. What I share with you today cannot deter what appears to be inevitable. Possibly, I can fathom for you some understanding of what is taking place, since I bring a unique perspective to the issues. My mother was Filipino, my father was Japanese and they met in Manila, where I lived until attending college at San Jose State here in California. In time I received a doctorate in Political Science with a focus on the psychology of governance. That will be our focus today. We will try to understand why Tokyo and Washington act as they do, and the contradictions that define their relationship. One other thing before I start. We will look at the Far East crisis from the perspective of a third person. Perhaps in this way we can be more objective in appraising the facts.

Contradictions

"To begin... The United States finds itself today unprepared for a war it seems unable to avoid. Japan, though more prepared for war, finds herself trying to avoid one. What we have here are two statements that both mirror and oppose each other; that is, the statements are riddled with inconsistencies and contradictions. For example, recently President Roosevelt told Harold Ickes, a trusted adviser, that in helping Britain against Germany it was:

> ... *terribly important for the control of the Atlantic for us to help to keep peace in the Pacific. I simply have not got enough Navy to go a round and every episode in the Pacific means fewer ships in the Atlantic.*

"Of course, the question arises: how do you keep peace in the Pacific when you are overtly assisting Japan's ally, the Nazi regime?"

"That's a paradox."

"Freda, that's what I'm getting at. American naval ships are needed in the Pacific to deter Japan. At the same time the convoys to England must be protected. Going on, the more the United States tried to halt an expansive, aggressive Japanese foreign policy in Asia, the more she provoked Tokyo. The more Japan pursued her sense of 'manifest destiny' in Asia the greater the American resistance, leaving both countries heading for a collision."

"They couldn't extricate themselves from their policies?"

"Harlan, policies can take on a life of their own."

"Self-justifying?"

"To some extent, yes. Another example ... Unable to reach some sort of compromise (or accommodation) with the moderates in the Japanese government, American resistant policy encouraged the militarists in Tokyo to take over the reins of power. General Tojo is now in power, representing an uncompromising military authority, and exactly what the United States wanted to avoid. This hardliner wants to pursue the war in China, and is prepared to seek a military advantage in Southeast Asia, knowing full well that this will mean war with the United States. Washington will not permit Japan to take over the Dutch East Indies, Indo-China, Thailand, and continue to oppose Japan's invasion of China."

"Does President Roosevelt have any other option?"

"He does, Harlan, and he has used them. The American embargo of exports to Japan, including oil, scrap iron, and steel, attempted to influence Tokyo to alter its policies. The same is true of the boycott of Japanese goods and the freezing of Japanese assets in the United States. The hope was Japan would mollify its policies. Unfortunately, this is not the case. Economic policies have disturbed Japan, but not intimidated her. The net result is a Japanese resolve to free herself of dependence on America oil (80%) by finding and controlling alternative sources, mainly Southeast Asia. Though the use of boycotts and embargoes was used by the United States to peacefully influence Japan that has not happened. On the other hand, Tokyo viewed such policies as a form of 'economic warfare, perilously close to an official declaration of war."

"America is pursuing the wrong policies, Dr. Flores?"

"Not necessarily wrong, Estelle. Rather, policies with inherent contradictions. This, however, is also true of the Japanese."

"Neither government understands this?"

"Whether they do, or don't, that know longer matters. Each side is unable to break the cycle, Freda. They are habituated to their own rhetoric, the aims and goals of their foreign policy are held hostage to a cycle of action and reaction with each side persuaded it is on the right side of history. Another example comes to mind.

<u>China</u>

"What's at the heart of the crisis in the Far East?"

"Good question, Harlan. In a word China. The United States is trying to maintain peaceful relations with Japan while providing military and financial aid to China, Japan's sworn enemy. America is an active ally of China and is indirectly already at war with Japan. After years of fighting in China at great expense and troop losses, Japan cannot end her invasion of the country. To renounce her incursion into China would be a disastrous 'loss of face.' More than that, it would be a victory for an American hegemony in Asia as the Japanese see it. Japan's desire for a new order in the Pacific would end. The imperialists would maintain the status quo, imposing on Asia an American-sponsored and supported 'world order.' Under these conditions, and according to the militarists, Japan would revert back to being a 'third rate nation,' dominated by the United States."

"If we relinquished our support of China, would that not mollify Japan?"

"Yes, Harlan, but the pro-China forces in the United States would see it as appeasement out of fear of provoking Japan. Roosevelt would find it difficult to defend such a policy, especially after the 'rape of Nanking.' Of course, even if the President altered direction, Japan would still covet the oil and foodstuffs of Southeast Asia. There would be no guarantee against an aggressive move in Indo-China and the Dutch East Indies. However, there is still another problem."

"Which is?"

"John Hay's Open Door Policy still influences the White House. The United States requires a Chinese market open to all countries. America wishes to sell some of her surplus products in Asia and to obtain raw materials, such as rubber. A China under total Japanese control would dominate the country and control trade. This was not a hypothetical case. It was already happening. Japan had placed restrictions on foreign business firms."

"Tokyo won't modify its policies?"

"Freda, not in an appealing way to the United States. The American Secretary of State, Hull stated his country's case as such:

The United States has its rights and interests there just as Japan. American opinion believes it to be incompatible with the establishment and maintenance of American and world prosperity that any nation should endeavor to establish a preferred position for itself in another country.

"Hull amplified this position with what was called the **Four Principles.** They include:

1. The territorial integrity of China must be maintained. Consequence: Japan must withdraw its army from China.
2. There must be non-interference in the internal affairs of China. Consequence: The government of China must be free and independent of any country.
3. There must be equal economic opportunity for all countries in China. Consequence: No one country should control commerce and business in China except for the Chinese.
4. Any alteration of the status quo in the Far East must be through peaceful means. Consequence: The use of force to settle disputes must be curtailed and subject to a peaceful resolution.

"Essentially, Hull was arguing the US position for maintaining the existing world order, based on a liberal, Western notion of internationalism. Japan could either join this new order or be isolated in an economic sense. The world order proposed by Washington was, of course, an updated **Washington System**, and contrary to Japan's position:

Japan's main concern was with having the United States recognize the fait accompli in Asia, thus acquiescing in Japan's control over China and possibly Southeast Asia.

Stated more forcibly, the Japanese were questioning America's role in Asia and elsewhere, stating:

The United States must stop trying to act a the world's policeman and refrain from intervening in other countries' spheres of living."

"Hull's policies were in opposition to Japan's hope to:

>...*build a **New Order or a Greater East Asia Co-Prosperity Sphere**, and this meant domination of the area by Japan so that she could obtain space for her surplus population, essential raw materials, and markets, and a buffer zone against the Europeans.*

"How can these views be reconciled, Professor Flores?"

"Not easily, even assuming all parties are sincere in their efforts to maintain peace, Freda."

"Does Japan really want a war with the United States?"

"No, Tokyo understands that in a protracted war with America, the Japanese cannot win. This outcome is even more certain if Japan is countered by the **ABCD** powers (America, Britain, China, and the Dutch). Moreover, if the Soviet Union jumped into the fray given its interests in Siberia and Manchuria, the equation becomes even more complicated and less inviting for Japan."

"Then Japan doesn't want a war."

"Not exactly. If war breaks out, Japan desires it to be short and in her favor."

"Is that possible?"

"Harlan, possible, but not necessarily probable."

"And that means what?"

"So much would be determined by the first six months of the war, and the involvement of other nations, plus the situation in Europe. In the final analysis, nothing is assured."

"Still, under the best of circumstances, what would victory look like for Japan?"

"At least three things: first, an early naval victory over the United States. Second, a quick and victorious military thrust into Southeast Asia. Third, the United States would accept Tokyo's dominant position in the Far East and agree to some form of settlement.

"Assuming that situation didn't occur, what about the United States improving her defenses in the Pacific to deter the Japanese, Professor Flores? Wouldn't that give the Japanese reason to pause?"

"Estelle, from a third party view, not necessarily. For example, the following actions have already been taken by the United States, or are contemplated:

- Inaugurating a peacetime draft.
- Passing legislation to modernize and expand the navy.
- Pushing immense defense contracts.
- Fortifying Pacific possessions, Hawaii, Guam, Wake Island, Midway, and the Philippine Islands.
- Tying down mutual defense agreements with Australia and New Zealand, the Dutch, the French, and the British in the Pacific.

"Each action can be seen by Japan as a provocation leading to an equivalent response. Each action is perceived by Tokyo as a preparation for a war that the United States hopes to avoid. That is the great paradox."

Sean Murray had listened with rapt attention, obviously dismayed by the relentless case for war no matter how unintended. Finally, unable to contain himself, he asked, "What about Nazis? Will they support Japan?"

"Yes, short of fighting the United States, Sean. What would they do? First, they do not want direct American involvement in the European conflict. Berlin recalls what happened when Wilson sent the 'doughboys' to France in 1918. Second, a war in Asia would distract America from aiding Britain and the Soviet Union to an even greater extent. That was in Berlin's interests. Third, Hitler knows the United States wants to avoid a two-front, two-ocean war. He's encouraging Japan to expand into Southeast Asia, hoping to draw American forces into a Pacific war. He's counting on that. Let the Americans fight and die in the Pacific. Keep them out of the Atlantic."

"You paint an ugly picture."

"I do, Sean."

"Then where are we?"

"Each side is playing for time, but for different reasons. The United States needs time to build up its military, at least another year. The Japanese, on the other hand, are running out of time. They cannot wait for the Americans to achieve overwhelming superiority in the Pacific. They understand the implication of the Vinson-Trammel Act, which will be discussed in a moment. But first; as often occurs, the expenditures for defense can lead to an alternative view. What can be used for defense may also have offensive capabilities. What appears to be a strategy to maintain the peace may also be seen as aggressive and war-threatening. \"

A Two-Ocean Navy

"Though they never graduated from Annapolis, Admirals Pacific and Atlantic were always in the forefront of American defense plans. The two oceans did separate America from the wars in Asia and Europe, but they also had to be defended. That meant a two-ocean navy. In 1934, the Vinson-Trammell Act provided for a major increase in naval strength --- 102 new warships over an eight-year period with a heavy emphasis on aircraft carriers and submarines. This construction, once completed, provided for a near equivalence with Japan's navy, assuming Tokyo didn't respond in kind. A second Vinson Act in 1938 mandated a 20% increase in naval strength. This legislation was in direct response to Japan's invasion of China and Hitler's annexation of Austria. A third act, the Vinson-Walsh Act of 1940, just a few months ago in July, increased the size of the Navy by 70%. Harold Stark, the Chief of Naval Operations, had requested $4,000,000,000. By a majority vote of 316 – 0, Congress authorized $8,555,000,000 with an even stronger emphasis on aircraft carriers. Representative Vinson stated:

> *The modern development of aircraft has demonstrated conclusively that the backbone of the Navy today is the aircraft carrier. The carrier, with destroyers, cruisers, and submarines grouped around it, is the spearhead of all modern naval task forces.*

"As I said earlier, each side was watching the clock. Both sides understood the meaning of the American military buildup, and the strategies each country might use in case of war. By mid-1940, there were few secrets."

"Strategies?"

"The results of war games played on both sides of the Pacific."

"Which influenced policy?"

"Decidedly. We'll review them after lunch. I'm somewhat famished after cross-crossing the Pacific so often. The world crisis will have to hold off until after lunch if you approve, Estelle?"

———————

Lunch turned out to be a sort of do it yourself affair. The conspirators, Dr. Ramos, and Sean Murray gathered outside in the backyard, which afforded a picturesque view of the Golden Gate Bridge and the headlands of Marin County. Javier was at the BBQ cooking thick, juicy hamburgers, while Maria was bringing out the fixings --- buns, lettuce, onions, pickles, mustard and catsup. Already on the large picnic table was a bowel of baked beans and a container of chips. To the delight of some there were bottles of Rainer Beer, and Coco Cola for others. Not to be outdone by these bourgeoise offerings, there was also a chilled Riesling wine from Napa County.

"We took a chance that the oft criticized weatherman might be right for once and a sunny day would envelop the city for a true all-American meal, including chunks of apple pie for dessert. So "pirates all, join in our little fest."

"Sean, you certainly know how to treat your guests."

"Freda, I try."

"And what a view, the straits of the Golden Gate and the Pacific beyond."

"Indeed, Harlan, and if you look keenly a friend heading westward."

Sean was pointing at a large aircraft carrier just now approaching the famous bridge, planes latched to every available space on the deck. Accompanied by a trio of destroyers, the ships passed under the Golden Gate Bridge in single file.

"Headed for our base at Pearl Harbor in Hawaii, I suspect, and dressed in war paint."

"To strengthen our forces, Estelle."

Eating quietly, those present watched the ships for a long time, then, as they disappeared over the horizon, wondered what fate awaited them. For some reason the moment felt spiritual, transcending the usual dismal news from the Far East. Young men were embarking on ships that hope to keep the peace, even as other young men on other ships were doing the same. Somewhere out there beyond their ties to home and family, work and school, their jobs and professions, they might meet to settle issues beyond the political skills of their leaders. Somewhere...

Planning for War

In time lunch was over and Dr. Ramos resumed her lecture. The burgers were eaten. The ships were gone.

"It was called Plan Orange. It referred to a series of options developed by the American War Department to deal with a possible war with Japan after the 1918 squabble n Europe. The plan took into account that Japan would attack the United States and the following would happen:

1. The Japanese would blockade and invade the Philippines.
2. Wake Island and Guam would be attacked.
3. A possible attack might be made on the Panama Canal.
4. Ships would be mobilized in California and Hawaii to sail westward to relieve areas attacked.
5. The fleet would then sail northward to crush the Japanese in one decisive battle.

"The Japanese had an equivalent plan. It was sometimes referred to as the Southern Strategy. It included:

1. The Philippines, Guam, and Wake Island would be attacked.
2. Another force would invade Indo-China, the Dutch East Indies, and Malaya.
3. Hong Kong and Singapore would be attacked.
4. Japanese based land planes would attack the advancing American fleet.
5. Submarines would also whittle down the battle fleet.
6. A final decisive naval battle would be fought near the home islands where Japan would have naval superiority.

"In 1939 and 1940 adjustments were made in the Orange Plan based on two realities: first, San Francisco was 7,000 miles from Manila. Second, Hawaii was 5,000 miles the Philippines, and longer yet to Japan. The distances demanded refueling stations in the Pacific. Beyond Pearl Harbor in Hawaii, Japanese held islands in the Central Pacific would have to be captured and turned into forward bases with air cover for the fleet. The advance across the Pacific would take and year or more, and be bloody. The Japanese also accepted these revisions as probabilities and carefully planned for them in their war games.

"Both sides envisioned a final major ship-to-ship battle between large opposing forces. After all, wasn't this the way naval war had been conducted for 300-years? Isn't that what Admiral Mahan had taught to generations of sailors. However, according to some naval experts, and rebellious young Turks, neither side fully appreciated the technological advances in submarine warfare and naval aviation, which would affect their preconceived notions of warfare. Nor has either side fully anticipated how a pre-emptive strike by either side might alter their calculations."

"Pre-emptive?"

"An attack, Harlan, without a previous declaration of war."

"The Americans would do this?"

"If pushed to the extreme, an attack from the Philippines has a logic. Of course, this works in reverse. A Japanese attack on the archipelago is also in the realm of possibility."

"But would either side do it?"

"Harlan, a better question might be: 'Why not?'"

Quiet descended as all considered the possibilities of a pre-emptive strike. There was something frightening and dark about such an action, which led to even greater suspicions of a potential enemy. Freda finally broke the silence.

"With the Pacific full of warships, doesn't that guarantee the peace, Professor Ramos?"

"Not necessarily. Of course, both nations feel the very existence of their fleets precludes either country from going to war. You're right, Freda. The events, however, leading up to the European war in 1914 suggests otherwise. That proposition --- armaments mean peace --- is again being tested, not only with arms but also with economic warfare. Recently, the

American ambassador to Japan, Joseph Grew warned President Roosevelt against the use of sanctions, pointing out:

> *If we once start sanctions against Japan, we must see them through to the end. If we cut off Japanese supplies of oil, Japan in all probability will send her fleets down to take the Dutch East Indies.*

"At this point it appears that both the United States and Japan are dancing to the same tune. Each side has sidestepped a cycle of escalating moves that 'provoked but failed restrain the other.' Undeterred by this, both sides continue to escalate the level of confrontation in ever risker ways. As one historian stated the case:

> *Tokyo calculates what aggression it can pursue without precipitating open conflict with Washington. The Americans gamble that they could pressure Japan by economic means without driving Tokyo to war.*

For each side, the attitude of the other remains a secondary consideration. Japan's highest priority is still China and her control of that country. America's priority is to keep this from happening. Any possible middle ground is seeping through diplomatic fingers in both Tokyo and Washington.

"Then war will break out in the Pacific?"

"It already has in all but name, Estelle. The war plans are in place. The ships are built. The treaties are signed."

"Treaties?"

"Our next topic."

CHAPTER 29

SCRAPS OF PAPER

NEWS HEADLINES

Japan today rejected the latest U.S. proposals as "fantastic and unrealistic."

U.S. President Franklin D. Roosevelt cut short his vacation in Warm Springs, Georgia and returned to Washington due to the critical situation in the Pacific.

"Our topic today focuses on treaties, and the twin bookends of diplomacy, outright cynicism as opposed to heartfelt idealism. By definition, a treaty is a formally concluded and ratified agreement between countries. A pact is a formal agreement between an individual and parties, and can have the weight of law behind it. An agreement is a negotiated contract typically binding on both parties as a legal arrangement. Keep those terms in mind as we discuss two treaties."

Dr. Flores was in Sean Murray's spacious, book-lined library in the Sea Cliff residence. Sean had left right after breakfast, suitcases in hand

and a gentle Irish smile on his face. As he departed he left the conspirators with an old Celtic blessing to keep the devil at bay and the joy of life in their hearts.

> *May God give you …*
> *For every storm, a rainbow,*
> *For every care, a promise,*
> *And a blessing in each trail.*
> *For every problem life sends,*
> *A faithful friend to share,*
> *For every sigh, a sweet song,*
> *And an answer for each prayer.*

The BBQ weather of yesterday was long gone, replaced by fog in the morning, sun in the afternoon, and increments of transition in the interval, leaving San Francisco with a cool 65 degrees and a cloudless sky. That being the case and with a stiff breeze off the Pacific, the conspirators were meeting in Sean's study as that was the most appropriate thing to do.

The Tripartite Pact

"Time to deal with two treaties. The date is September 27, 1940, a little over a year ago. The location is Berlin. The invited guests of Adolf Hitler are the representatives of Japan and Italy. The purpose of the gathering is to sign a mutual self-defense agreement, the Tripartite Pact. War had broken out in Europe with the Nazi invasion of Poland and the Far East was about to explode. That being the case, this agreement was in response to an expanding American assistance to Britain as well as increased resistance to Japan's invasion of China. The stated purpose of the agreement was that its members would:

> *… support one another should any nation not currently at war in Europe, or involved in the Second Sino-Japanese War, attack one of them.*

249

"They were thinking, primarily, were they not, of the United States, Dr. Ramos?"

"Without doubt, Estelle."

"And for their mutual benefit."

"That's the fact of the matter, Harlan. If attacked by the United States, Japan wanted allies. Berlin and Rome had the same desire in case America ended up in the European fracas. There was something more at work here. All three countries believed that every nation had a proper place in the world. With that in mind, Rome and Berlin would 'cooperate with Tokyo other in Japan's efforts to create a new order in the Greater East Asia region. Japan would do the same with respect to Europe and North Africa respectively It was their prime purpose to:

> ... *establish and maintain a new order of things, calculated to promote the mutual prosperity and welfare of the people concerned.*

"In other words they wanted the United States to mind its own business."

"That's one way of saying it, Freda."

"Accept Nazi rule in Europe and Japan's place in China?"

"Yes."

"And if America chose to interfere in the Far East, Germany and Italy would be at war with us?"

"A big of a gray area here, Harlan. Neither country was explicitly bound to declare war on the United States in order to aid Japan. Berlin might reason it was best to stay out of that one, at least on an official basis. Why push the Yankees?"

"And Italy?"

"Not really a factor, Estelle."

"Exactly what did the Pact say?"

"There were six articles, including:

Article 1 - Japan recognizes and respects the leadership of Germany and Italy in the establishment of a new order in Europe.

Article 2 - Germany and Italy recognize and respect the leadership of Japan in the establishment of a new order in Greater East Asia.

"Essentially, they were dividing up the world. Berlin would dominate the European continent. Japan would do the same in the Far East. America would be left alone to do the same in the Western Hemisphere."

"Would that arrangement last, Dr. Ramos?"

"Difficult to determine. It hasn't yet been tested. If America accedes to this, than yes, at least in the short run... If America intervenes, and this is the current case, than no... One other point... This was a cynical treaty among three nations with little love for each other. Each was using the other for reasons particular to their situation. Japan needed friends in a potential war with the United States. Italy needed an ally to save her hide in North Africa. Germany wanted a friend in Asia to distract the United States and keep her out of Europe. Beyond military authoritarianism, the three nations shared little beyond an acceptance of a Darwinian world where only the strong survive by oppressing other countries in a vicious form of ethnic and racial imperialism. They offered the world little more than the sword."

Whether Dr. Ramos was sharing an editorial or simply articulating prejudicial views was difficult for the conspirators to discern. That her objectivity as an academic was compromised was also an open issue... What was evident, however, was an abiding dislike for the three regimes in question.

"We're also dealing with a second treaty?"

"Oh, yes. To get at it, we'll being with a battle unknown to almost every American, the Battles of Khalkhin Gol - September 15, 1939 to September 17, 1939. Just two days of furious fighting between Russian and Japanese forces on the border between Mongolia and Manchuria.

"You're right, Professor Ramos, I never heard of it."

"Not to worry, Freda, you're about to get acquainted. The Russian named the battle after the Halha River that passed nearby. The Japanese called it the Nomonhan Incident after the small village on the border of Mongolia (under Russian control) and Manchuria (under Japanese control). It was for both sides a decisive victory for the Russians after years of border incursions and small and deadly firefights. The Russian victory led to Japan being expelled from Mongolia."

"This has something to do with a treaty?"

"Indeed. The Japanese learned three lessons: first, the heavily armed Soviet Siberian troops were tough soldiers. There would be no Japanese advance into Mongolia. A stalemate existed. Second, Moscow, if it decided to do so, would continue to assist the Chinese government with military aid in order to keep Tokyo preoccupied. Third, both the Russians and the Japanese needed to avoid a two-front war. For Japan that meant peace with the Soviets in case of war with the United States. For Moscow the same approach was necessary, peace with Japan, and a focus on Nazi hoards already invading the Soviet Union. Necessity required an agreement to neutralize each other in case of wear with a third party."

"No philosophical or political attraction, Dr. Ramos?"

"None. This marriage was a matter of need, nothing more, Harlan."

"Basically, cynical reasoning to achieve an end. Once the need was gone, any agreement would be scrapped. Each side knew that."

"Exactly, what was the agreement?"

Soviet-Japanese Neutrality Pact

"This was a non-aggression pact signed on Aril 13, 1941, again only a few months ago. Article 1 avowed that 'both parties agreed to maintain peaceful and friendly relations.' Short and sweet, this was an attempt to forgo past hostilities, at least temporarily. Article 2 was more complicated. It stated:

> ... *that if one party became embroiled in hostilities with a third party the other party to this agreement would remain neutral.*

"Recall that Japan is already an ally of Germany and Italy through the Tripartite Pact. If honored, Japan would need to take up arms in support of the Soviet Union. Scrumptiously, however, Japan had avoided this action. The new agreement with Russia merely confirmed what was already a reality."

"Both sides were wary of each other?"

"To say the least, Freda. When the time was right they would break the agreement."

"This is like the Nazi-Soviet Non-Aggression Pact of 1939?"

"Exactly. Temporary stability, nothing more."

"As you said, merely a scrap of paper."

"Dr. Ramos, I'm beginning to see the relationship between the Battle of Khalkhin Gol and the Soviet-Japanese Neutrality Pact. The border stalemate required forced the issue. Stability was needed in order to deal with other problems."

"Exactly, Estelle. And let me add this; there was a side agreement with each side pledged to:

> ... *respect the territorial integrity and inviolability of Manchukuo for Japan and the Mongolia People's Republic for the Soviet Union.*"

"In closing, it's important to understand four things. First, the Soviet Union would, regardless of consequences, never let Japan control Mongolia since that would be a dagger aimed at the heart of Soviet Siberia. Second, for the same reason, Japan would deny Russian control of Manchuria; that dagger would not threaten the Japanese. Third, Moscow could now deal with the Nazi blitz. Fourth, Japan was now free to focus on Southeast Asia and the Philippines. In Washington the government understood the implications of the 'neutrality pact.'"

"Another step toward war?"

"More, I think, that an undeclared wars already existed, not only with guns, but also trade policies, which happens to be our next topic."

"You're saying, are you not, that America was already at war, Professor Ramos?

"Estelle, an undeclared war, yes."

CHAPTER 30

TIGHTENING THE SCREWS

December 2, 1941 – Tuesday – San Francisco

NEWS HEADLINES

President Roosevelt sent Japan a request for an explanation for the heavy Japanese troop concentrations in French Indochina, exceeding the 25,000 agreed upon between Tokyo and Vichy France.

The storm began in the Aleutians, a mere speck in the North Pacific, almost unnoticed. Then it slowly gathered strength before heading southward toward the west coast of Alaska. As it did the storm drew in a plume of moisture from the warmish Japanese current, so much so that eventually torrential rains would soon pound Fairbanks and Juneau. As the storm grew in size it rumbled with thunder and lit of the sky with bolts of lightning. The ocean turned angry. High waves battered the coastline, smacking into moored boats and sleepy fishing villages. Still the storm moved southward, clawing its way past British Columbia, and then the Puget South area, abetted slightly by the polar jet stream. Seattle was pelted with golf ball size hailstones. Portland was swamped by heavy showers. There at the "Rose City" the storm paused for a long minute as it gathered strength for a headlong dash along the California coast, first pelting Crescent City, Eureka, and Napa. The winds picked up, great invisible currents in the sky, now flowing into the Bay Area before barging into San Francisco and drenching the city. For three days the storm stalled over the "city of Saint Francisco" and then, unobtrusively it wheeled seaward to slowly disappear over the horizon.

The storm was gone for now.

Breakfast was over. Nothing too special: Maria's pancakes, light and moist, heated New Hampshire maple syrup, butter from a local California diary, and strips of crisp bacon courtesy of the non-rabbinical world. A side dish of cleaved fresh strawberries was just the thing for the conspirators, along with refills of coffee. As always, Julio quietly removed dishes, refilled empty cups, always with an enchanting smile and quick hands. Outside the rain fell and fell.

Dr. Ramos pushed aside her notes, rose, and said, "Today we take a hard look at President Roosevelt's economic policies toward Japan. By necessity, we will have to ask some difficult questions, which, I'm afraid, might lead to uncomfortable answers. Before we do so, however, it's time to define three words, each of which bears upon our topic: an embargo, a sanction, and a boycott. Let's begin.

"An embargo is an official ban on trade or other commercial activity with a particular country. It is an official prohibition on an activity. By way of example, the United States might proclaim an oil embargo with Japan to deny Tokyo the 'black stuff' that powers ships and tanks. A boycott is an official withdrawal from a commercial or social relation with a country, organization, or individual. Again, using Japan as an example, the United States might refuse to trade with the Far East powerhouse. A sanction occurs when a penalty is threatened for disobeying a law or rule. The United States might coerce Japan to stop threatening Indo-China or the Dutch East Indies by placing restrictions on trade in order to gain a change of policy. In all of these examples, there is a high risk. Countries don't like being pushed around, not by the threat of guns or economic policies. More often than not, they may respond in an unexpected way."

"Which is at the heart of your lecture today?"

"Yes, Estelle. Today we deal with the nature of unpredictability, what might be called unintended consequences. Shall we begin?"

Chronology

"Background information is always useful. That being the case, we begin in 1911,

1911 Treaty of Commerce and Navigation with Japan

This treaty provided for a most-favored nation clause between the signatories. It also established a legal basis for commerce, navigation, property rights, travel, and access to courts of the nationals of each country. The treaty went into effect on July 17, 1911, providing mutual benefits to all parties.

In the 1930's problems emerged with the agreement. Congress was unhappy with the export of American goods to Japan at a time when Tokyo was aggressively expanding into China. There was also unease over Japanese violations of US property and citizens in Japanese-occupied areas of China. In addition, the most favored-nation clause made it illegal to adopt retaliatory measures against Japanese commerce to stem Tokyo's China policies. The United States wanted out of the treaty.

In July 1939 the United States gave notice to Japan that it would terminate the agreement. This would be done at the end of a six-month period prescribed by the agreement. Once terminated, the last obstacle to a legal embargo by the United States on exports to Japan.

Two questions emerged for us. First, were economic conditions or political concerns motivating American policy? Second, would Japan alter its policies in China in response to the termination of the treaty? Keep those questions in mind.

1938 – Moral Embargos

Exports of airplanes, aeronautic equipment, and other items that might have a military use were denied to Japan. This sanction, if you will, did not have the force of law. President Roosevelt asked for voluntary support, arguing it was immoral to ship planes to Japan, which would be used to kill Chinese citizens. Compliance was generally good given the horrors of the "Rape of Nanking" and other atrocities.

1940 Export Control Act

Under this law a license was needed to purchase certain products from the United States. No license, no purchase. Though supposedly nondiscriminatory, the law was really directed toward Japan. Exports could be closed to the Japanese if their China policies continued. The items included:

Oil	Aviation Gas	Copper	Quality Scrap Iron
Pig Iron	Iron Ore	Brass	Tungsten
Lead	Zinc	Aluminum	

The legislation became law on July 25, 1940. The key export was oil without which Japan's war machine, particularly the navy, would be adversely affected. Japan's oil inventory under non-wartime conditions was good for about 81-months. Also, about 80% of Japan's oil came from the United States, providing Congress, or so it thought, with real leverage over Japan.

The text said, the "President deemed it necessary in the interest of national defense to prohibit or curtail the exportation of military equipment, munitions, tools, and other materials to Japan." No question about this action; Japan was being punished for her aggressiveness in China.

All this must be seen against the European situation. France and the Netherlands were overrun by Germany in 1940. They were in no position to protect their colonial possessions in Southeast Asia, what some were referring to as "orphan colonies." With this in mind, a third question emerged: if cut off from American oil exports, would Japan grab the oil of the Dutch East Indies and the resources of Indo-China? And if she did, what would the United States do?

September 1940 – Japan's Response

1. Japan, showing a willingness to use force, extorted from the Vichy government of France a number of bases in Indo-China. If necessary, these forward bases might be used by the Japanese Imperial Army to move into the Dutch East Indies.
2. Japan joined the Tripartite Pact, which was aimed at the United States in order to protect herself in case of war.

September 26, 1940 – Tightening the Embargo

The embargo is no longer non-discriminatory. It was aimed directly at Japan. Oil, scrap iron, and aviation gas would not be sold to Japan. They can only be sold to countries in the Western Hemisphere, or shipped to Britain by way of convoys.

April 13, 1941- Neutral Treaty with Russia

On a temporary basis both countries remove the threat of a two-front war. To a degree, Japan now had a freer hand in the Pacific. What she would do with it was the question.

July 25, 1941 – Japan's Assets Frozen

Tokyo was stunned. She was cut off from oil; she could not access her funds in the United States. Given the cost of her military expenditures, this could drive the country into bankruptcy, certainly a stark reality.

Assumptions

American economic actions against the Empire of Japan were based on a number of unproven assumptions:

1. Japan will be deterred from striking Southeast Asia.
2. Japan will observe some sort of compromise in China short of total withdrawal.
3. Japan wouldn't dare challenge the United State by going to war.

Many disquieting questions also emerged:

1. Was the United States actually pushing Japan toward war?
2. Did the United States really want Japan to strike first in order to justify a Pacific war?
3. Was bankrupting Japan by freezing her assets a ploy to pressure Tokyo into a corner?
4. Did the United States want to get into the European War, and needed to do so through the backdoor of a Japanese attack?
5. Would Japan, feeling her national survival was at stake, see no option other than war?
6. Would the Japanese willingly live under an American imposed order in the Far East?
7. Was there really a rational distinction between a battleship's guns and Congress' restrictive economic policies advanced by President Roosevelt?

———

"There you have it, my friendly conspirators."

"You want us to answer these questions?"

"A few, at least, Freda."

"I'll take a stab at #1 and #4."

"Harlan?"

"FDR wanted Britain to survive. He wanted Russia to resist the Nazis. He needed the US in the war to help make this happen. Public opinion was supportive just shy of actual fighting. He needed Japan to push the American public into a war. Sanctions were the means by which he would do this. At this point, appeasement was no longer possible."

"I'll take a shot at #6."

"Freda?"

"The Japanese would eventually oblige Roosevelt. Tokyo's China policy was fixed. No Japanese government could survive withdrawal from the country. Accepting a US dominated world order in Asia was tantamount to surrender and an inconceivable 'loss of face.' It was now a 'either or' situation. Both countries were boxed in, their rhetoric notwithstanding."

"That leaves #5 for me."

"Estelle?"

"Japan will have to go to war. Cut off from American oil exports, Tokyo will need another source. That can only mean the Dutch East Indies. It's only a question of when, not if. In short boycotts and sanctions, no matter their initial intent, had succeeded in leaving Tokyo without any real option acceptable to the military government."

"Then Roosevelt is consciously accepting this reality?"

"More than that, Dr. Ramos. FDR needs American in what is becoming a second global conflict. There is no misunderstanding in Washington or Tokyo as to what the stakes are. The only question is under what circumstances will the war begin?"

"You have an answer, Frieda?"

"Only this. The actual incident, perhaps something unanticipated, my be very much like 1914 when the Archduke and his wife were killed in faraway and little known Sarajevo, causing the world to explode. Something like that, I think."

"You have a view, Professor Ramos?

"Oh, yes. You're all right and the clock is ticking."

"We think you begged the question."

"Harlan, I did."

"We can't let you off that easily. Was Roosevelt in the right? Did Washington occupy the high moral ground?"

"Morality in wartime is difficult to judge. Each side claims truth and evokes language to support its position."

"There is no absolute 'right?'

"Estelle, you are seeking a most elusive commodity."

"If it right doesn't exist, what does?"

"A basic Darwinian need to survive. A world dominated by the Nazis and the Gestapo, abetted by Hitler's Italian lackeys was an acknowledged threat to the United States. Like a disease, the totalitarian pestilence could only be contained by force. It had to be eradicated. Japanese occupation and control of the Far East was another epidemic of butchered civilians for the sake of Tokyo's ambitions. America, if she went to war, would be fighting for survival, pure and simple. That was already established by Britain surviving the blitz, even as Moscow battled in the frozen wastes of Russia. Survival was what was at stake. Notions of good and evil held by all belligerents were forceful arguments to prepare the populace for war, to motivate civilians, to provide them with a higher calling for the sacrifice necessary in destroyed cities and loss of life. But in the end it was about survival in a world of howling wolves."

"Such a stark appraisal, Professor Flores."

"Unvarnished, as they say, Estelle."

Outside, the storm raged, and the city endured. Raincoats and umbrellas were worn and held, and people went about their business oblivious to the issues weighing on the conspirators. Most would sleep reasonably well that night, though alarmed by the daily headlines suggesting America was in her last days of peace. A few others in a Sea Cliff residence would toss and turn throughout the night, awakening only to see the clock ticking. And perhaps in their fitful sleep they recalled the words of the Secretary of State, Cordell Hull: "I am certain that, however great the hardships and the trials which loom ahead, our America will endure and the cause of human freedom will triumph."

CHAPTER 31

BALLOTS AND BOMBS

———————— ⟡ ————————

December 3, 1941 – Wednesday – San Francisco

NEWS HEADLINES

Japanese naval forces are at sea, destination unknown.

US Secretary of State Cordell Hull gave a press conference expressing a pessimistic view of US-Japan relations, saying that the months of discussions to this point had never reached a stage where actual negotiations toward a peaceful settlement could take place.

———————

A light breakfast was over. Harlan had a bowl of Kellogg's PEP, a corn flake cereal promising to revive your energy. That was okay with him. Estelle preferred an old-fashioned whole grain cereal composed of little letter O's and a claim to be the "breakfast of Champions." As with Harlan, that was okay with her. Cream of Wheat was the choice of Freda, cooked cereal known throughout the South as grits. Raisins and strawberries were available to those who wanted a colorful flourish to their cereal. For those who wanted it, and everyone did, half a grapefruit was on the table, already neatly cut compliments of Javier. As for Professor Ramos, two pieces of toasted sourdough French bread layered with a generous streak of butter and marmalade jam, plus a steaming cup of hot chocolate, satiated her needs.

Outside the storm hammered the city, lightning streaking the sky, thunder rolling through the hills of San Francisco. And, of course, there was no letup in the rain causing storm drains to overflow and in some areas cross streets emulating Lake Tahoe. It was nice to be in a warm home with friends and a nearby fireplace alive with reddish coals and an occasional "crack" as the dry logs burned.

"Estelle, you have that look again."

"You know me well, Harlan."

"Poker players recognize cues.

"And mine?"

"You twist your left ear."

"No wonder you're an excellent attorney. You note details."

"Flattery, I accept. Now, what has W.T. Stead communicated to you, dear lady?"

"Twice last night he approached me."

"Automatic handwriting?"

"Yes. Two words again, as before:

TOO LATE

"You've deciphered it?"

"Freda, I think so, but not a more recent one... About an hour later, my hand wrote:

TVA

"As to the two words... I sense our struggle to avoid war in the Pacific is beyond us. Japan and America seemed ordained to fight. We cannot stop it."

"We should halt in our efforts?"

"No, that we cannot do, but we must redouble our efforts to create a second Ark, one more durable than the first."

"Learning from this tragedy and the first one?"

"Exactly, Freda."

"And the three letters?"

"No idea. Harlan?"

"Possibly, I do."

"Possibly?"

"Your father, Estelle, W.T. Stead, has somehow found his way into my topic for today?"

"The presidential election of 1940?"

"I'm not a historian, nor am I an academic, and certainly not an expert in the realm of political science. I am, however, an astute observer of the political scene, perhaps sufficient for our needs. No matter, Professor Ramos has given me the floor. I'll try not to slip.

"Our election system has a sometimes unwanted peculiarity. This is particularly true of presidential elections. They occur every four years regardless of any domestic or foreign crisis. Quite unlike Britain's parliamentary system, where Churchill replaced Neville Chamberlain this year when he failed to carry a 'vote of confidence.' Our elections are tied to the calendar, not to a vote of confidence. Recall Lincoln runs for reelection in1864 right smack in the middle of the American Civil War, FDR wins in 1932 and 1936, again in the middle of a crisis, the Great Depression. The calendar, you see, controls events, not the other way around."

"As it was for Roosevelt a year ago."

"Freda, yes, and with the world at war."

"Your topic?"

"Yes. Of course, any presidential election is important, but not all such elections are of the same importance. For example, Abraham Lincoln's victory in 1860 over three other candidates was immeasurably significant in its consequence. Some would argue that FDR's decisive victory over President Herbert Hoover in 1932 ranks right up there. If Lincoln saved the Union, Roosevelt saved the economic system. Each preserved the nation. With Lincoln, at a frightful cost in treasure and flesh... With

FDR by using the power of government to challenge the near collapse of capitalism."

"Harlan, you're suggesting another such pivotal election was in 1940?"

"I am, Freda, so much so that the fate of the civilized world, according to some, was in the balance."

"You were satisfied with the outcome?"

"Yes, Estelle. True, I'm a lifelong Republicans, but in the recent election I made an exception."

"Why?"

"The other three candidates were not to my liking."

"Three?"

"Three, Freda, FDR had to face Wendell Willkie, the Republican upstart from Elwood, Indiana."

"The other two?"

"Hovering in the background, a malevolent presence in the case of Adolf Hitler, and a major irritant in the case of Charles Lindbergh."

"Some exposition is needed, Harlan."

"Adolf Hitler's military successes in Europe had brought the continent to its knees. Only the Russians were still fending off German hoards. The British were barely surviving the daily bombing raids over London, even as they held on tenuously in North Africa against Rommel. Halfway around the world, the Japanese were consolidating their victories. In the last polls before the 1940 presidential election, the public was of two minds: assuming the British and the Russians might decisively turn the tide, the Republicans had a better than fair chance to defeat FDR, leading in the polls by 5% points. If, however, Hitler continued to prevail, the polls indicated stronger support for the occupant of the White House. In a war crisis the public wanted an experienced person. The lunatic in Berlin was very much like political wallpaper, present yet, as in this case, not directly on the ballot. As one historian stated the case:

> *When confronted with the possibility of fighting, they preferred Roosevelt by far larger percentage. By election day many voters had obviously made their reckoning wit the*

dread prospect of war. They had decided it was no time to exchange the reliable Roosevelt they had known through eight years of depression, reform, and ratcheting international tensions for the edgy Willkie they had seen I in the campaign.

The Isolationists

"And Charles Lindbergh?"

"Estelle, 'the Lone Eagle,' the first man to fly across the Atlantic Ocean to Paris in 1927, a hero to America's youth, and a defiant isolationist and foe of President Roosevelt, was the face of the America First Committee."

"I've heard of the group, Harlan. They're non-interventionist to the core, right?"

"That is the case, Estelle, along with a less than quiet streak of anti-Semitism and pro-fascist sentiments, an unfortunate undercurrent to the group's more acceptable themes. The organization got its start on the Yale University campus. A fellow by the name of K. Douglas Stuart, a student, started the group on September 4m, 1940. Originally, the American First Committee stood for:

1. The neutrality policy should be upheld.
2. Opposed Lend-Lease legislation.
3. Opposed American naval ships escorting convoys.
4. Opposed economic boycotts against Japan.
5. Favored an impregnable military defense of the US
6. Favored draft legislation for America's defense.

"Of course, isolationists were motivated by many things:

Many found justifications for Germany's behavior; many denied that the conflict was a struggle between good and evil, and many stressed British and French vices, especially their imperialism. Some also denied that the United States had the power needed to promote desirable results in Europe, such as peace and democracy.

"In these views many of the isolationists were sincere and fearful for the country:

> *They battled against efforts to weaken the neutrality legislation and to supply aid to the belligerents. They argued that economic aid would weaken national defense by depriving American forces of weapons they needed and would led to unnecessary involvement in the fighting.*

"One of their most powerful lines was 'arms would be followed by dollars and dollars by troops.'"

"Some truth to that, Harlan."

"Ah, Professor Ramos, I haven't put you to sleep."

"Far from it. Please continue."

"Many isolationists feared for our democratic institutions, believing that war would destroy 'private enterprise, democracy, and civil liberties. Some went further:

> *War might lead to the establishment of an authoritarian government, even a totalitarian regime.*

"In summary, the isolationists detested FDR's interventionist moves to get the country into war. They accused the President of lying to the American people about getting into war. At the height of their influence, over 800,000 dues paying members were following and accepting these views, including the idea that Roosevelt was power *hungry*:

> *Many emphasized political rather than economic motives and the dangers of presidential, not economic power. According to this view, Roosevelt was leading the American people into war in order to maintain and enlarge his power and to conceal hi failures at home.*

"Lindbergh was an excellent spokesperson for the American First Committee, tall, handsome, heroic in stature and accomplishment, he rallied millions to the non-interventionist point-of-view. He claimed Roosevelt's call to "defend England was really a call to defeat Germany.'

On September 11, 1941, just a few days ago, Lindbergh identified the forces pulling America into the war as 'the British, the Roosevelt administration, and American Jews.'"

"His views were accepted, Harlan?"

"By many, Estelle. Unfortunately, anti-Semitism existed and Lindbergh catered to it, unconsciously or not, when he said: 'The greatest danger to this country lies in their (Jews) ownership and influence in our motion pictures, our press, our radio, and our government.'"

"Ugly. As a flyer, I don't understand his view of an 'impregnable America.' He knew the potential of modern air technology, didn't he?"

"He did, Freda, but political fervor perhaps clouded his reasoning, as when he said:

> *One need only glance at a map to see where our true frontiers lie. What more could we ask than the Atlantic Ocean on the east and the Pacific Ocean on the west? An ocean is a formidable barrier even for modern aircraft.*

LINDBRGH SPEAKING

"In 1940, though Hitler and Lindbergh weren't on the ballot, FDR was faced with two powerful influences in his decision to seek reelection for a second time."

"A controversial decision on his part, was it not, Harlan?"

"Estelle, no president had ever defied the two-term tradition established by George Washington. Nothing about the restriction in the Constitution, or in criminal law, just a tradition honored over the years. As the 1940 election neared, Roosevelt played it coy, never sharing what his true intentions were, not even with his wife, Eleanor. He did remind people, however, that he missed his Hyde Park home on the Hudson and was thinking about a presidential library for his papers. He also needed to make some money, pointing out he had signed a lucrative contract with *Collier's Magazine* for a series of articles."

"But he really meant to run?"

"Yes, but not overtly. He wanted the what is called a 'draft;' that is, others at the Democratic Convention in Chicago would --- in a well-organized way --- provide an instantaneous and inspirational demand that FDR receive the nomination. In responding to the planted delegates, he would humbly accept the decree of the Convention. He would run again."

"We're down to this fellow Wendell Willkie, that is the case isn't it, Harlan?"

"Indeed."

The Unknown Factor

"Question, how does an interventionist in the Republican Party get the party's nomination on the sixth ballot? How does a guy with rumbled hair and suits avoid the presidential primaries and become the standard bearer for the Grand Old Party? How does a lifelong Democrat change his party affiliation and gather Republican support? How does a former CEO of a large electric utility, who mirrored FDR's foreign policy become the Republican champion?"

"Okay, Harlan, how does he do it?"

"He stops fighting the Tennessee Valley Authority and turns his mind to presidential politics, Estelle."

"I don't understand."

"Freda, Willkie was in charge of the Commonwealth and Southern Corporation, which supplied electricity to six states. The TVA, a government agency, was seen as a competitor to private industry, a socialist enterprise promoted by Roosevelt's New Deal."

"Tennessee Valley Authority... **TVA**... Harlan, was that what my father was alluding to? Was he reminding us to pay attention to this guy?"

"It appears so and I think I know why. After defeating Thomas E. Dewey, his only competition from New York, who was considered too anti-New Deal, too isolationist, and too haute, if not wooden in his campaigning, the Republicans took a chance on a dark horse. The archconservatives weren't happy about this, nor was President Roosevelt, but for different reasons. Sure Willkie was pro-business and opposed to big government and too much regulation of business. Republicans liked that. But his foreign policy, that was the problem. On the other hand, the President had expected a full-fledged isolationist to contest him. Instead, here comes Willkie, who is an interventionist, a supporter of Lend-Lease legislation, a foe of Nazi Germany, concerned about Japan's aggressive moves in the Far East, and willing to keep the 'destroyer deal' out of the political debate. In some ways, it was like Roosevelt debating Roosevelt. Here was a challenger who wanted to keep Social Security, accepted most of the New Deal, sought full employment, and had a winning motto: "I pledge a new world.'" Millions of Americans (some 60% according to one poll) considered Willkie a potentially excellent president. Even the President had a kind word for him, stating, "The avowed leader of the Republican Party himself --- Mr. Wendell Willkie --- in a word and in action is showing what patriotic Americans mean by risking about partisanship and rally to the common cause."

"How did FDR win?"

"In the main two factors. First, the economy was beginning to prosper. Unemployment was down to 14% as the large war contracts, especially for ships, planes, tanks and trucks, ramped up in addition to other war-related materials. Second, the Nazis appeared to be winning in Russia, England was barely hanging on, and the Japanese were on a roll in Asia. The war news wasn't good. The public chose experience over youth; it was just as simple as that. The final score was:

	FDR	WILLKIE
Popular Vote	27,000,000	22,000,000
	(55%)	(45%)
Electoral College	449	82
States Won	38	10

"The President won reelection for the second time, and famously said this of his victory: I'm happy I've won, but I'm sorry Wendell lost.'"

"As to those who watched the results from the sidelines: Hitler and Tojo were disappointed. Lindbergh was dissatisfied, as were most isolationists. Churchill, who had watched the campaign 'with profound anxiety,' said of the results

No newcomer into power could possess or soon acquire the knowledge and experience of Franklin Roosevelt. None could equal his commanding gifts."

It was over. The 1940 campaign was history. Americans had rolled the dice, as they did every four years, and ringing in their ears was the fervent promise FDR made at a Boston campaign stop:

> *I have said this before, but I shall say it again, and again and again. Your boys are not going to be sent into any foreign wars.*

But he had also said:

> *There is a mysterious cycle in human events. To some generations much is given. Of other generations much is expected. This generation of Americans has a rendezvous with destiny.*

CHAPTER 32

FOLLY

December 4, 1941 – Thursday – San Francisco

NEWS HEADLINES

It appears that large convoys of Japanese naval ships have departed for destinations in Malaya and Thailand.

The Washington Times-Herald published top-secret government war plans alarming isolationists who took it as proof that President Roosevelt was preparing to lead the United States into war.

"Professor Ramos, I return the floor to you."

"Which I accept with great reluctance given the nature of our topic today."

Again, the conspirators were congregating in Sean Murray's library having enjoyed another scrumptious breakfast. Maria and Javier had outdone themselves with homemade waffles, scrambled eggs, and slices of fried honey ham. A beaker of home squeezed orange juice was just the right drink. As always, hot brewed coffee was present.

"Soon you will be writing your new Ark. In it you will provide the wisdom and lessons you've learned to avoid still another war if the survivors will but listen. That being the case, we need to spend considerable time asking a simple question; if war breaks out between the United States and Japan, why will it have happened? Or said more pointedly, what's causing a potential war in the Pacific?"

"Others asked the same question in 1910, Professor Ramos."

"And how did they answer the question, Estelle?"

"With the usual suspects: secret treaties, the alliance system, the armaments race, imperialistic rivalries, and super-heated patriotism."

"And how did the first Ark respond?"

"President Woodrow Wilson's Fourteen Points, which incorporated the first Ark and placed great emphasis on the League of Nations."

"Which leads us to the flip side of the same question; what's gone wrong, first in Europe and soon, it appears, in the Far East? Why couldn't the post-war generation keep the peace? That's our challenge today? Why are swords overwhelming treaties and the peaceful resolution of disputes?"

Outside the rain had slackened to a steady, almost comforting shower, even as the wind had abated. The storm was receding and would soon be gone. Unfortunately, the latest weather report indicated another storm was brewing in the Central Pacific and heading eastward with predicted torrential rains carried to California by an armada of dark smudges in the sky. The storm was supposed to arrive Sunday or Monday.

Inevitability

"Where do we start?"

"With still another question, Freda. Is war inevitable between the US and the Empire of Japan?"

"Inevitable meaning something must happen?"

"Yes, that it can't be avoided."

"That the diplomats have lost control of events?"

"Again, yes, Freda."

"But they seem to be in charge, Professor Ramos. FDR is the Commander and Chief. He makes decisions. He has advisors. The Japanese government is in the same boat. Issues are discussed; decisions are made."

"Still, Harlan, if each country wants peace, but war confronts all of us, who is really in charge, if anyone?"

"You have an answer?"

"Yes. Each decision is taken within a specific institutional and social framework; that is, within the political culture of a country, and every decision is based on assumptions influenced by the values of that government. In most cases, the assumptions made are untested and given to unpredictable consequences."

"In every day English?"

"An example, Freda. The China question... The United States is determined to see China free of Japanese troops. Japan is equally determined to maintain and enhance its military control of the country. The US wants a free and independent China. Japan wants 'living room, what Hitler calls Lebensraum. He desires this in order to make Germany economically self-sufficient and militarily secure. Tokyo makes the same argument about China. Of course, the only problem is that the 'living space' is in someone else's backyard. The United States is prepared to see foreign enclaves reduce their presence in an evolutionary way, short of war, and by treaty. Japan appears willing to use force --- is using force --- to remove the last vestige of European imperialists from China. Embedded in all these views are world views ingrained with the cultural influences and political realities of each country.

"They can extricate themselves from these views?"

"They haven't."

"But they could."

"It is difficult to renounce that which explains your world in a world that can defy explanation."

"Are you saying diplomats are trapped by their own rhetoric?"

"Freda, consider this. They are protagonists, the United States and Japan. Are they, for example, part of some historical; process working itself out: imperialism in Asia ending; nationalistic urges surging; Asian cultural force thriving once more; a Spangler notion of nations rising and falling? Are these inexorable forces at work beneath the surface, difficult to discern and perhaps impossible to fully control?"

"The diplomats have lost control, Professor Ramos?"

"It appears so, but perhaps that is the great illusion, Estelle. Did they ever really have control? As one historian argued:

> *The tragedy of political decisions derives from the fact that again and again politicians find themselves in situations in which they are constrained to act in ignorance of the consequences and without being able to access calmly the probable results.*

"How does our new Ark deal with that?"
"Indeed, how does it?"

Analogies

"It is difficult to determine a general explanation for war, though patterns do emerge, what might be called long-term causes, or origins. These can include conflicts of interest, psychological tensions between societies, and unresolved territorial disputes. Analogies are helpful here. If you accumulate enough inflammable materials, a single spark might light up the night. Subjecting even the sturdiest concrete dam to too much water may test the dam beyond its capacity to safely hold back a floodtide. In other words, causes, very much like explosives may appear inert, yet blow up in our faces.

"An example would be helpful."

"Certainly, Harlan. Think of the FDR's boycotts, embargos and sanctions against Japan as water rising behind a dam. The last three drops may have been stopping oil and scrap metal shipments to Tokyo, and the freeze of Japanese funds. Recall the reasoning behind this was to deter Japan's aggressive in China and Southeast Asia short of going to war. But now the water is slopping over the edge and the dam is vulnerable to giving way. On the other hand, Japan's refusal to leave China and her continuous aggressiveness toward the Dutch East Indies and Indo-China are, it might be said, drops of water too, lapping now at the top of the dam. The next drop behind either dam, so the scenario suggests, may cause one of these dams to burst."

"But each side can see the water rising, can they not?"

"Certainly, Estelle."

"Yet, they do nothing to stop it."

"Or what they do is ineffective. Perhaps they are like a man who consciously and rationally is aware that he is going crazy. What is he to do, dear friend? Swirling around our leaders and diplomats may be forces they cannot fully appreciate, or understand, much less control." Historians ask in the quiet of the night::

> *What are these forces? Obvious possibilities may be found in the movement of ideas, and the clash of ideologies, in economic pressures and opportunities; and in changes in military technologies and strategic thinking*

"But the cost of war, Professor Ramos? The destruction. The loss of life and the financial costs… The disruption of society… How can war be preferable to peace?"

"Freda, my loveable idealist, I must shepherd you into another realm. If Japan, for example, feels its China policy is constrained by the ABCD powers led by the United States, that she is being isolated and punished for wanting to emulate the European imperialistic powers, that there is an international coalition to stop her, the risk factor may sway her toward war. Again, the flip side finds a mirror image. With all its potential hazards and sacrifice is war preferable to America surrendering the Far East to Japan? Difficult as it may be to accept, war be perceived as an acceptable justifiable policy."

"I can't accept that."

"Perhaps another analogy … Think of water as tension, a combination of anger, suspicion, and stress, relentless and unrelieved. Everyone knows that war is bound to come, sooner or later. Neither side no longer has the will to take an alternative path. The war strategies are set. Mobilization has taken place. The public is prepared for war. There is no deterrent sufficient to stop the drums of war. For some, as a French historian said long ago:

Better war than this perpetual waiting.

"There is relief in war?"

"Yes, but that's before the horrors of war come home to roost."

"But there's still time to stop this mad dash?"

"Estelle, time is working against all of us. Our government is being overtaken by events and so to is the public. Neither has, I contend, the opportunity to completely grasp what is happening. Everyone, including the Japanese, is caught up in the crisis. Both countries are reaching (or have) the conclusion that only through war can they survive."

"Difficult to accept."

A Moral War

"As is this next point, one I personally find objectionable, but understandable. For many, the news of war is stimulating and exciting, and, as we learned earlier, thankful relief."

"Impossible."

"No so, Harlan. After years, if not longer, of patriotism inculcated into our daily lives, war is seen as an outlet for the wellsprings of '*My country tis of thee*.' Governments are very good in convincing their citizens that they are the 'victims of aggression and in appealing to immediate feelings of patriotism and self-preservation." Fear and love are used judiciously; fear the enemy, love your country, prepare to make sacrifices, and above all be loyal."

"We are all subject to this appeal, Dr. Ramos."

"All, Estelle. No country goes to war feeling responsible for starting the conflict."

"There is no aggressor, no country in the wrong, no guilty party."

"That I didn't say. Only that each country sees itself as a victim, not as a perpetrator even if it attacks first."

"But..."

"The universal explanation: what I did I was forced to do."

"Than what is a moral war? What is right?"

"Exactly, Estelle. But, of course, the winners get first stabs at writing the history."

A Darwinian World

Along with all this, there are Darwinian undertones supporting heated patriotism and excessive chauvinism. Nations are seen in a constant struggle for survival and only the fittest will survive. Violence is viewed not only good, it is absolutely necessary in a world of fierce competition. Everything is and must be subordinated to this struggle. We are not really separated from the natural world. In the starkest terms, we live in a world of kill or be killed."

"I cannot accept this."

"But Tokyo does. Without American oil, Japan's economy will implode. Without Texas crude, Japan's war machine will grind to a halt. That being the case Japan will go to war rather than change her policies. She will attack the Dutch East Indies. She cannot make war in China without oil. She cannot be a great industrial power without oil. Yes, she will kill to survive, as will America, her liberal tendencies notwithstanding. Roosevelt will go to war when, if public opinion supports him, he can. Already American destroyers are killing German submariners, and shipping weapons to England and China for the same purpose. This is not about romanticizing war. Killing is not extolled. It is cold-blooded reality. Emile Zola stated the case in 1911:

> *War is life itself. Nothing exits in nature, is born, grows or multiplies except by combat. We must eat and be eaten so that the world may live. It is only warlike nation, which have prospered: a nation dies as soon as it disarms. War is the school of discipline, sacrifice, and courage.*

"Unacceptable!"

"Tell that to the Russians defending Moscow. Tell that to Poland, a nation unprepared to battle both Berlin and the Russians. Tell that to the Chinese and the people of Nanking. Tell that to Londoners."

"Ugly."

"It gets uglier. Darwin's ideas are now used to support Hitler's racial beliefs as tied to the survival of the fittest. The Japanese have a variant of this about the Koreans, Manchurians, and the Chinese. One might argue the Anglo-Saxon world has an affinity for this. Colonial possessions, for example, can only exist in a world of superior-inferior relationships, whether of guns or race. Even America needed to care for the Filipinos and the Cubans until they are "ready for independence."

"Professor Ramos, even if I accept your arguments, how would our new Ark deal with all this?"

"Another question to be answered, I'm afraid."

A New World Order

"The causes of war are complicated."

"Even more so, Estelle, when you factor in how individuals define themselves; that is, what gives meaning to their lives? What inspires them? What ambitions drive them?"

"You're getting at what?"

"The members of the Imperial Japanese Army and Navy. They occupied a preferential place in Japanese society, respected and esteemed, proud men who identified their success with the country's greatness and military exploits. Though war had hardships, it also led to advancement and near celebrity status for some, especially if there was success on the battlefield. In a paradoxical sense war was an alluring friends; peace was a problematic foe."

"You're going where with this?"

"The need to establish a new world order, or what the Romans called an 'imago mundi,' a new image of the world. Related to that a new 'axis mundi,' a new center of the world, shifting power from Washington to Tokyo, at least in the Far East."

"That will need explanation?"

"We must go back to the Washington Naval Conferences of 1921-22. To some degree the major naval powers accepted a formula resulting in a workable agreement for naval equity: 5-5-3, US, Britain, Japan. Though not perfect, it stabilized military conditions in the Pacific. At the same time an effort was made to do this in the political world through the Nine Power Agreement, which was embedded with Secretary of State Hull's vision of how China should be treated: (1) international cooperation in China; (2) uphold Chinese independence; (3) provide equal economic opportunity; and (4) create an environment for the peaceful development of a stable

Chinese government. Though not legally binding and, as always, there was no enforcement provision, the signatories did covet what was called the 'spirit of Washington.' Contrary to some, it did not freeze the Pacific into one point in time. Change was probable, even necessary in the region on the basis of gradualism and peaceful, acceptable increments lawfully implemented.

For a decade the Washington System worked. China renewed its efforts to become an independent nation-state and disagreements were settled peacefully. In Japan, however, there were forces opposed to the Washington System and maneuvering to disrupt the stabilizing agreement:

- Army and Navy Officers
- Right-wing Organizations
- Nativist Elements
- Some Businesses
- Ambitious Politicians

"What did these groups want? First, end Japan's adherence to and cooperation with the principles of the Nine Power Treaty. Two, remove from power liberal leaders supporting internationalism. Third, defy the Washington System and act independently of its principles with regards to China. Fourth, establish a new world order (an imago mundi) in the Far East with Japan as its axis mundi. In this way the military would prosper, as would the nation. Only in this way would Japan be free of Western entanglements and self-sufficient as she defined that need. Only in this way would Japan live out her historic mission in the world as determined by the gods. Japan would do in the Pacific what Hitler was doing in Europe, freeing Germany from the Versailles Treaty and, unshackled, fulfilling her historic role."

"War in the Pacific boils down to this?"

"Among other factors, yes, Freda. Once the military came to power, the die was cast. Japan embarked on reshaping the Asian world order. Nothing else was possible in the execution of her China policy. Japan, very much like Italy and Germany, was willing to disrupt the status quo regardless of consequence in pursuit of her goals.

Of course, all three countries were aided, at least to some extent, by appeasement policies in London and Washington. Here we must be quite clear. Appeasement never meant the 'pursuit of peace at any price.' That is a misunderstanding. Here Berlin failed to understand the British, as the Japanese doing with the United States. Both countries, once pushed too far, would fight to preserve their vital interests." The Germans pushed too far when they invaded Poland. Japan is making the same mistake threatening the ABCD powers."

"Are the Japanese aware of this?"

"To a degree, yes, Estelle?"

"They could change their policies, lessen the pressure."

"As could Washington. Both could, neither will."

That's where America is today?"

"It is. It gets down to this. Japan will not halt its invasion of China unless forcibly resisted. She will not back down and the United States will not desist."

"As simple as that?"

"Harlan, as straightforward as one, two, three."

"I..."

"One, Japan expands her influence and empire. Two, the United States shows a willingness to accept such expansion for so long that only an armed clash can stop it. Three, America finally resists even at the cost of war."

"Yet, another challenging task for our Ark, Professor Ramos. How do we deal with 'historic missions and all the rest?"

"I don't know."

Outside the sky was clearing, providing a short interval before the next storm relentlessly crossed the Pacific. Lunch was novel, a half-bowl of hollowed out French bread filled with creamy clam chowder, a San Francisco favorite. Strawberry ice cream added a nice touch. Then it was back to work.

"Before moving on, a last word about the Washington System. As it played out in the excited Japanese press, it implied that Tokyo, contrary to others, was actually protecting the status quo by 'dealing decisively with Chinese lawlessness and irresponsible attacks on treaty rights.' It was a 'police action,' nothing more. The Chinese countered with a different view. They were confident that world public opinion would condemn 'Japan's barbarism and censure its violation of international public justice.' On this basis, China identified herself with international law and order and 'sought its salvation through the support of other nations.' Authoritarian governments lined up behind Japan, others with China."

"Is it wrong to subscribe the 'Devil's Theory' as a cause of war in addition to all you have related, Professor Ramos?"

"Not necessarily, Estelle. Armament manufactures on both sides of the Pacific favored a strong national defense. Inevitably, such a stance did lead to profitable war contracts, but alone the 'merchants of death' did not cause the present crisis. A factor, yes... The actual cause, no..."

"Gerald Nye would not be in agreement."

"He's entitled."

"What about competition for colonies, Professor Ramos. Certainly, that was an underlying cause, if not more."

"Freda, a Frenchman once said, 'to remain a great nation or to become one, you must colonize.' The Japanese took this too heart, first Korea, then Manchuria, and now China, even as she looks southward toward the East Indies. Though late on the imperialistic scene, she covets an empire, a sort of rite of passage to join the big boys, France and Britain in particular. And, of course, the United States was not immune to this attraction. The Spanish-American War originates in Havana Harbor, and ends up with the Philippines, Guam, and Puerto Rico, plus the annexation of Hawaii and the construction of a canal across Panama. Tokyo would argue it's simply following a script written by others.

"The Japanese have acquired a *'White Man's Burden?'*"

"In Asia a somewhat different complexion, yet centered on the justification often used by London:

> *If we chose... the Empire might be self-sustaining; it is so wide, its products are so various, its climates so different that there is absolutely nothing which is necessary to our existence, hardly anything which is desirable as a luxury which cannot be produced within the boundaries of the Empire itself. The Empire at the present time derives the greatest part of its necessities from foreign countries, and exports the largest part of its available produce, also to foreign countries.*

"Beginning with oil, the Japanese wish to accomplish what the British have done?"

"In a nutshell, yes, Harlan. A large navy, as with Japan, is also justified in the name of empire. As a dignified official of Parliament stated the case:

> *Now these fleets and this military armament are not maintained exclusively or even mainly, for the benefit f the United Kingdom, or for the defense of home interests. They are still more maintained as a necessity of Empire, for the maintenance and protection of Imperial trade all over the world.*

"Imperialistic ambitions led Japan to this crisis?"

"Ambitions, to some extent, yes. Or perhaps it was the map and Tokyo's proximity to China that was the culprit. Had Japan advanced into Africa... Or South America...The European and American response would have been different. Exactly how is open to speculation. But she didn't. And if the United States didn't possess the Philippines and become a Pacific power... So many 'if's,' Harlan."

"Perhaps history is the real villain here, Dr. Ramos."

"That's tantamount to blaming God for man's folly."

"I retract my statement. The deity is off the hook. As to the other, I'm not sure. As you have pointed out, the currents today flow from the past."

"True, deep and dark they run."

"As asked earlier, where are we? What is the root cause of this impending war?"

"Freda, perhaps the *roots* is a better term with all of them leading to China. The Japanese have their ambitions. They have their grievances. And they have, if they can hold it, China. But, as we have seen, the United States will not acquiesce."

"Then it's war."

"Unless..."

Outside the sun peeked through the lingering haze, suggesting a few days of enjoyable weather. It was all an illusion.

CHAPTER 33

POLLS AND POLITICS

December 5, 1941 – Friday – San Francisco

NEWS HEADLINES

Japan responded to Roosevelt's inquiry of December 2 by saying that foreign repots of the number of Japanese troops in French Indochina were exaggerated and the troop concentrations were in full accord with the agreement between Tokyo and Vichy.

───────────

Professor Ramos was introducing her colleague, Bailey Thomas. The conspirators listened attentively in the study, which had become a sort of poor man's bunker as the Pacific storms passed overhead.

"Professor Thomas is a statistician at San Jose State. He's very good with numbers, which has always been my Achilles' heel. He also advises the Roper and Gallup polling folks. Essentially, both companies attempt to ascertain public opinion at a given moment about a particular issue, or how well a political candidate is doing against the opposition. He's going to help you understand the current mood of America about the European situation and the threat of war in the Pacific."

Professor Bailey was a jolly, rotund sort of fellow with fuzzy hair that seemingly defied any hairbrush. At about 5 foot flat, his appearance seem to grow as he bantered around numbers, statistical equations, and the results of polling samples.

"Now understand this, you pirates attempting to alter history. Yes, I have been told of your enterprise, one I endorse. To begin with, polls are not perfect; they are not completely error free. We don't even know if the responders are telling the truth or just telling us what they think we want to hear. The questions themselves can influence the response in the way they're written. Even the pollster must be careful to not give away a prejudice. That's why those of us in the game always qualify our results, saying the results are always plus or minus 3 to 4%. What we really offer is the most objective understanding of public opinion possible at a given moment. Where possible, we try to catch changes in opinion, or find tendencies that might be turned into projections. We can often tell you what people are thinking, but we have greater difficulty explaining the why they're doing it. True, we use a scientific approach, but that only takes us so far. So don't bet the house on us."

"How accurate are you?"

"Pretty good most of the time, Estelle. That is your name?"

"Yes."

"If we have an acceptable sample… If we have a good survey… If we are analytical in our conclusions… Well, given all that, we're not bad."

"And you have your hand on America's pulse concerning war?"

"You must be Freda. Yes we do. We've been at it for almost three years. Practice makes for improvement, I remind you, not perfection.

"So where are we?"

"The last of the three… You're Harlan. Okay, let's get into it, polls from 1939 to 1941. Peruse the batch of materials I've passed out to you.

Gallup Polling

Each polling question listed below was tied to a situation. The first question concerns the outbreak of war in Europe. The polling suggests that a majority of Americans didn't want to get involved. Let Europe stew in its own juices. In question #2 the opposition increases even after the war has turned badly for England and France. That pattern continues with question #3 as Belgium and France are invaded.

Situation:_Poland has been invaded. France and Great Britain have declared war on Germany.

Question #1 – September 1 – 6, 1939: If it looks within the next few months as if England and France might be defeated, should the United States declare war on Germany and send our troops abroad?

YES 42%   NO 48%

Situation: Poland is defeated. France and Great Britain refused to agree to Hitler's demands.

Question #2 – October 6 – 10. 1939: If it appears that Germany is defeating England and France, should the United States declare war on Germany and send our army and navy to Europe to fight?

YES 27%   NO 71%

Situation: German armies invade Belgium and France.

Question #3 – May 18 – 23, `1940: Do you think the United States should declare war on Germany and send our army and navy abroad to fight.

YES 7%   NO 93%

The next series of questions provide only two answers, HELP or KEEP OUT... Though the actual situation Europe and the Pacific may have changed, we were trying to compare apples to apples in terms of the possible answers. We were forcing respondents to select from two standard choices. Pears and pineapples were not invited. Question #4 indicates the peak of opposition to involvement based on this format. Questions #5 through 9 indicate increasing support for military involvement in relationship to the changing world situation. Question #10 ups the ante, even rigs the polling a tiny bit for those of us in the business. See what you think."

286

Situation: France is defeated. Great Britain stands alone.
Question #4 – June 27- July 3, 1940: Which of these two things do you think is the more important for the United States to try to do --- to keep out of war ourselves or to help England win, even at the risk of getting into the war?

HELP 35%   KEEP OUT 61%

Situation: Congress passes the first peacetime draft in American history.
Question #5 – September 19 – 26, 1940:

HELP 52%   KEEP OUT 44%

Situation: Roosevelt is elected for an unprecedented third term as president.
Question #6 – November 21 -26, 1940:

HELP 60%   KEEP OUT 40%

Situation: Congress passes the Lend-Lease Act.
Question #6 – March 9 – 14, 1941:

HELP 67%   KEEP OUT 33%

Situation: Germany invades the Soviet Union.
Question #7 – July 1941

HELP 62%   KEEP OUT 33%

Situation: A German U-boat fires on the USS Greer. American ships are authorized to fire on German vessels on sight.
Question #8 – September 19 – 24, 1941:

HELP 64%   KEEP OUT 30%

Situation: Japan and the United States are on the verge of war.
Question #9 – November 21 – 26, 1941:

HELP 68%   KEEP OUT 28%

Situation: Japan is threatening the British and the Dutch in Southeast Asia, and possibly the Philippines and other American bases in the Pacific. **Question #10** – December 6, 1941: If Japan attacks should the President declare war on Germany and Japan?

HELP 91%   KEEP OUT 7%

"Contrary to what many people believe, the American people were paying attention to the news headlines since that Berlin bloke beat up on Poland. They know a knucklehead when they see one. They were watching newsreels in the local theaters. Warsaw bombed. Refugees fleeing the Nazis… Same in Asia… Tokyo's thugs trampling over Chinese peasants… They were hearing about the atrocities in Europe from those able to leave the continent, or flee from China. They were following President Roosevelt's speeches and reading between the diplomatic lines of carefully chosen words by Secretary of State Hull. They knew something was up on both sides of the globe. The polls showed it."

"As I considered your results, I found myself amazed how closely they mirrored my own evolution. I started out adamantly against involvement, a sort of pacific, isolationist, noninvolvement mix of feelings, and slowly, because of events, altered my perspective. Today though, I hope to avoid war. I certainly want America engaged to rein in the dictators."

"I also followed Harlan's road, though perhaps I held out a little longer. What about you, Estelle?"

"Freda, Nanking and Warsaw did it for me."

"Our latest poll suggests you're right where most Americans are at this moment. Check the next series of polls on your paper."

The Mood of America

Poll #1: 1940 – Regardless of what you hope, what do you think the chances are that the United States will be drawn into this war in Europe?

Sure	9.9%
Probable	29.2%
Fifty-Fifty	22.8%

Unlikely	22.2%
Impossible	4.0%
Don't Know	11.9%

Poll #2: 1940 – In the trouble now going on in Europe, which side would you like to see win?

England and France	83.1%
Germany and Italy	1.0%
Neither Side	6.7%
Don't Know	9.8%

Poll #3: 1941 - No matter what happens, do you think that we should immediately increase our:

Air Force	Yes	88.3%
Army	Yes	84.8%
Navy	Yes	86.8%

Poll #4: 1941 - Would you favor a term of compulsory military service for all young men of eighteen or nineteen?

Yes	31.3%
Yes, If Necessary	11.6%
No	48.8%
Don't Know	8.3%

Poll #5: 1941 - What were your main reasons for opposing military training for young men?

Opposed to Compulsion	21.6%
No Immediate Danger	19.7%
Un-American	11.6%
Like a Dictatorship	11.3%
Creates a War Spirit	11.0%

The next two polls are subject to inquiry.

Poll #6: 1941 - Who is more of a menace to the United States, Germany or Japan?

Germany

Does Japan have a long-term plan to attack the United States?

Yes	24%
No	70%
Other	6%

These questions, asked in early 1941, suggest a greater knowledge of the European situation, or certainly a greater degree of fear concerning the Nazis. Apparently, it is more difficult for Americans to perceive Japan taking on the United States in a shooting war. Our latest polls, however, show that this perception is slowly changing."

"So where are we Professor Bailey?"

"I have no crystal ball. As we head toward Christmas and a New Year, the country is no longer divided on the need to improve our defense, or even our assistance to Britain and China. No question about that. Neutrality has been cast aside. We're for the Brits and the Chinese. The isolationists, though fervent in their views, are no longer so influential in our politics. We are already in a dangerous, undeclared war in the Atlantic and Asia. Acceptance of a coming war is past tense. The only question remaining is when we will jump in with both feet. There is only a matter of when, and perhaps what finally provokes us. The public had heard their president.

Courage is not the absence of fear, but rather the assessment that something else is more important than fear.

Professor Bailey excused himself from lunch, and with a buoyant smile headed wherever pollsters go, but not before saying in a most optimistic voice, "Best of luck, my dear pirates."

Again, up to their high standards, Maria prepared another fine lunch harkening back to her New Mexico past, homemade tacos, do it yourself style. On the big kitchen table were all the ingredients --- soft taco shells, chopped hamburger and diced chicken, shredded lettuce, refried beans, and salsa. Of course, Maria did provide impromptu instructions on how to pull everything together. The conspirators, suddenly prompted by inward stirrings, were quick learners of the Hispanic culture. Once lunch was over they would resume saving the world.

Last Ditch Negotiations

"Dr. Ramos, we're ready. Where do we start?"

"With Secretary of State Hull's fateful note to Japan, November 26, 1941, only a few days ago. In what many are calling a consequential correspondence, but what the Japanese are describing as a declaration of war, Hull outlined the final American position:

1. Japan must remove all military forces from China.
2. Japan must lend her support to the nationalist government of China under Chiang Kai-Shek
3. Japan must enter into a multilateral, non-aggression pact with the United States to guarantee stability in the Far East.
4. Japan must guarantee the territorial integrity of all countries and possessions in the Pacific.

"If agreed to by Japan, the United States would quickly unfreeze all Japanese assets and resume exports of oil to Japan. The Japanese, as expected, refused. They could do little other. As one historian stated the case:

> *The Japanese, after four-and-a-half years of bloody losses, would suffer an intolerable loss of face and position if they did so In the last analysis, Washington forced a showdown over China.*

"As to why Hull took this position at the insistence and approval of the White House"

This policy could hardly be justified by America's relatively small stake in China, whether missionary, investment, or trade. The only reasonable justification was that the continued militaristic expansion of Japan in the Far East --- with its challenge to law, order, peaceful processes, and territorial integrity --- posed an intolerable threat to the future security of the United States.

"Another factor may have been at play. If the United States agreed to Japan's continued presence in China, the Chinese might have sued for peace. In that situation a million Japanese soldiers currently bogged down in China would have been available for Tokyo's ambitions in Southeast Asia, or even the Soviet Union, which, of course would complicate Moscow's effort against Germany. As Churchill told Roosevelt: 'If China collapses, our joint dangers (in the Pacific) would enormously increase.'

"On September 6, 1941,the Japanese developed a document entitled *Guidelines for Implementing National Policies*. This document represented the equivalent of a declaration of war against the United States if the terms listed below were not met:

1. The Anglo-American powers desist from extending military and economic aid to the Chiang Kai-shek regime. (Japan wanted a free hand in China.)
2. The Anglo-American powers refrain from establishing military facilities within Thailand, the Dutch East Indies, China, or the Far Eastern provinces of the Soviet Union. (Japan wanted to be the preeminent military power in Asia.)
3. The Anglo-American powers should restore the resources needed for Japan's existence. (Japan wanted an end to trade restrictions and the freezing of her funds).
4. Japan promised to undertake no further military expansion in Asia and to withdraw troops from Indo-China upon establishment of a just peace in the Far East.
5. Japan would guarantee the neutrality of the Philippines.

"Talk about being far apart."

"Estelle, the gulf was wide and widening."

"In summary, what did the Japanese really want?"

"If war came, Japan would define the war as:

> ...*one against the ABCD powers, its purposes being expelling their influences from East Asia, consolidating Japan's sphere of autonomy and security, and constructing a new order in greater East Asia.*

"From the perspective of Tokyo, my conspirators, the ABCD power stood for the status quo in the name of the defense of democracy. In reality, as Japan saw it, they were trying to prevent Japanese growth and development. If Japan should give in, America's military position would be further strengthened, and Japan would become even more subordinate to its influence."

"As always, where does that leave us?"

"Estelle, at the edge, balanced precariously."

CHAPTER 34

OMENS

———————— ⌒ ————————

December 6, 1941 – Saturday – San Francisco

NEWS HEADLINES

It was reported that Japanese nationals were being hurriedly withdrawn from Panama, British North Borneo, Malaya, India, Ceylon, and other countries, just as they had already begun withdrawing diplomats from Mexico.

————————

The Pacific storm stalled 250-miles northwest of Hawaii leaving San Francisco, if the weather reports were accurate, with a clear and sunny weekend. The forecast suggested an unofficial holiday and the local were more than willing to indulge themselves.

As always, Golden Gate Park would be full of walkers and picnickers, all out to enjoy the sun in one of the world's great parks. Others would be at the Park's aquarium for a glimpse of exotic sea life, while some would stroll into the planetarium to view distant stars. Some families would head for the famous San Francisco Zoo, there to gaze at the elephants, gorillas, and giraffes, or to watch the trained seals frolic in ice-cold water joyfully balancing rubble balls on their snouts. Of course, no one missed Monkey Island where the chimps were the center of attraction, jumping, jabbering, and up to all sorts of antics. For the romantic types, Stow Lake and Park rowboats beckoned, and perhaps a few kisses would be exchanged beyond the shore. All that was in the Park.

At the beach sunbathers were expected to enjoy sand and surf, and to watch the Pacific rollers splash at their feet. Nearby, Play Land at the Beach invited amusement park visitors, especially those who wanted to test their nerves on the giant, creaky old wooden roller coaster called the "Big Dipper." Lots of folks would be content with the merry-go-round and other less demanding rides. Those who wanted a delightful lunch would visit the Cliff House overlooking the Great Highway and those enjoying a weekend holiday.

The conspirators, however, were not among those at leisure that weekend. Spurred on by Estelle and prodded by their own self-inflicted desire to construct their Ark, the conspirators carried on, clear skies or not. They did so with a sense of urgency that they could not fully explain, nor even wanted to admit. Perhaps it began the night before when Estelle announced still another visit from her father, W.T. Stead. Once more he had left her with an inscrutable message:

NOW

Now what, of course, was the first thing that quickly came to mind? Other questions jostled with each other. Was something happening now? Was something about to happen? Had something already happened and was already history?"

"Estelle, nothing?"

"Not even the vaguest, Freda.

"Estelle, your father is always one step ahead of us. He must be up to, as always, something, don't you think?

Professor Ramos now got into the Q and A.

"If it has already happened, we can do nothing about it. If it's happening at the moment, we're still unable to respond. If it's about to happen, perhaps its there we must focus."

"Logical. Okay, what might about to happen, Harlan?"

"Hostilities."

Harlan's answer suggested no particulars and none was necessary. Intuitively, the conspirators accepted the premonition; the Pacific was about to boil over. That being the case, they worked furiously all day, stopping only for a quick meal and the call of nature. Beyond that, they explained, debated, and crafted their Ark, almost as if it needed completion that day. Harlan led the way.

Assumptions

"We have to assume the United States will be drawn into a global, two ocean war against the Tripartite nations, Rome, Berlin and Tokyo. We must assume it will be a long war if it is a fight without compromise and to the bloody end. Because of that Europe will be devastated, as will the Japanese homeland if the Allies win, Washington, London, and Moscow. Millions will be killed; other millions will be homeless; still others by the millions will not have work. If that business about splitting the atom and constructing a super bomb proves true, that will only add to the destruction."

"You paint a dreary picture, Harlan."

"In this worst case scenario, I can envision nothing else, Estelle."

"What do you propose?"

"Our Ark must do two things: first, it must deal with the devastation. Second, it most offer some form of institutional hope to avoid still another war, one that just might end civilization as we know it."

"You don't overstate the case?"

"Freda, have you known me to be given to hyperbole?"

Reconstruction

"We can assume that Great Britain and Western Europe will be nearly broke when the guns fall silent. How will they rebuild their economies? Stated another way, how will they avoid ongoing deep depressions that leads to civil disorder, even anarchy and invite the unwelcomed influence of Soviet communism?"

"Your answer, Harlan?"

"Untouched physically by the war and now prosperous beyond belief, only the United States is in a position to fund the rehabilitation of Europe and Japan."

"Taxpayer's money to fund both our friends and foes?"

"Yes, Freda. Recall what happened with Germany and the reparations issue. We will need to avoid that."

"You're asking a lot of Americans, helping Nazi Germany."

"Not Nazi Germany! A new Germany, democratic and prospering, as hopefully it will also be in Japan."

"But Germany started the war!"

"Estelle, I agree, but reverting to a 'guilt clause' again solves nothing. That was a mistake then. We shouldn't repeat it."

"Wouldn't we be harming our own industries and agriculture by reviving Europe's economies?"

"No. A healthy Europe is essential for our economy. Our excess production demands markets abroad. For the Europeans to buy, they must be able to sell. It's a two way street."

"You mentioned communism earlier. What were you getting at?"

"Professor Ramos, if I am right, Moscow will end up a dominant force on the European plain. If so, the Russians will want to expand their ideological influence. Hopefully, a healthy Western Europe would halt that expansion."

"This is a new type of warfare?"

"It is; democratic capitalism, if you will, against totalitarian control of the economy and citizens."

"You have a name for this program of assistance?"

"How does the Roosevelt Plan of Assistance sound to you?"

A Common Economy

"What do you mean by this, Harlan?"

"A European economic system, Freda, must emerge with our assistance, one that incorporates the continent's nations into some sort of common economy, where all countries are interdependent, and prosperity is based on mutual success. As I would envision it, trade barriers (think tariffs) would be reduced, perhaps even ended. Common trade regulations would, I hope, emerge, along with a common currency."

"Like we have in the United States?"

"As one possible model, yes. In Asia Japan and her neighbors would so something similar."

"The objective?"

"End national competiveness that leads to war. Make resources available to all countries, as they are available to all states. Oil, the resource that led to so much trouble, will not be a threat in the world I foresee. Free trade and the peaceful exchange of currency will determine the market."

"You're not being overly optimistic?"

"Hopefully, no, Dr. Ramos."

"That being the case, what about the German army and armaments in general?"

National Defense

"Here we walk a difficult path. How do we maintain national defense forces while incorporating them into some sort of larger entity?"

"Your answer?"

"Estelle, as with the common economic market in Europe, blend national armies together into a mutual defense force. French and German and British forces, along with Italians, and others, including the United States, would exist under one flag with a least one common objective."

"Which is?"

"To halt the Soviet expansion into Western Europe by military means in necessary."

"You fear Moscow?

"If Nazi Germany is defeated, Moscow will be the continent's super power."

"America would be in this common military alliance, right?"

"She must be, Freda. There is no choice for two good reasons. First, we will be the strongest military force in Western Europe and Asia. We must be the backbone of the new force. Secondly, by incorporating Germany into the alliance as a legitimate member, she will be less likely to go off the rails as she did in 1932."

"In other words, we can closely watch her?"

"That's one way of stating the case."

"The Europeans will buy into this?"

"If they wish to avoid the mistakes of the past, yes."

"You have a name for this defensive organization?"

"How about the Atlantic Alliance?"

Philosophical Underpinnings

"My turn. We need to determine what ideas should be the solid foundation for our new Ark. That has been my cross for the past few months."

"Then, Estelle, I happily sit down."

"And deservingly, Harlan. We, of course, need a point of departure, ideas and concepts that will enhance our Ark. For me, that means Woodrow Wilson's Fourteen Points and the Covenant of the League of Nations. What started out with the best of intentions has come to this bitter moment. The peace has not been kept. Our new Art must include a new international body uniting all nations and realistically including an updated Fourteen Points. That can be done, I think. We have time to work on this. The Senate will have, I trust, an opportunity to finally redeem itself for the 1919 rejection of the League of Nations."

"Beyond that, Estelle?"

"We can look at the universality of President Roosevelt's Four Freedoms: the freedom of speech and religion, and the freedom from want and fear. They must be the essential ingredient in creating our new Ark and a justification for a Covenant of Peace in the post-war period."

"Idealistic!"

"True, Professor Ramos, with a strong tinge of realism if we are to have a more just world."

"You spoken to me about the Kellogg-Briand Pact. How would that affect the new Ark?"

"A little background first. In 1927, Aristide Briand, the French Foreign Minister sent a note of acceptance to Secretary of State, Frank Kellogg. The French agreed to enter into a pact for the mutual outlawing of war. Inherent in the Pact was the view that the best way to stop wars was to simply outlaw them, that instead of laws of war there should be laws against war. The public support for the proposal was great around the world and eventually 27-nations participated in the agreement. The final treaty permitted only defensive wars but outlawed war as 'an instrument of national policy. In January 1929, the Senate passed the Pact by a vote of 85 to1 with certain reservations, among which were: (1) reserving the right of self-defense; (2) reserving the right to protect the Monroe Doctrine; and (3) reserving the right not to enforce the treaty against violators. Still, the treaty passed and suggested a concept for the new Ark ---just outlaw war."

"But the Pact didn't hold up?"

"True. No treaty holds up when it's not supported and enforced. That, as always, is the great challenge."

The conspirators spent the next hours, as they had each day, working out what would go into a new Ark. Urgent or not and spent by their effort, they agreed to an early dinner, a few hours of rest, and then back to the grindstone around 9:00 p.m. Had they checked, they would have noticed the time at the White House where it was midnight --- EST --- and a new day, Sunday, December 7, 1941

Later

"Estelle, you're pale as a ghost."

The conspirators and Dr. Ramos, now an honorary co-conspirator, were gathered at a large dining room table where they were prepared to continue fastening flesh to the bones of the their new Ark. However, one glance at Estelle raised another concern.

"I had another visit."

"Your father?"

"Yes."

"More writing?"

"No!"

"What then?"

"In my dreams, Freda, a manifestation so distinct as to almost seem real."

"He communicated to you?"

"Yes, Harlan, and in a manner dripping with urgency."

"What did he say?"

"Not words really. Just letters, over and over, the same letters."

ZZZZZ

"Nothing else, Estelle?"

"Only a flashing image, blurry, very indistinct."

"Which you think was?"

"A pineapple."

Harlan and Freda were completely at a loss. On the one hand, the image was almost humorous. On the other hand, W.T. Stead was not known for this sort of levity. Unsure as what to say, they looked at Professor Ramos for a tactful response. Once glance and they knew something was terribly wrong. The professor was ashen. Her eyes were slammed shut and her fingers were trembling. Her breathing seemed to be labored.

"Professor Ramos, what's wrong?"

The good professor didn't answer. She seemed to be working her way through a thicket of thick mud full of thistles that pulled and scratched her, leaving her frightened and exhausted, as if she had encountered some terrifying specter in her unwelcomed delirium. Then suddenly her eyes flashed open, her hands balled into fists, and she literally screamed, "My god, they wouldn't. Not again."

"Who wouldn't, Professor Ramos? Wouldn't do what?"

Instead of answering Freda, she stared hard at Estelle before saying, "Your father, has he ever deceived you with his communications across the void?"

"Never."

Not once?"

"Never!"

"No deception?"

"No."

Professor Ramos was calming down. Historicity was taking over, rationally considering the information, challenging the possibilities, and finally accepting the only explanation possible for Stead's communication.

"He knows."

"What?"

"Harlan, Estelle's father knows."

"Knows what?"

Rather than answer the question, Professor Ramos got up, saying, "I must use the telephone in the next room. Please forgive me, but it's an emergency."

Professor Ramos was gone for at least an hour before returning, her face flushed and her lips trembling.

"They don't believe me."

"Who?"

"They think I'm a kook, Harlan? They won't listen."

"Who want?"

"They say everything is quiet out there."

"Where's there?"

Professor Ramos finally settled down, as if finally accepting the inevitable. The tears in her eyes suggested a terrible understanding.

"My friends. What Estelle shared with us startled me. In a moment, I'll explain why. Please understand, I've done my best. I called a friend in the army stationed at the Presidio. He was patient, understanding, and disbelieving. He would do nothing beyond making a few inquiries. I called a friend who called a friend in the Navy Department in Washington. He got nowhere either. It wasn't what I said that was the problem. It was the source of my information that put people off. Once I mentioned Stead, they sent for the white jackets. I also checked with a former colleague, now at the State Department. Unhappily, I had to wake him up. This time I didn't mention your father, Estelle. His response was highly bureaucratic, "There's nothing happening out there, but I'll check again in the morning."

The vagueness of Professor Ramos' statement only encouraged greater curiosity.

"You must tell us what's going on."

"Estelle, the **Z**'s referred to that letter alphabet. However, it can also refer to a flag venerated in Japan, the **Z-flag**. On May 27, 1905 that flag flew bravely on the battleship *Mikasa* during the famous naval battle of Tsushima, a strait of water between Japan and Korea. Admiral Togo hoisted on the yardarm where it definitely fluttered in the breeze for all to see. By prearrangement, every ship in the attacking fleet understood its meaning:

> *The fate of the Empire rests on the outcome of this battle. Let each man do his utmost.*

If ever a group listened intently, it was the three conspirators. They didn't interrupt. They waited for the professor to continue.

"The Russian Baltic fleet had sailed 14,000 to confront the Japanese at Port Arthur on the coast of Manchuria. There a major naval battle would be fought, the first decisive battle between modern steel ships, and where the use of radio (wireless telegraphy) was first used. This battle would be the last in human history where the defeated navy surrendered at sea, and it would end the Russo-Japanese War of 18005 with a stunning Japanese victory."

"But what does that have to do with Stead's communication?"

"Harlan, on the night of February 1904 a squadron of Japanese destroyers crept up on the Russian fleet moored in the outer harbor of Port Arthur. Technically, there had been no declaration of war by either side. The Russian officers had been told to hold their fire if they encountered the Japanese fleet. So, that night with ship lights on and the crews sleeping soundly in the protected harbor, all seemed well. With the **Z-flag** flying, the Japanese attacked without warning, severely damaging the Russia fleet with a spread of torpedoes.

"I don't see…"

"Estelle, it was a 'sneak attack! The Japanese attacked without a declaration of war."

"I still don't understand."

"You're father told you what's going to happen and soon. There will be an attack on American naval forces. There will be no declaration of war."

"I can't believe it. But if it is true, where…"

He also told you."

"He mentioned no location!"

303

"He did with a symbol."

"The pineapple?"

"Yes."

"Hawaii?"

"Yes, the greatest military base in the Pacific is going to be attacked tomorrow. Pearl Harbor is the target."

Earlier in the day at 6:00 p.m. EST, and, of course, unknown to the conspirators, President Roosevelt sent a telegram directly to the Emperor Hirohito, seeking to avoid hostilities. He ended his message with these words:

> *I address myself to Your Majesty at this moment in the fervent hope that Your Majesty may, as I am doing, give thought in this definite emergency to ways of dispelling the dark clouds. I am confident that both of us, for the sake of the peoples not only of our own great countries but for the sake of humanity in neighboring territories, have a sacred duty to restore traditional amity and prevent further death and destruction in the world.*

CHAPTER 35

THE Z FLAG

December 7, 1941 – 7:00 a.m. - Sunday, San Francisco

NEWS HEADLINES

Americans believe that war in coming according to the latest Roper and Gallop polls.

The conspirators were having breakfast, not that they relished eating anything. Their appetite was kaput. Black coffee, a slice of toast, and a bit of strawberry jam, that was about it.

To a person, they had not slept well, tossing and turning and more wakeful than asleep as the night hours past. Alarm clocks were not set; there as no need. By 6:00 a.m. they gave up the host, dressed, and gathered themselves for the God-awful events Dr. Ramos had predicted, and which they now accepted.

It was a terrible thing to know that a ponderous locomotive and passenger cars tugging along behind were headed toward a damaged bridge constructed high over a fast running river hundreds of feet below. They could see the train rounding the last turn before the long straight-a-way leading to the bridge. And, if they peered hard enough, they saw a lone sentinel rotating a red warning light, back and forth, trying desperately to advert a disaster. But, of course, by the time the train engineer saw the danger it was too late. The fates would not be denied.

"Harlan, what time is it in Washington?"

"About 10:00 a.m., Estelle."

"And Hawaii?"

"4:00 a.m.

"Awake at the White House, asleep in Honolulu."

"And we're in the middle, neither here or there."

"As you say, Freda, unwilling spectators to a great tragedy."

Professor Ramos sat quietly listening to her new friends. Against all odds, she had spent a good portion of the night calling people, who might call people, but it was to no avail. "No sight of any Japanese ships in the Pearl Harbor area according to the patrol craft sent out yesterday." That was one report. Another voice spoke to Professor Ramos, "Japanese tasks forces have been seen heading toward the Dutch East Indies, or Indo-China, maybe even Thailand. No one is sure." Still another message came to her during the long night, "Nothing to report. Apparently, no Japanese warships headed toward the Philippines."

By morning, Professor Ramos was trying to feel better. No reports of Japanese forces headed toward Hawaiian waters. But one thing did disturb her, a thought that jabbed at her, "Where was the main Japanese fleet, which the people in intelligence has lost sight of days earlier?"

8:00 a.m. – San Francisco

"Estelle, we could be wrong, couldn't we?"

"My father misleading us, Harlan?"

"Or we read the tea leaves wrong. That possible, isn't it?"

"But Professor Ramos is so certain, the **ZZZZZ** and the blasted pineapple."

"Maybe it just refers to people slumped in their beds, worn out from a too much good food and happy drinks at the luau?"

"You don't really believe that, do you?"

The question was not answered. What was there to say?

"When will it happen, Professor Ramos?"

"I'm no naval strategist, but I would assume in the early morning when the crews are just getting out of their cots. Perhaps around 8:00 a.m. Hawaiian time."

"That's less than three hours from now."

9:00 a.m. – San Francisco

"Freda, turn on the radio."

"There's no news, Estelle. There wasn't any at 7, or 8 either."

Pacing back and forth, Professor Ramos finally came to rest, only to say, "I want to bounce something off all of you."

"What?" Freda asked quickly and perhaps too abruptly.

"We all know President Roosevelt wants to get into the war and snuff out Nazi Germany. We also know he'll never get a declaration of war out of Congress unless the United States is first attacked. The Germans have been reluctant to play along. They want the US out of things for as long as possible or until Russia is defeated."

"And the Japanese?"

"Pretty canny to this point. Pushing up to but not beyond the line leading to war."

"Well then what are you getting at?"

"Just this, Harlan. If the White House could get the Japanese to do something, just bad enough to arouse the American people, but not serious enough to compromise our military, that might solve Roosevelt's problem, wouldn't it? I mean by racketing up the economic stranglehold on Japan, he might be manipulating them into a military confrontation."

"Force them to think they had no choice but war?"

"Exactly, Estelle."

"How would he do this, assuming he was doing it?"

"How do you catch a fish?"

"With bait."

"Very good, Freda."

"What's the bait?"

For a moment it was quiet as all looked at each other. Estelle broke the silence.

"Pearl Harbor?"

"Why not? The fleet is there. Cripple it and Japan has a free hand in the Pacific."

"Not possible, Professor Ramos. Roosevelt's no mad man. Destroying our fleet while we're still unprepared, that would be insanity."

"Estelle, supposed there's a twist to this?"

"Such as?"

"American aircraft carriers are waiting to pounce on the Japanese fleet before it attacks.

"Tokyo is being set up?"

"It's possible."

"If we have an edge, yes. If we've broken their communication code, it would be possible."

10:00 a.m. – San Francisco

"Still no news."

"That's a good sign, Estelle."

"Hopefully, Freda."

"I need to make a point."

"Harlan?"

"No matter what happens today, we must still finish constructing our new Ark. We must have it, I hope, completed by Christmas, certainly by the

New Year. This will be our gift to humanity. Agreed?"

"Agreed."

"Professor Ramos?"

"Of course, Harlan."

"Let's listen to the Philharmonic. I always enjoy their Sunday morning show."

"Dial it up, Freda."

The conspirators slumped in their deep cloth chairs, twisting a bit at times to find a more comfortable position. The music was comforting, suggesting a more civilized world. Freda, exhausted by the whole business, fell into a half sleep. Harlan, unable to drift off, enjoyed the music while working on an unfinished crossword puzzle. Estelle looked out at the Golden Gate Bridge and mumbled to herself, "W.T., what's really going to happen?" Professor Ramos simply stared out the large French window at the Pacific, wondering aloud, "I wonder what's going on out there? Checking her watch she saw that it was 10:50 a.m., 7:50 a.m. Hawaiian time.

Thirty minutes later, the music was interrupted by a hesitant voice, saying, "We interrupt this broadcast for a special announcement:

The Japanese have attacked Pearl Harbor.

EPILOGUE

NEWS HEADLINES

Japan Wars on U.S. and Britain;
Makes Sudden Attack on Hawaii;
Heavy fighting at Sea Reported
The New York Times

———————

"Sean Murray just called. He's headed home by way of the Central Pacific."

"Good to be in your own home at a time like this, Estelle."

"He doesn't have too much love for London, but he doesn't want Ireland to sit this one out, as they did in 1914, Freda."

"We'll all be going home,"

"Back to your law practice, Harlan?"

"Yes, though it seems so unimportant now. What about you, Freda, back to fighting racial injustice?"

"My cross to bear."

"And Estelle, I think I know what you'll be doing?"

"Oh?"

"Working on the new Ark, as did your father, that would be my guess."

"And a good one, Harlan."

"That only leaves Professor Ramos."

"I will, I think, try to write a history of the last few days with you and how we had a ringside seat to a slow motion nightmare."

"We'll be in it?"

"If you agree, Estelle, and all the information you gathered long before I arrived. I've already parsed together a possible introduction."

"Perhaps you would share."

I will argue this was an unnecessary war, that the multitude of crises and confrontations in the late 1930's should have been handled differently, that two great nation, one expanding westward to the Philippines, the other throughout the Far East, were not inevitable enemies, though that is difficult to accept at the moment of national rage.

I will contend that too many recurring misunderstandings combined with an element of racial prejudice, made it increasing difficult to deal with the challenging problems in the Pacific. Of course, I'll have o ask the key questions: Why did the Western powers appease Japan when she took over Manchuria, while risking war over China only a decade later? Why was Japan determined to upset the Washington System in the Far East, supported by the Nine Powers Treaty that provided stability? Why was the United States unwilling to permit this?

Why did Japan tie her national survival to creating a new political order in the Far East, and why did America perceive her survival as threatened by this? Why weren't Tokyo and Washington able to make the drastic concessions necessary to avoid a war? And finally, between Hull's note dated November 26, 1941 and the Pearl Harbor attack yesterday, an eleven-day period, why wasn't it possible to provide a different outcome in this prelude to war?

"Professor, our Ark will have to deal with these questions."

"Which you will do, Estelle."

"You have a title for your history of these events?"

"I do."

In the Wake of the Empress of China

312

Printed in the United States
By Bookmasters